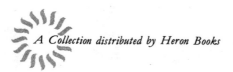

THE
GREATEST MASTERPIECES
OF
RUSSIAN LITERATURE

MAXIM GORKY

THE
ARTAMONOV
BUSINESS

Translated from the Russian by Alec Brown
with an Introduction by
R.D.B. Thomson, M.A. (Oxon), D. Phil. (Oxon)

Original frontispiece by Jean-Pierre Chabrol

Original illustrations by Bernard Duffield

Distributed by
HERON BOOKS

13 005 20

Maxim Gorky

INTRODUCTION

Maxim Gorky (pen-name of Alexey Mikhaylovich Peshkov) is not only a great writer; he occupies a unique position in the history of Russian culture. His career straddles the crucial year 1917 which witnessed the overthrow of the Romanov dynasty and the establishment of a new Government headed by Lenin and his Communists; Gorky participated directly in these events. Already world-famous as a writer, he was to make a new name for himself by his words and deeds in the critical years that followed.

Gorky's life is a remarkable story. He was born on 16 March, 1868, in the big trading city of Nizhny Novgorod (later re-named Gorky in honour of its most illustrious son). His father, Maxim Peshkov, was a skilled craftsman, with many admirable qualities, among them a lively sense of humour and a strong personality; but these qualities did not endear him to his wife's family who stubbornly opposed the match. Soon after the birth of their child the young parents moved down the Volga to Astrakhan. Here tragedy struck the family. In 1871 Gorky's father caught cholera and died; the mother was shattered by the loss of her beloved husband and is said to have blamed young Alexey for his death ever after. She decided to return to her family in Nizhny Novgorod, and so it was that the boy spent the next eight years of his life in the home of his maternal grandparents. This experience was to have a profound influence on his future development. His grandfather was a harsh and bigoted despot, who ruled his family with a rod of fear; his grandmother on the other hand was a complete contrast. It was she who introduced the young boy to the riches of Russian folklore, and first planted the seeds of literature in his heart. Gorky wrote of her later that "she filled him with strength for his long and difficult life." In one form or another these two figures frequently re-appear in his later works.

As a child Gorky had only a few weeks formal schooling, and at the age of eleven he was sent out to earn his own living. In the next few years he tried an amazing variety of jobs and trades: household servant, shop assistant, ship's boy, iconpainter, baker, nightwatchman, to name only a few of them. But the drudgery and sheer physical exhaustion of this life did not hinder the boy's inner development; on the contrary it seems to have assisted it, or at least to have intensified his determination to educate himself, and break free of his miserable existence. Gorky observed his surroundings and his neighbours with an insatiable curiosity, which enabled him to write about these experiences more than thirty years later in his autobiographical trilogy, Childhood, Apprenticeship, My Universities, *with such freshness that the events seem to have happened only yesterday.*

But the boy was not only observing life during these years. He became a voracious reader and spent all his spare time and money on books. Helped by some discriminating adults, but chiefly by his own native unspoilt taste, Gorky gradually came to find in literature a defence against the hardships of his everyday existence. At first he naturally preferred romantic tales of adventure and gallantry, which offered a complete contrast to the life he knew, and enabled him to escape from it, but gradually the boy's taste came to appreciate the subtleties of more realistic literature, which seemed to take the world as it was, imperfect and unadorned, and yet find some order and beauty in it. It was this second type of literature which most influenced Gorky in his own writings.

Gorky's ambition to become a writer was already forming, but first he was to spend several years tramping the length and breadth of Russia. In this way he came into contact with an extraordinary variety of people, some of them worthless or even criminal, but others sensitive and intelligent. Gorky was never to forget these experiences, and all his life long he was tormented by the paradox that contemporary Russia seemed unable and unwilling to employ the talents of so many remarkable people. When, with the Populist leader Mikhail Romas, he tried to convert a village of peasants by good example and simple common sense, they responded by setting fire to the house in which Romas and he were sleeping. On another occasion he saw a woman who had been convicted of adultery, being horsewhipped through the streets of a small town to the mockery and abuse of the populace; but when he tried to intervene to protect her, the crowd turned on him, beat him up and left him for dead. At the same time the Tsarist authorities were distrustful of this young man who asked too many questions, hobnobbed with too many suspicious characters, and who talked naively of reforming life and society. In the face of such discouragements, Gorky felt at times like giving up the struggle; on one occasion he even tried to shoot himself, and survived only thanks to his extraordinary constitution.

It was during these years that Gorky first tried his hand at literature. To begin with he tried to write poetry, but without much success. His literary debut is usually dated from 1892 when his first story Makar Chudra *came out in a Tiflis newspaper. For this auspicious occasion the young author chose the pen-name "M. Gorky" (a Russian word meaning "bitter"). He could hardly have foreseen that within a few years this pseudonym would have become so famous that it would obscure his real name. For the next few years he managed to keep himself by his pen, mostly by journalistic writings, but his reputation was steadily growing; in 1895 his story* Chelkash *was published in the important magazine* Russian Wealth, *which had a national circulation. Three years later he had written enough to justify publication of two volumes entitled* Sketches and Stories. *They sold out so quickly that in the following year the publishers had to bring out an enlarged edition in three volumes. From that moment Gorky's name was made all over Russia, and in the next few years translations into the leading European languages were to give him a worldwide reputation.*

Gorky's sudden rise to fame owed much to the novelty of his writings. They were unconventional in style and subject-matter. He based himself primarily on his own experiences, describing the people that he had met during his wanderings round Russia. Naturally, these were very different from the aristocratic and intellectual personages that we find so often in earlier Russian writers. The heroes of Gorky's stories were taken from the outcasts of society, tramps, criminals and prostitutes, and the resulting picture was a very different one from that given by his predecessors. This in turn affected the style : where previous Russian writers had based themselves on the cultivated speech of the nobility and the educated classes, Gorky introduced the plain and often coarse language of the lower strata of society.

Fame brought Gorky into contact with a wide variety of outstanding figures in the Russia of his time. He met famous writers such as Chekhov and Tolstoy, whom he has described for us in his memoirs of them, and nearly all the writers of his own generation, through whom he found his way into literary salons and so into smart society. At the same time his unvarnished portrayal of the terrible realities of life in Russia brought him close to the reformers and revolutionaries who wished to democratise the autocratic system of Government under the Tsars and to assist the cultural and industrial development of their country.

This wide range of acquaintances was of immense importance to Gorky, and few writers have been on familiar terms with the people of so many different classes and walks of life. It broadened his outlook, and gave him some of the cultural and intellectual polish he had hitherto lacked. But at the time it was the political side that dominated Gorky's interests. His works of the next decade, particularly the novel, Mother, and the play, Enemies were deliberately designed as political, rather than as literary, statements, and as such were welcomed by Lenin. The proceeds from his works he would donate generously to the funds of various opposition parties; he even used his influence with rich merchants to extract money from them for revolutionary organisations. During the revolution of 1905 his fearless activities in the name of liberty and democracy led to his arrest and imprisonment by the Tsarist authorities, but a wordwide campaign of protest soon forced them to release him, on condition that he left the country.

The years 1906-1913 were spent abroad mostly in Capri. He continued to write prolifically and to maintain his contacts with the revolutionaries, and in particular Lenin, the leader of the Bolsheviks. The two men were to remain on close terms until

Lenin's death in 1924, although they did not see eye-to-eye on every matter and indeed frequently quarrelled furiously. In 1913 the proclamation of an amnesty on the occasion of the tricentenary of the Romanov dynasty enabled Gorky to return to Russia. A few months later the Great War broke out. Gorky took a pacifist line throughout these years : ever a humanitarian he was appalled by the suffering and wanton destruction that the war entailed, even when, as in the early months of the war, the Russians seemed to be victorious.

When the Tsar was overthrown in February 1917, Gorky greeted the news with enthusiasm. His initial fears that anarchy might ensue and sweep away the democratic liberties so peacefully and unexpectedly achieved, soon gave way to admiration for the calm and stability of the Russian people at this unprecedented turningpoint in their history. But from the summer onwards he realised that Lenin and his party were trying to undermine this stability and to overthrow the new Government. In his newspaper, New Life, *he warned against this danger, and he continued his denunciations of his former friends, the Bolshevik leaders, even after their successful coup in October 1917. He maintained his fearless criticism of the Bolsheviks' disregard for human life and their contempt for individual liberties in the face of threats, abuse and general obstruction from the Communist regime, until his newspaper was finally forced to close in the summer of 1918.*

Having failed to save Russian democracy from the hands of the Communists, Gorky proceeded less provocatively to work for the cause of Russian culture, which had always remained his first concern. He tried to protect works of art against the vandalism of the mob ; he interceded on behalf of aristocrats, scientists and artists who had been arrested on suspicion or were being held as hostages by the Communists. Here his wide circle of acquaintance among intellectuals and inside the Communist Party was of immense value. He instituted a publishing-house, World Literature, *an ambitious project for translating the classics of the world's literatures into Russian. Whether Gorky ever seriously envisaged the eventual realisation of this grandiose scheme or not, it is undeniable that in the short span of its existence its achievement was enormous. In the prevailing* conditions of Civil War and the general breakdown of normal life it provided work for Russian intellectuals, who would otherwise have been utterly lost ; and by finding work for them he enabled them to qualify for food-rations, fuel and accommodation, which were all in pitifully short supply.

But Gorky's efforts on behalf of Russian culture were not to the taste of the Bolshevik leaders. They regarded his requests with increasing intolerance, and the Party boss of Petrograd, Zinovyev, openly threatened Gorky with trouble should he persist on this course. Exhausted at last by official obstruction as much as by his own overtaxed health, Gorky had to emigrate once again to Western Europe ; he finally settled in Sorrento, because Mussolini's Government would not allow him to return to his old home in Capri.

During the years of his second emigration, Gorky did all he could to keep in touch with events in Russia. He founded a magazine, Colloquy, which was intended to inaugurate a dialogue between Soviet Russia and Western Europe via the Russian emigration, but this venture collapsed when it became clear that the Soviet censors would not allow Colloquy to enter the country. In spite of this Gorky's reputation was such that Russians instinctively wrote to him : young writers would send him their manuscripts for comment and advice. Gorky read their works carefully and wrote back conscientiously and frankly. These activities took up an immense amount of time and energy, yet Gorky also contrived to write his own original works, mostly short stories, and the novel, The Artamonov Business, the last he was to complete.

The idea for The Artamonov Business, the degeneration of a family over three generations, had long been in Gorky's mind. As far back as 1902 he had mentioned his plans for the work to Tolstoy, and the older writer had expressed his interest. A few years later he had spoken of it to Lenin, who had approved the theme, but had urged him to wait a few more years until revolution should enable him to depict the final chapter in the degeneration of the Artamonovs.

This prolonged postponement (Gorky did not finally begin work on the book until 1924-25) inevitably affected the development of the novel. As Lenin had predicted, a revolution *had indeed intervened to add historical confirmation to Gorky's judgment on his fictional characters. And in the meantime his own artistic and intellectual personality had deepened and matured. This can be seen by comparing* The Artamonov Business *with Gorkys' earlier novels. The action is now far more concentrated and less episodic. The flow of narrative is better sustained, and the author's psychological penetration has become much keener. The fortunes of Gorky's fictional heroes are now carefully placed in their historical context. Important events such as the assassination of the reforming Tsar, Alexander II, in 1881, the humiliating defeats in the Russo-Japanese war of 1904, the revolution of 1905, and the outbreak of war in 1914, chart the passing of time and the inexorable march of history towards 1917.*

Basically The Artamonov Business *is cast in the form of a family chronicle. It describes the rise and fall of three generations of merchants in a Russian provincial town, Dromov, (the Russian name means "dozy"). Gorky was always fascinated by the merchant class, and he had frequently depicted characters from it in his earlier short stories, novels and plays. What attracted him in these people was their extraordinary physical vitality; but this, combined with their lack of education, and indeed of any kind of breeding, made them often boorish and arrogant. The founder of the Artamonov dynasty, old Ilia, who dominates the first part of the novel, is a good example of this type in both his good and his bad qualities. For all his faults, his energy and industry win the respect and affection of his workers, and so long as he is on the stage the reader is swept along in the torrent of his activity, and of Gorky's obvious admiration for his hero.*

It is not surprising, however, that Ilia's dominating character somewhat overpowers his children. Peter, who takes over the business after his death, is only his shadow. Never having dared to stand up for himself in his father's presence, he has little self-respect or self-confidence. He has none of his father's passion for work; he regards the factory as something alien and hostile to him. The workers sense his inadequacy, and the business begins to slip out of his hands.

Peter has two sons. Yakov, who occupies the centre of the stage in the fourth and final section of the novel, carries the degeneration of Peter to its logical conclusion. He resents the growing power of the workers, but he is unable to do anything about it. Panic-stricken by the events of 1917, he tries to escape to the West, but he is murdered before he can leave the country. Peter's other son, Ilia, is very different. As his first name suggests, he has inherited his grandfather's character. He rebels against Peter's mechanical and unimaginative handling of affairs, and runs away from home to study; eventually he joins the Bolsheviks. If old Ilia stands for those who had brought Russia into the nineteenth century, his grandson is meant to represent those who have forced her into the twentieth.

Like Gorky himself, the novel is the product of two utterly different historical epochs. If the subject-matter belongs to the pre-revolutionary period, which he knew so well, his treatment of it owes more than a little to Marxist theory and the hatred of capitalism which it fostered. It is therefore a measure of Gorky's artistry that he managed to combine these two aims so successfully that The Artamonov Business *is no less highly regarded in the West than it is in the Soviet Union. Even so, it is noteworthy that the novel ends abruptly with the outbreak of the October Revolution, and although this can be partly explained by the fact that Gorky was primarily concerned with the collapse of the Artamonovs, the reader is still entitled to ask what became of their business. Even more surprising is the total disappearance of young Ilia from the book; as a young Communist one would have expected him to return in the final pages to emphasise the changing destinies of the Artamonov clan. Partly, of course, this was due to Gorky's ignorance of life in the Soviet Union since his departure in 1921, but there are probably also psychological reasons, connected with his own unhappy experiences of the Bolshevik leaders.*

Be that as it may, the appearance of The Artamonov Business *following on his eulogistic memoir of Lenin, written in 1924, did much to redeem Gorky in the eyes of the Soviet authorities. Hitherto he had been regarded as a renegade, but he was now treated more favourably in the Soviet press, and a campaign was initiated to persuade him to return to Russia. This he did in 1928 for the celebrations of his 60th birthday. After a few more visits he finally settled for good in 1933, and*

INTRODUCTION

*remained in the Soviet Union until his death in 1936, when he
was given a State funeral and his ashes buried in the Kremlin
wall. Since then he has generally been regarded as the father
of Soviet literature, and his name and his works are treated
with special reverence in the land of his birth, which he served
so devotedly all his life. His literary style and the ideas he
advocated are now recommended as models for budding writers.
His works sell in huge editions, and there is hardly a Russian
alive to-day who has not read something by Maxim Gorky.*

R. D. B. Thomson

London, April, 1968.

PART ONE

A YEAR or two after the Liberation of the Serfs, at communion on Transfiguration Day, the congregation of St. Nicholas on the Ladder observed a stranger in their midst. The fellow actually elbowed his way very rudely into the thick of them—to light expensive candles at the most venerated of the ikons of the town of Dromov. He was powerfully built, with an immense curly beard, well shot with grey; his pate well capped with a fleece of dark, rather gipsyish curly hair; his nose huge; and grey eyes with a touch of blue in them, defiant under the dense ridges of his eyebrows. People noticed too that, when he dropped his arms, his immense fists reached to his knees.

When it came to kissing the cross, there he was with the town *élite*! That they found particularly displeasing, and when they came out from communion the leading citizens of Dromov gathered at the church porch to discuss the stranger. Some thought he must be a meat and fish wholesaler, others—an estate bailiff; but the mayor, Evgeny Baimakov, a peaceable man whose health was as poor as his heart was kind, cleared his throat gently and said: 'I should put him down to be a member of some nobleman's household staff—groom, or something else to do with sporting life.'

But Pomialov the draper, known as the Widowed Cockroach, a restless sensualist, a lover of foul language, pockmarked and altogether a nasty piece of work, said maliciously: 'Any of you notice his paws—those long arms, I

1

mean? Look at him there, stalking along as if the belfries were all a-pealing for him.'

The broad-shouldered, large-nosed stranger was pacing steadily down the street as if the soil he trod belonged to him; he was dressed in a knee-length peasant frock-coat of good blue stuff, good-quality soft Russian leather knee-boots; hands thrust deep into pockets, elbows snug at his sides.

Telling Mrs. Yerlandsky (who made the church wafers) to find out all about the man, the citizens went their ways, while the bells still rang. Meat pasties awaited them. Pomialov invited them all to drink tea with him that evening in his raspberry garden.

After dinner the unknown one was seen by other Dromov citizens; he was then on the other side of the river, on that tongue of land belonging to the Prince Ratskis and known as the Cow's Tongue. There he was, in and out of the willows, pacing out that sandy point with even strides, shading his eyes and peering first at the town, then at the Oka itself and that twisted and silted little tributary, the Vataraksha, with its marshlands.

Now the Dromov folk are cautious. Nobody was likely to go so far as to shout over to the man to ask him who exactly he was and what he was about. All the same, they did send the town drunkard and town fool, Mashka Stupa, a police constable. Without turning a hair, in front of everybody (including the women folk), Stupa slipped off his uniform trousers, and waded across the muddy Vataraksha, his crumpled peak-cap cocked on his head. Sticking out his huge tippler's belly, he waddled up to the foreigner and —very loudly, to give himself pluck—asked: 'Who be you?'

The stranger's answer was inaudible, but Stupa came straight back to those who sent him and said: 'He just said

2

to me, "And who might you be, you impudent rascal?"
There's evil in that man's bulging eyes, there's no doubt—
he's a bad lot.'

That evening, in Pomialov's raspberry garden, Mrs.
Yerlandsky—a woman with a goitre, famous as a fortune-
teller and all that—rolled her eyes terribly, and reported to
the *élite*. 'He says his name's Artamonov, Ilia Artamonov;
he says he means to settle down here, he's going to set up
something, only he didn't tell me what he's going to set up.
He came in by the Vorgorod road, and he's left that way
too, at three o'clock.'

So they did not really find out anything special about the
stranger, which was not very pleasant; it was like somebody
tapping on your window in the dark and disappearing; it
foreboded ill.

About three weeks passed, and the scar had almost knit
in the memory of the Dromovians, when there was the
Artamonovs, four men strong, driving straight to Baimakov's. Like an axe coming down on a branch Artamonov said
right out: 'Well, Yevsey Mitritch, we shall be new-comers,
under your wise hand. No doubt you'll do what you can
to see me start off on the right foot.'

Concise and businesslike, he explained that he had served
the Prince Ratskis on their estate on the River Rata in the
Kursk Government; he had been Prince George Ratski's
bailiff. After the liberation he had gone his own way. The
Prince had looked after him well, and he meant to set up on
his own. He was going to build a linen factory. He was a
widower. His children were Peter—the eldest, Nikita—a
hunchback, and Alexey, the youngest—really a nephew,
whom he had adopted.

'The peasants about here don't plant much flax,' Baimakov observed thoughtfully.

'Then we'll get 'em to plant more.'

3

Artamonov's voice was thick and rough, like a big drum booming. Baimakov on the other hand had always trodden gingerly, and talked in a low voice as if he was afraid of stirring up a ghost. With his sad, kindly eyes, a sort of lilac in colour, he blinked at Artamonov's sons, standing stolid by the door. There were not two alike. The eldest was like his father, deep-chested, beetle-browed, with little bruin eyes; Nikita had a girl's eyes, large and blue as his shirt; Alexey was a fine curly-haired, ruddy-cheeked lad, fair-skinned, who looked you with a cheerful smile straight in the face.

'Is one going for a soldier?' Baimakov asked.

'No, I need them all myself; I've got them all freed.'

Artamonov waved one hand. 'Be off!' he ordered.

One by one, in order of seniority, they trooped out, and then Artamonov placed a hand on Baimakov's knees, and said:

'Yevsey Mitritch, now we're about it, I want to be your in-law: let your daughter marry my eldest.'

Yevsey Baimakov was indeed taken aback. He bounced up and down on the bench, waving his hands.

'What's that? Good lord! I've never set eyes on you before; I don't know properly who you are, and you putting a question like that! My girl's an only child. She's young to be marrying. Why, you haven't even set eyes on her, you don't even know what she's like. . . . What are you thinking of?'

But Artamonov only smirked into his curly beard, and said: 'As far as I go—ask the police inspector, he owes enough to my Prince; the Prince wrote and told him, too, to do all he could to help me. You'll hear no evil, I swear it on the holy ikons. As for your daughter, I've been about here, in your town, I know her, everything; I've been here four times on the quiet, I've found out everything. My eldest has been here too, he knows what the girl looks like —don't you fear!'

Baimakov felt as if a bear had got him down. All he could do was ask his visitor to bide a bit.

'I can't bide long; though man may wait, the years don't,' was all the implacable stranger replied; then he turned to the window and called out: 'Come in, pay your respects to the master of the house!'

When they had all taken their leave, Baimakov turned to the ikons, crossing himself, muttering, 'Lord—have mercy on me! What breed is this? Lord preserve me from misfortune.'

He stumbled out on his stick into the garden, where his wife and daughter were making jam under the lime tree. His plump, good-looking wife asked him: 'Whose lads were those waiting in the courtyard just now?'

'Don't know,' he grunted, 'where's Natalia?'

'Gone to the stores for sugar.'

'Sugar, eh?' Baimakov repeated dourly, and sat down on a turf seat. 'Sugar. . . . Ah, there's truth in what folk are saying—this Liberation 'll cause a deal of trouble.'

His wife took a keen look at him. 'What are you getting at?' she asked him anxiously. 'Feeling poorly again?'

'It's a bad go! I can't help feeling that fellow has come to take my place on this earth.'

She tried to soothe him. 'Don't be so silly,' she said, 'he isn't the only countryman come into the town lately.'

'Ah, that's just it . . . they keep coming in. . . . I'm not going to tell you anything—till I've thought it over. . . .'

Five days later Baimakov took to his bed. Twelve days later he died, and his death cast a still darker shadow on Artamonov and his children. During the mayor's illness Artamonov called twice, and they had a long face-to-face talk each time. The second time Baimakov finally called in his wife. Wearily clasping his hands on his breast, he said: 'Well, you take it up with her, it's clear I no longer play any part on this earth. Let me—rest a bit.'

'Let's go out, Ma'am,' Artamonov said to her; without bothering to see if she was following, he strode out of the room.

'Yes, go, Uliana; no doubt it's all laid down in the books,' was the subdued advice of the mayor, when he saw that she could not quite bring herself to follow Artamonov. She was a clever woman, strong-willed, who never made up her mind on the spur of the moment; but this time she was back with her husband an hour later, shaking away the tears from her lovely, long lashes, and saying: 'Well, it seems it is written in the books; give your blessing to our lassie.'

The same evening she brought the daughter to her father's bedside, dressed all in her best. Artamonov gave a shove to his son, the lad and the girl clasped hands without looking at one another, and Baimakov, wheezing, held an ancient pearl-studded family ikon over them. . . . 'In the name of the Father, and Son . . . Lord, show Thy mercy on my only child . . .'

To Artamonov severely, he said: 'Don't you forget! You answer before God for my little one!'

Artamonov bowed low before him, till his hands touched the floor. 'I shall not forget.'

When the young couple, receiving the blessing, had gone, Artamonov sat down on the sick man's bed, and said firmly: 'Put your mind at rest, everything will be as it should. I served my Princes thirty-seven years without a fault, and humans aren't like the Almighty, they aren't indulgent, it isn't easy to please another man. As you for, Mother-in-law, you'll be all right, you'll mother my kiddies, and they'll have their orders to show you respect.'

Baimakov listened, without a word, his eyes on the ikons in the corner and tears running down his cheeks. His wife gave a whimper too, and Artamonov, with a note of annoyance in his voice, said: 'You're going early, Yevsey Mitritch, you didn't take enough care. You don't know how much I counted on you!' He drew his fingers across his throat, to emphasize what he was losing, heaved a tremendous sigh, and said: 'I know what you've done; you've been pretty decent, as well as clever, I could have done with your company for another five years; together, we'd have made things hum . . . but the Lord's will be done!'

There was a pitiful cry from the wife. 'Oh, you croaking raven, frightening us so. . . . Who knows . . .'

But Artamonov had risen; he bowed very low before Baimakov, as if Baimakov were already dead. 'I thank you for your confidence,' he said. 'Good-bye, I must run down to the river; there's a barge of stuff just come in for me.'

When he had gone, Mrs. Baimakov was dissatisfied. 'The loutish clod, not one nice word for his son's future bride!'

Baimakov halted her. 'Please don't start, don't upset me.' Then, a moment later, 'You stick to him; there's likely more in him than in any other here.'

Baimakov was laid to earth with great honour by the whole town, assisted by the incumbents of five churches. The Artamonovs came next after the widow and daughter in the funeral procession; the Dromovians did not think much of that; hunchback Nikita, who was behind the others, heard one of the crowd grousing. 'Nobody knows a thing about them, and—straight to the first place.' Pomialov rolled his acorn-tinted eyes, and whispered: 'Both the departed and his good lady were always cautious folk, they must have had some reason. So there's more in it than meets the eye. That vulture must have bewitched them, or they'd never put themselves on a level with the likes of him.'

'You're right, there's something fishy . . .'

'That's just what I mean. Forged money, I expect. And when you come to think how straight poor old Baimakov lived, eh?'

Head bent and back up, as if expecting somebody to hit him, Nikita heard all this. It was a windy day, the wind behind them, and the dust raised by the hundreds of feet pursued the procession and laid thick powder on the greased hair of the men. Somebody said: 'See how our dust has peppered Artamonov—the gipsy's gone white . . .'

On the tenth day after the funeral, Uliana Baimakov and Natalia retired to a nunnery, handing over the house to Artamonov. A whirlwind took possession of the man and his sons. From morning till night you could see them everywhere, striding swiftly through the town, even in a hurry with the sign of the cross if they passed a church. The father was noisy and demoniacal; the eldest son taciturn, dour, and evidently either timid or shy; handsome Alexey was insolent to other lads and had saucy winks for all the girls. As for Nikita, as soon as day was up he'd taken his sharp-pointed hump over the river to the Cow's Tongue, where a flock of carpenters and stone-masons had settled, erecting a long barrack-like brick building and, close at hand, down by the Oka, a large two-floored house of eighteen-inch timbers, just like a prison. In the evening the Dromovians would gather on the bank of the Vataraksha, chew pumpkin and sunflower seeds, listen to the whine and screech of the saws, the rustling sound of planes, the dull dead thud of sharp axes, and deliver themselves of witticisms about the folly of building a tower of Babel, while Pomialov soothed everybody with prophecy of all manner of misfortune for the strangers.

8

'Ha! The Spring'll waterlog those rotten buildings. They'll have a fire before they know where they are; the carpenters smoke—with shavings all about!'

The consumptive Reverend Basil chanted the response: 'They that build upon sand . . .'

'They'll bring in factory workers. Then there'll be drink —theft—vice.'

Luka Barsky, huge, fat-packed all round and in every limb, took a milder view. In his hoarse bass voice he mused: 'If it brings people in, feeding'll be better. There's no harm in it—let 'em do business.'

The Dromovians got great amusement out of Nikita Artamonov. He cut down and rooted up the willows in a huge square plot. Then for days on end he shovelled out the greasy Vataraksha mud. After that, he cut turf from the marsh. Hump in the air, he wheeled it up in a barrow and piled it here and there on the sand.

'It's going to be a garden,' the Dromovians guessed at last. 'What a fool! As if you could turn sand into good soil!'

When the Artamonovs came back over the river at sunset, in Indian file, father in front, and their shadows floated down the greenish water, Pomialov would point and say: 'Look, look at that hunchback's shadow!'

Anybody in fact could see any day that Nikita's shadow —he went third—quivered more than the others; it also seemed heavier than his brother's shadows. Once, after a heavy downpour, the river had come up, and the hunchback caught his foot in the undergrowth, or trod in a hole, and went under. All the watchers on shore were delighted, and roared with laughter. Only thirteen-year-old little Olga Orlov, daughter of the tipsy watchmaker, cried out pitifully: 'Oi! Oi! He'll drown!' She got a good cuff for that, 'Don't call out when you're not told!'

9

Alexey, who always brought up the rear, dived in and got his brother on his feet again. When the two of them, soaked and muddy, had clambered ashore, Alexey made straight for the gapers. They fell back out of his way, and somebody who was scared muttered: 'You savage beast . . .'

'We aren't liked here,' Peter observed, but the father, without breaking step, looked him in the eyes and said: 'Give 'em time and we shall be.' Then he cursed Nikita. 'You scarecrow! Look where you're going. Don't make a fool of us! We can't live on laughter, you nitwit!'

The Artamonovs lived to themselves, making no acquaintance. They were looked after by an elderly woman, very stout, who tied her black kerchief so that the ends stuck up like horns, and spoke in a shapeless sort of way, so that you might really have thought she was not Russian. Nobody could ever get a word out of her about the Artamonovs.

'The scoundrels—anybody'd think they were monks.'

News did get round that the father and eldest son often drove out round the local villages, getting the peasants to sow flax. On one trip Artamonov was set upon by deserters. One of them he killed with a two-pound iron ball he carried at the end of a stout strap, another got a cracked skull. The third escaped. The police inspector praised Artamonov for that. The young incumbent of the poor living of Ilinsk only imposed a penance for manslaughter— forty nights' prayer in the church.

When the autumn evenings came, Nikita read out to his father and brothers the lives of the saints and the homilies of the fathers, though the old man frequently interrupted him. 'Now what lofty height of wisdom that is, more than our intelligence can master. We're common labouring folk, that's not for us, we were born for common things. Now

10

the late Prince George Ratski had read all of seven thousand books, and had gone so deep into thoughts like these that he had even lost his faith in God. He had travelled in every country, and been received at all the Courts—he was a famous man! But when he built a linen factory, it failed. Whatever he tried, came to nothing. So if it hadn't been for what his peasants produced . . .'

When he made these pronouncements he would utter every word precisely, with profound thought, as if listening to himself. He would try to instruct his sons. 'Life will be hard for you . . . you must be your own law, your own defence. You see, I didn't have to make decisions, they were made for me. When I saw things going wrong, I couldn't put them right, it wasn't my business, but my master's. I wasn't only afraid to do anything on my own; I didn't even dare think for myself, in case my brain got confused with the master's. Hear what I say, Peter?'

'Yes, father.'

'That's right, lad. Take it all in. We used to exist without living, so to speak. Of course, you had less responsibility. Your steps were guided for you. It's easier to live like that —but there's no sense in it.'

On occasion he would go on like this for as much as a couple of hours, every now and then saying: 'Hear what I say, children?' He would sit, legs dangling, on the stove, his fingers twisting the curls of his beard, and steadily hammer out link after link in the chain of words. There was a warm obscurity in the huge, clean kitchen, with the tempest raging outside or running silkily over the window-panes. Then came the frosts, the air blue-cold and brittle; Peter would be at the table with a tallow dip, rustling papers, clicking the balls across his abacus, Alexey helping him, Nikita nimble-fingered making baskets.

'That's how it is—Our Monarch the Tsar has given us

11

our liberty. We need to get clear what the intention is. You can't even let a sheep out of hurdles without intention, and here it's thousands of thousands have been let out. As I see it, His Majesty grasped that it wasn't taking much from the gentry, they were frittering it all away anyhow. Now Prince George tumbled to it. Before the liberation came, he said to me: "Compulsory labour isn't profitable." In other words, they're trusting us to work at liberty. From now on even a soldier won't shoulder a musket twenty-five years on end—it's work's the word. It's up to every man to show what he's fit for. The nobility's written off. Do you get that? Now it's you who are the nobility!'

Uliana Baimakov spent nearly three months in the nunnery. When she came home, the very second day Artamonov asked her: 'Shall we have the wedding soon?'

She was shocked. Her eyes flashed angrily. 'What are you saying—don't forget yourself! Less than six months from her father's death, and you . . . Don't you know what's right and wrong, man?'

But Artamonov silenced her, sternly. 'Mother-in-law, I don't see anything wrong in it. The gentry do far worse, and the Lord puts up with it. I need the girl: Peter must have a wife.'

Then he asked her how much money she had. Her answer was: 'I won't settle more than five hundred on my girl!'

'You'll give more than that,' the towering mouzhik replied, unruffled, confident, and looking her straight in the eyes. They were sitting at table, facing one another, Artamonov with his elbows on the table and his fingers buried in the dense mat of his beard, while the woman knit her brows and drew herself back, as if fearful of something. She was well over thirty, but looked much younger, with steady, intelligent, greyish eyes set bright between rosy cheeks. Artamonov stood up, and stretched himself. 'You're a fine woman, Uliana Baimakov,' he said.

'Anything else to say?' She mocked him, nettled.

'Not a word.'

He dragged his feet, as if unwilling to go. Watching his back, she slipped a swift glance at a mirror, then angrily muttered: 'Shaggy devil, interfering . . .'

She felt afraid of him, and went upstairs to her daughter. But Natalia was not there. Through the window she caught sight of her—in the courtyard, by the gate, Peter Artamonov beside her. She ran downstairs, out on to the porch, and shouted: 'Natalia—come indoors at once!' Peter saluted her.

'That's not the way, my fine young fellow, talking to a maid without her mother, let it not happen again!'

'She is my betrothed,' Peter reminded her.

'All the same. It's no custom here,' the mother replied, asking herself why she lost her temper so. As if young people should not court. It was not very nice of her—as if she envied Natalia.

Indoors, she pulled Natalia's hair hard, and whatever her own thoughts were, forbade any more such meetings. 'Though he is your betrothed, don't forget there's many a slip 'twixt cup and lip,' she said harshly.

She was very troubled at heart. A few days after this she called on Mrs. Yerlandsky to have her fortune told. All the women of the town went to that old barrel of a witch to get their fears and their sins and their disappointments off their chests.

'There's nothing very hard to see in it,' Mrs. Yerlandsky said: 'I'll tell you straight, dearie, you stick to him. It's not for nothing I'm pop-eyed, I know the inside of people like my own pack of cards. See how successful he is, everything he touches comes easy; all the talk against him here is only envy. No, dearie, don't you fear him, he's no fox, he's a bear.'

'That's just the point, he is a very big bear,' the widow agreed. With a sigh she told the fortune-teller: 'I was afraid first when he asked for Natalia's hand for his son; very afraid. Out of the clouds, nobody knew him, marrying his family into ours. Was it seemly? When I think how he talked at me, and I looking into his big impudent eyes, saying yes, yes, yes to everything, consenting to it all, as if the man had me by the throat.'

'The significance of that,' the wise old wafer-maker explained, 'is his faith in his own power.'

But nothing she said relieved Uliana Baimakov's mind, not even when seeing her out of her dark herb-stuffy room Mrs. Yerlandsky said: 'Don't forget, it's only in fairy stories that fools get on . . .'

There was something suspicious in this loud praise of Artamonov—so loud that it seemed bought. And a friend of hers, Matrena Barsky—tall, swart, and dried-up like salt cod—had quite a different view. 'Uliana, darling, the whole town is talking about you. Aren't you afraid of those newcomers? Surely . . . it's not for nothing one of the boys is a cripple, it won't be for a little sin the parents produced him like that. . . .'

They were hard days for widow Uliana. More and more frequently she snapped at her daughter, though she knew quite well there was no reason. She tried to see as little as possible of her lodgers, while they for their part seemed to be more and more in her path, darkening her every hour with alarm.

Winter came on them before they could think, and the town was assailed with deafening blizzards. The world froze hard. Houses and streets were lost behind mountains of sugary snow. The starling roosts on the houses and the church spires were capped in white wool. The rivers and the rusty waters of the swamps were rivetted together with white iron sheeting. On the frozen Oka boxing and wrestling tournaments began between the townsmen and the neighbouring peasants. Every single holiday Alexey fought; every single time he came home angry and defeated.

'What's the matter, lad?' Artamonov asked his son, time after time. 'Surely they aren't better fighters here than you?' And Alexey would hold a copper piece or a lump of ice to his bruises, but always kept a stubborn silence. Only his eagle eyes now and then flashed—till, one day, Peter said: 'Alexey fights very well; it's our own side, chaps of the town, who beat him up.'

Artamonov laid his fist on the table—'And why?'

'We aren't loved.'

'We?'

'Yes, we. They don't love any of us.'

Artamonov's fist came down on the table so that the candle sprang out of its socket and went out. He bellowed into the darkness: 'What are you always talking to me about love for, like a silly girl? I don't want to hear another word!'

Nikita lit the candle. Quietly he said: 'Alexey ought not to go fighting.'

'So that people could laugh, eh? Say an Artamonov was afraid, eh? You shut up, you scarecrow, you—snot!' He carried on for a long time. But, some days later, at supper, he suddenly turned gruff and kind. 'What about a bear hunt, lads, eh, it's good sport. Before your time I went bear hunting with Prince George Ratski in the Riazan forests; we used to take 'em with pikes, that was sport!'

He warmed up, and told them a number of stories of successful expeditions. A week later he took Peter and

15

Alexey into the forest with him. They got an old man bear. Then the brothers went on by themselves and put up the mother; she slit Alexey's short fur coat and he got a torn thigh, but the two lads mastered her, and, leaving her in the forest for the wolves to sup off, brought a pair of young bears back with them.

'Well, and how are your friends the Artamonovs?' Dromovians would ask Uliana Baimakov.

'All right.'

'Pigs are no trouble in winter,' was Pomialov's observation.

To her surprise, the widow latterly had begun to feel the hostility to the Artamonovs as a personal affront; the chill hatred struck at her too. She could see what sober lives they lived, pulling all together, stubbornly getting their big enterprise going, and she could see nothing bad in them either. She had kept a sharp eye on Natalia and Peter, and come to the conclusion that the taciturn, stocky lad was unusually well behaved for his years, never trying to get Natalia in a dark corner to tickle her, or whisper highly-seasoned things in her ear, like the young men of the town to their girls. She was even a trifle troubled by that incomprehensible, dry, yet attentive and, you might say, even jealous attitude which Peter took up towards her daughter.

'He won't be a tender husband.'

But one day, coming downstairs, she heard her daughter's voice in the hall. 'Bear-hunting again?'

'Getting ready. Why?'

'It's dangerous. Alexey got hurt.'

'His own fault. Keep calm. So—you think about me?'

'I didn't say anything about you.'

'You little rogue,' the mother said to herself, with a smile and a sigh. 'And what a clumsy lout he is!'

Meanwhile Artamonov was getting ever more insistent

on the wedding. 'You'd better hurry, or they'll forestall you!'

She could see for herself that it ought to be speeded up. The girl was sleeping badly, and could not hide how her body's desire was wearing her down. When Easter came, Uliana took Natalia away to the nunnery again. When she came back, a month later, she found her abandoned garden spick and span, paths clean, trees stripped of lichen, the soft fruit garden cut back and tied; a skilled hand had been at work.

Going down the path that led to the river, she came on Nikita. The hunchback was repairing a wicker fence damaged by the spring floods. The bones of his hump stuck sorrowfully up under his long canvas tunic, nearly hiding the huge head altogether, with its straight, fair hair; to keep his mop from falling over his eyes, Nikita had tied it with a birch twig. A grey figure, set among the succulent green foliage, he suggested an aged hermit, completely absorbed in his task. With axe swinging silver in the sunlight, he was neatly trimming a stake, singing some church thing to himself as he did so, in a tiny girlish voice. Through the withies the silken water gleamed greenish, the sun played in it, darting golden flashes.

'God's greeting,' she suddenly said softly, to her own surprise.

Nikita's blue eyes flashed softly back, and he responded: 'And with you.'

'You tidied my garden?'

'I did.'

'It's beautifully done. You are fond of gardens, aren't you?'

Kneeling there he told her briefly how the prince, his master, had apprenticed him at nine to the gardener—he was now nineteen.

17

'He's a hunchback,' the woman said to herself, 'but he seems to have a sweet nature.'

That evening she was drinking tea in her room upstairs, Natalia with her, when there was Nikita in the doorway with a bunch of flowers and a smile on his rather ugly, sombre, sallow face.

'Please accept this posy.'

'But why?' She was astonished, and examined the well-chosen flowers and greenery with some suspicion. Nikita explained that when he was in service it had been one of his jobs to present the princess with flowers every morning.

'Really,' Mrs. Baimakov said. Then she coloured a little, and held her head high. 'Am I then like a princess? She was surely a beauty . . .'

'But so are you.'

Blushing still deeper, Uliana Baimakov asked herself if the father had not put him up to saying this. 'Well, I am very grateful for the honour,' she said, but did not offer him a cup of tea. When he had gone, she said aloud: 'He has nice eyes; they aren't his father's, they must be his mother's.' And heaved a sigh.

She made little more effort to persuade Artamonov to wait till the autumn for the wedding, when it would be a year after her husband's death, but simply said, with determination: 'All I ask, Mr. Ilia Artamonov, is for you to leave the whole thing to me, let me make all the arrangements according to our good old-time customs. That will suit you too, because it will introduce you to all our leading people at once; it will give you prominence in the town.'

'Hm,' Artamonov grunted, rather piqued, 'I'm pretty prominent, even at a distance, without all that.'

His touchiness hurt her. She said: 'You are not liked, you know.'

'Then let 'em fear me!' He smirked and shrugged his

18

shoulders. 'There's Peter too, always talking about being *liked*. What queer people you all are!'

'But a lot of that dislike hits me; not only you, but me too.'

'Mother-in-law,' he said, 'don't you worry! He held up his huge hand, clenched his fist till the circulation stopped, and said: 'I know how to break people, they won't dance their tune round me for long! I can do without love.'

She held her tongue. There was an eerie alarm in her heart as she thought, 'What a savage!'

So her comfortable house was filled with her daughter's friends, all girls of the best families in the town. They were all luxuriously clad in old-world brocade sarafans, with billowing white sleeves of muslin and fine lawn, slashed and cross-embroidered in coloured silks, with lace wristlets and goatskin and morocco leather shoes, their long maiden hair plaited with ribbons. The bride, breathless in a heavy silver brocade sarafan with gilded filigree buttons from yoke to hem, and a gold brocade cape on her shoulders, all white and blue ribbons, sat petrified in the principal corner of the living-room. Wiping her perspiring forehead with a lace handkerchief, she led the singing in a loud voice:

> Over the green meadows, —
> The flowers like the sky—
> Poured the spring waters,
> Muddy and icy . . .

Her comrades all together caught up the dying groan of the maiden lament:

> They sent me, a maiden
> To bring the house water,
> Me their barefoot
> Naked daughter . ..

Alexey, deep in the covey of girls, laughed loud and

shouted: 'That's a queer song! Pack a lass in brocade like a turkey in a saucepan, and then all yell, "Oh my naked daughter!" '

There was Nikita, sitting, close to the bride-to-be. His new tunic was piled up in freakish blue folds across his hunch on to the nape of his neck; his blue eyes were staring wide, fixed on Natalia with a strange anxiety in them, as if fearing that at any moment she might melt and vanish from sight.

In the doorway stood Mrs. Barsky; she filled it all, rolling her eyes, booming in her gruff bass voice: 'You don't put enough wail into it, girls!' and strode into the room like a draught mare, to tell them—severely, too—how those old songs should be sung and with what trembling a young maid should approach the altar.

'The saying has it: marriage builds a stone wall round you, so you bear in mind your husband is a wall you'll never break and never climb beyond. . . .'

But the girls had little ear for her. It was cramped and stuffy in that room, and they ran past the old thing through the yard into the garden. There Alexey was, too, in their midst like a bee quick from flower to flower, with his gold-shot silk tunic and broad plush trousers, all talk and laughter, as if he were drunk.

Mrs. Barsky was very put out. She pouted her thick lips and her eyes started from their sockets. Gathering up her homespun skirts in front of her, she was off upstairs like a cloud of dense smoke, to explain, with a far-seeing look on her face: 'That girl of yours, she's happy, that's all wrong, that's not custom. Happy beginning—sorry ending!'

Natalia's harassed mother was on her knees at a massive, iron-bound chest; all round her the floor and the bed looked like stalls at a fair, with the scattered stuff—lengths of tweed, tussore, red fustian—Cashmere shawls, ribbons and embroidered toilet cloths. Athwart the brilliant colours lay a broad beam of sunlight, and they glowed like a glorious evening sky.

'It's all wrong too, the groom living in the bride's home before he goes to altar . . . the Artamonovs ought to move out. . . .'

'You should have spoken earlier, it's late now,' snapped Uliana Baimakov, and bent again over the chest, to hide away the annoyance on her face. Then she heard that bass voice persisting: 'People used to say you were a clever woman, that's why I held my tongue. I thought you'd see it yourself. What's it to do with me? As far as I'm concerned I don't mind what anybody says, there will be justice in Heaven.'

And Matrena Barsky stood her ground, like a statue, her head held stiff as if it were a goblet brimful of wisdom. But when she saw she was not going to get any answer, she slunk out of the room. Uliana, on her knees amid the gay finery, full of malaise and fear, muttered: 'Oh Lord God, succour me, and keep me sane!'

There was a new rustle at the door. She stuck her head quickly deep into the chest to hide her tears. It was Nikita. 'Natalia sent me, to ask you if you want any help.'

'No, thank you, dear boy. . . .'

'In the kitchen Olga Orlov has spilled treacle all over herself.'

'No—not really? She's a clever lass—— Now, you ought to find a good girl . . .'

'Who would marry me?'

Meantime, in the garden under the weeping willow, over pots of beer about the round table, were gathered Artamonov senior, Barsky—who was the bride's godfather—Pomialov, Zhiteikin (the tanner) with his vacant stare, and Voroponov (the wheelwright). The groom-to-be was leaning against the tree. His dark hair was well plastered down with grease. His head might have been an iron casting, and he was deferentially listening to the conversation of his elders.

'Our customs are different,' his father had said pensively, and Pomialov answered bombastically: 'We folk in Dromov are deep-rooted. Great is Mother Russia!'

'We aren't exactly side-horses, either!'

'Our customs are ancient . . .'

'There's a lot of Mongol blood about here, you know, and all that . . ."

All shrieks and laughter, jostling, the girls came racing into the garden. They wound a bright wreath of sarafans about the table and chanted:

> Oi, great father of the groom,
> Ilia Vassilievitch,
> First step—you break your leg,
> Second step—the other leg,
> Third step—you twist your neck . . .

'Is that your custom!' Artamonov cried, in astonishment, turning to his son. Peter, not sure of himself, one eye on the girls, smirked and plucked at one ear.

'You—wait!' Barsky counselled, roaring with laughter.

> That's too little for the villain
> Who abducts a helpless maiden . . .

'Little, you say?' roared Artamonov, He did not exactly like this atmosphere; his fingers drummed the table, while the girls got more and more worked up, singing:

> May this company hurl and break you
> From the heights on to the rocks,
> Never reckon to deceive us
> Never either sing the praises
> Of your distant foreign parts,
> For your freedoms are not decent
> But by sorrow are they sown
> And by weeping are they watered

'Ah, so that's how it is!' Artamonov suddenly cried, with a shake of the head. 'All very well, young ladies, still I've a word to say for my own country, saving your grace; we're a bit more gentle and a bit more hospitable in our parts. . . . As we say, "The Svapa and the Usozha don't flow into the Oka, but, thank God, into the Sein." '

'Don't you speak so fast,' said Barsky, half-boasting, half-threatening, 'you don't know us yet. Now you've got to tip the girls.'

"How much should I give?'

'Ah! that's up to you.'

But when Artamonov handed the girls two silver roubles, Pomialov was annoyed. 'Flinging money away, making yourself big!'

'You aren't easy folk to please, are you!' Artamonov cried, quite nettled in his turn. Barsky roared with laughter —Zhiteikin's falsetto cackle also cut into the silence.

This party, the 'maiden party', did not end till day broke. The company had all departed, and the house was almost asleep, but Artamonov sat on in the garden with Peter and Nikita, stroking his beard, his eyes roving all round him, touching flowers and shrubs and plucking at the rose-lined clouds, while he quietly discoursed: 'They're a tough crowd, these folk, there's no sweetness in 'em. All the same, Peter my lad, you do everything your mother-in-law wants; mind, whatever silly petticoat drivel you may think it—to-day it goes! Alexey's seeing the girls back to town, is he? They like him enough, if the lads don't. That Barsky lout's got a down on him, all right. . . . Yes . . . Nikita, it's up to you to do the gentle stuff, you know how. You caulk up the cracks I make, boy!'

He glanced aside at the huge beer vat, and went on morosely: 'Guzzled every drop of it; drink like horses. What do you say, Peter?'

Peter fingered the silk belt his betrothed had given him, and said, in a low voice, 'It would be simpler and quieter in the country.'

'Ah, but where's the *simpler* if you miss the boat.'

'They keep putting off the wedding.'

'Patience, lad.'

At last the great and difficult day came for Peter Arta-monov. He was seated now in the principal corner of the living-room, well aware that his forehead was knit in a sullen frown, conscious how unseemly it was, what a bad figure he was cutting in his bride's eyes, but do what he could the frown would not lift, it was too tightly stitched down. He cast sly looks at the company and tried to toss the hair of his forehead; hops were scattered over the table and over Natalia's wedding veil; Natalia was hanging her head too, her eyes were half-closed, she was worn out, pale, frightened, trembling like a little child.

'Bit-ter be it!' for the twentieth time the ring of flushed and hairy faces with staring teeth yelled at him.

Peter turned towards her—neck stiff, like a wolf's. He raised the wedding veil; his nose and his dry lips pecked at her cheek. He felt the satin coolness of her skin; he sensed how her shoulders quivered and shrank, and he was both sorry for Natalia and ashamed of himself, while the slightly tipsy figures surrounding them shouted: 'He doesn't know how!' 'Shoot at the lips, boy!' 'Let *me* have a go!' A drunken female voice rose above them all: 'I'll learn you how to kiss!'

'Bitter be it!' came Barsky's hard voice.

Peter set his teeth and to the girl's moist lips pressed his own. A shiver ran through them. She seemed to melt and shrink, like white mist in the sunlight. They were both of them hungry, fasting since the day before. What with the

excitement, the sharp tang of liquor and the two glasses of
tangy red wine he had drunk, Peter himself felt he was intoxicated, and was afraid of her noticing it. Everything
round him was unsteady; at moments he saw nothing but a
multicoloured mass; then it would all dribble to left and
right, the leering faces like swollen red bubbles. His father
swung a glass into the air; hair wild, eyes drawn into
Uliana Baimakov's ruddy cheek—'Come on, In-law, each
other's health in good mead! Your mead's sweet as the
hand that brewed it . . .'

She reached her full white fingers towards him, her gold
bracelet with its coloured stones flashed in the sunlight, and
across her lofty bosom gleamed the milk of pearls. She too
had drunk more than one glass. There was a sensuous smile
in her grey eyes and her lips, parting, quivered seductively.
Their glasses touched; she drained hers and bowed to him.
Artamonov was beside himself. Shaking his shaggy head,
he cried: 'Oh, what style you have, In-law! The style of a
Princess, or I'll be damned!'

Peter was dully aware that his father was overstepping
the mark; amid the tipsy din of the company he was still
acutely aware of the spiteful exclamations coming from
Pomialov, or Mrs. Barsky's gruff reproaches, and Zhiteikin's
snigger of a laugh.

'Marriage?—We're on trial,' he thought, as he heard a
voice say: 'Just look—what eyes the devil's making at
Uliana—*oi-oi!*' and another voice: 'There'll be another
wedding yet, only without parsons. . . .'

But as those words caught his ear he forgot them, for
Natalia's knee—or was it her elbow?—touched him, and
through his whole body flooded a disturbing faintness. He
tried not to see her, held his head rigid, but he could not
master his eyes; they were stubbornly tilted her way.

'Will it be over soon?' he whispered, and Natalia whispered back, 'I don't know.' 'On show like this,' he began, and when she quickly murmured assent he was happy; they felt the same sense of shame.

Alexey and the girls were having their own party in the garden. Nikita was sitting with a lanky parson who had a sodden beard and coppery eyes in a pock-marked face. Through all the windows and doors, from courtyard and street, people from the town were staring in. There were dozens of heads swaying and interchanging in the bluish air; mouths agape, whispering, hissing, yelling; the windows were bulging bags out of which at any moment those noisy heads might come tumbling into the room like so many water-melons.

Nikita noticed particularly the head of a navvy named Tikhon Vialov. It was a big, bony head with dense ginger hair and red blotches. The eyes, which at first glance seemed colourless, glittered strangely as they blinked; it was the pupils which blinked, not the lashes—they were motionless. Motionless too were the thin, close-pressed lips of the man's tiny mouth, half hidden in curly whiskers. The ears were clumsily attached to the skull. The fellow was leaning full on a window-sill. He made no noise, uttered no oath when people tried to push him aside; he merely shifted them instead, with easy movements of his shoulders and elbows. His shoulders were a massive rounded block, into which the neck was sunk, so that the head seemed to spring straight from the trunk. He, also, seemed to be hunched, and Nikita could see something in the man's face that was good and predisposing.

The crooked lad all of a sudden gave his tambourine a tremendous smack, then drew a firmly-pressed finger across the parchment; the instrument rumbled and wailed; another man uttered a piercing whistle, flicked open a two-bank harmonica on to his knee, and there was one of the bride's

26

old friends, plump curly-haired Stephen Barsky dancing a wild fling in the middle of the room, crying in time with the beat:

> "Hi! You maidens standing against him,
> All you clever ones, leading the band,
> Tell me if my money is worthless,
> Come and try your prowess with me!"

Barsky's father rose to all his great stature, and thundered: 'Stephen lad! Don't let the town down, show these chicken!' Then Artamonov was up, tossing his tousled head, blood flooding his cheeks, nose afire, throwing back into Barsky's face; 'Steady on there, we're no chicken; game cocks we are! We'll see who can dance! Alexey!'

Alexey's features lit up with a smile; he shone as if varnished, while he took the Dromov dancer's measure; and then, dead white of a sudden, was off himself, at an incredible speed, high-pitched shrieks whirling from his lips.

'He's got no words!' the Dromovians cried.

Instantly came Artamonov's desperate howl: 'Alexey—God damn you!'

Alexey did not slacken one step of his wild tattoo, only stuck two fingers to his lips, sent out a deafening whistle and pronounced:

> "Lord of the manor Mackey
> Had half a dozen lackeys;
> Now the lordly Mackey
> Himself is but a lackey!"

'What about that!' Artamonov barked victoriously.

'O-ho!' the priest declared significantly, demonstratively raising a finger and with it turning his head discreetly away.

'Alexey will outdance your chap,' said Peter to Natalia, and Natalia timidly answered: 'He's nimble.'

The two fathers spurred on their sons, as if they were fighting cocks. They were both of them well lit, standing

27

shoulder to shoulder; the one enormous, clumsy as a sack of oats, with tears of drunken enthusiasm trickling from narrow slits beneath his brows—the other, all taut, as if himself about to spring, his long fingers alive, playing against his thighs, his eyes mad. Peter then noticed quivers running through the flue of beard on his father's cheekbones, and said to himself: 'Grinding his teeth. Any moment he'll strike somebody . . .'

'The Artamonov lad dances frightfully, no figure work, very poor.' It was Mrs. Barsky's bass voice, and Ilia Artamonov turned and guffawed into her swart squat-nosed frying-pan face. Alexey had won. The Barsky boy was staggering to the door. Then Artamonov plucked roughly hold of Uliana Baimakov's arm. 'Come on,' he ordered, 'come on, In-law, out you come!'

The colour left her. With her free hand she protested. Furiously, but lost, she tried to refuse. 'No, no, come. . . . You and me—together—it's not done . . .'

There was a general hush—smirking faces—Pomialov exchanged glances with Mrs. Barsky. There was an oiliness in his words: 'Why not? Better let him have his own way, Uliana, dance! God will forgive . . .'

'I take full responsibility,' bellowed Artamonov.

He had somehow become completely sober. He frowned. He stepped forward, as if propelled against his will, as if going to battle. She was pushed forward towards him. She was a trifle drunk herself; she stumbled, missed her step, then drew herself straight, flung back her head, and her dancing feet circled the floor. Peter could catch the whisper of horror. 'Heavens! And her poor husband not a year in the ground; and she marrying her daughter too!'

Without looking at Natalia, he realized how ashamed she was of her mother. He whispered: 'Father shouldn't have danced.' 'Mother too,' the bride murmured sadly, standing on a bench, to be able to see over the dense ring of heads. She swayed, and caught hold of Peter's shoulder. 'Steady!' he said tenderly, holding her by the elbow.

Through the open windows, over the heads of the on-lookers, played the last gleams of the sunset, and the man and the woman went on circling, like two blind creatures, in that ruddy glow. In the courtyard, in the garden, out in the street, there was loud laughter and shouting, but in the stifling room the silence grew more intense. The tight-sprung parchment of the tambourine drubbed darkly, the harmonica whined, while with jerking limbs those two twirled like burning puppets, close-held now by the young folk crowding round them, silently and seriously observing their dance as if it were a task of unusual import. The sober citizens among the adults had gone out into the yard, and only those owlishly held by their drink remained.

At last Artamonov gave a final double stamp and was still. 'You've got me beat, Uliana Ivanovna!' he cried. With a shudder Uliana Baimakov too was still, as if she had suddenly come against a wall. She bowed, turning to the whole circle of them, and murmured: 'Think twice before you condemn me.' With that, fanning her cheeks with her handkerchief, she left the room.

Mrs. Barsky at once took her place. 'Time to dispatch the young couple,' she commanded. 'Come, Peter, come this way—boys, take his arms.'

Artamonov pushed them aside a moment. His enormous hands rested on his son's shoulders. 'Go along, then,' he said, 'God grant you fortune! Kiss me!' He gave his son a push, the other lads took his arms. Mrs. Barsky led the way, spitting to left and right and muttering: 'Nor ail nor wail, nor envy nor dishonour . . . Fire and water timely come, not for sadness but for gladness.'

When Peter had followed her into Natalia's room, where

a magnificent bed stood waiting, the old woman slumped on the chair in the middle of the room. 'Listen to me,' she commanded exultantly, 'and don't you forget, here are two half-rubles; put them in your boots, where your heel goes; when Natalia comes in, she will kneel to pull off your boots, but don't you let her.'

'Why not?' Peter asked morosely.

'That's not your business. You refuse her three times, but the fourth time you let her, then she must kiss you three times, and you give her the money then, and say: *I make you this present, my slave, my fate!* Got it? Then you undress, and get into bed; but back to her, mind; she will say: *give me shelter*, but you don't say a word; you only offer her your hand the third time—got me? And then. . . .' Peter looked in amazement into the swart broad face of this woman who was teaching him, with gaping nostrils and slavering lips.

Mrs. Barsky took her kerchief and wiped her greasy chin and her bosom. Authoritatively, snapping out each coarse, shameless word precisely, she pursued her instructions to him, ending up: 'If she yells out, don't take any notice, if she bursts into tears, don't take any notice'—and waddled unsteadily out of the bedroom, leaving behind her only a whiff of alcoholic breath.

A wave of fury came over Peter. He wrenched off his boots and flung them under the bed, tore off his clothes and mounted the bed like a horse; teeth clenched, afraid he might even break into tears himself because of the tremendous sense of wrong that choked him. 'The marsh devils . . .'

It was hot in the feather bedding. He got out and went to the window, opened it wide. A confused, tipsy rumble flooded into the room, guffaws, girls' shrieks; there were dark outlines of bodies moving hither and thither in the bluish darkness under the trees. The slender spire of the

THE ARTAMONOV BUSINESS

church stuck like a copper finger into the sky; the cross had been taken down for gilding. Beyond the roofs showed the river, a mournful ribbon, with a fragment of moon pouring soft light over it, and after that came the sombre banks of the endless forest. To Peter's thoughts came country so different—the great space of golden grain lands, and he sighed.

Suddenly there were footsteps on the stairs, and giggles; he leapt back into bed. The door opened; there was a rustle of silk and creaking slippers; then sobs, somebody crying; then a bolt slipped back into place. Peter cautiously raised his head. A white figure was standing by the door, lost in the darkness; one arm was moving, in measured beat, and the figure was bending nearly to the floor. She was praying —and he had not prayed. But he felt no impulse to pray. 'Natalia,' he began timidly, 'don't be afraid. . . . I am afraid myself . . . I am miserable.'

With both hands he smoothed his hair tightly back; plucked at his ears; murmured: 'You needn't do anything, taking off the boots and all that. It's nonsense. My heart was aching. She revelled in it. Please don't cry.'

She edged with great caution to the window. She whispered: 'They're still about.'

'Yes,' he said.

Both of them afraid, and worn out, it was a long time before they could do more than exchange empty words at a distance.

At daybreak there was a creak on the stairs. Then a hand felt at the wall. Natalia went to the door. 'Keep that woman out,' whispered Peter.

'It's Mamma,' Natalia replied, and opened the door. Peter sat on the bed, legs dangling. He was dissatisfied with himself and depressed. 'I'm a poor thing,' he kept thinking, 'I'm afraid; she will make a mock of me some day . . .'

31

The door opened again. 'Mamma wants you,' Natalia whispered, and leant on the stove, lost against the white tiles. Peter went outside. There in the darkness he was assailed by the frightened, burning, and indignant whisper of his mother-in-law: 'What are you thinking of, Peter Artamonov, do you really want to put me and my daughter to common shame? It's nearly daylight. They will soon come to waken you, and you will have to put out Natalia's shift for everyone to see her virtue!'

She held him by the shoulder with one hand and pushed him away from her with the other. 'What's the matter? No spunk, no will? Don't keep me on tenterhooks, out with it. . . .'

Peter said in a hollow voice: 'I don't want . . . to . . . hurt her.'

He could not make out his mother-in-law's features, but he seemed to hear her give a short laugh. 'That's all right,' he heard her say, 'off you go, lad, off you go, and do your man's job . . . pray to Christopher the Martyr. . . . Off you go—come—give me a kiss!'

She drew a warm arm about his neck, and in a haze of winey breath kissed him with sweet, sticky lips; but he missed his time, and the smack of his kiss was wasted on the air.

He went back into the bedroom and closed the door behind him. Determinedly he held out his arms; the girl responded, was in his arms, was whispering uncertainly: 'Mamma's had a drop or two.'

Peter scarcely expected those words. He fell back towards the bed, muttering: 'Don't be afeared . . . I'm not much to look at, but my heart's good . . .'

She pressed closer and closer into him, and whispered suddenly: 'My poor legs . . . they're giving way . . .'

They liked parties in Dromov. The wedding lasted five whole days and nights. From early morn to midnight they were at it, madly, a whole crowd of them proceeding from one house to another, in a vortex of alcoholic fumes. The Barskys put up a particularly lavish show, going all out to be first, but Alexey beat up the son for saying something insulting about Olga Orlov, and when the Barsky parents laid their complaint to Artamonov, all they got was his amazement that they should fuss: 'Where on earth don't lads fight?'

Artamonov was lavish to the girls with ribbons and gew-gaws, and tips of money for the lads. He made their fathers and mothers roaring drunk. His arms were about everybody, he shook them all up thoroughly, with his constant 'Glory: my dears! We're living, eh?'

Altogether he went wild, putting away much liquor, as if he thought to quench some inner conflagration; but for all he drank he was never intoxicated, becoming only noticeably thinner. He kept his distance from Mrs. Baima-kov, yet his sons could not help noticing how imperiously and furiously he eyed her. He made great show of his physical strength, tugging on the pole against the garrison soldiery, and wrestling with a fireman and three stone-masons, throwing them all. Whereupon the navvy Tikhon Vialov went up to him and insisted: 'Now try me.'

Artamonov was taken aback by the man's tone, and measured the rugged body with his eye. 'What do you think you are?' he asked, 'tough, or boastful?'

'Don't know,' came the solemn answer.

They seized each other by the belt, and for a long time trod the ground without moving. Artamonov's eyes fol-lowed the womenfolk over Vialov's shoulders; they were shamelessly making eyes at him. He was taller than the navvy, but not so stoutly built, though better proportioned.

Vialov got his shoulder into Artamonov's chest, and strove to get his feet off the ground, for a throw. But Artamonov knew this. 'Too simple, old boy, too simple!' he cried. All at once he himself gave a deep grunt, and Tikhon flew over his head and met mother earth with such force that his legs were momentarily paralysed. There on the grass, wiping the sweat from his face, and somewhat ashamed, Vialov admitted: 'You're tough.' 'So it seems,' the onlookers replied, mocking. 'Healthy,' Vialov went on.

Artamonov held out his hand. 'Up we get!' Vialov tried to get up without Artamonov's hand, but could not. He stretched out his legs again. His eyes followed the departing onlookers with a strange, feeble look in them. Nikita went up to him, full of sympathy. 'Hurt? Can I help?'

Vialov grinned. 'It's my bones. I am stronger than your dad, but not so clever. Let's catch 'em up, friend.' He tucked his arm snugly in that of the hunchback, and they made after the others, Vialov stamping now and then with his feet, no doubt hoping to lessen the pain.

Worn out by sleepless nights, the young couple drifted for all to see about the town, surrounded by the gaily rigged, noisy, tipsy crowd—eating, drinking, driven to shame at the spicy jokes showered on them, trying hard not to look at each other, inseparably arm-in-arm, inseparably side by side wherever they sat, yet speechless as if two strangers. All this delighted Matrena Barsky, and she would turn to Artamonov and Uliana Baimakov and ask if the lad had not been well prepared, eh? 'I told you I would . . . See, Uliana, how well I schooled your lass. Just look at your son-in-law, proud as a peacock, beside himself he is, and sore-strained . . .'

But when at night they withdrew into their own room, Peter and Natalia shed with their clothes all drunken merry-making, which was forced on them and dutifully borne, and exchanged their own thoughts about the day that was done.

'I must say folk know how to put it down here in Dromov.'

'Do your folk drink less, then?' his bride asked him.

'You didn't think *mouzhiks* had all that to drink, did you?'

'But you don't seem like *mouzhiks*.'

'We were household serfs, you see . . . that's something like nobility . . .'

Or, they were sitting embraced at the window, drinking in the garden scents in silence, when she whispered: 'Why so quiet?' and he whispered back: 'I don't want to say any ordinary words, just now.'

He would have liked to hear words that were not ordinary, but Natalia knew none. When he had tried to tell her of the endless space, the openness, of the golden steppes, she only said: 'Aren't there any woods at all? Oh, how terrible that must be!'

'Terrors live in the woods,' Peter observed flatly. 'How can the steppes be terrible? Nothing but earth, and sky, and yourself!'

One day, some time later, while they were at the window, speechlessly admiring the starry night, there was a scuffle down in the garden, near the bath-house; then running, crashing through the raspberry bed; then a hushed, but enraged cry: 'What are you about, you devil!'

Natalia, frightened, leapt up. 'Mamma!'

Peter leant out of the window, filling the frame with his broad back, and saw his father, arms round his mother-in-law, holding her to the wall of the bath-house, trying to get her down. Her arms beat like flails on his head; in a breathless hoarse whisper as she cried: 'Let me go, or I'll scream!' Then, beside herself, 'Please, sweet, don't . . . please don't . . .'

35

Quietly Peter closed the window, took Natalia and drew her on to his knee. 'Don't look,' he said. She struggled. 'What is it, who?' 'Father,' Peter said, holding her tight. 'Don't you understand?'

'*Oi*, how can they?' she whispered, in terror and confusion. Peter carried her to the bed. Meekly he said: 'We are not our parents' keepers.'

Natalia clutched her head in her hands, and rocked to and fro, howling: 'What sin, what sin!'

'Not ours,' Peter said, and back to his mind came his father's words: *The gentry do far worse, and the Lord puts up with it.* 'It's better like that," he went on, 'he won't try to interfere with you now. . . . Old men are coarse, they think it's a trifle to have a bit of fun with the daughter-in-law . . . don't cry . . .'

Through her tears Natalia said: 'Remember when they danced together? I was afraid then. . . . If he forces her, what will life here be like?'

But, worn out by excitement, she was soon asleep, still dressed. Peter then opened the window and looked all about the garden, but there was nobody there. He took deep breaths of the little wind that comes before dawn, when the trees shake off their scented darkness. Leaving the window wide open, he lay down beside his wife, but did not close his eyes, turning over and over that what had just happened. How good it would be to have a small farm somewhere, he and Natalia. . . .

Natalia soon wakened. Sorrow for her mother, and indignation—so she felt—wakened her. Barefoot, as she was, she hurried downstairs. The door of her mother's room, always bolted at night, was half open. This frightened her still more. But when she looked at the bed in the corner she saw the white shape under the sheets, and the dark hair strewn over the pillow.

'Sleeping,' thought Natalia, 'tired out by tears and grief...'

She had to do something to console her outraged mother. She went into the garden. The dew-damp grass tickled her bare feet. The sun had just topped the forest fringe, and the low rays dazzled her. There was already a touch of warmth in them. She plucked a dew-silvered leaf of burdock and put it to her cheeks. Refreshed by this, she plucked strings of red currants, using the leaf as platter, thinking the while of her father-in-law, though without bitterness—of his regular way of clapping her on the shoulders and with a genial smile asking: 'Well, how are we, lass? Full of life, eh? That's the way!'

He clearly had nothing else to say to her. Those slaps of his had always offended her a little, it was just like slapping a mare's flanks. 'The old villain!' she said to herself, and tried to think harshly of him.

The finches, the tits, and the linnets were at their music, the foliage rustled like silk, far away on the outskirts of the town a shepherd was piping, and from the shore of the Vataraksha, where the factory was slowly rising, the sound of men's voices floated slowly across the glimmering silence. Something snapped overhead. Natalia started and looked up—it was a bird-trap hanging from the apple tree, and a linnet fighting to get out of the wall of twigs. Nikita's work? A dry branch cracked.

When she went back indoors she looked into her mother's room. Uliana was awake, on her back, arms behind her head, forehead puckered in surprise. 'Who . . . who is it . . . oh, *you*,' she said agitatedly, and sat up, leaning on one elbow.

'I only . . . brought you some currants . . . for your morning tea.'

On the table beside the bed she saw a large kvass bottle,

nearly empty. There was kvass spilled on the cloth. The cork lay on the floor. Round her mother's steady grey eyes lay a dark shadow, but they were not swollen from tears, as Natalia had expected; they merely seemed to have grown deeper and darker. That slightly haughty look, too, was gone; her mother seemed to look out from a great distance, absently.

'The mosquitoes keep me awake,' Uliana said, drawing the sheet close round her neck, 'I'm going to sleep in the barn in future. I'm bitten to death. What got you up so early? Barefoot, too, on the wet grass? Your shift is all wet. ... You'll catch cold ...'

Her mother seemed to speak unwillingly, without feeling; lost in her own thoughts. Natalia's concern began to change to the sharp, even hostile curiosity of a woman. 'Dreaming of you woke me,' she said.

'Dreaming what?' the mother asked, eyes on the ceiling.

'I mean ... sleeping here all alone ... without me.'

Natalia detected a deepening of colour on her mother's cheeks; she could see through the false smile as Uliana said: 'I'm not timid, you know,' then, closing her eyes, 'run along now, your darling's awake—I seem to hear him upstairs.'

As she slowly went back upstairs, Natalia thought, scornfully and almost hostile to the idea: 'He spent the night with her, it was he drank the kvass. Those blood-spots on her neck were not made by mosquitoes, but kisses. I won't say a word to Peter. Sleep in the barn—hm! And shouting out too ...'

'Where've you been?' Peter asked, looking keenly at her. She felt guilty, and lowered her glance. 'Gathering currants ... I went to see mother.'

'Well?'

'Seems all right.'

'Oh!' said Peter plucking at his ear, 'oh!' With a grin, he stroked his tawny little beard and said: 'Seems that old fool Barsky was right—don't believe the shrieks or the tears.' Then he asked: 'Seen Nikita?'

'No.'

'Not seen Nikita—but he's out there in the garden, trapping birds—look!'

'*Oi!*' cried Natalia, in horror, 'and me out there like this!'

'Just what I was thinking.'

'When on earth does he sleep?'

Peter, pulling on his boots, cleared his throat noisily, while Natalia, with a smile, said: 'Though he is a cripple, Nikita's nice, nicer than Alexey.'

Peter cleared his throat again, but not quite so loudly.

Every day, as soon as the sun was up, and the herdsman, mournfully blowing his long horn, was assembling the animals, the beat of axes began across the river, and the Dromovians, turning out their cattle and sheep, would turn to each other and say scornfully: 'Off they go again, no peace, no quiet . . .' or, 'Greed's the sworn foe of rest.'

At times Ilia Artamonov thought he had at last overcome the sluggish hostility of Dromov. People now respectfully raised their hats to him; they listened with attention to his stories about the Prince Ratski family, though nearly always there was somebody to observe proudly that: 'Our gentle folk are simpler and poorer, but stricter than yours.'

On Sunday evenings and other holidays he would sit on in the well-planted, beautiful gardens of Barsky's Inn down by the Oka, and try to persuade the rich and powerful of Dromov that: 'You'll all profit by my enterprise.'

'God grant,' Pomialov answered him, on one occasion, with his ingratiating grin, from which it was hard to know if he was going to slobber over you or use his teeth. His

39

nubbled face was clumsily concealed in his flaxen beard while his pasty nose sniffed suspiciously at everything about him, and his brown eyes watched spitefully. 'God grant,' he repeated, 'though we didn't do so badly without you, but perhaps we'll get along with you.'

Artamonov frowned. 'That's a bit two-edged,' he said, 'not friendly.'

Barsky laughed loudly. 'Our Pomialov's like that,' he said.

Barsky looked as if somebody had slapped together a few scraps of purplish flesh; his huge head, bull neck, cheeks, arms—all of him was thickly covered with a dense, bear-like fleece; his ears were invisible, his diminutive eyes hidden in billows of fat. 'All my guts have run to fat,' he would say, and guffaw, opening wide a mouth full of stumpy teeth.

The wheelwright, Voroponov, peered closely at Artamonov with his excessively bright eyes, and in a dry voice tried to teach him: 'It's good to do business, yes, but the Lord's tasks should not be neglected. As 'tis said, "*Martha, Martha, for all your cares, one thing only is lacking*." '

Those eyes, bright and at the same time apparently empty, looked at him, as if Voroponov had guessed something and was about to astound them all. There were times when he would start: 'Of course, Christ too ate of the bread, so that Martha . . .'

'Now, now,' Zhiteikin the tanner halted him, for he was an elder of the church. 'Don't forget yourself!' and Voroponov was silent, his sallow ears twitching.

Artamonov then asked Zhiteikin: 'So you know all about my enterprise, do you?'

'Oh no,' Zhiteikin cried genuinely surprised, 'that's your business, not mine—you're a queer fellow. . . . We've every man of us our own worries.'

Artamonov sipped the thick beer and gazed between the

branches at the dull belt of the river—and then more over to the left, where the writhing Vataraksha traced its green snake-like arabesque, creeping from the pine forest through the marshes. There, on the point, a golden tongue of sand, among the rich heaps of chips and wood-shavings were red bricks, and set in a clearing of the willows stretched a long factory building, like a ruddy coffin without a lid. A warehouse, its corrugated roof still unpainted, its golden rafters sprung high in the burning sky, flamed in the sunlight; and the yellow frame of a two-floored house shimmered in the heat.

It was neat of Alexey to compare the house seen from a distance to a guitar. Alexey was living down there, to get him away for a bit from the lads and lasses of the town; he was difficult—quick-tongued, quick-tempered too. Peter was more sluggish; there was something missing in Peter; he still had not the least notion how much a man could do if he had the drive. A shadow darkened Artamonov's face.

He lowered his bushy eyebrows and smiled at the Dromov men; poor stuff, these Dromov men, with little or no urge to real work, no guts either.

When night fell, and the town was fast asleep, Artamonov stole like a thief down the river bank, by back ways, to widow Baimakov's garden. There were mosquitoes droning in the warm air, as if it was they that spread over the world the tasty mingled odour of cucumbers, apples, and fennel. There was the moon rolling on its way among the grey clouds, and shadows smoothing the water. Stepping over the wattle fence into the garden, he crept across the yard—then he was in the dark barn, and from the corner came the frightened whisper greeting him: 'Nobody notice you?'

As he wrenched off his clothes, he groused and grumbled: 'I'm sick of this hiding—what, am I a kid?'

'You started it.'

'And what? If God brought us together.'

'Ohhh! You godless creature! It's against God's law.'

'Then let it be! 'Tis long to that reckoning. Your Dromov folk are the first worry.'

'Shh! Say no more!' she whispered, and long into the night, driven by a burning thirst, she soothed him with her caresses. Later, waking from a short sleep, she again spoke of the Dromov folk: beware of this one; remember that one's cunning, that one's a liar, that one's got money and to spare. She said: 'Pomialov and Voroponov are trying to buy up the timber all round, since you'll need so much, so they can beat you down.' 'Too late,' he replied, 'I bought the lot from the Prince in good time.'

They were wrapt from all sides in impenetrable darkness. They could not even see one another's eyes. All their talk was in hushed whispers. The air was redolent of hay and birch besoms; from the cellar below came a damp and pleasing coolness. A sombre silence had wrapped the little town in leaden casing. The only sounds were the nimble scamper of a rat, or the squeaks of a litter of mice, between the hours marked by St. Nicholas' church scattering the sickly uncertain echoes of its cracked bell into the darkness.

'Ah, what splendid flesh,' Artamonov exulted, palping the lavish and burning body of the woman, 'what power! How came you to have but one child?'

'There were two others,' she said, 'but they were weaklings and died.'

''Twas your husband who was no good . . .'

'You won't believe me,' she whispered, 'when I tell you, I never knew what love meant till I knew you. Other women used to talk about it, but I never believed, I thought they lied to save their faces! I tell you, he only gave me shame; to go to bed was like lying on the block. I'd pray for him to fall asleep without touching me! He was such a decent man too, so quiet and clever; but God did not grant him any gift for making love . . .'

This astonished Artamonov and excited him too; his hands cupped and crushed her full breasts, and he growled: 'So that's it. . . . I never knew . . . I thought it was all the same to a woman, who the man was.' Beside her he felt more powerful, more intelligent.

By day she was always the same even-tempered, calm and wise housekeeper, respected throughout Dromov for her brains and her literacy.

One day, thoroughly wakened by the youthful fury of her caresses, he said: 'Now I know what you were after. We were fools to marry our children, we should have married ourselves . . .'

'Your boys are good lads; I don't mind if they find out . . . but the town . . .' She shuddered. 'Don't worry, lass!' he whispered in her ear.

One day she suddenly said: 'Tell me, sweet—that deserter you killed . . . doesn't he trouble your sleep?'

He was unperturbed. Stroking his beard, he replied: 'N-no . . . I sleep quite well. Why shouldn't I? I hadn't even time to see the man—they got in first blow at me, nearly had me down, so I swiped the nearest with my cudgel and then the second—the third got away.' He heaved a sigh, and growled: 'Fools set on you, and you're responsible . . . ugh!' He was indignant. He lay on for some time, without speaking.

'You asleep?' she asked, at last.

'No.'

'You must go . . . it's getting light . . . going down to the site? . . . Oh, how all this must wear you out . . .'

He strode through the chill and pearly half-light of breaking day, pacing his own land, hands clasped at his back beneath his cloak, thrusting the tail out like a cockbird's, trampling the shavings and the sawdust. He was thinking: it was high time he gave Alexey opportunity to work a little steam off; Alexey was a good lad, indeed, though a hard nut.

His eye sought out a handy patch of sand and wood-shavings, for a nap. He was soon asleep. The fire of sunrise burned gently to a blaze in the greenish heavens; the glorious sun proudly flourished its peacock tail of light over the world and then stately glided into full vision.

The workers woke and nudged one another, pointing out the giant lying there—'He's come!' Bullet-skulled Tikhon Vialov shouldered his crowbar. His eyes glinted at Arta-monov, as if he would have liked to tread over him—but dared not.

All the ant-swarm hither-and-thither of the men, their cries, their noisy tools, were powerless to waken that massive body lying, his snores like the scroop of a blunt saw, face to the sky. Vialov shambled away, looking round and blinking as if somebody had cracked him on the skull. From the house Alexey appeared in white canvas tunic and blue trousers; light as air he went down to bathe, making a circle round his uncle as if afraid that a slight rustle of wood-shavings might waken him.

Nikita had gone off into the forest before daybreak. Nearly every day now he brought in a couple of waggons of leaf-mould, piling it on the plot he had cleared for the garden; he had already planted birches, a sycamore, a rowan, a wild cherry; now he was digging deep holes in the sand and filling them with a mixture of leaf-mould, clay, and river mud—for fruit-bearing trees. Out of working hours Tikhon Vialov helped him. 'Making gardens is a decent sort of job,' Vialov declared.

Peter Artamonov acted as overseer, plucking at his ear

Bernard Duffield

as he went about the work. There was the rich sigh of the
saws as they ate into the timber, the slithering whistle of
planes, the ring of the axes, the rich slopping of gobs of
mortar, and the whine of the grindstone as it licked a
cutting-edge back on to the axes. As the carpenters raised
a beam they sang its song—*The Oak Beam*—a young voice
ringing with the introit:

> "Godson Zachary came to Mary,
> With his fist he felled her squarely . . ."

"Tis a coarse song,' Peter remarked to Vialov; but Vialov, knee-deep in the sand, only answered: 'It don't matter,
what they sing.'

'Why not?'

'Words aren't men,' Vialov answered.

'A strange *mouzhik*,' thought Peter, as he walked away.
He recalled how his father had wanted Vialov to be foreman, but Vialov kept his eyes on Artamonov's feet and
merely said: 'I'm no good for that, I can't manage other
men . . . make me your yardman. . . .' Upon which Artamonov had cursed him roundly.

Autumn came in cold and wet, the gardens rusty, the
woods like iron, with spreading blotches of rust; the winds
howled rain, and swept the dirty, trodden wood-shavings
on to the water. Now not a day passed but mangy nags
dragged the peasant wagons up to the warehouse with loads
of flax.

Peter booked it in, carefully watching out, in case the
grim, shaggy peasants slipped in a sweated bale, or goods
damped for weight, or even common flax instead of long
staple. His job was no easy one. Alexey, quick-tempered,
was never slow to start a quarrel with the peasants.

Artamonov had gone to Moscow. Soon after him the
mother-in-law went away too, ostensibly to retire to a

nunnery for a while. When evening tea came round Alexey would complain. Life was getting him down. He did not like the local folk. This got Peter's goat. 'As if you're a paragon yourself! You rub everybody up the wrong way . . . always bragging.'

'Why not, when I've reason to?' was Alexey's answer to that.

He would toss back his forelock, straighten his shoulders, puff out his chest and, with a cock-o'-the-walk squint, stand challenging his brothers and Natalia. Natalia kept out of his way, as if there was something in him that frightened her; she was always sharp with him.

After dinner, when Peter and Alexey had gone back to the factory, she took her sewing to Nikita's monastic little room, and sat by the window in the birchwood armchair which the cripple had so neatly made for her. The hunch-back was the clerk of the mill, from morning to night at his books, but whenever Natalia came he would break off and tell her stories of the life of the nobility, and of the strange flowers in their greenhouses. His high-pitched girlish voice was vibrant and kindly, his blue eyes looking past Natalia out into the open; she would bend over her stitching, lost in thought, as if oblivious of him. They might sit like that two whole hours without exchanging one glance, though from time to time Nikita would feel compelled to take his sister-in-law into the kindly warmth of his blue eyes; his clumsy ears would then flush noticeably.

Sometimes his glance had compelled her to glance back at him, and give him a smile full of grace, a strange smile, in which Nikita had sensed more than once that she guessed his troubled heart; at other times he had felt that he had offended her, she was angry, and he lowered his head guiltily.

To-day the rain was beating at the window, washing

from the garden its faded summer colours; they could hear Alexey shouting, the roars of the young bear chained a day or two ago in a corner of the courtyard, and the ceaseless tattoo as the workgirls flayed the flax.

Alexey burst into the room cap awry; though he was wet and smeared with the autumn mud, it was like a sudden intrusion of spring. Laughing, he told them about Vialov— Vialov had just chopped off a finger. 'He makes out it was an accident, ha-ha, but it's clear as daylight—he's getting out of military service. And we who'd give anything to get away from all this into uniform . . .' He frowned, and bellowed like the young bear: 'To hell with it all!'—then imperiously held out his hand: 'Let me have a bit of cash, I'm off to the town.'

'What for?'

'Mind your own business.' And he was gone, singing:

> "Trips a lassie down the lane,
> Taking cakies to her man . . ."

'Ah me, he'll come to no good one of these days,' said Natalia. 'Little Olga Orlov and the other girls see a great deal of him, but Olga isn't fifteen yet, and no mother, only that drunkard of a father.'

Nikita did not like the way she said this; there was too much feeling and an excessive sorrow—even jealousy—in her words. He stared fixedly out of the window. The firs reached out their hands in the damp air, shaking mercurial drops of rain from their green needles; his firs; every tree about the house was his work.

Peter came in, morose and tired. 'Tea not ready, Natalia?' 'It's early.' 'Tea, I said,' he shouted.

Natalia went out. He took her chair and started complaining. 'All this father's put on my shoulders,' he growled. 'Round and round, but I don't know where it all leads; and if anything goes wrong, he will take it out of me.'

Gently, cautiously, Nikita told him about Alexey and the little Orlov girl, but he did not want to hear, took nothing in. 'I've no time for admiring the girls,' he said. 'My own wife I only see half-asleep, at night; my day's blind as an owl. You're filling your head with twaddle . . .' He plucked at his ear, hesitated, and went on at last: 'This factory business isn't for us. We ought to have bought a bit of land in the steppes and farmed. Less worry and more profit.'

Ilia Artamonov came back from Moscow in great spirits. He had grown younger, trimmed his beard close, grown still broader in the shoulder, it seemed, and his eyes were brighter; altogether he was like a plough with a brand-new coulter. He stretched himself out on the divan like a gentleman, and told them their business was going to go like clockwork, without fail—'Work enough for you and your children and your grandchildren. For three hundred years ahead. We Artamonovs are destined to bring about a tremendous advancement in our country's economic prosperity!'

His eyes ran over Natalia's figure, and he cried out: 'Getting big, Natalia, eh? Let it be a boy—and there'll be a fine present for you!'

Going to bed that night, Natalia said to her husband: 'The old Dad's pretty nice, when he's in a good humour.' But Peter looked askance at her, and said roughly: 'No doubt, promising presents.'

But after a little more than a fortnight, Artamonov's humour swung the other way, and Natalia asked Nikita what was making him so sore. 'I don't know,' Nikita said. 'Nobody can make head nor tail of him.'

It was the very same evening, over tea, that Alexey suddenly came out, loud and bold: 'Dad, let me join the army.'

'W-w-what?' and Artamonov choked in astonishment.
'I don't like the life here.'

'Outside!' Artamonov ordered the family, but when
Alexey went with them: 'Stop, Alexey!'

At great length he looked the lad up and down, up and
down, hands behind his back, only his eyebrows twitching;
then he muttered: 'And I telling myself you were my eagle!'

'I can never fit in here.'

'Rot! Your place is here. Your mother put you in my
charge—off you go!'

Alexey turned to go, awkwardly, like a hobbled horse,
but his uncle grabbed him by the shoulder: 'That's not the
way you deserve to be talked to, either—my father talked
to me with his fist. Out!' Then, calling him back once again,
he said to him, very seriously: 'Ye could be a big man, see?
Don't let me hear any more puling from ye!'

When Alexey had left the room, Artamonov remained
rooted at the window, clutching his chin, watching the
damp grey snow float down. Soon it was dark as the grave
outside, and he went down to the town. Uliana's outer
gate was already locked. He tapped on the window. She
herself opened the door to him, asking angrily what he was
thinking of, coming 'at such an hour'.

Without a word, without taking off his coat, he went
straight indoors, flung his cap on the floor, leant his elbows
on the table, and talked to her about Alexey. 'He's not one
of us,' he told her, 'my sister had business with her master;
it's coming out.'

Uliana had looked to see that the shutters were well
closed, and put out the candle. In the corner of the room the
bluish flicker of the silver ikon-light alone thinned the
darkness.

'A quick marriage—that would hold him down,' she
said.

'Right enough,' he replied, 'but that's not all. There's no drive in Peter, that's the misfortune. Without drive you can neither get sons nor kill a man. . . . You'd think he was working for somebody else, still for a boss as if he were a serf, he's not got the liberation in his bones—get me? Nikita—well, poor lad, no wonder all he thinks of is gardens and flowers. So all this time I'd thought it would be Alexey who would get his teeth into it.'

Uliana tried to calm him. 'You're too impatient. You'll get the wagon going in time; and once it starts, they'll all knuckle under, and put their own shoulders to the wheel.'

They stayed talking till midnight, side by side, in the warm silence of her room. The soft bluish radiance of light, which the feeble little petal of flame in the ikon lamp dispensed, hovered to and fro. Artamonov's complaint was not limited to the lack of business drive in his sons; he could not get the townsfolk out of his mind. 'Mean-souled cusses they are,' he said. She replied: 'They can't stand you because you're successful; we women folk may like it, but to the men the success of another is a beam in the eye.'

She was clever at calming and consoling him, and even when she said: 'The only thing I am afraid of, terribly afraid, is you giving me a baby,' he only grunted.

'In Moscow,' he said, getting to his feet and embracing her, 'the shop's going ahead like a house a-fire. Oh, if you were only a man!'

'Good night, dear one,' she said, 'you must go!' and, kissing her passionately, he obeyed.

At Shrove-tide Mrs. Yerlandsky brought Alexey home from Dromov on a timber drag—tattered, beaten up, unconscious. With the help of Nikita, she massaged him at great length with horse-radish macerated in vodka; he only groaned. Artamonov paced up and down the room like a wild beast, rolling up his sleeves every few minutes and letting them down again, grinding his teeth; the moment Alexey came to himself he brandished his fist and shouted at him: 'Who was it? Out with it!'

Alexey pitifully half-opened one angry, swollen eye. Spitting blood, he gasped, then cried hoarsely: 'All right, finish me off!'

Natalia, terrified, broke into loud sobs. The old man stamped with mortification. 'Enough of that! Outside!' he yelled.

Alexey clutched his head in his hands as if he would have wrenched it off, and groaned. Then, flinging his arms wide, he rolled over on to his side, and was silent, his bleeding, wheezing lips wide apart. A candle flickered on the table, over the mutilated flesh the shadows crept; it seemed to swell and darken. At the feet stood the brothers, hushed, crestfallen; the old man still strode about the room, asking at large: 'Tell me—can he—will he pull through—tell me!'

But a week later Alexey was up again, with a moist cough, and spitting blood. He took frequent steam baths; and drank pepper-seasoned vodka; a grim sombre fire smouldered in his eyes; he was the handsomer by it. He refused to say who had done it, but Mrs. Yerlandsky found out—Stephen Barsky, two firemen and a Finn who was yardsman to Voroponov. But when Artamonov put it to Alexey, he replied: 'I don't know.' 'Don't lie!' 'I did not see them,' Alexey said, 'they flung a big cloak over me from behind.'

'There's something you're hiding,' Artamonov insisted, trying to get to the bottom of it, but Alexey only flashed a dangerously burning glance at him and said: 'I shall get over it.' 'That's not enough!' was Artamonov's opinion. Into his beard he growled: 'They deserve a bit o' red paint for a thing like that—singe their whiskers for 'em.'

He became still more attentive—gruffly kind to Alexey—and toiled demonstratively, not trying to hide that purpose of all this new spurt of activity was to inspire his children with a passion for labour.

'Do everything yourselves, don't scorn anything!' he tried to teach them, and himself did many a thing he could have left to others, on all sides revealing keen-eyed, animal skill. That way he always knew exactly what the principal obstacle was, and the easiest way to master it.

Meanwhile Natalia's pregnancy ran unnaturally past its time. When at last, after more than two days of childbed, she gave birth to a daughter, he could only say, bitterly: 'Come, what is the meaning . . .'

'You should thank the Lord for his mercy,' Uliana solemnly counselled him, 'with to-day being St. Helena the Flaxen . . .'

'No? Not really?' He grabbed the calendar of the saints, to check it, keen as a child—'Where is the sweet babe?' On Natalia's bosom he laid ear-rings with rubies, and five ducats: 'There's y' present!' he bellowed. 'Though it's not a boy, you've done well.' And turning to Peter: 'You, you cold blooded cod, aren't you glad? I was when you were born.'

Peter stared in alarm at the bloodless, agonized, almost unrecognizable face of his wife; her exhausted eyes were deep sunk in black hollows, and looked out on living and lifeless things as if they reminded her of a time long forgotten; slowly her tongue moistened her bitten lips.

'Why is she so silent?' Peter asked his mother-in-law.

'She's cried out enough,' Uliana told him, pushing him out of the room.

Two days and nights he had heard his wife's cries. At first he had been sorry for her, and afraid she would die. Then the cries deafened him, he was stupefied by the coming and going about the house, and wearied with fearing and pitying. He tried only to keep as far away as he could, where the howls of Natalia could not reach him. But nowhere could he get away from them; those shrieks rang out somewhere inside his own head, and awakened the most extraordinary ideas. Wherever he went he seemed to come across Nikita with his axe, or his shovel—hewing down, shaping timber, digging pits, scampering away noiseless as a mole—as if the two of them moved in a circle, to meet at every turn.

'I don't suppose she will pull through,' he muttered. Nikita thrust the shovel into the sand. 'What does the midwife say?' he asked. 'Hopes for the best. You're all a-shiver —what's the matter with you?' 'Neuralgia,' Nikita replied.

The evening after the child was born Peter had been sitting on the porch steps with Nikita and Vialov. With a dreamy smile he had said: 'Mother put the little babe into my hands, I was so glad that I didn't feel its weight at all, I nearly threw my little daughter up to the ceiling. Can't make out how such a little thing should give so much pain . . .'

Tikhon Vialov scratched his head and in his usual droll way observed: 'All human troubles start from little things.'

'I don't see what you mean,' Nikita asked, with great seriousness. Vialov only yawned: 'Well, you see, that's how it seems to me.'

They were interrupted by a call to come in to supper.

The child was well developed, and heavy. All the same, five months later it was dead—of green sickness. Natalia fell sick with it too, and nearly died.

When they laid the babe to earth, Artamonov tried to console his son: 'After all—she'll bear you others. What's more, from now on we've our own plot in the churchyard, we've cast our anchor deep. What you have's your own, what you command's your own, your own on earth, your own under earth—it rounds you off!'

Peter nodded, but his eyes were on Natalia. Back strangely bowed, she stared below her at the little mound which Nikita was meticulously levelling with a shovel. With an unnaturally quick movement of her fingers, as if afraid she might burn her fingers against her red, swollen nose, she wiped the tears from her cheeks and muttered: 'Dear God, dear God, dear God . . .'

Alexey was sauntering about, reading the inscriptions on the crosses of other graves; he had grown thin and looked older than his years. His features, with their flue of dark hair, so distinct from the other peasant faces, might have been scorched and blackened by fire. The insolent eyes, sunk deeper under the black brows, looked out on all the world with hostility; his voice echoed hollowly, he spoke haughtily and indistinctly—as if on purpose—and when anybody asked him to repeat his words, irritably snapped at them—'Can't you understand?'

He had taken to swearing too; there was now a nasty, mocking note in any dealings with his brothers. Sometimes he shouted at Natalia as if she were a common work-girl. When Nikita one day took him to task, asking: 'Why hurt our Natalia so?'—his answer was: 'I'm a sick man.' 'But she is so gentle,'—'Then let her put up with it!'

He often talked like that of being 'a sick man', invariably with a touch of pride, as if his infirmity were a merit marking him off from the common herd.

Returning from the burial, he said to Artamonov: 'We ought to make our own graveyard, these people won't even suffer our dead to lie beside them.'

Artamonov smiled. 'We will, too,' he said, 'our own

church, and our own cemetery; we'll have our school and our hospital, too—you wait!'

As they went over the Vataraksha bridge, they came on a fellow dressed in a long, rusty, tattered coat, clinging to the rails; a beggar to all appearance; it might have been a civil servant gone to the dogs. The hairy lips, set in the neglected grey growth of bristle of the flabby face, were mouthing soundless words, baring the black stumps of teeth; there was a dull light in the watery little eyes. Artamonov had just turned aside and spat when he saw Alexey nod to the down-and-out with unusual goodwill. 'Who's that?' he asked.

'The watchmaker—Orlov. . . . A clever fellow . . . *They* drove him to this.'

Artamonov shot his nephew a silent sidelong glance.

The summer turned out dry and hot. Forest fires broke out across the Oka. All day an opal pall of acrid smoke hung in the air; at night the horned moon was ominously red; the stars in the haze ceased to twinkle, but stood out like the heads of copper nails; the expanse of the river, mirroring the troubled heavens, was like a stream of cold, dense underground smoke.

The Artamonovs were drinking after-supper tea in the garden, in a semi-circle of sycamores; the trees had taken root well, but the magnificent foliage of elegant leaves which capped them cast no shadow, for the whole night was hazily aglow. Cicadas chattered, cockchafers boomed noisily about, the samovar simmered. Natalia, the upper buttons of her blouse undone, poured out. The flesh of her bosom had the warm tint of fresh butter. The hunchback sat bent over the twigs he was peeling to make bird-cages. Peter plucked at the lobe of his ear, and said slowly: 'It's bad to taunt folk—father's always doing it.'

Alexey, with his dry cough, stared out towards the town,

reaching towards it as if he expected something. At that moment the church bell began to toll mournfully. 'What's that? A fire?' he asked, at once, putting his hand to his forehead and leaping up.

'What an idea! It's the watchman, sounding the hour.'

Alexey left them. After a pause, Nikita said slowly: 'He's always seeing fires nowadays.'

'He's bitter,' Natalia said cautiously, 'and how jolly he once was . . .'

Then, assuming authority, Peter turned to his brother and Natalia—'You're both of you a bit silly about him; he only takes offence at your pity . . . Natalia, bed!'

Nikita followed them out with his eyes. Then he too went to bed—out to the summer-house, where he had a pile of hay. But instead of sleeping, he seated himself on the threshold. The summer-house stood on a hummock which he had banked with turf; the view from it topped the fence and gave on to the sombre roofs of the town, herded together, watched over by the church steeple and the firemen's look-out tower.

Indoors, the servants were clearing the table and there was a rattle of crockery. Weavers were passing by on the other side of the fence, one with a casting net, another carrying buckets, a third trying to strike a spark from a flint to light his tinder for a pipe. A dog howled. Tikhon Vialov's steady voice rang in the night—'Who goes there?'

The silence was drawn down over the world, tight like the skin of a drum; however softly it broke against that surface, the crunch of the weavers' feet in the sand jarred on the ear. Nikita loved this soundlessness of night. The more complete it was, the better could he bring all the powers of his imagination to flutter around Natalia, and the brighter then did her dear eyes, always a little startled and apprehensive, glow before him.

It was easy, too, in the dark silence, to make up all manner of strokes of good fortune for himself. He discovered rich hidden treasure, gave it all to Peter, and in return Peter gave Natalia to him. Or there was a band of robbers attacking, and he achieved such marvels against them that his father and his brother agreed that Natalia should be his. Or an epidemic descended on them; Natalia and he were the only ones to survive, and at last he could tell her what was in his heart.

It was some time after midnight when it struck him that above the herded houses and still clustering orchards was another shape, slowly rising into the dark grey depths of the heavens. A minute later the shape was limned with a ruddy glow from below—a building on fire. He ran up to the house; there he saw Alexey already clambering nimbly up the fixed ladders on to the warehouse roof.

'There's a fire!' cried Nikita, and his brother, without stopping in his climb, called back: 'I know . . . what about it?'

'Yes, you were expecting a fire,' Nikita said, stock still as he remembered.

'Well, and what of that?' Alexey replied. 'Drought like this brings fires, doesn't it?'

'We should get the men up!' Nikita said—but Vialov had already done so, and they were beginning to run down to the river, shouting merrily one to another.

'Come up here with me,' Alexey said, as he straddled the ridge of the roof.

Nikita obediently followed him up. 'I hope this doesn't frighten Natalia,' he said.

'Aren't you frightened of Peter putting another hump on your back?' Alexey asked.

'Why should he?' Nikita murmured, and the answer came: 'Keep your eyes off his wife!'

It was some time before Nikita could find an answer. He felt he would slither down off the roof and crash to the ground beneath. 'What an idea,' he said at last, 'you'd do better to think twice before you speak.'

Alexey laughed: 'All right, all right. I'm not blind . . . Don't you fear . . .' He had not been so happy for a long time, peering under his sheltering hand at the broad tongues of flame licking up into the still air, filling it with a dull roar. 'It's the Barskys' house,' he cried excitedly. 'There's twenty barrels of pitch in their yard. It won't catch the neighbours, though, with the gardens in between.'

'To get away, to get away from all this' was in Nikita's thoughts as he peered into the fire-shattered distance, where wrought-iron trees stood out in the ruddy air, and little toy human figures ran fussily to and fro over soil which was rust as ruddy, and thrust at the fire with long thin poles.

''Tis burning fine,' said Alexey.

'Away into a monastery,' the hunchback told himself.

Down below in the yard stood Peter, half-asleep, grousing angrily. Vialov's answers came unhurried. Natalia stood, framed in a window, crossing herself.

Nikita sat on the roof until all that remained on the Barsky site were gilded and glittering coals piled round the blackened columns of the chimneys. Then he climbed down. Going out of the gate, he came on his father, wet through, hatless, blackened with smoke, his coat torn.

'Where are you off to?' Artamonov barked at him, with a fury which was not usual, pushing him back into the courtyard. Then, sighting the white shape of Alexey up on the roof, he cried out still more furiously: 'And who stuck you up there? Come down, you nincompoop, you know you're not fit to be out like that . . .'

Nikita went through into the garden and sat down on the seat under his father's window; in a few moments he heard

58

the door bang fiercely and then his father's voice, hushed but ringing—'You want to ruin yourself, do you? And bring me to shame, eh? I could slay you . . .'

He caught Alexey's whining answer: 'It was you put the idea in my head.'

'Not a word!' the old man cried. 'You can thank God that wastrel's lost the power of speech . . .'

Nikita quickly and stealthily slipped away to the summerhouse in the corner of the garden.

Over morning tea the next day Artamonov said: "Twas no accident. They've found out it was that drunken watchmaker. They've beaten him up; he won't live. It's said Barsky was his ruin, and he had a down too on young Barsky; it's a dirty business.'

Alexey calmly drank his milk. Nikita's hands shook so that he had to hold them between his knees. But the old man noticed it. 'What are you shivering for?' he asked.'I don't feel well.' 'You're a puny lot . . . Look at me!'

Angrily Artamonov pushed his cup away and went out.

The Artamonov works rapidly drew in men. About two versts from the factory, on some rising heather-covered ground, squat little huts began to spring up among the conifers—bare houses with no fence, no garden, from a distance so many beehives. For lonely bachelor workers Artamonov put up a long low building with a lean-to roof just above a shallow ravine—the river long dried-out and forgotten. Three stoves dispersed the length of it served for heating; the windows made small, to conserve the warmth, made it look like a stable, and the workers indeed called it *Stallion Court*.

Artamonov had become even more given to lordly shouting, but money did not put his nose in the air; he was natural with his men, one of the family at weddings, godfather to the children, and on holidays loved a long chat with the elder weavers. It was they who got him to persuade the peasants to sow flax on old pasture land and the clearings of forest fires, with good results. The older workers were very proud of their hail-fellow-well-met master; in him they saw a fortunate *mouzhik*, and would tell the younger men to look at him,—'That's the way to get on!'

And Artamonov lectured his sons. '*Mouzhiks* and workers are more intelligent than townsfolk. Townsfolk's blood's watery, their brains are stripped, they're greedy but they've no guts. Petty dealings, nothing solid. They don't know when to stop, either, but your *mouzhik* sticks within the limits of what's right, he's not all over the place. His right's straightforward: God, f'r example, or corn, or the Emperor. He's plain all through, is your *mouzhik*; so stick to him, lads.

'Peter, you're too cut-and-dried with the men, that's no good, you've got to know how to pass the time of day with 'em; make 'em laugh too; 'tis easier to get what a cheerful man means.'

'I can never think of witty things,' said Peter, his hand as usual going to his ear.

'Learn! A laugh only takes a minute and a half, but it charges a man up for a whole hour. Alexey's a blunderer, too, with the men, always nagging and complaining.'

'They're a lot of rascals, bone-lazy,' Alexey answered him back.

'What do you know about the men?' Artamonov barked.

He was deadly serious. Yet he could not restrain a smile, which he tried to hide, pressing his beard up into his face; to his mind had come how wisely and stoutly Alexey had argued it out with the townsfolk about the cemetery. Dromov had refused to bury any of Artamonov's men in the town cemetery. He had been obliged in the end to purchase

a biggish plot of alder-covered ground from Pomialov and
start his own graveyard. Vialov and Nikita together had
cleared it of timber.

Vialov was a puzzling character. Nikita could see that he
was a quick and skilful worker; there was far more intelligence in his labour than in the unexpected tortured
oracular pronouncements he was given to making. In one
respect Vialov reminded Nikita of his own father—he had
a knack of always finding the weakest point of resistance,
doing a job by his wits, to the preservation of his strength.
Apart from that one enormous difference stood out: whatever he did Artamonov did it with enthusiasm; Vialov
always worked with a sort of indifference, in a condescending way, as if fully aware he was worthy of better things.

His talk was the same: scanty, condescending, portentous,
with an air of indifference, as if to say: 'There's a lot more
I know, that isn't all I might say.'

Moreover, Nikita always seemed to catch a kind of hint
in what Vialov said—a hint which made him irritated with
the man, instilled fear of him and also a disturbing curiosity.

'You know a lot,' he said to Vialov once. Slowly Vialov
answered: 'That's why I am alive—if I know something,
where's the harm, so long as I keep it to myself . . . My
know's put away in a miser's chest, well hid, don't you
worry . . .'

You would never hear Vialov asking other men what
they thought. He merely stared persistently into them with
those blinking bird's eyes and then, as if he had sucked out
their thoughts, he would suddenly blurt out something he
should never have known. There were moments when
Nikita wished the man might bite out his own tongue, or
else chop it off, as he did his finger—but he hadn't even done
that properly. Instead of chopping a finger off his right hand,

he had taken one off the left, and the fourth finger, too.

Artamonov, and Peter—in fact, everybody else—thought Vialov stupid; Nikita saw him differently. His mixed feelings of curiosity about Vialov and fear of that bull-headed, inscrutable peasant grew more and more intense. His sense of fear particularly increased one day when they were on their way back from the forest. Vialov suddenly said: 'It's eating your heart out of you . . . You silly fellow, why not tell her—she might have pity on you, she seems a kind sort.'

Nikita stopped short; his heart failed him; alarm petrified his legs, and he stammered: 'Tell what—whom . . . ?'

Vialov merely glanced at him, and strode on. Nikita clutched at his sleeve; Vialov scornfully plucked the hand off him. 'What's the use of pretending?' Vialov asked.

Nikita slipped the young birch he was transplanting off his shoulder, and looked about him. He would have given anything to plant his fist in the man's shaggy face; but how was he to silence him?

Vialov kept his eyes fixed straight ahead and continued, no more ruffled than ever: 'Even if she isn't kind, she might well pretend to be, for your sake. Women are inquisitive, there isn't one who doesn't want to try another man, to see if there's anything sweeter than sugar. Does our good brother need much? One or two shots and he's all set—and you, burning away for the want of it. Have a try, tell her, I wouldn't mind betting she'll say *yes*.'

In the man's voice Nikita caught a note of friendly compassion. This was something he had never known; there was a bitter pricking in his throat—but also a sensation as if Vialov was stripping him naked.

'What nonsense comes into your head,' he said.

At that moment the church bells began tolling for late communion. Vialov heaved the birch tree on to his own shoulder, and strode on, using his shovel as a stick and continuing calmly as before: 'Don't be afeared of me. You must know I'm on your side, you're a decent fellow, and you're interesting. All you Artamonovs are devilish interesting. You aren't even like a hunchback—yet you are one.'

Nikita's fears dissolved in a burning mortification, which half-blinded him. He stumbled on like a drunkard; he could willingly have laid down on the spot to rest. Hesitatingly he begged: 'Don't you talk to anyone about that.' 'I told you it's as good as locked away,' Vialov replied. 'Forget it all; don't let a word slip to her!' 'I never do have any talk with her. Why should I let it slip?' They did not say another word to each other all the way to the house.

From now on Nikita's blue eyes grew still larger, and more sorrowful; he looked past people and through them, more taciturn, more retiring, than ever. Natalia's eye noticed it. 'Why are you so down in the mouth?' she asked him. 'I've a lot of work,' he answered and hurried away, leaving her offended.

This was not the first time Natalia had felt a new roughness in her brother-in-law's attitude towards her. Her life was monotonous. In four years she had borne two daughters and was already pregnant again.

'Not another girl—what do we want with 'em?' Artamonov had growled, when the second was born, and he made her no present. To Peter he had complained: 'I want grandsons, not grandsons-in-law. Do you think I built this business up for strangers?'

His every word made her feel at fault; she knew that her husband also was dissatisfied. In bed beside him she would stare out into the night at the far-away stars and feel her belly and pray for it to be a boy, though at other times she felt an impulse to shout at them both: 'I shall go on having girls, just to spite you all!'

She longed now to do something astounding, that nobody could have expected of her—something good, to make them all more kind to her, or outrageous, to make them fear her. Only she could never think of anything, either good or bad.

She would be up at daybreak, and down in the kitchen helping the cook prepare breakfast, then upstairs again to nurse the children, then waiting on father-in-law, husband, brothers-in-law, then back to the children again, then sewing and mending for them all. After dinner she would take the little ones out into the garden till evening tea. From time to time buxom lasses from the spinning mill would pop into the garden to say what lovely lovely babies they were, and Natalia would smile back, though she never believed a word of it—they seemed ugly children to her.

Sometimes she would catch a glimpse of Nikita through the trees. He was the only one of them who had ever been kind to her, but now if she asked him to join her for a minute, he would always have a guilty look and say: 'Excuse me, I've no time.'

The mortifying notion gradually formed in her mind that Nikita had been merely pretending to be kind, that Peter had set him to spy on her and Alexey. She was truly afraid of Alexey, because Alexey appealed to her. She knew that she could have refused that handsome fellow nothing. But he showed no desire, did not even seem to notice her presence, and from the hurt caused by his indifference came hatred for him and his impudent dashing ways.

Evening tea was at five; at eight they supped; then Natalia bathed the children, fed them, and put them to bed. Long kneeling prayers followed; and she always went to bed full of anxiety to bear a son. But if Peter wanted her, he would break in on her devotions. 'That's enough; come on!'

Hastily she would cross herself, interrupt her prayer, and go to him, humbly entering the bed. Very rarely he would try to turn it with a touch of humour, such as: 'Why so much praying? You'll never get all you want, there isn't enough to go round . . .'

In the night the infant woke her, crying. She suckled it and soothed it. Then she went to the window and gazed for some time on the garden and night sky; through her mind passed hazy thoughts of her mother, of Artamonov, of her husband, of all that the hard day which had slipped by unnoticed had brought. It was a strange world, robbed of the customary voices, the workgirls' songs, now sad, now cheerful, or the countless noises and murmurs of the factory, its subdued beehive roar. That incessant lively din had filled the whole day; echoes of it were in every corner of the house, rustling in the foliage of the trees, fluttering against the window-panes; the mutter of labour forced itself on her and prevented thought. But in this stillness of night, with all living things given to somnolent silence, to her mind came Nikita's eerie tales of women abducted by the Tartars, and the lives of women hermits and martyrs, stories too of lives full of happiness and jollity. But most frequently all that memory prompted was a sense of injury.

Artamonov usually looked straight through her, but that would even have been satisfactory had there not also been rare meetings by chance with him indoors, with nobody else about, when his keen eyes shamelessly palped her body from breasts to knees, and his breath quickened menacingly.

Her husband was cold and curt with her. Sometimes it seemed to her she stood in his way; because of her he was unable to see something hidden behind her. Very often, when he had undressed, he would loll a long time at the foot of the bed, leaning on one elbow and plucking at his ear, or else stroking his cheek with his beard, as if he had toothache.

His ugly face would fall into wrinkles—angered, aggrieved —and Natalia would be afraid to get into bed.

He had little to say to her, and that only about domestic matters. Now it was only very rarely indeed that he spoke of a farming life or how the squires lived, about all of which she knew nothing. In the winter, when the holidays came round, or for any wedding, or in Shrovetide, he drove her in the sleigh through the town, with his huge black stallion in the shafts. This animal, with its copper-yellow eyes, outlined with blood-shot veins, tossing its head and snorting loudly, terrified Natalia, especially as Vialov made things worse by saying: 'That's a nobleman's horse, it doesn't take to a stranger's hand.'

Her mother was a frequent visitor, and Natalia envied her the free life she led, and the festive light in her eyes. Her envy became still more biting and painful when she observed the youthful turn that the light banter between her mother and Artamonov would take, the self-satisfaction with which he would stroke his beard as he gazed at his mistress—her mother strutting about like a peahen, with swaying hips, shamelessly vaunting her beauty before him. The liaison had long been known to all the town. Uliana was harshly condemned and decent people cut her, forbidding their daughters even to call on Natalia, once their playmate, because she was the daughter of a fallen woman, daughter-in-law of an obscure peasant outsider, and wife of a creature puffed with pride—her dour husband. Now the petty delights of her maiden life were magnified and glowing in her sight.

It hurt her too to see that her mother, who had once been so straight, had learnt to be cunning and false. Clearly Uliana Baimakov was afraid of Peter. To keep on the right side of him she flattered him with her tongue, making much of his alleged businesslike powers. She must also have feared

Alexey's scornful glance; she was always chaffing with him, exchanging whispers, making him presents—on his last birthday it was a porcelain clock with sheep on it and a woman in flowers, a lovely and well-made piece which everybody admired.

'I got it for a debt,' she had explained to them all, 'only three rubles silver, too, it's old-fashioned, it won't go; but when Alexey gets married, it'll make a nice ornament . . .'

'So it would for me,' thought Natalia.

Her mother was always poking her nose into the housekeeping, and making her sick with instructions. 'Don't put napkins out on ordinary days, the men's whiskers dirty them so!'

She pursed her lips now whenever she saw Nikita, though she had once liked him, and spoke to him like a paid clerk suspected of dishonesty. She warned Natalia: 'Don't be too forthcoming with him—hunchbacks are sly.'

More than once Natalia would have liked to unburden herself to her mother about Peter—how he did not trust her, and had set Nikita to spy on her, but something always held her back.

But the worst came when her mother, feeling worried like the men because there was no grandson, began one day asking details about her night business with her husband, such shameless details too, with plain words. The mother's moist eyes, her smile, her eyes a little screwed up, her voice softly purring, and her curiosity upset Natalia terribly, so that she was relieved when Artamonov called out: 'In-law —shall I have the carriage ready?'

'I would prefer to walk, dear,' her mother replied.

'Right; I'll see you down.'

All Peter had to say was: 'Your mother's a smart woman; how she manages to hold father! Having her, he's more gentle with us all. She ought to sell the house and come to live here.'

'No, no, not that,' Natalia would have liked to say, but did not dare; and when she thought of how popular and how happy her mother was, that hurt her still more.

One day, seated by the garden window, sewing, she caught snatches of Nikita's and Vialov's conversation. They were busy working on the other side of the strawberry bed, by the bath-house, and the yardman's calm voice penetrated the dull murmur of the factory.

'Boredom—men make it themselves. They herd together and then time hangs heavy.' Once again, he played on Russian words, and Natalia thought: 'How true!' when there was Nikita's gentle voice—objecting: 'You run words to death; what about dancing and singing parties, eh? No, you can't be jolly without people.' Natalia listened in astonishment—that was equally true.

She came to realize that everybody else was sure of his own words, everybody knew some one thing thoroughly. In particular, she saw that common, solid words, when close packed one to another, furnished everybody with his own special fragment of universal right. One man differed from another in the kind of words he used. Words also served men as ornaments; they were flourishes, things to toy with, like gold or silver watch chains. She herself had no such words, nothing in which to dress her innermost thoughts; the result was that those thoughts remained hazy and indefinable, like autumn fog, and merely weighed her down, made her more stupid, so that in the end she told herself, angrily and bitterly, that she was really a fool, ignorant, and dull-witted . . .

'*Medved*—bear—means a *vedun*—a knower—because he *knows* where the mead is,' babbled Vialov, in the raspberry plot. 'How right he is,' she thought—then shuddered as she called to mind how Alexey had killed her pet.

It was a bear. For a whole year and a month, tame and gentle as a dog, it had had the run of the courtyard, lumbering into the kitchen, rising on its hind legs, softly grunting and begging for bread, with its comically blinking eyes. It was such an amusing animal and so sweet and intelligent when others were kind to it.

Everybody was fond of Bruin. Nikita used to look after him, curry out the lumps of his thick, felted hair, take him down to the river to bathe. The bear became so fond of him that whenever Nikita went out, the animal would lift its snout and sniff the air with anxiety, race snorting about the yard, and more than once broke into the office, where his protector worked, even smashing in the window to do so.

Natalia had loved giving the bear bits of wheaten bread with treacle—he had even learned to dip his own bread in a mug of treacle. Then he would rock on his shaggy hind legs and bellow with delight, stuff the bread into his toothed and pinkish jaws, suck his sticky-sweet paw from all sides, then nuzzle Natalia's knee, to have her play with him. You could even talk to the pet, he was just beginning to understand.

But one day Alexey treated the bear to vodka. The drunken beast danced and rolled about, climbed on to the bath-house, took the chimney pipe to pieces, then began bowling down the bricks. A crowd of the workers gathered, roaring with laughter at the sight. From then on, every off-day Alexey would make the bear drunk, to please the men, and the animal got so used to booze that it would pursue any of the men who smelt of liquor; Alexey could not show his face in the yard, but the bear would make a bee-line for him.

So they chained it up. But it smashed its kennel and got

loose in the yard, with the chain round its neck and a big timber at the other end, waving its front paws, head rocking to and fro. They tried to catch it. It tore Vialov's leg, bowled over Morozov, one of the young workmen, then with a blow of its paw on the thigh, knocked down Nikita.

At this point Alexey ran up with a long pike, and with all his force ran it into the animal's belly. From her window Natalia saw the bear sit back on its hind legs, waving the fore legs at all the men shouting madly all round it, as if begging for forgiveness.

Somebody was ready at hand to slip into Alexey's grasp a sharp carpenter's axe. Alexey sparred about, then got in one blow on one paw, one on the other. The animal uttered a terrible cry, sank on to its butchered stumps, and the blood spurted from them in all directions, leaving thick red patches on the ground. Howling piteously, it thrust its head under yet another blow, when Alexey, straddling wide, brought the axe down on the back of its skull as if it were a block of wood. The bear now buried its muzzle into its own blood, the axe going so deep into the bone that even when he got some purchase with one foot on the shaggy body, Alexey could hardly free the blade.

They all lauded his skill and pluck. Artamonov clapped him on the shoulders, and shouted: 'And you say you're a sick man? You rogue!'

All that was horrible. But it was still more horrible to Natalia to know that her intrepid, clever-handed, gay rascal of a brother-in-law was in the grips of a worthless hussy, and had no eyes at all for herself.

Nikita ran out of the yard. Natalia burst into tears. Peter gaped at her in astonishment. 'What on earth would you do if it was a man killed in front of you, eh?' he asked her in exasperation. 'Stop, you ninny!' he yelled, as if she were a little girl. She thought for a moment he was going to hit

her. Holding back her tears she recalled their bridal night—
how good and how timid he had been. Then she told herself that even so he had never beaten her, as all husbands
beat their wives. Stifling her sobs, she murmured: 'Forgive
me, I was so sorry for it . . .'

'You should be sorry for me, not for a bear,' he replied
calmly, and a little more kindly.

The first time she had complained to her mother about
his roughness, how well she remembered the answer she
got.

'Your man's the bee—for a man we're the flowers—they
drink our nectar, that's what you have to see, and learn to
bear it, dearie. Men are the masters in everything; they have
more on their minds than we have—such as building
churches and factories. Only look at what your father-in-
law has built up out of waste ground. . . .'

Latterly, as if sensing that he had not much time left,
Artamonov had begun to make supreme efforts to speed up
the development of his enterprise and to get it on a sure
footing.

A little before St. Nicholas' Day in May, a steam boiler
for the second block of the factory arrived. It was brought
by barge. The barge was moored against the sandy bank of
the Oka, a stone's throw from where the muddy waters of
the green Vataraksha sluggishly seeped into the bigger river.

They now had a hard task—to haul that boiler some
three hundred yards up the sandy slope. On St. Nicholas'
Day, Artamonov gave all the workers a good solid dinner,
with vodka and beer, the tables laid in the yard. The womenfolk made them very festive with twigs of larch and birch
and the first spring flowers—and by their own presence, too,
all decked out as they were, like so many blossoms.

The master, with his family and a few guests, sat at the

table of the old weavers. Spicy banter flashed to and fro between him and the brazen-tongued spindle-girls. He drank heavily, and worked up the merriment, with artful skill. Passing his hand with a flourish through his grizzled beard, he shouted, with some emotion: 'Ah, good folk, we live, don't we?'

They all admired him, admired his style; he was well aware of it too; he was doubly intoxicated at the thought of what a man he was. He shone, glistened, like the sunshiny springtide day; like the whole earth, gaily decked in the tender green of grass and leaf, and sweet with the odour of the birches and the young pines which thrust their gilded candles into the azure heavens. This year spring had fallen early and hot; the wild cherry and the lilac were already abloom. Everything was festive together, everything rejoicing; even human beings, this day, seemed to be thrusting forth all that was best in them.

That ancient, Boris Morozov—one of the weavers—a frail litle old man with a waxen face tucked snug away in a greenish-grey beard all scrubbed and white like a corpse, rose to his feet, with one hand on the shoulder of his eldest son—a peasant of about sixty. At the top of his voice, flourishing a bony, fleshless hand, he yelled: 'Look at me—I'm ninety, I am, ninety and over, mark you! When I was a soldier I fought Pugachev; I rebelled in Moscow the year of the plague, I did, I fought Bonaparte . . .'

'And whom did you sleep with?' Artamonov yelled back, in his ear—Morozov was very deaf.

'Apart from t'others, two wedded wives. Look: seven lads, two daughters, nineteen grandchildren, five great-grandchildren, I've weaved the whole lot! You can see 'em, they be all here, look-ee!'

'Breed us some more!' shouted Artamonov.

'You'll get 'em! I've outlived three emperors, and one

-empress, I have; just think of that! I couldn't tell you how many masters I've had. They're all of 'em dead. But I'm alive. I've wove miles of cloth, I have. Now, you're a real man, Mr. Artamonov, you'll live long. You're a real master, you love the whole work and the work loves you. You never insult a man either. You're a branch of our own timber, long life to 'ee! Success is your lawful wife, not your mistress, who sleeps with a man, then quits him. More power be to 'ee! And keep y'r health, man, that's what! Keep y'r health, I tell 'ee!'

Artamonov grabbed Morozov in his arms, swung him up off the ground, kissed him. He was very moved. 'Thanks be, young-un!' he cried, 'I'll make you master foreman . . .'

The men yelled, roared with laughter, while the old weaver, thoroughly tight, held high above them, waved his skeleton arms; his voice falsetto: 'I say he's everything, I say—everything . . .'

Uliana made no effort to restrain herself. From her cheeks she wiped tears of joy. 'How wonderful!' her daughter said to her. She cleared her nose and answered: 'Of course, a man like that, the good God created him for wonders!'

'Take a tip, lads,' Artamonov cried to his sons, 'how to get on with your men. See, Peter?'

After the banquet, the tables cleared, the womenfolk sang while the men tried their strength, at tug-of-war, and wrestling. Artamonov was everywhere, dancing, wrestling. The festivities went on all night.

At daybreak some seventy of the men made their way in a noisy crowd down to the river, with Artamonov at their head, singing, whistling, tipsy—a regular riot—bearing with them oak timbers, rollers, ropes; and with them hobbled the old weaver, muttering to Nikita: 'He'll master it; I know he will . . .'

They got the squat, red monster off the barge safely;

it was like a headless bull. Then they reeved ropes round it, and with much heave-ho-ing and levering, dragged it on to the rollers, with planking beneath them, next the sand. Rocking to and fro the boiler started on its way. It looked to Nikita as if its stupid round jaws were gaping in amazement at that throng of high-spirited men. Artamonov, in liquor, put his shoulder to it with straining cries: 'Stead-y, lads, stead-y!' Then he slapped the red flanks of the iron monster: 'She's off, she's off!' he bellowed.

There were less than a hundred yards left to the factory, when the swaying boiler suddenly gave an extra violent tip, and slowly slid off the front roller, thrusting its squat muzzle into the yielding sand. Nikita could see the round jaws puff a spurt of grey dust over Artamonov's feet.

The men clustered angrily all round it, and strove to slip a roller under it, but they had exhausted every ounce of strength, and still the boiler was fast in the sand; if anything all they had done was to plunge it in deeper than before. A lever in his arms, Artamonov was in the thick of his men. 'Come on, lads, altogether, hea-ve!'

The boiler stirred a trifle, unwillingly, then settled back heavily again. Nikita now saw his father leave the men, treading strangely, his face altered, one hand under his beard, clutching at his chest, the other clutching at the air, as if he was blind. The old weaver was hopping along at his heels, crying: 'Swallow some earth, swallow some earth!'

Nikita ran to his father. Artamonov gulped, spat blood at his feet and said, in a hollow voice: 'Haemorrhage . . .'

His cheeks had gone grey, his eyes blinked with fear, his jaw shook and his massive, clever body seemed to have shrunken with alarm.

'Hurt yourself?' Nikita asked him, taking his hand. Artamonov staggered a step nearer, gave him a push, and said in a low voice: 'Must have broke a blood vessel.'

'Swallow some earth, I tell you . . .'

'Enough! . . . Go away!' Artamonov muttered, spat again, a large quantity of blood this time, then, in astonishment, gasped: 'It does flow! Where's Uliana?'

Nikita would have run to the house, but his father held fast to his shoulder. Bending his head, Artamonov shuffled in the sand, as if trying to hear the rustle and crunch of it against the angry cries of the men.

'What can it be?' he asked, and started out, treading gingerly, as if crossing high over a river on a framework. Uliana happened to be at the front door, Natalia seeing her off. Nikita noticed her handsome face on first sight of Artamonov—it seemed to swing like a wheel, first right, then left, then turned dead white.

'Get some ice,' she cried, when Artamonov, clumsily folding his legs under him, had sunk to the steps, hiccuping up more and more blood. As if in a dream Nikita caught Vialov's even tones: 'Ice is but water; water won't take the place of blood . . .'

'He ought to swallow a mouthful of earth . . .'

'Tikhon, run for the priest.'

'Let's get him up, carry him indoors,' commanded Alexey. Nikita took one elbow, but somebody trod on his toes so heavily that he saw stars. Then he seemed to see everything more vividly than before. With sickly greed he began to take in every detail, from the porch to his father's room, engraved in memory for all time. There was Vialov, on the big black horse, curvetting about the yard, out of hand. The animal would not go through the gateway, prancing, swinging this way and that, its evil jaws high, scattering the men—frightened maybe by the sudden conflagration of the blinding sun in the sky—then at last was off at the gallop, only to shy violently at the ruddy trunk of the boiler, tossing its rider, and coming back to the yard, tail flicking, breathing hoarsely.

Somebody had the gumption to send some of the boys: 'Come, you boys, run . . . !'

On the window-sill sat Alexey, twisting his pointed black beard. His unpleasant features, so different from the peasants, had grown more keen. They looked dusty, as he stared fixedly over the heads of the others at Artamonov, prostrate on the bed, saying, in a strange voice· 'I must have ruptured myself . . . 'Tis God's will. Boys, I command you —treat Uliana as your own mother; hear me? For Christ's sake! Ahhh! I don't want anybody in the room but ourselves.'

'Don't keep talking,' Uliana pleaded pitifully with him, and stuffed pieces of ice between his lips. 'There isn't anybody else.'

He gulped down the ice, heaved an uncertain sigh, and said: 'You are not the judges of my sin, and it's no fault of hers. Natalia, I've been rough with you—don't take it amiss. Boys! Peter—Alexey—don't quarrel. And don't be so hard with the men. They're good stuff. The best. You, Alexey, you marry that girl of yours . . . it's all right!'

'Dad! Don't leave us alone!' Peter begged, and knelt. But Alexey poked his back. 'What's the use . . . I don't believe . . .'

Natalia cut up the ice in a brass bowl with a kitchen knife; the rustling jabs of the knife were accompanied by the ring of the metal and Natalia's sobs. Nikita watched her tears dripping on to the ice. A yellowish ray of sunlight thrust into the room; it caught the mirror and thence fell back quivering shapelessly on the wall. It might have been trying to obliterate the shapes of the long-moustached red Chinamen on the night-blue sky of the wall-paper.

Nikita had taken his stand at his father's feet, expecting

Artamonov to think of him. Uliana Baimakov combed out the dense, curly hair, and regularly wiped the incessant trickle of blood from the corner of the mouth, the beads of perspiration from forehead and temples. Inaudibly she whispered into the clouded eyes, whispered passionately as if she prayed. With one hand on her shoulder and the other on her knee his tongue, grown clumsy, turned the last words: 'I know. May Jesus watch over you. Bury me in our own graveyard, not out there. I don't want to be among those Dromov . . .' Then, submerged by a great wave of yearning, he whispered: 'Ah, I must have ruptured myself . . . God, ruptured myself . . .'

A tall, round-shouldered priest, with Christ-like beard, and sad eyes, arrived. 'Give me a minute more, parson,' said Artamonov, turning back to his sons—'Boys—don't split! Stick together. Business doesn't like splitting. Peter, you're the eldest—you will be responsible for everything, understand? Now you can go . . .'

'Nikita . . .' Uliana reminded him.

'Where is Nikita? Take care of Nikita. Go now . . . After . . . And Natalia too . . .'

He died of the haemorrhage that afternoon, the sun still glowing mercifully in the west. There he lay, head high, the waxen face frowning and troubled, the eyes, not perfectly closed, seeming to be contemplating the massive forearms obediently crossed on his breast.

To Nikita it seemed that the household was not so much stricken by grief or consternation at this demise as by astonishment. He felt the same dull amazement in everybody, except Uliana Baimakov. She sat on, silent, tearless, beside the departed, as if life in her had died down, deaf to everything, hands on knees, eyes fastened on the marble face set in its snow-white beard.

Peter had straightened his back. He was talking too much,

loudly, in and out of place. Coming into the room where his father lay and where together with an obese sister from the nunnery Nikita was reading from the Psalms, he peered suddenly into his father's face, questioningly, crossed himself and stood there two or three minutes. Then he went out again, and his thick-set shape appeared first in the garden, then in the courtyard, as if he were looking for something he had lost.

Alexey was fussily busying himself with the funeral arrangements. He galloped off to town; then there he was back again, straight into the room, to ask Uliana what to do about the burial and its ceremonies.

'There's time yet,' she told him; worn-out and perspiring, he rushed away again. Natalia appeared. Timidly, pathetically, she tried to get her mother to take some tea, and eat. Uliana heard her out, then said: 'There's time yet.'

While his father was alive, Nikita never knew whether he loved him. He was conscious only of awe, though that did not prevent him marvelling at the inspired manner of working of that man who was so unkind to him, scarcely seeming even aware whether his hunchback son was still alive, or dead. Now, though Nikita felt that he had been the only one who really loved his father deeply, he was completely overcome by a dark mood, unable to think. He was cruelly, harshly hurt by this sudden death of so strong a man: He could not even breathe freely. He just sat on a corner chest, waiting for his next turn at the Psalms, mouthing the familiar words silently while he waited and stared about him.

The warm dusk filled the room; small bright flowers shimmered in the gloom,—yellow petals of the wax candles. All round him the long-moustached Chinese materialized from on the walls; they carried bales of tea on yokes over their shoulders; there were eighteen of them, two by two, on each piece of the wallpaper; those on one side going up, on the other coming down. The oily moonlight touched the wall and the Chinese there immediately acquired new life, and ran more swiftly up and down.

Of a sudden, against the monotonous flow of the words of the Psalter, Nikita caught a hushed, insistent voice: 'Not —really—dead? Oh Lord God!'

Uliana Baimakov's voice was so devastatingly desolate that the nun broke off her reading, and answered her, guiltily: 'Yes, dear lady, dead; the Lord's will be done.'

That was so unbearable that Nikita stumbled noisily from the room, full of bitter, aching resentment against the woman.

Outside the door was Tikhon Vialov, on a stool. He was breaking splinters of wood off a chip, sticking them in the sand, and driving them home, out of sight, with his heel.

Nikita sat down beside him, and silently watched; it made him think of the weird Dromov loony, Anton, overgrown with hair, swarthy, one leg twisted at the knee, with the eyes of a tawny owl, making circles in the sand with his stick, building little cages of chips and twigs inside the circle, then trampling what he had made into the sand, and singing in a revolting way:

> "Chirist is born, good Chiristian men,
> Waggon's broke a wheel agen,
> Bumbledy, bumbledy, bum–dy man,
> Bumbledy bum–dy, Chiristi-an!"

'What a business, eh?' Vialov said to Nikita, as he gave himself a slap on the back of the neck, killing a mosquito. Wiping his hand on his knee, he shot a glance up at the moon, caught in a spray of willow over the water; then his eyes rested on the fleshy mass of the boiler.

'That insect', he continued calmly, 'was hatched this year early; a mosquito lived, and now . . .' Nikita was afraid to let him finish the thought. 'Now you killed it,' he interrupted, and hurried away.

A few minutes later, not knowing what to do with himself, he was back in his father's room where he took over from the nun and read. He poured his own yearning into the words of the Psalms, so that he did not hear Natalia come in, only, all at once, the subdued drip-drip of her voice.

Natalia was never close to him, but he felt liable either to say or to do something extraordinary, and perhaps terrible; even now he was terrified lest in spite of his will some tell-tale word slipped from his lips. He bent his head low, hunched up his hump, and hushed his breaking voice; against the words of the eighty-ninth Psalm the two women's sobbing voices came to his ears.

'See—I've taken the cross he wore from his neck; I shall wear it.'

'Mother, darling, don't forget—I too am all alone.'

'In an alien nest, alone . . .'

'*How long, O Lord, wilt Thou hide Thyself for ever? How long shall Thy wrath burn like fire?*' Nikita painstakingly chanted that wail of terror and despair, and to his mind came the sorry saying he had once heard: '*To live, hating life, is sorrow, loving life—double sorrow.*' He was dismayed to find himself feeling that Natalia's sorrow was a ray of hope for his own happiness.

The next morning, Barsky and the mayor, Zhiteikin, drove out. Having saluted the dead man, bowing before him, each in turn peered into Artamonov's darkening features—cautiously, uncertain of him; they were clearly taken aback by Artamonov's sudden death.

Then Zhiteikin, in a biting, acid voice, tackled Peter. 'I hear you've the idea of burying your father in your own graveyard; now, is that so? Mr. Artamonov, that would be an insult to Dromov. It would be taken as an indication that you don't want anything to do with us, don't want to get on with us—now, is that not so?'

Alexey ground his teeth and whispered to his brother: 'Turn 'em out!'

Barsky then tackled Uliana. 'Friend,' he boomed, 'what's the meaning of this? It's an insult.'

Zhiteikin tried to cross-examine Peter. 'Is it Parson Gleb's idea? Whatever you may think, bear in mind your father was the biggest manufacturer in the district, founder of a new enterprise, a personality and an ornament to our town. Even the Police Inspector has expressed his astonishment. "Are they not Orthodox folk?" he has been asking.'

He kept up a flow of argument, oblivious of the fact that Peter was trying to say something; but when Peter was at last able to get in a word and say it was his father's wish, Zhiteikin piped down at once. 'Well, that be as may be,' he said, 'we shall not be missing at the graveside.' It became obvious that he had really come on some quite different errand.

He crossed the room to where Barsky, having got Uliana up against the wall, was muttering away at her, but before he had reached them, Uliana suddenly cried out loud: 'My good friend, don't be a fool, get out!'

Her lips and eyebrows were a-quiver. Tossing her head proudly back, she turned to Peter: 'These two, in company with Pomialov and Voroponov, want me to try to persuade you boys to sell them the factory; they're offering me an annuity if I do . . .'

'Gentlemen . . . Get out of here!' cried Alexey, pointing to the door.

With a smirk, clearing his throat, and with nudges of his elbow, Zhiteikin edged Barsky towards the door, while Uliana Baimakov sank on to a chest and broke into sobs. 'They want to wipe out his memory . . .' she cried.

Alexey, full of menacing dignity, eyes on Artamonov's face, declared: 'However rotten I may be, I'd smash my own skull in rather than be like them.'

'Yes, a fine time to start bargaining,' Peter agreed, also looking at his father.

Natalia went up to Nikita, and whispered: 'Why are you so silent?' He was touched that somebody thought of him; overjoyed that it was Natalia. He could not restrain a smile of pleasure as he whispered back: 'What can I do. . . . We two . . .'

But lost in thought, she had already gone out of the room.

Practically all the *élite* of Dromov came to the funeral, the police inspector, tall and scraggy, clean-shaven but with grey side-whiskers and a magnificent limp, paced down the sandy path side by side with Peter Artamonov. Twice he said exactly the same thing: 'His Highness Prince George Ratski specially recommended your late father to me, and he has shown himself thoroughly worthy of it.' But a moment or two later he announced to Peter that it was hard work carrying a coffin uphill. He slipped out of the procession, pursing his shaven lips, and stood in the shade of a fir tree, letting them all go past him, townsfolk and workers, as if it were a march-past.

It was a hot day, with genial sunshine illuminating the multicoloured crowd as it made its way across the oily patches of yellow and green light. They slowly made their way between two small hills to a third, patterned already by something more than a score of crosses thrust towards blue heaven in the shelter given by the broad limbs of an ancient, crooked pine. The sand sparkled with a diamond-like glitter, crunching underfoot. The sonorous descant of the clergy flowed over them in waves. Loony Anton followed at the tail of the mourners, stumbling and hopping along; his browless staring eyes were intent on his feet; every now and then he bent down to pick up a twig from his path, collecting them under his arm; at the same time in a penetrating voice he sang:

> "Chirist is born, good Chiristian men,
> Waggon's broke a wheel agen . . ."

Pious men among the mourners struck him, told him to stop his song. The police inspector wagged a threatening finger at him and shouted: 'Shhh! You fool!'

Loony Anton was not liked in Dromov. He was of some sort of Mongol tribe, and so it was impossible to look on him as one of God's blessed ones. Nevertheless, they feared him, considered him a harbinger of evil, and when he appeared in the Artamonovs' courtyard just as the funeral service was beginning, and passed round the tables, bawling out his rubbish:

> "The devil sat on the weathercock,
> Ai, ai, the rain is wet
> It will rain a bitter flood,
> And the poukie bitter wept."

quick-thinking people exchanged whispers: 'They're in for bad luck, the sons are!'

The whisper did not escape Peter Artamonov. Some moments later he saw Tikhon Vialov pin the loony in a corner and try to get out of him what a *poukie* was . . . 'You don't know? I thought not. Get out of here! Off you go, go on!'

A year slipped quickly by, like turgid mountain water in autumn. Nothing particular happened, except that Uliana Baimakov went very grey, and pitiful little age-wrinkles came on her temples.

Alexey underwent a noticeable change, became gentler, kinder to others, though with it came an unpleasant impatience. He seemed to be whipping everybody on with his merry quips and wisecracks. Peter Artamonov was seriously worried by Alexey's challenging attitude towards the factory—he seemed to be drawing it on, as he had done the bear which in the end he himself killed. He developed a strange passion for things—the things gentry use: apart from that clock Uliana had given him, in his room he began to collect all manner of useless, even if pretty, *objets d'art*—including a picture of a peasant girls' round dance, embroidered in seed pearls.

Alexey was saving—so why should he spend money on such trifles? He also took to dressing fashionably and expensively. He kept his dark beard trimmed neatly, shaved his cheeks, and anything in him which had suggested the rough peasant vanished bit by bit. Peter felt something definitely alien, which he could not define, in his cousin, and as he began cautiously observing him, on the sly, his mistrust increased.

Peter's approach to the works was a slow and wary one —like his approach to people. He developed a slow gait and used to go slinking about with his eyes screwed up like a bear's,—you might have thought he was afraid things would slip away as soon as he got near them. At times, when the worries of the factory got him down, he felt as if he was enveloped in the chilling cloud of a peculiar, disturbing desolation. At such moments the works turned into a wild beast made of stone which was at the same time alive—the creature was crouching close to earth, its shadows cast like wings, and only its tail—the factory chimney—thrusting up. The snout of it was snub, but menacing—the windows by daytime were teeth of ice; on winter evenings, they were iron teeth, red-hot with their fury, and he had the illusion that the real purpose of the factory was a hidden one, not to weave miles of textiles, but in some mysterious way to be hostile to him, Peter Artamonov.

Bernard Duffield

On the anniversary of the father's death, after a memorial service at the cemetery, the family foregathered in Alexey's bright, lavishly furnished room. With great emotion Alexey said: 'Father's will was for us all to stick together. That's right enough; but we are like prisoners in this house.'

At this, Nikita saw Natalia, sitting next to him, start; she shot a surprised look at her brother-in-law, while in a gentle voice he pursued his theme: 'But I don't see why we shouldn't stick together without getting in each other's road. The factory is our joint concern, but we've each of us his own life, haven't we?'

'And so?' Peter demanded warily, staring far beyond him.

'You all know about my affair with Olga Orlov,' Alexey replied, 'well, I want to take her to the altar . . . Don't you remember, Nikita, she was the only one sorry when you tumbled and fell into the river?'

Nikita nodded assent. It was almost the first time he had sat so close to Natalia, and it was so good that the last thing he wanted to do was to make a movement, speak or even listen to what the others were saying. And when Natalia, starting like that, just touched his elbow, he smiled, and his eyes, beneath the table, sought her knees.

'I seem to think Olga and I are made for one another,' Alexey said. 'She makes life different altogether. But I'm not going to set up house with her here, I'm afraid she and Natalia would not hit it off.'

Uliana raised her eyes, heavy with grief, and came to his assistance. 'I know Olga very well,' she said, 'she's a rare one with her hands; she's good with her books, too. Ever since she was a kid she's maintained herself and her drunken father. The only thing is, she is headstrong by nature, and I can't see her, either, getting on with Natalia . . .'

'I can get on with anybody,' Natalia insisted, with some

indignation, while Peter, with a sidelong glance at her, turned to Alexey and said: 'After all, it's your affair, isn't it?'

Alexey looked at Uliana, then asked her if she would sell him her house. 'What's the use of it to you, now?'

But Peter restrained him. 'Come, why not make this your home?'

'Anyway, I'll be going,' Alexey said, 'to tell Olga the news, she'll be so happy.'

When he had left them, Peter gave Nikita a shove. 'Here, what are you mooning about, eh? What's on your mind?'

'How wise Alexey is, I was thinking.'

'You were, were you? We'll see . . . and you, mother, what do you really think?'

'Of course, it's wise for him to marry her,' Uliana replied, 'though how they'll make their home's another question altogether. She has her own funny ways—even seems a bit queer in the head, sometimes.'

Peter gave a wry grin. 'Hm! That's a fine addition to the family!' he observed.

'Perhaps I ought not have said that,' Uliana replied, and her eyes might have been staring into a darkness where everything was confused, where the eye could not quite make out the outlines. 'She's no fool, anyway . . . the old man had a lot of valuables—Olga hid the lot—at my place—so he shouldn't spend them on drink. She'd come along to me with them, at night, and then I would pretend to make Alexey a present . . . All he's got is hers . . . her dowry. Some very valuable stuff, too. Yet all the same I don't like her very much—she's too much one by herself."

His back turned to his mother-in-law, Peter gazed into the garden; the starlings were busy, teasing everything about them. Something Vialov once said came to his mind: 'I don't like starlings, they're like demons . . .' What a fool that man was—that was why so much notice was taken of him, he was such a fool.

Meanwhile, not once raising her voice—with evident reluctance, as if preoccupied by other thoughts—Uliana Baimakov told them how Olga Orlov's mother had been a squire's wife, who had lived wildly and taken up with Orlov while her husband was still alive, and lived with him five years.

'He is a clever craftsman; he used to make furniture as well as mend watches; he carved wooden dolls too—I've got one somewhere—a naked woman, it represents; Olga thinks it's her own mother's portrait. Then the husband died—they married—and the same year she lost her life, drowned, when bathing in the river, drunk . . .'

'Now, there's love for you,' Natalia suddenly said. This gratuitous interjection drew a reproachful glance from Uliana. Peter smirked, and put in: 'We are not talking about love, but about drunkenness.'

They were all silent. Observing Natalia, Nikita had noticed how the Orlovs' story had upset her; she was plucking nervously at the edge of the fringe of the tablecloth, and her simple, kindly face, flushing deeply, assumed a foreign, angry expression.

After supper, while sitting in the garden in the lilac thicket which was beneath Natalia's window, Nikita heard Peter overhead saying pensively: 'There's no doubt, Alexey's got his head screwed on straight.'

Immediately came Natalia's voice, in a heartrending wail: 'Yes, you're all of you so clever! Only I am a fool! He was right; we're in a prison here. I am a prisoner . . .'

Nikita's heart failed him; racked with alarm and pity, he clutched with both hands at the bench on which he was sitting; an unseen force was raising him up, driving him forward—but where?—while over his head still rang the

voice of the woman he loved, stirring up a feverish yearning in him.

Natalia had been plaiting her hair, when her husband's
words suddenly set light to the malicious fire within her.
She put her back against the wall, trapping behind her those
hands which suddenly itched to strike out and to tear. The
words choked in dry sobs in her throat; she no longer knew
what she was saying, or even caught the cries which broke
from her astounded husband; out it all poured, how she was
still a stranger in that house, a stranger whom nobody
loved, just like a servant.

'You don't love me, you never even talk to me at all, all
you do is roll your great body on to me like a stone whenever it comes up your back to do so. Why don't you ever
show me tenderness—am I not your wife? What's wrong
with me?—tell me that! Look how mother loved your
father . . . I used to think my heart would break from
envy. . . .'

'Come on then, you love me the same,' was all Peter
said, and sat on in the window embrasure, taking in every
feature of his wife's distorted face, lost in the dark gulf of
the room. He found what she said was senseless, yet to his
astonishment, at the same time felt some justification for
her grief, and knew there was deep wisdom in it. The worst
of all in her grief was that it foreboded an endless chain of
disagreements, of cares and upsets, and he had more than
his fill of worries without this to add to them.

Natalia stood swaying in the same spot, draped shapelessly in her white nightgown, an uncertain, elusive outline,
which seemed to float up and then down again, as if she
were swinging on a swing, while her voice either rose to a
shriek or died down again to a whisper: 'Look at Alexey,
how he loved his Olga . . . And how easy to love him—he
is so jolly and dresses like a decent man, and look at your-

self! You never have a nice word for anyone, and never a laugh. I could have lived oh so close to Alexey, but I have never dared say a word to him; you set the hunchback to keep his eye on me for you, disgusting sly little creature . . .'

Nikita bent his head down and lurched away from that blow, into the darkness of the garden; the branches of the trees caught at him; he brushed them aside and rushed on.

Meanwhile Peter rose to his feet. Going close up to Natalia, he grasped her plaits in one hand and wrenched back her head so as to look straight down into her eyes. 'Close to Alexey, eh?' he queried, in a subdued, thick voice. He was so amazed at this thing his wife had just said that he could not be angry with her, or strike her; it was steadily becoming clear to him that she had merely told him the truth: life was dreary to her. He understood dreariness. Yet it was essential to mollify her, and to do that, he began banging the back of her skull against the wall, whispering again and again: 'What was that you said, eh? you fool? Close to Alexey, eh?'

'Let me go! Let me go! I'll scream! . . .'

With his other hand he gripped her by the throat, hard; her face turned purple, her voice came hoarsely. 'Trollop!' he said, pressing her hard against the wall, then stepped sharply away from her.

She seemed to rebound from the wall herself, and swept past him, to the cradle—the baby had been whimpering for some time. Peter felt as if she had trodden on him. Swaying to and fro before him, slithering from side to side, was a dark blue plot of the sky, with dancing stars. Beside him, quite close, sat his wife, and without moving he could easily have given her a swiping blow. Her expression had gone dead, as if turned to wood; only tears slowly, idly trickled down her cheeks. She was suckling their little daughter, her eyes, through the glassy film of tears, fixed

89

on the far corner, oblivious that the child could not easily get at the breast, the nipple, sticking straight out, slipping beyond reach of its lips, so that through its whimpers it sucked at the air and turned its head this way and that. Starting back to life, as if from a nightmare, Peter suddenly growled: 'Give it your tittie, woman, can't you see?'

'I'm only a fly,' Natalia muttered, 'a fly with its wings torn off.'

'Well, am I not lonely, too?' he asked her. 'There aren't a couple of Peter Artamonovs.'

He was vaguely aware that he had not expressed himself very precisely, had even said something unfair. To calm his wife and avoid the danger which threatened, he should have expressed the real truth, very simple and indisputable too, so that she grasped it at once and submitted to it, instead of encumbering him with stupid complaints and snivelling— why, hitherto she had not produced all this female folly. He watched how carelessly, clumsily, she put the child to sleep, and said: 'I've work on my hands! The factory! That isn't the same as just sowing wheat or planting potatoes. It needs thought. And you—what've you got to worry you?'

Sternly, persuasively, he began, making efforts to get near to that elusive fairness; but it avoided him, and an almost plaintive note began to creep into his voice.

'The factory isn't such a simple business,' he repeated, with the feeling that his words were drying up, and it was pointless going on. Natalia did not utter a sound, merely stood, with her back to him, rocking the cradle. It was Tikhon Vialov's calm, quiet voice came to his rescue. 'Mr. Artamonov!' it called out.

'What do you want?' he demanded, going to the window.

'Come out here a moment!' the yardman replied, with an insistent note.

'Ill-mannered lout!' Peter growled to himself, and threw a reproach at Natalia: 'See? I've no peace even at night, and you whining about . . .'

Vialov met him at the porch, cap in hand, eyes glinting; the man shot a glance round the yard, brilliant in the moonlight, then in low tones said: 'I've just taken Mr. Nikita down . . . he'd hung himself . . .'

'Why . . . how on earth?' Peter sank in a heap on to the porch steps; the earth could have swallowed him up.

'Don't you sit 'ee down,' Vialov grumbled, 'come on; he asked for you . . .'

But Peter did not move, only whispered: 'What can be the meaning of it? Eh?'

'He's come to now; a sowsing did it . . . Come on, now . . .'

Vialov helped Peter up by the elbow, and took him into the garden. 'He managed to fix it in the bath-house, in the anteroom; a noose from the roof, from the ridge-beam; if I hadn't come along . . .'

Peter stood stock still again, repeating: 'But why? Grieving for father, do you think?'

The yardman faced him, waiting, then said: 'He got to such lengths he would take her chemise and kiss it . . .'

'Whose chemise, you babbler?'

Peter's bare feet dug into the earth. The yardman's dog caught his attention. It had come out of the shrubbery and was looking at him inquiringly, wagging its tail. He was afraid to go to his brother. He felt so empty. He had no idea what he could say to Nikita.

'Ah, you might as well be blind,' Vialov muttered. Peter was silent, wondering what Vialov would say next.

'Her chemises, your missus's chemises, when they hung up there, on the line.'

'But what for . . . Wait a minute!' He gave the dog a

kick, picturing his brother's stumpy, hunchbacked shape
kissing a chemise on the line; it was ridiculous and he spat
scornfully—he could do nothing else. But the next instant
a scorching doubt struck at him. He took hold of Vialov's
shoulders and shook the man violently, gritting out: 'Those
two . . . You've seen them together, have you?'

'I see everything,' Vialov replied. 'Your missus doesn't
even know a thing about it.'

'You're lying, aren't you?'

'What good would that do me? I don't expect any reward from you.'

Then, as if hewing a clearing through the darkness, Vialov briefly told his master of Nikita's misfortune. Peter
could see that the yardman was telling the truth, for he himself had long since noticed something in Nikita's eyes, and
the attentions, insignificant, but persistent, which Nikita
showed Natalia.

'So that's how it stands,' he whispered, speaking his
thoughts aloud, 'I never had time to grasp it.'

Then, giving Vialov a push: 'Come on,' he said.

He could not bring himself to face Nikita at once, but, as
they entered the bath-house through the narrow doorway,
kept behind Vialov and, before he could distinguish his
brother in the darkness, in a voice which trembled he said:
'Nikita, what are you thinking of?'

The hunchback did not answer him. He was only just
visible, lying on the bench by the window, with a dull light
falling on belly and legs. Then Peter distinguished that his
brother was sitting with his back up against the wall, his
head sunk on his chest, his shirt torn from top to bottom
and sodden, clinging to the mis-shapen chest. The hair of
the head was also wet, and there was a dark wound, with
radiating swellings, on the jaw.

'You're bleeding, you've hurt yourself?' Peter muttered.

'No,' came Vialov's answer senselessly loud—'I hurt him a bit, in my hurry.' Vialov stepped to one side.

It was terrible to go near his brother. His own voice sounded like that of a stranger; he plucked at one ear, complaining, reproaching. 'You ought to be ashamed . . . 'Tis unnatural before God . . . You shouldn't have done this . . .'

'I know that,' came Nikita's voice, as unnatural as his own, rasping. 'But I couldn't bear it any longer. Let me leave you all . . . I'll go to a monastery . . . Hear! I beg you . . .' He coughed; there was a whistle in his throat, and he was silent.

Now Peter felt moved to tenderness, and his reproaches became more kindly. At last he said: 'As for this about Natalia, why, of course, that was only the power of Satan over you, no more . . .'

'Tikhon, Tikhon,' cried Nikita—a wail of desperation, then, with a sickly groan—'But Tikhon, didn't I beg of you never to say a word? At least keep it from her, for the love of God, I implore you—she would laugh—I could not bear that. . . . At least have that mercy on me . . . Don't forget I am going to serve the Lord all my life for your sakes . . . Don't tell her, never a single word . . . Tikhon, this is all your fault, oh, Tikhon . . .'

He muttered away, his head held with unnatural stiffness, staring straight ahead, and that in itself was horrifying. Vialov said: 'I wouldn't ever have let it out, had it not been for this. She'll never learn anything from me . . .'

More and more moved to tenderness, and himself shame-faced now, Peter promised faithfully: 'On the cross I swear it, she shall never know.'

'That is good of you,' Nikita breathed his gratitude, 'now I can become a monk.' He was then so still that he might have fallen asleep.

'Does it hurt?' Peter asked him; and then, again, getting no answer: 'Your throat—hurts?'

'Not so bad,' Nikita answered hoarsely. 'Now you two leave me . . .'

'You stay with him,' Peter whispered to Vialov, as he fell back, past him, to the door.

But when he was outside, in the garden, and had drawn a deep breath of the intoxicatingly warm scents of the sweaty earth, his sense of tenderness was swept right away by disturbing thoughts. He strode down the path making every effort not to crunch the gravel; he had to have great quiet, or he could never sort out these thoughts. They were hostile, and terrified him by their numbers. They did not seem to arise from within him, but rather to force their way into him from outside, from the darkness of the night, and flit to and fro like so many bats. One took the place of another so swiftly that he was unable to seize on any one of them and shape it into speech; all he could grasp was a sensation of crafty twists and loops and knots which tangled him in themselves, and with him Natalia, Alexey, Nikita, and Tikhon Vialov, in a confusing chain of dance which wound and unwound so swiftly you could not pin it down, —and he was in the very centre of that writhing chain.

What took precise form was only the crudest thought, that his mother-in-law should move in as soon as possible, and Alexey out. He would have to show Natalia some tenderness. 'See how they love each other!' Yet, after all, that neck was put in a noose not from love, but from its own misery . . . it was a good thing Nikita had chosen to go away, to a monastery, there was nothing for him in the outer world . . . It was a good thing . . . and Vialov was a fool, he should have spoken of it before.

But it was those intangible, unformulated thoughts which troubled him to shame and frightened him, making him peer timorously ahead into the dense, moist darkness of the night. In the distance a thin trickle of mournful singing rose, from the touch of light of the factory hamlet. The mosquitoes droned. He was acutely conscious of a pressing need to work the alarm out of himself and crush it at the earliest possible moment. He never knew how he came to the lilac thicket under his bedroom window, but sat there a long time, elbows on knees, head sunk on hands, staring into the black soil, till under his feet it began to pulsate and swell like a boil on the point of bursting.

How wonderfully, he had to admit, Nikita had mastered the sand. Now he would depart, and be gardener in the monastery he adopted. He should be content.

He did not notice Natalia creep up to him, and so, when she suddenly seemed to spring from the ground just before him, he started violently back, in momentary fright, till the familiar voice calmed him a little: 'Forgive me, for the Lord's sake, for carrying on so . . .' she whispered.

'Hm, what does it matter,' he said graciously, 'God will forgive you; after all, I said a word or two as well.' He was really very pleased that she had approached him; now it was up to him to find the soft words which might fill and plaster over the fissure caused by their quarrel.

He sat down. Natalia, hesitatingly, sat down beside him. Now was the time to say something soothing, so he said: 'I know how dull it must be for you. There's little enough jollification in our house. What have we to be jolly about? Father used to find it in work. As he saw things, you might say, there are no human beings at all, only workers, except for beggars and the gentry. We all live merely to work; work overshadows everybody.'

He spoke cautiously, lest his tongue run away with itself. His own impression, hearing his own words, was that he was talking like a serious, businesslike man who is a real master. Yet he felt that it was still all only on the surface; he was slipping over his thoughts, not opening them up, powerless to get his teeth into them, and he felt he was sitting on the edge of a deep pit into which any minute he might be hurled by an unknown person who was following everything he said and whispering insistently: 'You're not telling the truth.'

At the crucial instant Natalia lay her head on his shoulder and whispered to him: 'Don't forget you're mine till death us do part, what does that mean to you?'

In a trice his arms were round her, pressing her to him, and he was listening to her burning whisper: 'It's all wrong not to know that. To take a girl, and she bear you children, and yet there's no *you*, you're heartless towards me. Peter darling, it's all wrong. Who is nearer to you than I am, who will be sorry for you in an evil hour?'

He felt she had lifted him off the ground and turned him over in the air; he luxuriated; she had robbed him of all strength. He revelled in a sudden coolness, which revived him, and, with a sort of gratitude, exclaimed: 'I promised him not to say a word, but I must!' In a few words he told her what Vialov had said about Nikita. 'He's even kissed your chemises drying in the garden . . . that's the sort of madness it's come to! How can you not have known, or noticed anything?'

He felt his wife's shoulders, under his hand, give a powerful shudder. 'Is she sorry for him?' he asked himself, but in a flash, indignantly, she replied: 'I never noticed the least trace of desire! Oh, how secretive he has been. Hunchbacks really are cunning!' And Peter Artamonov asked himself whether she was merely scornful, or playing a part.

'But he used to be so attentive to you,' he said.

'Well, and what of that?' she countered challengingly. 'Touloun too shows me attention.'

'Oh, come . . . Touloun's only a dog.'

'Well, didn't you make Nikita your watchdog, to keep an eye on me, and keep me out of the way of my brother-in-law Alexey—I'm not blind, you know. Oh, how disgusting, and how offensive, I used to find him . . .'

It was clear that Natalia was hurt and indignant; he could tell that by the way her skin twitched, and the spasmodic jerking of her fingers as she plucked and twisted her sleeve. But the indignation seemed excessive to him, and, not convinced by it, he struck his wife a final blow. 'Just now Vialov cut him down—hanged himself—he's lying there now—in the bath-house.'

Natalia went limp and strengthless under the weight of his arm; with unconcealed fear she cried: 'No . . . no . . . not that! O Lord God!'

'So she was lying,' Peter decided. But, jerking back her head as if she had been struck on the forehead, she suddenly whispered, with angry sobs: 'What are we coming to! We have scarcely had a little freedom from people's condemnation since your father's death; now the tongues will all be wagging again . . . Oh God, what for? One brother hangs himself, another marries nothing better than his mistress—what are we coming to? Oh, Nikita Artamonov, how dirty of you! So that's what we had to expect of you, that's what you do for us, you heartless creature!'

With a sigh of relief, Peter gave his wife's bent shoulders a rough squeeze. 'Don't worry,' he said, 'nobody's going to know anything. Vialov won't let on, because he likes Nikita; besides, he's nothing to complain of, against us. Nikita's going away, going into a monastery . . .'

'When?'

'That I don't know.'

'Ah, as soon as ever possible! How can I face him after this?'

For a moment Peter did not speak, then said: 'You go and have a look at him now, see how he is . . .'

But she leapt to her feet as if stabbed, and almost yelled at him: 'Oh! don't tell me to do that, I won't go! I can't—I am afraid . . .'

'Why?' came Peter's swift question.

'A would-be suicide . . . I won't; do what you like, I am afraid!'

'All right; let's go to bed!' Peter said, standing upright, feet apart. 'We've both of us had enough for one day.'

As he strode slowly side by side with his wife, he somehow felt that this day had brought him both evil and good —he, Peter Artamonov, had hitherto been an unknown quantity to himself, whereas he was really very clever and wily, he had just managed with great skill to get the better of some unknown who had persistently troubled him with foul ideas.

'Of course, you are the nearest person to me,' he assured Natalia. 'Who is more close? That's what you have to keep in mind—the nearest to you—then everything else will work out . . .'

The twelfth day after this night, at daybreak, Nikita Artamonov set out, staff in hand, leather bag at his back, down the yielding sandy track, which was dark from the abundant dew. He stepped out quickly, as if eager to waste no time escaping from any memory of the way the family saw him off.

All of them, but half-awake, had previously assembled in the dining-room, next the kitchen. By custom they had sat there, stiff, even talking stiffly, and it had been abundantly clear that not one of them had a single heartfelt word for Nikita. Peter, however, had been kindly, one might almost say, in good spirits, as if he had just completed a good deal;

two or three times he said: 'Well, we Artamonovs will now have someone in the family to pray for our misdoings . . .'

Natalia poured out tea, frigidly, all her attention on the cups; her small, mousey ears were noticeably flushed and crumpled; she kept frowning and going in and out of the room. Her mother maintained a dreamy silence, every now and then moistening a finger, to stroke back the grizzled hair over her temples. But Alexey was the only one unusually troubled; he kept jerking his shoulders and asking: 'But Nikita, what made you decide on it? All at once, like this? I can't make head or tail of it . . .'

At his side sat Olga Orlov, a small, peaky-nosed woman. Without the least care to conceal it, she arched her dark eyebrows and inspected them all in a way which Nikita did not like at all—her eyes were too big for her face; they were too sharp and kept snapping too much for a decent unmarried girl.

He found it very hard to sit, surrounded by them like that, and could not help wondering with apprehension whether in the end Peter would not tell everybody. Why didn't they get on with the last embraces more quickly?

Peter was first to bid his farewell. He went up to Nikita, put his arms about him, then, very loudly, in an unsteady voice, said: 'Well, brother, dear fellow, fare thee well . . .' But Uliana Baimakov halted him. 'What on earth are you about?' she cried, 'you should sit a while first, without a word, then you should pray, and only afterwards bid him farewell.'

All this was done at high speed, then Peter approached him again, and said: 'Forgive us. Write about your contribution, and we'll send it off at once. But don't agree to take the higher orders. Fare thee well. Pray frequently for us.'

Uliana made the sign of the cross over him, kissed him

thrice on forehead and cheeks, then strangely enough burst into tears. Alexey gave him a great hug, looked him straight in the eyes, and said: 'Well, God be with ye! We each of us have our own path to tread. Though for the life of me I still can't make out why you suddenly got this into your head . . .'

Natalia was the last to go up to him. She paused before she reached him, pressed her hands to her bosom, bowed low, and murmured softly: 'Fare thee well, Nikita . . .' Though she had suckled three children her breasts still stood erect and firm.

And that was all.

No, there was still Olga Orlov. She stuck out a hot little hand, hard as a chip of wood; at close quarters her face was additionally repulsive. She asked him rather stupidly, 'had he really made up his mind to take the tonsure.'

Outside, thirty or more of the elder weavers were waiting to bid him good-bye. Deaf old Boris Morozov waggled his head and yelled: 'Soldiers and monks—they're the first in the service of this world; I'm telling 'ee!'

Nikita went up to the cemetery, and took farewell of his father's grave. He knelt before it, not praying, but lost in wonder at the turn his life had taken. When the sun came up at his back and a broad angular shadow, like that of the ferocious watchdog's kennel, lay across the dew-washed turf of the grave, Nikita bowed down to the earth and murmured: 'Father dear, farewell.' His voice rang hollow and hoarse in the delicate early morning stillness. For a moment he was silent, then he repeated: 'Father dear, farewell,' and bitter tears sprang to his eyes; he sobbed like a girl, the pain was unbearable when he thought of the clear ringing voice he once had had.

He was about half a mile away from the cemetery when he suddenly noticed Tikhon Vialov. Shovel on shoulder, hatchet at his belt, Vialov was standing like a sentry in a thicket by the roadside.

'Off?' he asked.

'I am. What are you doing here.'

'Going to dig up a rowan to plant outside my hut, beside the window.'

They stood looking at each other in silence some moments, then Vialov's swimming eyes glanced away. 'Off you go,' he said: 'I'll keep you company a little way.'

They set out, silent; the first to say anything was Vialov. 'How heavy the dews seem. 'Tis bad, they bring drought, and famine.'

'God grant not.'

Vialov muttered something that he could not catch. 'What?' he asked, not a little alarmed,—he always expected to hear something extraordinary from this man, something which would upset him.

'Well, he may grant it, was what I said,' Vialov replied.

But Nikita was convinced Vialov had said something he did not wish to repeat. 'What are you getting at?' he asked reproachfully, 'you mean you don't believe in God's mercy?'

'Why should I?' Vialov answered him calmly. 'This is the time when we need showers. These dews are bad even for mushrooms. A good management sees that everything is to time.'

Nikita sighed deeply, and shook his head. 'Sometimes you have very bad thoughts, Tikhon,' he said.

'No, my thoughts are good. I don't think with my eyes.'

They continued another fifty paces without a word, Nikita with his eyes on the ground, following his own lengthy shadow, Vialov tapping on the shaft of his hatchet in time with their steps.

'Next year, Nikita, or such time, I'll come and have a look at you—eh?'

'Do. You're interesting.

Vialov took off his cap and halted. 'Well, then,—fare-ee-well, Nikita Artamonov.' He gave his head a scratch and said thoughtfully: 'I like you—heart to heart . . . You're gentle by nature. Your father had a clever body, but you're full of soul—your heart is good . . .'

Throwing down his staff and giving a shrug with his hump to level his bag, Nikita embraced Vialov without a word. Vialov flung his immense arms around him. Loudly, insistently, he cried: 'Then that's fixed—I'm coming!'

'Thank you,' Nikita replied.

At the point where the road takes a sharp dive into the pine forest, Nikita looked back. Vialov, cap under arm, stood in the middle of the road leaning on his shovel, as if determined to let no one pass him by; the morning breeze caught at the hair on his ugly head and played with it.

Afar off, Vialov looked not unlike Anton the loony. Nikita quickened his pace. His thoughts were full of Vialov's sombre character, but in his memory there persistently echoed:

"Chirist is born, good chiristian men,
Waggon's broke a wheel agen."

PART TWO

IT was not till the ninth anniversary of the death of their father that the Artamonovs finished building the church, and had it consecrated to St. Elias the Prophet. They were seven years building it. That was Alexey's fault. 'God will bide a while, he's in no hurry,' would be his cheerful if rather unseemly quip, each time he used the bricks set aside for the church; once it was for a third shop, another time for a hospital.

After the consecration, a memorial service was held at the family burial plot for the father and the various grandchildren buried there; the family then waited till the general congregation had made their way from the cemetery. At last, tactfully ignoring the fact that Uliana Baimakov had remained behind, within the enclosure, seated on the bench beneath the birch trees, they slowly made their way homewards; there was no need to hurry, the celebration banquet for the clergy, their friends and all the factory staff and hands, being fixed for three o'clock.

It was one of those dull, grey days, the sky frowning like autumn, the damp wind wheezing like a worn-out nag and lashing at the tips of the fir trees, auguring a downpour. Down the reddish strip of sandy path the dark toylike outlines of the men bobbed to and fro as they wended their way back to the factory, the three blocks of which, built radially, clung to the earth like tense outstretched red fingers.

Alexey swung his stick. 'Wouldn't Father have been happy, could he but see how we're forging ahead!'

'He would have been pained when the Emperor was assassinated,' replied Peter, after a moment of thought—not wishing merely to agree with his brother.

'Hm, he wasn't very fond of being pained by things . . . And it was his own wit he lived by, not the Tsar's.'

Alexey pressed his cap deeper on to his head, and gave the womenfolk a look; his own wife, small but well-built, was wearing a plain dark frock; as she tripped nimbly over the much-trodden sand, and wiped her spectacles with a handkerchief, she looked like a village school-teacher, beside Natalia, plump and dressed in a long black silk cloak with jet on shoulders and sleeves, a dark lilac toque elegantly covering her luxuriant auburn-tinted hair.

'Natalia gets more and more beautiful,' Alexey said, but Peter did not reply. 'So once again Nikita has not turned up at the anniversary,' Alexey continued. 'Do you think perhaps he is angry with us?'

On damp days Alexey had trouble with his chest and his leg; he was limping now, leaning on his stick. He felt a need to try to erase the mournful impression produced by the memorial service and this miserable grey day. Stubborn in everything, he was determined to make his brother talk. 'My mother-in-law's stayed behind to have a weep,' he went on. 'She can never forget him. She's a good old dear. I've given Vialov a nod to stay behind and see her back; her wind's not too good now and again, she finds it hard to get about, or to talk.'

'It is hard,' Peter observed.

'Are you dreaming? What's hard?'

'I shall have to get rid of Vialov,' Peter replied, looking to one side at the rising ground, bristling with conifers.

'Whatever for?' cried Alexey in surprise. 'He's an honest fellow, reliable, not lazy either . . .'

'Because he's a fool,' Peter said.

The women came up with them. 'I'm trying to talk Natalia into sending Ilia away to the *lycée*—she's afraid to . . .' Olga said to her husband; her voice was pleasing and surprisingly powerful for so small a body.

Natalia, pregnant, had the waddle of a well-fed duck. With the tone of the senior speaking slowly and through her nose, she said: 'In my opinion these *lycées* are a harmful fashion. In her letters Elena uses such words, you really can't understand what she means.'

'Everybody ought to go to school, everybody!' Alexey declared severely. He took off his cap and wiped his perspiring forehead and prematurely bald pate—the bare area stretched in a clear-cut oblong from forehead towards nape, elongating his whole face tremendously.

With an inquiring glance at her husband, Natalia disputed the point. 'I think Pomialov's right,' she said, 'learning makes people wild.'

'That's so,' Peter agreed.

'You see,' she cried, with great satisfaction, but her husband only went on, dreamily, to finish his thought— 'people ought to go to school.'

Alexey and Olga laughed. Natalia reproached them. 'Come! Is your memory so short? You've just come from a memorial service!'

They linked their arms in hers, and quickened their pace. But Peter hung behind. 'I'll wait for mother,' he said.

That disturbing creature, Tikhon Vialov, was a thorn in his flesh. Just before the service, at the cemetery, looking down over the factory, Peter had said out loud, but to himself, not to boast, simply recording what he saw: 'It *has* grown!'—and immediately, there at his back, was the calm voice of the ex-navvy: 'Like mould in a cellar—of itself it 'grows,

Peter had not said a word, did not even look round, but the obvious and insulting stupidity of that pronouncement really did upset him. A fellow toiled and moiled, and found a living for more than one hundred other fellow men—day and night his mind on the enterprise, forgetting himself entirely in his care for it,—and then there comes a fool to declare that it lives 'of itself', and not by the master's intelligence. The fool, what was more, was always muttering things about a man's soul and about sin . . .

Artamonov sat down for a moment beside the road on the stump of a pine, plucking at his ear and recalling how he had once complained to Olga that he had no time 'to think about his soul'. He had then heard a strange question. She asked him 'if his soul really lived a separate existence from him?'

He had seemed then to see a spark of some kind of woman's humour in it, only Olga's birdlike face had been solemn, her sombre eyes behind the spectacles with a kindly light in them.

'I don't get you,' he had said.

'Nor can I understand,' she had replied, 'when people talk about their soul as if it was something separate, a sort of orphan.'

'I don't get you,' Peter had repeated, and with that any desire to talk to her vanished. She was too alien and incomprehensible; yet, despite himself, he liked her simplicity, even though it inspired him with apprehension lest behind it was concealed cunning.

But Tikhon Vialov he had never been able to stand at all. He found the mere sight of that blotchy, massive skull, with its peculiar eyes and those close-stuck ears hidden in gingery hair unpleasant; he disliked that tightly-curled beard, and the man's very gait, so lethargic; the whole of that clumsy, but knotted body was repugnant to him. The man's calm was unpleasant to him,—and made him somehow envious; even Vialov's reliability as a yardman irritated Peter. Vialov worked like a machine; it was scarcely ever necessary to tell him off for anything, but even this diligence excited Peter's annoyance. Moreover, it was increasingly displeasing to observe the man year by year taking ever deeper root in the whole Artamonov establishment, clearly feeling himself to be an indispensable spoke in the wheel. It was strange to see that children were as fond of him as dogs and horses were. The old wolf-hound Touloun, now chained up, and for that reason vicious, would let nobody but Vialov go near him; Peter's eldest, too, Ilia, a headstrong child, was more obedient to the yardman than to either his father or mother.

In an effort to get Vialov out of his sight, he had offered the man first the job of sexton, then that of forester, but Vialov only shook his heavy head. 'I'm no good at that,' he always said, 'if you're tired of me, have a rest from me, give me a month's leave, I'll go and see Mr. Nikita.'

He said just plainly that: *have a rest from me!* Those words, so stupid and so insolent, together with the reminder of Nikita, cloistered away in a poverty-stricken forest priory beyond the marshlands, roused a perturbing suspicion in Peter's mind. He feared that Vialov knew not only what he had told Peter about Nikita, when he cut him down, but most likely some other shameful thing as well; and he felt Vialov was awaiting some new misfortunes, his glittering eyes suggesting: 'You leave me alone, you need me!'

Vialov had already made three visits to the priory. He would sling a bag on his back, take a staff in his hand, and set off at an unhurried pace. You would think it was a concession to the earth, for him to put down his foot on it; everything the man did seemed to be done as a concession. And when he returned, he answered questions about Nikita unwillingly and unconvincingly; he always seemed to be keeping something back.

'He's well. They think highly of him. He said I was to thank you for the presents you sent him.'

'What had he to tell you?' Peter had inquired.

'What has a monk to tell?'

'All the same, what did he say?' asked Alexey impatiently.

'Talked about God. And the weather. The rains, he said, they're out of season. Complains of the mosquitoes; they've a terrible lot of mosquitoes over there. He asked about you.'

'Asked what?'

'He was concerned about you, worried.'

'About us? But why?'

'Altogether. You see, you're rushing ahead, he's stopped still where he was—well, he's concerned about you and all your restlessness.'

Alexey roared with laughter. 'What twaddle!'

The pupils of Vialov's eyes swam, all expression vanished.

'After all, I don't know what his thoughts are, I only tell you what he said. I'm a simple man.'

'Yes, you are!' Alexey agreed scornfully, 'simple as loony Anton.'

The wind enveloped Peter Artamonov with its scented warmth, and the day lightened; the sun peered out from the bottomless blue of a gap in the clouds. Peter looked at it; it blinded him, and he sank back, deeper than ever, into his meditation. He could not help a feeling of grievance that Nikita, after investing a thousand roubles in the priory and getting an agreement for one hundred and eighty a year for life, should renounce his portion of his father's estate in favour of his brothers.

When the news had come, he had growled: 'What's he

making us presents for?' Only Alexey was pleased. 'After all, what does he need money for?' Alexey demanded. 'To fatten his fraternity of paupers? Whereas we've the business —and families.'

Natalia had even been sentimental about it. 'You see, still he couldn't forget how much he wronged us,' she had said smugly, with one finger brushing away a lonely tear from her ruddy cheek. 'It'll make a dowry for Elena.'

But Nikita's decision cast a shadow over Peter; the town talk about Nikita's tonsure had been malicious enough, not at all flattering to the Artamonovs.

Peter got on well with Alexey, even though he could see his gay brother taking the lighter part of the burden: it was Alexey who did the annual trip to the Nizhgorod Fair, and went to Moscow twice. Peter never forgot how he came back full of highly-coloured talk of the scale on which Moscow captains of industry lived.

'They cut a great dash—not one whit less than the nobility.'

'It's easy to do that,' Peter replied. But Alexey was slow to catch his meaning, and went on excitedly: 'When a business man runs up a house, it's a regular palace,' he said, 'and his children have the best education.'

Though he had aged considerably, his youthful fire flooded back, and the eagle eyes were alive with light.

'What are you so down at the mouth about?' he asked his brother, on another occasion, and tried to instruct him: 'You've got to take business lightly, business doesn't tolerate dreariness.'

Though Peter was aware of a resemblance to his father in Alexey, Alexey still became less and less comprehensible to him.

'I'm an ailing man,' he would still keep reminding one—

yet he took no care of himself, drank a great deal, gambled at cards a lot, all night, and quite clearly was loose with women. What took first place in his life? Apparently, neither he himself nor his own nest. The house he had taken over from Mrs. Baimakov needed a general overhaul, but Alexey never gave it a thought. His children were born weakly, and all but one died before they turned five; the survivor, Miron, was a nasty, bony brat, three years Ilia's senior. Both Alexey and his wife were infected with a curious greed for useless things. Every room of their house was cram full of the most heterogenous upper-class furniture. Both of them liked giving pieces of it away. They gave Natalia an interesting cabinet with porcelain inlay, and her mother a huge leather armchair and a magnificent bed of Karelian birch and bronze. Olga was clever at embroidering seed pearl pictures—yet Alexey used to bring her home from his trips about the country identical pieces of embroidery!

'Extravagant notion!' Peter declared, when Alexey gave him a monumental desk with intricate carving and a multiplicity of drawers, but Alexey clapped him on the back and cried: 'It's a poem—and things like that aren't made any more, the Moscow folk knew that!'

'You'd better buy up silver, the nobility had a lot of silver!'

'Give me time—I'll buy up everything. In Moscow. . . .'

If Alexey was to be believed, the people of Moscow were all half-demented, concerned to a man not with real work, but with how to ape the gentry, and to that end they were buying up all they could from the nobles, from whole manors down to tea-cups.

Whenever he called on his brother, Peter felt hurt and envious to find he was more comfortable there than in his own home, though it was as difficult for him to make out why as it was to understand what attracted him to Olga. Beside Natalia she looked like a little skivvy—but she was not idiotically afraid of paraffin lamps, nor did she believe that university students made paraffin from the fat of suicides. Her soft voice was pleasing, and she had kindly eyes—spectacles could not hide the heart-warm light in them; on the other hand, when it came to business or affairs of the wider world, she was tiresomely infantile, as if far removed from it all—and that he found surprising and irritating.

'So am I to take it that by your reckoning nobody's to blame for anything?' he once asked her scornfully.

She replied: 'Oh, some people are to blame, but I don't like judging others.' Which Peter did not believe at all.

She treated Alexey as if she were the senior of the two, and knew herself to be more clever than he was. This did not worry Alexey in the least. He called her 'Auntie' and it was only very rarely that he lost patience with her. 'That's enough, Auntie,' Peter once heard him mutter, 'I'm sick of it . . . I'm an ill man, I need a bit of spoiling.' 'You're quite spoiled enough, that's the end of it,' she answered, and threw him a smile such as Peter would have given anything to see on Natalia's face.

Natalia was a model wife and a clever housekeeper, a marvel at salting down cucumbers, marinading mushrooms, and boiling jam; her servants, too, worked as accurately as the cogwheels of a watch. Natalia never faltered in her calm love for her husband—a love which had clotted like kept cream. She was painstaking. She would fret and ask him how they stood at the bank. 'You see the bank's sound, and won't crash.' When she got some cash in her hands her handsome face would grow stern, her raspberry-red lips tight, and a light at once oily and acrid showed in her eyes. As she counted the multicoloured, dirty scraps of paper, her podgy fingers would handle them as carefully as if she thought they might slip out of her grasp and fly away like so many flies.

'Tell me,' she said one night, in bed, when she had saturated Peter with her caresses, 'do you split all we get with Alexey? Are you sure he isn't cheating you? He's spry, and he and Olga are greedy, such ones for grabbing everything they can, everything . . .'

She felt she had rogues all round her. 'I don't trust anybody except Tikhon Vialov,' she said.

'Then you trust a fool,' muttered Peter, worn out.

'Even if he is a fool, he's a conscientious one.'

When they first went to the Nizhgorod Fair together, and Peter, astounded by the huge dimensions of that all-Russian market, said: 'Well, what do you think of it, lass?' her reply was: 'Very cheap indeed; there's lots of everything, and it's all cheaper than back home.' Immediately she began to reckon up what they ought to buy: 'Two pounds of soap, a case of candles, a bag of sugar, a sack of refined sugar too . . .'

When they went to the circus, she shut her eyes every time the acrobats came on. 'Oh, the shameless creatures,' she cried, 'showing all they've got! *Oi*, I doubt whether I ought to look at them, is it good for the child? You ought never to have brought me to see such terrible things, it may be a son I'm carrying.'

In moments like those Peter Artamonov felt stifled by her stodginess; it suggested the thick green slime of the Vataraksha, in which the only fish that could survive was the greasy *Cyprinus tinca*—a sort of carp, a stupid fish.

All these years Natalia had persisted in long, serious bedtime prayers—after which she would lie supine in the bed, tempestuously summoning her husband to have his pleasure with her lavish flesh. Her skin was redolent of the storeroom, with its pots of salted preserves and its marinades, its smoked fish and its hams. More and more frequently Peter felt she was excessive in her appetite, her caresses were wearing him away. 'Let me be, I'm tired out,' he suddenly said, one night.

'Sleep, then, God bless you,' she responded humbly, and was asleep in no time herself, eyebrows arched as if in surprise, and a lingering smile on her lips, as if through her sealed lashes she could see some delectable thing she had never beheld before.

At such moments, when Peter was most clearly—and painfully—aware that he had no desire for Natalia, he tried to force his memory to revive that gruesome day when she came to bed of their first son. Her sufferings had been going on nineteen hours when her mother, with frightened face, tears in her eyes, led him into the room, which was full of a peculiar stuffiness. Writhing on the crumpled bed, eyes wildly starting from their sockets from the intense pangs, her hair tangled, dripping all over with perspiration and unrecognizable, Natalia howled like an animal at him: 'Peter —darling—I'm dying—it'll be a boy—Peter—all over— good-bye . . .'

Her lips were bleeding from her own teeth—they scarcely moved; the words seemed to come not from her throat, but straight from her belly, enormously swollen towards her thighs, indecently puffed up as if on the point of bursting. Her purple cheeks were puffed out too, and from her lips thrust a swollen, bitten tongue; she kept clutching at her hair, tearing it, wrenching her head about, all the time howling like an animal, bellowing, trying to persuade, to master some unknown who either could not or would not give way to her, that it would be a boy.

It was a windy day, the wild cherry outside rocked and rustled loud, the shadows danced on the window-panes,

Peter saw their leaping, heard their voice, and was beside himself: 'Put a curtain over the window! Have you no eyes in your head?' he shouted. And then he fled in fear, pursued by Natalia's shrieks: 'Eeee-ooooooh! Eeee-ooooh!'

It was half an hour later than his mother-in-law, speechless now from happiness and fatigue, had once again brought him to his wife's bedside, and Natalia had received him with the impatiently flaming glance of one of the great martyrs, and in a weak, intoxicated voice said: 'A boy—a son.'

He had bent down and laid his cheek on her shoulder, and stammered: 'Ah, mother, I shall never forget this you've gone through, not to my dying day, I tell 'ee! Thank you . . .'

This was the first time he called her 'mother', giving the word all the fear and delight he had felt. She had then closed her eyes and stroked his head with weak, heavy hand.

'What a champion!' the pock-marked, big-nosed midwife said, holding up the boy as proudly as if she had borne it herself. But Peter had not been able to see his son at all; he was conscious solely of the corpselike face of his wife, with dark pits in place of eyes. 'She won't die?' he asked. 'Die?' the pock-marked midwife cried cheerfully, 'if they died of this, there'd be no midwives.'

Now this champion was in his ninth year, a tall, healthy lad named Ilia, with large, intensely blue eyes set between an upturned nose and a lofty forehead—eyes like those of Alexey's mother, and Nikita.

A year later, a second son, Yakov, was born, but since his fifth year lofty-browed Ilia had been the outstanding personality in the house. Spoiled all round, he was obedient to nobody, and lived just as he pleased, showing an astounding capacity for getting into scrapes and dangers. His escapades were almost invariably unusual ones, and that produced a sensation akin to pride in the boy's father.

One day Peter found his son in the stables, trying to fix a wheelbarrow wheel on an old trough.

'What's that going to be?'

'Steamer.'

'That won't go.'

'I'll make it,' the boy answered, in the challenging tones of his grandfather. All Peter's efforts to convince him that there was no possibility of its going were in vain, but, trying to persuade him, Peter Artamonov saw his own father in the boy.

Ilia was absolutely inflexible in getting whatever he wanted, but this did not enable him to succeed in making a steamer from a trough and two barrow wheels. All the same, he drew two paddle wheels with a piece of charcoal on the sides of the trough, dragged it down to the river, got it into the water—and then stuck fast in the mud. Even that did not alarm him; in a trice he was shouting to some women who were rinsing linen: 'Hi! You women, come and pull me out, or I shall drown . . .'

Natalia had the trough chopped up, and gave Ilia a good hiding. From that day he began to look through her, just as he looked through his little two-year-old sister, Tania. On the whole, he showed a practical turn, always trimming a piece of wood, chopping and breaking up something, fitting something together. Observing this, the father was sure: 'Something will come of him; he's a builder.'

There were times when for days on end Ilia did not pay the least attention to his father. Then suddenly, there he would be, in the office, climbing on his knee.

'Tell me a story.'

'I've no time.'

'Nor have I got time.'

With a laugh, Peter pushed his papers aside. 'All right then, once upon a time there were some peasants . . .'

'I know all about the peasants; tell me something to make me laugh.'

But that was beyond Peter. 'You run along to Granny.'

'She's always sneezing.'

'Mummy.'

'She'll give me a wash.'

Peter Artamonov laughed. This boy of his was the only being in the world who made him laugh, cheerfully, from the heart.

'Then I'll go and ask Tikhon Vialov,' Ilia announced, and tried to get down. But Peter held him back.

'And what does Vialov tell you?'

'Everything.'

'Well, for example?'

'He knows everything, he used to live at Balakhan, they build barges and ships there . . .'

When, one day, Ilia had a fall, and cut his face, Natalia thrashed him. 'Don't climb over the roofs!' she cried, 'you'll be deformed, you'll be a hunchback . . .'

Ilia went purple with indignation; he did not utter a cry, only threatened his mother: 'If you hit me, I'll do worse, I'll *die*.'

Natalia told Peter about it. He only smiled and said: 'Don't beat him, send him to me.'

Ilia came, stood against the door jamb, hands behind his back. With no other feelings but curiosity and a perturbing tenderness,—'What have you been rude to mother for?' Peter demanded.

'I'm not a fool,' Ilia answered him angrily.

'Not if you're rude?'

'But she beat me. Tikhon says that only fools are beaten.'

'Tikhon? Tikhon himself is . . .' But for some reason he took care not to call Vialov a fool. Instead he strode up and down, shooting keen glances at the young creature by the door, at a loss what to say.

'Well, you beat your little brother now and then.'

'Because he's a fool. It doesn't hurt him either, he's fat.'

'So you think fat people ought to be beaten?'

'He's greedy.'

Peter was aware of his inability to teach his son, and also that the boy knew it. Perhaps it would have been more simple and profitable just to box his ears. But his hand would not stir to strike that disturbingly dear and impulsive head. Under the steady, expectant stare of the precious blue eyes it was not easy even to contemplate punishment. The sunshine, too, was in the way. Ilia always did get into the worst trouble on sunny days. As he gave him a routine talking-to, Peter recalled the time when he himself had had to listen to the same words; they had never touched his heart and they left no trace in his memory; they had merely bored him and—for a very short time—frightened him. A thrashing, on the other hand, even if deserved, was hard to forget—that he also knew well.

His second son, Yakov, was plump and rosy-cheeked like his mother. He cried a great deal; he even seemed somehow to enjoy crying, his cheeks puffed out and his fists bored into his eyes. He was timid and ate enormously and greedily, and then, when he was over-heavy with food he would sleep or complain: 'Mamma, I'm bored.'

His daughter Elena only came home during the summer. She was a real young lady, and a stranger to him.

At seven Ilia was put to learn the rudiments under the Reverend Gleb, but when he found out that the son of one of the clerks, Nikonov, was learning from a picture book entitled *Our Own Tongue*, and not from the Psalms, he announced to his father: 'I am not going to learn, my tongue hurts me.' And only after a long and very gentle cross-examination did he explain that 'Pasha Nikonov learns our own tongue, not somebody else's.'

But there were times when that live wire came up against something or other, and then he would go away by himself and sit up on the hill under a pine tree, throwing dry cones into the dull-green Vataraksha.

'It's dull for him,' the father concluded. He too would go on for weeks, or months, senses deadened by the factory life, in a constant whirl; then suddenly a dense fog of obscure thoughts would descend on him, and he could never grasp what oppressed him most: cares concerning the factory, or the sheer boredom of bearing cares which were in fact so monotonous. On days like that he would often without any cause conceive hatred for a man merely because, coming up with him, he caught a sidelong glance or heard a word which rubbed him the wrong way. This particular miserable, grey day he felt something akin to hatred for Tikhon Vialov. Vialov came up holding Mrs. Baimakov's arm and Peter overheard him saying: 'We Vialovs were a large family. . . .'

'Why don't you go and live with them, then?' he snarled. He went up to his mother-in-law and took her by the elbow; Vialov did not utter a word, merely withdrew, but Peter insistently and seriously repeated his question to him. The yardman screwed up his colourless eyes and quite unruffled replied: 'Because there isn't anybody, not one of us left, they've all been done in.'

'What do you mean? Who's done them in?'

'Two brothers, them they drove to Sevastopol, and there they were killed. My eldest brother got mixed up in a rising when the Liberation went to the peasant's heads; my father —he did a bit of rioting too—wouldn't put up with potatoes, when they tried to force us to eat potatoes; he was going to be flogged, but he ran away, and the ice broke and he was drowned. Then there were two more my mother had, by her second husband, Vialov, a fisherman he was, that's me and my brother Sergey. . . .'

'But where's that brother?' Uliana inquired, her tear-swollen eyes fluttering.

'He was killed.'

'You reel it off as if you were reading from a memorial,' Artamonov said angrily.

'Madam likes to hear it . . .' Vialov replied. 'She was a bit down in spirits, so, you see . . .'

He broke off, however, without concluding, to bend down and pick up a dry twig and throw it to one side. They walked in silence two more minutes.

'But who killed your brother?' Artamonov suddenly asked.

'Who does all the killing? Another man, of course,' Vialov answered, still unmoved.

Mrs. Baimakov sighed. 'Sometimes it's lightning,' she added.

'Sometimes it's lightning . . .'

In high summer trying days set in. There was a crushing, pitilessly sultry silence throughout the smoky-yellow firmament stretched above the world; on all sides there were fires, in the turf-fields and the forests. Suddenly a dry, burning wind blew up wildly, with savage whistle and whine, rending the withered foliage from the trees, and last year's rusty needles from the conifers, raising clouds of sand and driving them before it, mingled with scraps of wood, and bark and goose-feathers. It buffeted and threatened to strip men's clothing off them; it plunged into the forest, fanning the fires more fiercely.

There was a long sick list at the factory. Above the whirr of the spindles and murmur of the shuttles Artamonov could hear dry, straining coughs; at the machines he saw wearied, angry faces, observed languid movements. Production went down, the quality of the goods fell noticeably; the number of days wasted grew, the men took to drinking, the women workers' children were ailing. One of the carpenters, rubicund little old Seraphim, was frequently busy now making tiny coffins—not infrequently too he turned deal planking into last resting-places for grown men who had completed their earthly time.

Alexey insisted that a jollification should be arranged: 'You want a bit of jollification, to cheer the people up!' And, setting off with his wife for the fair, he once again counselled: 'Arrange a jollification—that'll put life into the men. Believe me, good spirits can save a man from any misfortune!'

'See to it,' Peter instructed his wife. 'The best, and make it lavish.'

Natalia grumbled at the idea. He was angry: 'What?' he snapped. Taking the hem of her apron and clearing her nose in protest, she submitted: 'Very well.'

They began the jollification with prayers. The Reverend Gleb carried the little service through with pomp; he had grown still thinner and drier; his cracked voice mouthing the strange ancient words, rang melancholy, as if this was his last living plea. The grey faces of the consumptive weavers were sombre and grim; they stood reverently wooden; quite a number of the women were openly sobbing. And when the priest raised his sorrowful eyes heavenwards, the assembly followed him and also looked up through the smoke at the dim, ominous sun, thinking, no doubt, that the tender-hearted priest could really see somebody in the sky who knew him and was paying attention.

After the service, the women carried tables into the factory village street, and the whole human equipment sat down to business at wooden bowls brimful with greasy noodles and mutton, a bowl to each ten men, and a barrel of strong home-brewed beer and another of vodka to each table. This soon improved the fallen spirits of the exhausted men. The silence which had descended like a burning cover on the world shivered and moved off over the marshlands, towards the forest fires, and the Artamonov village rang out with cheerful voices, the ring of wooden spoons, the laughter of children, the shrieks of the women and the chatter of the younger people.

The rich, satisfying dinner lasted three hours. Then, when they had seen to their homes those who were drunk, the young people gathered round spick-and-span Seraphim. His blue striped shirt and trousers, washed to azure blue, and his tipsy, rosy little peak-nosed face all glowed rapturously, his undaunted, still youthful eyes glittering and winking. In that jolly little coffin-maker there was something of his own name—a seraphic, heaven-sent, fluid pulsation. He seated himself on a bench, settled his *gousli* on his bony knees, and, plucking over the strings with dark-hued fingers twisted like horse-radish roots, began singing, or rather chanting, like a blind beggar, with that special moaning and nasal catch of the voice:

> "And so good folk, I'll tell a story to amuse you,
> And all you wise-heads can interpret it . . ."

With a wink to the girls, in the midst of whom towered his own buxom impudent-eyed, handsome daughter, Zinaida, he pitched his voice a tone higher and wailed out more intensely:

> "And so Lord Jesus sat in radiant paradise
> In the sweetly-scented heavenly shade
> Of a lofty golden-blossomed lime-tree;
> In state he sat upon a lime-bast throne

Distributing his gold and eke his silver
Distributing also his precious stones
To all rich men and wealthy as reward;
Because such men are truly moneyed men,
The benefactors of the very poor
Who love their fellow men if they are poor
And lavishly feed the wanting and the lowly . . ."

He gave the girls another wink, and suddenly changed his whine to a dancing measure; his daughter put her hands gipsy-fashion behind her head and, shaking her breasts, uttered a whooping cry and began dancing to her father's ringing song and strumming strings.

"If a man accepts the silver,
Jesus take his legs away
If a man accepts the gold,
Jesus burn him to a cinder
All your jacinths and your pearls
On your eyes a cataract!"

The strumming of the guitar and jolly play of Seraphim's song drowned the whistles of the lads. Then the women, married and unmarried, all joined in the dance song:

"Shorewards speed the lively ships
Bringing presents to fair maidens"

and Zinaida, leaping and stamping, suddenly yelled, beating in against the rhythm:

"Jack to Jill
Matting for petticoats
John to Joan
Love-in-the-mist"

Ilia Artamonov was sitting with Paul Nikonov on a pile of deal planking—Nikonov was a scraggy little boy, with a thin neck, at the top of which sat uneasily a strangely old head, sparsely covered with hair; the scared, grey eyes set in the grey, unhealthy-looking face shifted uneasily to and fro.

Ilia liked the little sky-blue old man; it was nice to listen to his guitar twanging and to his comical, cheeky voice.

122

Then, all at once, that big woman in the red blouse went mad and spoiled it all. She was the cause of the wild whistling that suddenly engulfed the noisy, discordant song. ... He had already taken a firm enough dislike to her, when Nikonov whispered in his ear: 'You know, Zinaida is loose, she sleeps with everybody ... even your own father ... I've seen him squeezing her myself.'

'What was he squeezing her for?' asked Ilia, as if he did not understand.

'Ugh, you know ...'

Ilia lowered his eyes. He knew what men squeezed girls for, and he was very angry with himself for asking like that.

'It's a lie,' he said scornfully, and wouldn't listen to Nikonov's whispers.

Nikonov, being often beaten, was a funk. Ilia didn't like either his lack of spunk or his endless dreary tale-telling about the factory girls. But he knew a good bit about hunting pigeons, and Ilia loved pigeons; at the same time the pleasure that he got from protecting the weakling from the factory kids meant a lot to him. Besides, Nikonov did know how to tell you things he saw, even though he only saw nasty things, and talked about them as if he might be Yakov himself, always complaining about other people.

After a few more minutes, Ilia went home. They were all having tea in the sultry shade of the dusty trees. The visitors were at the large table: silent Reverend Gleb, Koptiev the engineer, swarthy and curly-headed like a gipsy, the firm's secretary Nikonov, who had so assiduously plied soap and water to his face that it was difficult to make out any expression on it. There was a minute nose set amid moustaches, a great dome of a forehead, and between the one and the other a splotch of a smile silting up the narrow eye-slits with ripples of flesh.

Ilia sat down beside his father; he could not believe that solemn person had any doings with the shameless spindle-tender. Without a word his father drew a heavy hand round his shoulder. Everybody was done up by the heat, running with sweat, the opposite of talkative, only Koptiev's sonorous voice reverberating as if it were a crystal-clear frosty winter night.

'Well, shall we go on to our village?' Ilia's mother asked.

'Yes, I'll go and get ready,' his father replied; and went indoors. The next instant, Ilia ran after him, catching him up at the porch.

'And what do you want?' his father asked him gently. But he too had his question—looking his father straight in the face—'Is it true you've been squeezing Zinaida, or not?'

It was Ilia's impression that the question frightened his father. That did not surprise him. In his view there was no doubt about his father being a timid man, afraid of everybody, which was why he was so taciturn. There were times when he felt that his father was even afraid of him—and this was one of them. So, to encourage the terrified man, he said: 'I don't believe it, I only asked to make sure.'

His father pushed him indoors, and down the corridor into his office, shut the door firmly, and then began pacing up and down, sniffing, as he did when he was angry.

'Come here,' said Artamonov senior, standing still by the table; Artamonov junior did as he was told.

'What did you say?'

'Pavlushka said so, I don't believe it.'

'You don't believe it? Hm.'

Artamonov puffed the rage out of himself, staring fixedly at his son's bullet head and solemn, hard face. He tugged at his ear, wondering whether it was a good thing or bad that Ilia did not believe the stupid chatter of another kid of the same age—did not believe it and clearly was trying to console his father with his non-belief. Peter simply did not know what to say to his son, or how, and certainly had no wish to give the boy a hiding. Yet he had to do something definite, and finally concluded that the most simple and comprehensible thing was to beat him. So, laboriously raising a not very obedient hand, he got a grip of his son's crisp curls, and, pulling at them, muttered: 'Don't listen to fools, don't listen to fools!' Then at last he gave the boy a hard shove and said firmly: 'Get along with you! Go to your room. And stay there. Do as I say!'

The boy went to the door, holding his head on one side, as if it did not belong to him, while Artamonov, watching him, found consolation in the fact that he did not cry; so he could not have hurt him much. He tried to be angry. 'The idea . . . *I don't believe it!*' he growled, 'I'll show you.'

This however was not enough to stifle a feeling of sorrow for the boy; he was aware of the boy's hurt feelings—and dissatisfied with himself. 'That's the first time I've laid my hand on him,' he said to himself, and looked at his beefy, hairy paw with disgust. 'I suppose I'd had a hundred hidings by the time I was ten.'

That however was no consolation. Glancing through the window at the sun, which was just like a globule of fat in cloudy water, and catching the call of the noise coming from the workers' colony, he dragged himself out to see the jollifications. On the way he met Nikonov. 'That step-son of yours,' he jerked out, 'has been putting stupid ideas into my Ilia's head . . .'

'I'll give him a good hiding,' suggested the clerk with evident readiness—even, it would seem, with some satisfaction.

'Yes, curb his tongue a bit,' Peter added, shooting a sideways glance at Nikonov and thinking how simple it all was.

The colony received the master and his company with a

deal of noise and goodwill; there were half-tipsy smiles all round, and flattering cries. Seraphim, in new bast shoes and white leggings laced with red strappings in the Mordvinian way, came dancing and prancing up to Artamonov, singing in his praise:

> "Oh, who comes here?
> It is he himself
> Who is't that he brings?
> 'Tis all his own he brings."

There was grey-bearded, flowing-haired old Morozov, the image of a priest, assuring him in profound tones: 'We've done well, I tell 'ee, you've done us well.'

Another old worker, Mamaiev, cried enthusiastically: 'The Artamonovs look after their folk royally!'

Nikonov said to Koptiev, so loudly that everybody could hear: 'Grateful workers know how to value their benefactors!'

'Mummy, somebody's pushing me!' wailed Yakov. He was rigged out in a pink silk shirt with circular patterning; his mother was holding him by the hand, graciously bestowing smiles on the women, and soothing Yakov: 'Look at the little old man dancing . . .'

The sky-blue carpenter rotated tirelessly, with constant springs, crying out his catches:

> "Eh, my good foot, tap it out,
> Tap it lightly as fast as it's played,
> Sandals of bast are better than a boot
> And a married woman sweeter than a maid!

This was not the first time Artamonov had listened to praise, and he had every reason not to believe a word of it, but all the same he was mollified by it, and with a smirk he cried: 'Now that's very nice, men, thank you! We don't get on badly together, do we?'—while through his mind flashed regret that Ilia was not there, to see what a high opinion the men had of his father.

Bernard Duffield

Now he felt a need to do something fine, anything to touch the worker's hearts. With a pluck at his ear and a moment's thought, he announced: 'The children's hospital shall be doubled!'

Spreading his arms wide, Seraphim leapt back from him. 'Did you hear that?' he yelled. 'Come on, three cheers for the boss!'

Though without much unison, the men did give a resounding hurrah. Surrounded by the women, overcome with sentiment, Natalia nasally intoned: 'Come, my dears, go and bring two or three more barrels of beer; Tikhon will let you have it, come on!'

That raised the enthusiasm of the women still further,— as for Nikonov, he waggled his head and smarmily declared: 'A bishop couldn't entertain better!'

'Mummm! I'm hot,' howled Yakov.

But the delight was somewhat diminished, if not destroyed altogether, by a black-bearded fellow with eyes like ripe plums—a stoker, named Volkov. He leapt up to Natalia, clumsily dangling in his left hand a wizened little infant, unconscious from the heat, with scabs all over its bluish little body: 'And what am I going to do?' he shouted hysterically, 'my wife's died. Died of this heat, poor dear! And left me this addition—what am I going to do?'

From his insane eyes trickled tears which looked yellow. The women pushed him away from Natalia; as if to apologize for him, they cried: 'Don't you pay any attention to him, you can see he isn't all there. His wife was a hussy. And consumptive. He's ailing himself.'

'Somebody take the child away from him,' Artamonov ordered angrily. Immediately many pairs of female hands were stretched out towards the child. But, with a foul oath, Volkov slipped away.

Yet taken altogether, everything went wonderfully—it

was very gay and jolly, as a holiday ought to be. Noticing some new faces among the workers, Artamonov, almost with pride, said to himself: 'Numbers are going up . . . if only father could see!'

All at once, Natalia said to him: 'It wasn't the time to punish Ilia. He can't see how much they love you!'

Artamonov held his tongue. He cast a furtive glance at Zinaida. She was leading a dozen other girls and singing—in a low-pitched, whining voice:

> "He passes near
> His looks are dear
> He longs, I see
> Oh, to kiss me!"

'Slut!' he said to himself, 'even the song's no good.' Taking out his watch, he looked at the time, then, with a blatant excuse: 'I'll run up to the house a moment, there ought to be a wire from Alexey,'—strode swiftly away, turning over in his mind what he ought to say to his son. He had invented something both severe and sufficiently kind, but the moment he quietly opened Ilia's door, he forgot it. The boy was kneeling on a chair, with his elbows on the window-sill, staring into the hazy, ruddy sky; the twilight was filling the room with brownish dust; a thrush in a large cage on the wall was busy preening himself before sleeping.

'In disgrace, eh?' he said. Ilia started, turned, then slowly got down from the chair. 'You see what happens? Listening to any rubbish . . .'

His son hung his head; Artamonov could see he was doing that on purpose to remind his father how he'd beaten him. 'What're y' hanging your head for? Hold your head straight!'

Ilia raised his eyebrows, but did not look at his father. The thrush had begun hopping about the bars, uttering little whistles.

'He's angry,' Artamonov said to himself, and sat down on the boy's bed, poking at the pillow. 'You shouldn' listen to twaddle,' he said.

'How can I help it,' Ilia replied, 'when people talk like that?'

His serious, pleasant voice delighted Artamonov; with more kindliness, he plucked up courage and said: 'Let them, only you don't listen! What you hear, forget! You hear somebody say something dirty—you forget it!'

'Do you forget like that?'

'Why, of course. If I had remembered everything I have heard, what would have come of me?'

He spoke slowly, painstakingly choosing the simplest words, though well aware that he could still have done without a number of them. Soon getting entangled in the confusing wisdom of simple language, he heaved a sigh and said: 'Come to me.'

Ilia went cautiously up to him. Artamonov took the boy between his knees, and pressed his palm gently on his broad forehead. Then, feeling that his son simply would not look up, he was huffed.

'You are pigheaded, are you? Look at me!'

Ilia at last looked him straight in the eyes, but that was even worse, because the boy said: 'What did you beat me for? When I said I didn't believe Pavlushka.'

Artamonov senior did not answer at once. He saw with astonishment that his son by some miracle had become his match, either by rising to a grown-up in authority, or else by reducing a grown-up to his own level. 'Touchy beyond his years,' flashed into his thoughts. Then, principally to achieve a reconciliation between his son and himself, he said hastily: 'You didn't get much. You must learn. You've no idea how my father used to beat me. Mother too. And the ostler and the bailiff. And the German butler. When

129

your own beat you it isn't so bad, but when it's a stranger, it really hurts. Your own blood makes it a light hand.'

Pacing the room, six strides from window to door, he was very anxious to bring this talk to an end, almost afraid his son might ask him something more. 'You see and hear more than you ought here,' he muttered, without looking at the boy, who stood pressed against the foot of the bed. 'You must go to school. To the *lycée*. Would you like that?'

'Yes.'

'Very well, then . . .'

He would have liked to pet the boy a bit, but something stood in the way. He could not even recall if his own father or mother had ever petted him, when they had hurt his feelings.

'Very well, off you go, and play,' he said. 'Only you'd better stop palling up with the Nikonov kid.'

'Nobody else likes him.'

'There's nothing to like him for, the little rotter.'

Artamonov went down to his own room, and stood at the window, deep in thought; he had managed that badly, he was spoiling Ilia, the boy had no awe in him. . . .

From the direction of the factory hamlet came the bright noise of jollification—girls shrieking and singing, a background of voices, the rasp of an harmonica. Near the courtyard gate he clearly caught Vialov's voice: 'Sitting at home, boy, when there's a jollification? Going away to school, you say? That's good. *An empty head might be dead* the saying goes. I'll miss you though, me boy.'

Artamonov would have liked to shout: 'It's not true, it's I will miss him. Skunk, making up to the master's son!'

When he had despatched Ilia to the town, to the Reverend Gleb's schoolmaster brother, who was to prepare him for the *lycée*, Peter did indeed feel a great gap in his heart and found the house dreary. There was something irksome, something out of place, just as if the ikon lamp in the bedroom had gone out; Peter was so accustomed to that tiny blue flame that if for any reason it did go out, at whatever point in the night it was, he woke up.

Before his departure Ilia got up to such pranks that one would have thought he was determined to leave as bad a memory as possible behind him. He was so rude to his mother that one day she dissolved into tears; he let all Yakov's birds loose and gave the thrush, which he had promised to Yakov, to little Nikonov.

'What are you thinking of, carrying on like this?' Peter asked him, but Ilia did not answer, only cocked his head on one side, and Peter had the impression his son was mocking him, yet again reminding him of what he had wanted to forget. It was strange to realize how much of his heart that little fellow had taken possession of. 'Is it really possible that my father worried about me like that?' The answer his memory gave was a confident one—that he had never felt his own father to be near and dear to him; in him he had felt only a severe master of the house, who had always given Alexey far more attention than himself.

'Can it be that I am a kinder man than my father?' Artamonov tried to find the answer, but could not decide whether he was kind or not. These thoughts, which would suddenly descend on him at the most inopportune moments, when he was at work, troubled him. The enterprise was going ahead magnificently, and watched him with its hundreds of eyes, demanding unceasingly active attention. But it only needed the slightest thing which reminded him of Ilia, for all thoughts of the factory to snap off short, like sweated warp-threads, and tremendous effort was needed to knot them firmly again. He did all he could to fill the emptiness caused by Ilia's departure, and paid more attention to his younger son, but to his grim mortification he came to the conclusion that Yakov was no consolation.

'Daddy, buy me a goat.' Yakov asked of him—Yakov always had something he wanted.

'What do you want a goat for?'

'To ride on.'

'That's no good; only witches ride on goats.'

'But Elena's given me a picture book and there's a good little boy in it, riding on a goat . . .'

Artamonov told himself that Ilia would never have believed a miserable picture like that. He would have insisted at once: 'Tell me about the witch.' Nor did he like Yakov complaining to him that the factory boys had ragged him, when he was always ragging them.

Ilia also was a great one for picking quarrels and scrapping, but he never once complained of anybody, even though his playmates of the colony often got the better of him; but Yakov was cowardly and lazy, and always sucking or chewing at something. At times there could be noticed in Yakov's behaviour an element of the incomprehensible, even the unpleasant. For example, once when his mother, pouring him out hot milk, caught a glass with her sleeve and scalded herself, Yakov simply grinned and boastfully declared: 'I could see you were going to tip it over!'

'You saw it, and said nothing,' cried Artamonov, 'that was bad. See, your mother's scalded her feet.' But Yakov, blinking and sniffling, simply went on silently chewing. It was only a few days afterwards that Artamonov heard him outside telling a story, his words tumbling over each other: 'I could see,' he said, 'I could see he was going to thrash him; he got nearer and nearer till he was right up behind him, and then, oh! what a crack!' Looking out of the window, Artamonov saw that Yakov, flourishing his fist, was deep in an excited conversation with that little Nikonov

132

rat. He called him in and forbade him to talk to the Nikonov boy at all; he was going on to give him a word of
advice too, but after a single glance at the bluish whites of
his eyes and strangely bright pupils, he heaved a sigh and
pushed him away. 'Off with you, empty eyes,' he said.

Carefully, as if on a slippery surface, Yakov made off,
elbows tight into his sides and palms held out, just as if he
were carrying something awkward and heavy.

'Clumsy, and stupid,' decided Artamonov.

In his daughter, grown-up, taciturn, there was also a
strain of woodenness and something in common with
Yakov. She liked lolling about reading books, at tea ate
quantities of jam, and after dinner would sit scornfully
crumbing a piece of bread between thumb and one finger,
or toying with her spoon in the plate, as if trying to fish a
fly out of the soup. She had a way of tightly pursing her
full-blooded and very beautiful lips and addressing her
mother in a way not at all fitting in a young girl. 'Nowadays,' she would say, 'people don't do so. It's gone out of
fashion.'

When Artamonov said: 'Well, Miss Cleverhead, why
not take a peep at the way the linen for your underclothes
is woven?' she answered: 'If you like.' She put on her best
frock and took the sunshade her Uncle Alexey had given
her, and obediently followed her father, taking great care
lest her frock touch anything. A number of times she
sneezed, and when the workers wished her the time of day,
she only blushed, and, without a word, or even a smile, gave
them a pompous nod. Artamonov told her all about the
work, but, soon noticing that her attention was not on the
machinery, but on where she was going to step next, he
shut up. He was deeply hurt by his daughter's indifference
to all the complexities of the works. Nevertheless, when

they came outside from the weaving-room, he did ask her: 'Well, what about it?'

'It's very dusty,' she answered, inspecting her frock.

'You didn't see much,' he said, with a smile, then cried in vexation: 'But what do you keep lifting up your skirt for, the yard's clean and your petticoats are short enough without that.'

She timidly withdrew the finger and thumb with which she had been holding up her skirt, and said guiltily: 'It all smells so oily.'

That delicate finger and thumb business particularly exasperated him, and he even growled once: 'Look 'ee, you'll never get much if you don't take your whole hand to it!'

One rainy day, when she was lying on the divan with a book, Artamonov sat down beside her, to find out what she was reading.

'About a doctor,' she said.

'Ah! Science, I see.'

Then, peeping at the book, he exploded. 'What are you lying for?' he cried. 'It's poetry. You don't tell me science is written in poetry?'

Hastily and in terror, she told him a cock-and-bull yarn about God permitting Satan to seduce a doctor—a German —and Satan sending a devil down to the doctor. Artamonov sat tugging at his ear, in a genuine effort to make head or tale of the yarn, but it was idiotic and exasperating to hear his own daughter talking to him in that tone of an instructress, it prevented him understanding.

'Was the doctor a toper, then?'

He saw that the question embarrassed Elena, and he gave up trying to hear her explanation, but said angrily: 'What a rigmarole! Fiddlesticks! Doctors don't believe in devils! Where'd you get the book from?'

'The engineer gave it me.'

134

Artamonov then remembered how Elena would sometimes gaze dreamily, with grey pussy-cat eyes, at some
point in space, and he thought it necessary to warn her.
'Koptiev's no match for you,' he said, 'don't you get
giggling too much with him.'

Yes, Elena and Yakov were duller, greyer than Ilia, that
became clearer every day. He did not notice that gradually,
in place of love for his son, there was born in him a hatred
for the Nikonov boy. One day, coming on the boy, he said
to himself: 'All through that little rotter I beat my son . . .'

The boy revolted him physically. He was round-shouldered, his head loose on the slender neck. Even when the boy
ran he seemed to Artamonov to be slinking along like a
cowardly rogue. Young Nikonov worked hard, cleaning the
boots and clothes of his stepfather, splitting and bringing
in firewood, fetching water, carrying the swill out of the
kitchen, washing out his little brother's nappies in the river.
Busy as a sparrow, a grubby and tattered little thing, he
would meet anybody and everybody with an ingratiating
grin, like a fawning dog. If he saw Artamonov he would
bow even a long way off, bending his goose-neck till his
head was down on his chest. Artamonov almost enjoyed
seeing the boy in autumn rain, or in the winter, splitting
firewood, blowing on his chilled fingers to get a little
warmth into them, or hopping like a goose on one foot, the
other in the air, with the down-at-heel, gaping boot slipping off it. The boy would sometimes clench both hands to
his chest and twist like a corkscrew, coughing. Learning
that he was keeping two pairs of pigeons in the loft over
the bath-house, Artamonov told Vialov to let the birds go
and see that the boy did not go up there. 'We'll have him
falling off the roof and breaking his bones—see what a poor
thing he is . . .'

One evening, going into the office, Artamonov found

the boy scraping at the floor with a penknife and trying to wash spilt ink out with a wet rag.

'Who spilled it?'

'Father.'

'Not you?'

'On my honour, no, Sir.'

'Then why's y'r snout all snivelling'

The boy crouched, head bent ready for a blow, and did not answer. Then, crushing him with a glance, Artamonov said, with satisfaction: 'Serves you right.' But all at once, after a few moments of thought, he smiled into his beard, and realized how infantile and ridiculous were such feelings against this insignificant kid. 'Good Lord, what am I about!' he asked himself, but indulgently—then tossed a heavy, copper five-copeck piece on the floor. 'There, go and buy yourself some gingerbread!'

The kid reached for the coin so cautiously with his dirty little bones of fingers that he might have been afraid it would burn him.

'Does your stepfather beat you?'

'Yes.'

'Well,—what of that?' Artamonov said, to console him, 'everybody's beaten.' And a few days later, when Yakov complained that Pavlushka Nikonov had done him some injury, it was not because he believed his son, but almost automatically that he said to the clerk: 'Give that stepson of yours a hiding!' 'I will, sir,' Nikonov respectfully assured him.

When the summer arrived and Ilia came home for the holidays, strangely dressed, his hair clipped short and his forehead still more prominent, Artamonov's dislike for the little Nikonov grew sharper, as he saw that his eldest stubbornly continue to associate with the puny raggamuffin. Otherwise, Ilia had become disgustingly polite, addressed both father and mother in the plural, strutted about with his hands in his pockets, behaved like a visitor in the house, teased Yakov to the point of tearful hysterics, and infuriated his sister till she threw books at him—in short, he behaved abominably.

'What did I say?' Natalia lamented to her husband, 'everybody says learning makes for insolence.'

Artamonov said nothing, but watched his son with concern. He had the impression that though Ilia was up to many tricks, he did so without enjoyment; he was being deliberately bad. Pigeons appeared once more on the roof of the bath-house, cooing up and down the ridge, and when they were not playing with the pigeons Ilia and Pavlushka Nikonov sat for hours against the chimney stack, busy talking. At the outset, when Ilia had just got home, Artamonov had made an overture: 'Well, come on,' he said, 'tell me what you've been doing; I once used to tell you things, now it's your turn.'

Very quickly, curtly, Ilia told him some quite uninteresting story about how they ragged their teachers.

'What do you do that for?'

'They make us sick,' Ilia explained.

'Hm! Doesn't seem right to me. Is it hard to do your school-work?'

'Easy.'

'Is that the truth?'

'Take a look at my marks,' Ilia said, with a shrug of the shoulders. His eyes meanwhile were fixed on the garden, on the sky.

'What can you see up there?' Artamonov asked him.

'A hawk.'

Artamonov senior sighed. 'All right, run along and play. Anyone could see I bore you.'

Alone, he recalled that he too, as a boy, had almost always been either bored or frightened when his father spoke to him. 'He rags his teachers,' he thought. 'That never came into my head when the church clerk lammed it into me with a strap. I suppose this damned life we live must have got softer for the younger generation.'

Before returning to school, Ilia made one request—his only request: 'Father, please let Paul Nikonov keep his pigeons in the bath-house loft . . .'

Vaguely, Artamonov replied: 'You can never satisfy everybody.'

'So he can!'—the boy decided the matter. 'I'll run and tell him—he'll be so pleased.'

Artamonov was mortified to find his son troubling about the pleasures of a miserable little brat, without having made the least real effort to try to bring a little pleasure into his own father's life, and when Ilia had gone, he found himself obsessed by a still more persistent dislike of the clerk's stepson. From now on, whenever, either at home, or in the works, or in Dromov, Artamonov lost his temper, automatically that grubby little ragamuffin forced his way into the core of Artamonov's anger, just as if inviting him to shed all his evil thoughts and malevolent sensations on to those fragile bones. Meanwhile little Paul Nikonov was unmistakably growing up. He grew like a mould, like an evening shadow, and, flitting all over the place, a furtive demon, ever more frequently got in Artamonov's way.

One serene autumn day, when the cobwebs were trailing the air, Artamonov, tired and out of humour, went into the garden. Evening was falling. In a greenish sky, clean-swept by the wind and washed by the rains, the exhausted autumn sun, devoid of warmth, was fading. Tikhon Vialov was busy, raking up fallen leaves in one corner; their soft, nostalgic rustle floated through the air; beyond the trees the factory muttered; grey smoke sluggishly fouled the transparency of the air. To avoid seeing or speaking to the yard-man, Artamonov took the opposite direction, towards the bath-house. The door was ajar. 'That creature's here,' he said to himself.

Cautiously peeping into the anteroom, there in the corner in the darkness, he espied the form of his enemy, spread-eagled on the bench. Head down, legs straddled, the boy was masturbating. For an instant this pleased Artamonov, but the next instant he thought, first of Yakov, then of Ilia. Full of sudden fear and disgust, he hissed out: 'What are you up to, you little rotter?'

Nikonov's hand ceased its spasmodic motion, and flew up; the whole form of the boy tore itself awkwardly away from the bench; the mouth opened, and uttered a stifled shriek; then he threw himself in a huddle at the huge man's feet. With real enjoyment, Artamonov kicked the boy in the chest with his right foot—then halted: the boy cracked, uttered a feeble cry, and rolled over on to his side. For a moment Artamonov felt that that kick had cleared out of his heart some foul rags, which had long nauseated him. But the next instant, with a glance into the garden, and listen-ing carefully a moment, he pushed the door to. He bent down, and said quietly: 'Well, up you get, come with me.'

The boy lay with one arm thrown forward, the other bent under his knee; one leg seemed much shorter than the other, as if he had slyly crawled up to Artamonov; but this outstretched arm was unnaturally, terribly long. Artamonov staggered, then steadied himself with one hand on the door-jamb, took off his cap and with the lining wiped his fore-head; it had all at once flooded with sweat.

'Up y' get, I won't tell anyone,' he whispered. But he was already aware that he had killed the boy, his eyes on the little trickle of dark, dusty blood which was winding out from under the cheek pressed to the boards.

'I have killed him,' he told himself. The brutally simple words seemed to deafen him. He slipped his cap into his tunic pocket and made the sign of the cross, staring stupidly at the pitiful screwed-up little body; in terror he played with the clumsy thought of how he would say: 'It was an accident, I knocked him down opening the door . . . Yes, the door . . . The heavy door . . .'

He turned and slumped on the bench—at his back stood Vialov; broom in hand, the man was staring at the boy with his colourless eyes, and thoughtfully scratching his bullet head.

'See,' Artamonov began, in a loud voice, holding on to the edge of the seat with both hands, but Vialov nodded and interrupted him: 'He was a weakling, and clumsy too. How many times have I not told him not to climb up there.'·

'What's that?' cried Artamonov, with mingled fear and hope.

'You'll break your neck, I told him. You too, sir, said the same, didn't you? Every sport requires skill. I suppose he's fainted.'

Squatting down, the yardman felt the boy's wrist, then the neck, put a finger to the cheek, then, wiping it to and fro on his apron, as if lighting a match, said: 'I really believe he's passed right out. He was a poor frail thing; it didn't need much, did it?'

Vialov spoke quite calmly, moved slowly and was exactly the same as he always was; Artamonov did not trust him, and was ready to hear menacing, condemning things. All the same, Vialov only glanced up at the ceiling and the trapdoor cut in it, listened a moment to the cooing of the birds, and began again calmly and unaffectedly: 'Trying to get at the trapdoor—one foot on the bench, t' other on the door-latch, then up on the top of the door, when he could grab the edge and pull himself up. But his poor little arms had no strength in them, so down he came; I suppose he caught the corner of the door with his heart.'

'I didn't see what happened,' Artamonov said, while the sense of self-preservation filled his mind with flashes of guess work—was the man lying? tricking? laying a trap to catch him? or had the fool simply not tumbled to the truth of it?

The last supposition was the most likely. Vialov altogether behaved like an idiot, tossing back his head, as if he had bumped his forehead on something, heaving a sigh and saying: 'Ah, dust of dust! Why should such as he ever exist? I'll go and tell his mother. I don't guess his stepfather will worry his head much, he never wanted the kiddie.'

Artamonov listened to the yardman with great suspicion, striving to catch a lying note, but Vialov spoke exactly as he always did, as if curiosity was quite unknown to him.

'Hark!' he said, his eyebrows quivering, and listening: somewhere outside a woman's voice was calling angrily: 'Paul, Pau-aul, Paul . . . !'

Vialov stroked his cheek. 'And there's your little Paul,' he said,—'get your weepers ready!'

This reassured Artamonov; the man after all was only a fool. He drew his cap from his pocket and carefully examining its broken peak, went out into the garden.

For two or three weeks he passed through the sensation of having waves of obscure fear stirring to and fro within him, menacing him daily with a new, unknown misfortune. At any moment the door might open, Vialov come in and say: 'Of course, I know all about it.'

But outwardly things went swimmingly; the workers all took the boy's death in simple, businesslike fashion—they were all well broken to births and deaths. Nikonov put a black tie on his sallow neck, and a humble self-importance appeared on his well-scoured face, just as if he had at last been awarded a distinction long due him. The mother of the murdered child, a tall, scraggy woman with a horse-like face, without a word or a tear set to work to expedite the burial of her son. She kept fiddling with the muslin ruche at the head, adjusted the wreath on the blue forehead of the corpse, carefully pressed the brand-new coppers covering his eyes down more firmly, and kept crossing herself, with an ugly sort of hastiness. Artamonov even observed that her hand grew so tired that twice during the service she couldn't lift her arm—twice she tried and twice it fell back, as if broken.

Yes, as far as that side of it went, everything passed off smoothly. The Nikonovs even thanked him with tiresome profusion for his contribution towards the funeral costs, although in point of fact, out of fear of exciting Vialov's suspicion, Artamonov had given them very little. But all the same, he still could not believe that the yardman was quite so stupid as he had appeared to be, in the bath-house. This was in fact the second time that the bath-house had given the fellow prominence, insinuating him deeper and deeper into Peter's life. Strange—and unholy. He even wondered if he should not burn the place down, or have it broken up, sawn up for firewood; for that matter, it was quite old and decaying. He ought to build another, on a new site.

He took to observing Vialov carefully, but saw that the man had not changed his way of life—there was still the same lack of will, as if he existed against his own wishes, to please somebody else; he was still just as reserved; he treated the workers roughly, like a policeman, and they disliked him; towards women he was specially rough, scornfully so; Natalia was the only woman he was different with, but not as if she were his mistress, rather as if she were a relative, an aunt or elder sister.

More than once he tried to find out something from her —'Why on earth do you make yourself so unusually pleasant to Vialov,' he said on one occasion, but she only answered: 'He's grown so into the household, hasn't he?'

Had Vialov had friends, gone out anywhere, he might have been put down as member of some religious sect; there had been a number of such about of late. But apart from Seraphim the carpenter, he had no friends, though he liked going to church and prayed furiously, for some reason always opening his mouth disgustingly wide to do so, just as if he were going to shout at God. There were times when Artamonov frowned, as he looked into the yardman's glittering eyes—there seemed to be a threat lurking in those colourless eyeballs: he would then be overcome with a desire to take the fellow by the throat, shake him up, and cry: 'Now, out with it!' But Vialov's pupils only melted and swam, and the stony calm of the man's bony face would allay all his alarms.

While loony Anton was alive, quite frequently he could be seen in the yardman's watch-house, or sitting with him in the evening on the bench by the gate. One day in particular Artamonov came on Vialov cross-questioning the loony.

'Stop jabbering all this nonsense, now think and tell me what you mean by *the bum-dy man*—who is he?'

'*Bumbledy!*' Anton had shrieked with delight, and sang:

"Chirist is born, good Chiristian men . . ."

'Half a mo!'

"Waggon's broke a wheel agen . . .'

'What are you trying to get at?' Artamonov had asked, with an annoyance which was incomprehensible to him.

143

'I want him to explain his un-human words.'

'Drop it! They're only loony nonsense.'

'Even a loony must have some kind of reason,' Vialov replied stupidly.

There was really no point in talking to him.

One sleepless, howling night Artamonov felt he simply could not bear the dead weight on his mind any longer, so he woke Natalia and told her. She sat without a word, blinking sleepily, till he finished, then she yawned and said: 'Now, I myself always forget dreams.' Then all at once she started up: 'Oh, I do hope Yakov doesn't do anything like that!'

'Do what?' he asked, in amazement, and then, when she had made quite clear to him what she was afraid of, he tugged at his ear, mortified. What had been the sense of talking? But this same night, while the blizzard howled and roared round the house, together with a deepening sense of his own isolation, he had a great idea which threw light on the murder, explained it: he had killed a perverted boy, who was a dangerous companion for Yakov to have, and he had done it through his great love for his son, out of apprehension for him. This gave his obscure hatred for the boy a reasonable justification, and that was some measure of alleviation. But he still wanted to get completely free from the burden, shift it all on to somebody else's shoulders. He sent for the Reverend Gleb, anxious to have an extra-confessional talk about this unusual sin, not mixing it up with repentance for ordinary sins.

The thin, round-shouldered parson came in the evening, and humbly took a chair in the corner; he was always tucking his lanky body into the darkest and narrowest possible corners; he might have been taking refuge from his own shyness. The outlines of his very old, sombre cassock were lost against the dark leather of the arm-chair, and only the lighter patch of his face showed—and that dimly—against the dark background; beads of water from melting snow glistened on the hair of his temples like grains of glass; as usual he clasped his sparse but long beard in one bony fist.

Unable to bring himself to start with the main thing, Artamonov began by observing how rapidly popular morals were deteriorating, how his workers exasperated him with their laziness and drunkenness and lechery. But that topic palled, and he was silent again, pacing the room. Then, from the parson's tenebrous corner, poured a river of his words, closely resembling a complaint:

'Nobody troubles himself with the people—the people on the other hand have never been accustomed to looking after themselves, they don't know how. Educated people . . . well, I won't take it on myself to lay down the law, but there are not very many educated men in Russia. And those there are don't get into real touch with ordinary life, the life the mass of people live. Though they try a lot, they don't try the principal thing. They're inclined to revolt, and that brings the authorities down on them. Altogether nothing seems to fit quite right in Russia. There's only one voice to be heard, louder than ever, over the babble of the crowd, appealing to the world conscience and authoritatively trying to awaken it, and that is the voice of a certain Count Tolstoy, philosopher and author. A most remarkable man, his pronouncements are courageous to the point of temerity, but since . . . well, you see, the Orthodox Church is challenged . . .'

He went on for a long time about Tolstoy, and although Artamonov did not fully understand, nevertheless the parson's sighing voice, rippling calmly out of the darkness, and depicting the almost legendary profile of that unusual man, did take Artamonov out of himself. Without losing sight of why he had sent for the priest, a sensation of pity

145

for the man gradually came over him. He knew that the poor creatures of Dromov considered the Reverend Gleb to be to all intents touched by God—a blessed half-wit—just because he was not self-seeking, because he was kind to everybody, as well as conducting his services well and being particularly moving when he chanted the service of the dead.

All that Artamonov considered natural—that was what a priest should be. His soft spot for the Reverend Gleb was excited by the general dislike of the town clergy and the Dromov *élite* for the man. But at the same time a spiritual pastor should be severe, he should know and use specially penetrating language, he should instil fear of sin, revulsion from sin. Artamonov was aware that the Reverend Gleb was devoid of such powers, and, listening to his indecisive tongue, full of hesitations, obviously as if apprehensive of giving offence, he suddenly said: 'Father Gleb, I have brought you out here like this to tell you I am not going to fast this coming Lent.'

'And why might that be?' the priest asked pensively, then, without awaiting any answer, added: 'You are responsible to your own conscience.'

It seemed to Artamonov that the Reverend Gleb spoke just as frivolously as Tikhon Vialov. Through his poverty, the priest did not wear goloshes, and pools of melted snow had formed off his heavy, peasant high boots. He shuffled his feet in the pools and went on in the same complaining tone, without a trace of condemnation: 'One looks around at the world, and only one thing offers consolation: as it increases, the evil of life concentrates in one point, as if to make it easier for us to overcome it. I have always observed it happen like that: first a little spindle of evil appears, then, like thread on a bobbin, more and more evil grows on to it. Scattered evil is hard to overcome—but when it's all together it is possible to cut it off all at once with the sword of justice. . . .'

Those words stuck in Artamonov's memory; in his ears they rang soothing, for the spindle was the little Nikonov —had not all his dark thoughts clustered round that creature, attracted by it? And now once again he told himself that he could charge a certain portion of his sin, quite righteously, to his son's account. He heaved a sigh of relief, and instead of confessing invited the parson to take tea with them.

It was bright and comfortable in the dining-room, the warm air saturated with tasty odours. A samovar was bene-volently bubbling and puffing out vapour on the table; Mrs. Baimakov was seated in an arm-chair, charmingly singing to her four-year-old granddaughter:

> "Good Saint Thunder
> Gave out presents:
> To Saint Peter
> Summer heat,
> To Saint Nicholas
> Power on the waters
> To Saint Elias
> A pike of gold . . ."

'Pagan notions,' murmured the Reverend Gleb, with an apologetic smile, as he seated himself at table.

When they went to bed Natalia told Peter that Alexey was back; she had seen him—'He's crazier than ever about Moscow . . . I'm so worried . . .' she said.

In the summer months Natalia had begun to get rashes— little red pin-points only, on her ruddy, smooth skin—but they worried her, and twice a week before going to bed she indurated her skin with digitalis ointment. She was busy with the massage at this very moment, seated at her mirror, both elbows working; the heavy swing of the globes of her bosom showed through her nightdress. Peter lay in bed with his arms behind his head, beard pointing ceilingwards, cocking one eye at Natalia and thinking that she was like a sort of engine, and her ointment smelt of boiled sturgeon. When at last, after praying in a persuasive whisper, she did get into bed, and, by the constant habit of her healthy flesh, offered herself to her husband, he pretended to be asleep.

'Spindle . . .' he was thinking, 'yes, and I'm the bobbin on it. Rotating. And what is spun on me? That was another of Vialov's wisecracks, that man spins fine but the devil weaves hessian . . . What a crazy mouth the man has!'

Puffed up by Alexey, the Artamonov works crept further and further over the sand dunes on the far side of the river. The ground lost its golden tint, the silvery gleam of the mica vanished, the sharp glint of the quartz was snuffed out as the sand was trodden hard down. As every spring came round the growth of weeds spread its brilliant green, plantain began to plaster its leaves on the paths, burdock hung out its huge ears, the trees of the garden powdered the ground round the factory with pollen, and the autumn fall of leaves, as they rotted, fattened the sand with their manure. The growl of the workshops grew louder, troubles and worries increased, while the spindles whirred in their hundreds, and the looms muttered; all day the engines puffed and wheezed, and there was an incessant unmistakable mutter of labour hanging over it all—it was pleasant to remind oneself that one was master of it all, astonishingly pleasant; Peter was almost proud.

But there were occasions, more frequent of late, when Peter Artamonov was overcome with weariness, and his childhood came back to him—the village, their limpid river set in the broad spaces, and the simple farming life of his home country. Then he felt as if invisible clawing hands had seized him and were whirling him about; the day-long din which filled his head allowed no place for any other thoughts than those which the works gave rise to; the smoke of the factory chimney, corkscrewing into the sky, cast a dark dreariness and gloom over it all.

While that mood was on him—for hours, or days—he particularly disliked his workers. They seemed to be getting more and more feeble, to be losing their peasant toughness, to be infected with feminine quarrelsomeness, to be excessively touchy, ready insolently to turn on you. A strain of unreliability and lack of responsibility to the job appeared in them. Years ago, in his father's day, they had been more of a team, more of a family; there had not been so much drinking, or so much shameless lechery. Now everything was at sixes and sevens. The men were admittedly more alive, he would even say they were more intelligent, but they were less careful about their work, and spiteful to one another,—constantly spying and playing one off against another like a lot of rogues. The younger men and girls had become particularly undisciplined and disrespectful; indeed, the Artamonov works now very quickly transformed the younger generation of peasants into something very different from what they had been.

The stoker, Volkov, was an example. The man had had to be sent to the County lunatic asylum. Only five years ago he had first turned up at the factory, with no more than he stood in, except good looks and health—and a brisk wife. A year later the wife got off the straight road, the husband began beating her, she contracted T.B., and now they were both gone. Artamonov had noticed a multitude of similar cases of the rapid destruction of his men. In five years he had had four murders—two in brawls, one from revenge, and one a case of a middle-aged weaver cutting the throat of one of the mill girls out of jealousy. There were frequent brawls with bloodshed and quite serious cases of wounding.

Alexey did not seem to be in the least affected by all that.

149

He became still more of a puzzle to Peter. He had something akin to the qualities of spick-and-span, waggish old Seraphim, who seemed to find it equally jolly, and put as much skill into, making pipes or bows-and-arrows for the boys as making coffins for them.

Alexey's hawk-eyes were always bright with assurance that everything was going fine—and would continue to do so. He already had three graves in the cemetery. Miron was his only child with a firm, tenacious hold on life; an ugly boy, hastily botched together from long bones and gristle; all creaks and rattles, with a trick of cracking his finger-joints loudly. At thirteen he already wore spectacles, though that did shorten his long beak of a nose a little and dim the unpleasantly bright eyes. You never saw the boy without a book in his hand, thumbed so tight you'd think it had grown to his hand. He addressed his parents as equals; even more—he argued the rights and wrongs of things with them. They liked it. But Peter, conscious that his nephew had no love for him, paid him back in like coin.

There was no dignity, no order, in Alexey's home life. In Artamonov's eyes the difference between his life and that of his brother was nearly the same as that between a monastery and a booth at a fair. Alexey and his wife had no friends in Dromov, yet on Sundays and holidays individuals of dubious quality gathered in his cluttered-up rooms,—they were like lumber rooms, they were so packed with scratched antiques. There would be the factory doctor, Yakovliev, with his gold teeth and irascible temper, an ironical fellow; then that noisy engineer Koptiev, a drunkard and a card-player; then Miron's teacher, a student barred from the universities by the police, with a pug-nosed wife who played the guitar and smoked cigarettes. As well as these there would be other queer misfits, all of them equally brazen-tongued against the Church and the Authorities, and it was clear that every one of them thought himself a first-rate mind. With his whole being Artamonov felt that these were not real people, and he could not make out what Alexey, half-proprietor of a large enterprise, saw in them. Hearing their clattering voices, he recalled the Reverend Gleb's complaint that people wanted a great deal, but not the principal thing.

He did not attempt to inquire what that principal thing exactly consisted in—he was sure it was work.

Apparently his brother's favourite was that noisy gipsy Koptiev. Koptiev always seemed to be drunk, but there was a tough element too in the man, even some brains; Koptiev's most frequent pronouncement was: 'That's all fiddlesticks, philosophizing—you want industry and applied science!'

At the same time, the elder Artamonov always suspected something heretical and destructive in Koptiev. 'He's a dangerous young fellow,' he told his brother, which surprised Alexey considerably. 'Koptiev? What are you getting at? He's a fine lad, and a great worker, inexhaustible—and clever. I wish we had a thousand like him!' And then, with a smile, 'If I had a daughter, I'd marry her to him, chain her to him!' After that Peter went away in a bad humour.

If they did not play cards, he would sit all by himself in his favourite arm-chair, broad and deep as a bed, watching the company and plucking at his ear, unable to agree with any one of them, yet wishing he knew how to dispute what they said; but he would never enter into the discussion, because, even though he was the senior partner, not one of them would take any notice of him, and also for certain other reasons. Those reasons were not quite clear to him, but he was anyway not good at talking, and it was only very rarely, with great effort, that he would put in a word.

'Now, as for that, the Reverend Gleb once told me about a Count . . .' he said once. But Koptiev immediately snapped: 'Why bother your head about a Count, you, of all people—your Count Ratski was the dying gasp of the Russia of villages . . .'

He went on nagging, most disrespectfully pointing his finger at Peter, and all the rest of the company, listening to him, were just like a gipsy tribe, homeless wanderers.

'Maggots,' Peter told himself. 'Spongers.'

On one occasion he said: 'The saying, *Work's not a bear, it won't run away to the forest* is not quite right. The work you undertake is a bear, and why should it run away to the forest, when it's got you gripped in its paws? It's your master.'

'There you are, there you are,' Koptiev's tongue began wagging. 'Who says so? Who, I ask you? That's the very danger,' while Alexey, his own brother, put in ironically: 'What's come over you?—been borrowing ideas from Vialov?'

This nettled Peter sorely, and when he got home he told his wife to keep a sharp eye on Elena—'That gipsy Koptiev is hanging round her. Alexey panders to the man. Elena's a juicy morsel, not for the likes of him. Start looking out for somebody for her at once.'

'How can I find a suitor for her here?' Natalia asked, in some trouble. 'We shall have to go farther afield . . . besides, she's young yet . . .'

'You try—they'll *young* you,' he said, with a grin, and prompted Natalia to a fit of playful laughter.

When Peter Artamonov did succeed in slipping out for a brief space, breaking beyond the magic circle of factory cares, he still found himself in a dense fog of enmity towards all men, and of dissatisfaction with himself. There was only one bright spot—his love for his son, but even this was darkened by the shadow of little Nikonov, driven deeper into him by the burden of that murder. When he was looking at Ilia he would sometimes feel a need to say: 'See what I did, out of fear for you.'

His intelligence was not sufficiently agile to hide from him that his apprehension had appeared only a second before the murder, yet he was equally clear that only his apprehension could to some extent justify what he had done. All the same, he never found the courage even to mention Ilia's comrade when talking to him; he was afraid of letting slip something about the crime he had committed, and now wanted to make out to be an heroic act.

Ilia meanwhile grew rapidly under his eyes—but somehow crooked. He had become quieter, and more gentle with his mother, nor did he tease Yakov, who was also a schoolboy now; he liked looking after his younger sister, Tatiana, and though he still twitted Elena, it was not offensively. But in everything he said could be felt an anxiety, a chill of afterthought. Miron had taken the place of the little Nikonov boy, and the cousins were practically inseparable, holding inexhaustible confabulations, with much mutual gesticulation; they studied together, read together, walked and sat together.

Ilia was scarcely ever at home. He would put in a brief appearance in the morning for tea, then down to the town to his uncle's house, or off to the woods with Miron and a swarthy, impetuous lad named Goritzvetov. This Goritzvetov was small and sly and prickly as burdock; he had a wriggling walk, and eyes which were comically cocked on one side, seeming to squint.

'You must want something to do, to pal up with a little Yid like that,' Natalia told the boy, scornfully. Artamonov saw the thin lines of Ilia's eyebrows twitch. 'Yid is an insulting word, Mamma,' Ilia said. 'Anyway you know he's

153

the nephew of our priest, the Reverend Gleb, so he's a Russian. He's first in his form, too . . .'

Natalia snorted disdainfully. 'The Yids always are on top.'

'How do you know?'—Ilia stood his ground—'There are four Jews in Dromov, and they're all poor, except the chemist.'

'Yes, and forty little Yids . . . There are Yids everywhere. Vorgorod's full of them too, and at the Fair . . .' But with vexed persistence Ilia repeated: 'Yid isn't a nice word.'

Natalia turned scarlet. Banging her spoon on her saucer, she cried: 'What are you thinking of, trying to teach me? Do I know or don't I how to speak? I'm not blind, I can see the way that little snider smarms up to everybody, even to Vialov; that's why I say *smarming as a Yid*, because smarmy people are dangerous. I knew one of them . . .'

'That's enough!' Peter suddenly snapped sternly. She turned to him, on the point of tears. 'What has come over you, Peter, may I not speak in my own house?'

Ilia sat without a word, frowning. Natalia reminded him —'After all, it was I who brought you into the world.'

'Many thanks,' said Ilia, pushing his empty cup away from him. Peter stole a glance at the boy, and smiled, plucking at his ear.

From the way his wife spoke he could gather that she was afraid of her son, exactly as she had once been afraid of oil lamps, and not so long ago was afraid of a fanciful sort of coffee machine that Olga gave her—convinced it would blow up. Artamonov himself, in fact, felt something akin to the mother's foolish fear of Ilia. He was a puzzling lad— all three boys were puzzling. Now what could they find interesting in the yardman? They would sit endlessly at the gate with Vialov in the late afternoon.

One evening Artamonov caught the peasant's sermonizing voice: 'That's how it is. The less you've got, the lighter

154

you go. But don't you believe that about angles—now, are there any angles in the sky? there aren't any walls to make angles.'

The schoolboys roared with laughter. Ilia's laugh was short and velvety—Miron's dry, biting—Goritzvetov's rather less willing. Suddenly he checked himself laughing and cried: 'Here, wait a moment, that isn't really funny at all!'

Vialov took up his confused story again, drawling his gruff words out: 'You kids ought to learn all you can about mankind, find out what man really is. Find out what everybody's designed for, what his lot is . . . That's what you want a bit of magic about. Language too. You've got to know every word through and through. For example, you —any one of you—often say "*konechno*"—you think it means just "of course", but it really *says* "*finally*"—"*in the end*"—yet there never is any end . . . !'

Then Vialov repeated that wisecrack Peter had heard so often: 'Man spins a fine thread, the devil weaves hessian from it. And so on, and on without any end . . .'

Again the boys laughed, Vialov guffawing with them, then, with a sign, saying: 'Oh you scholars—hard skulled!'

In the evening half-light the boys seemed smaller, less significant, than in the sun, but Vialov swelled large, and his babble seemed even more idiotic than it did by day.

These talks that Ilia had with Vialov confirmed Artamonov in his dislike of the man; they gave rise too to obscure fears. He inquired of the boy: 'What do you find in Vialov?'

'He's an interesting character.'

'But what's interesting in him? His idiocy?'

Ilia answered calmly: 'Even idiocy has to be understood.'

Artamonov liked that answer. 'True enough,' he said, we

all live idiotically,' and immediately, it occurred to him that that was Vialov's language!

Ilia stirred very special expectations in Artamonov. Seeing him, hands in pockets, stand looking out at the workers in the courtyard, whistling softly to himself—or strolling through the weaving shop—or briskly on his way to the workers' colony, Peter thought he could see in him a very smart future head of the Artamonov mills. 'Besides, it'll come to him differently from me—I was just harnessed in, and off you go!'

It was only a little vexatious that with him Ilia was so taciturn. Even if he did speak, he was curt with it, as if he had considered his words well before-hand, and they excited no inclination to continue the conversation. 'He's a bit hard,' Artamonov told himself, the only consolation being that it was also a good thing not to be like that loud-mouthed gabbler Goritzvetov, or like lackadaisical, lazy Yakov, or like Miron, who, rapidly shedding anything boyish, talked now in a bookish way, with an uppish bearing, just like a government official, convinced that books contained a special regulation,—and an immutable one, too—for every possible situation.

The weeks of the holidays flashed by with elusive speed, and already the children were preparing for departure again. Things seemed to work out so that Natalia lavished much genial counsel on Yakov for the journey, while Artamonov, talking to Ilia, said nothing of what he had really wanted. Yet how was he to tell him that living in that mosquito-swarm of monotonous worries about the business was a dreary thing? You couldn't tell a young lad of that.

Peter Artamonov came so to long for something quite out of the ordinary to happen to him, yet something as inevitable as seasonal snow, as rain, mud, summer heat or dust, that at last he did find it, or at least contrive it. He was caught one day, in a wooded corner of the district, back of beyond, by a July thunderstorm, with hail and thunder and lightning rending the clouds. Following the narrow forest track, he drove right into a torrent of water, indistinguishable in the darkness; the ground gave way beneath the horses' hooves and the wheels of the char-à-banc sank in up to the axles. It was awesome, when a cold blue light for an instant menacingly lit up the seething water-logged ground, and the black trees, leaping hither and thither in fear, seemed to be flying against him through the glassy screen of the rain. The horses, invisible, stopped short, snorting, their feet slopping about in the slime, his fat driver, Yakim, a mild fellow, hesitatingly and gently trying to soothe them. Filling the forest with its icy tattoo, the hail volleyed down, to be followed immediately by a heavy downpour of rain, lashing the foliage with its million heavy drops, and filling the darkness with its angry howling.

'We must make for the Popovs',' Yakim said.

So there was Artamonov, in somebody's else's clothes, wrapped so that he was afraid to stir, sitting shamefaced, as if in dream, at table in a warm room, in a dry, pleasant soft light. A nickel-plated samovar was purring, and a tall, thin woman, with a turban of auburn hair, and dressed in a dark, loose-fitting frock, was pouring out tea. The grey eyes were pleasantly bright in her pale face. In soft tones, very unaffectedly and retiringly, without a trace of complaint, she told him how her husband had recently died, how she wanted to sell the property, move to town, and open a preparatory school.

'That was your brother's advice,' she told him. 'He's an interesting person, your brother, so alive; not like anyone else.'

157

Artamonov cleared his throat and, peering cautiously about him, was envious. In his younger days, when he had travelled about the country with his father, he had been in many a manor house, but he had never seen anything much in them; both the people and the things in such houses had merely made him feel awkward—but here there was a kindly atmosphere, everything was just right. A large lamp with a pearl globe poured its milky light over the cups and silver on the table and on the tightly drawn-back hair of a little girl with a green shade over her eyes; there was an exercise book open in front of her, and she was drawing in it with a thin pencil and purring to herself, so softly though that it did not prevent him hearing all the mother said.

It was not a big room, and it was tightly packed with furniture, but everything looked as if it had grown naturally; yet each separate thing spoke for itself, about itself, just like the three very bright pictures on the walls. The picture opposite Peter depicted a fabulous white steed with haughtily curved neck, and mane unbelievably long, almost to the ground.

Everything in this house was amazingly comfortable and soothing, and the lovely voice of the mistress rang like a pensive song coming from afar. Now with such surroundings you could live all your life without a real care, and never do anything evil; with such a woman for wife, you could respect her and discuss everything with her.

Meanwhile the black heavens still blazed from time to time with bluish flashes which thrust in through a semi-circle of coloured panes on to the veranda beyond a french window, but the storm could no longer disturb him.

He left at daybreak, tenderly bearing with him the impression of a peace which caressed, an impression of comfort, and the almost disembodied image of the grey-eyed, quiet woman, who had created it all. Swaying through the waterlogged potholes, which equally reflected the gold of the sunlight and the dirty blotches of the wind-torn clouds, he said to himself with sorrow and envy: 'That's how people really live!'

On an impulse he did not tell his wife anything about his new acquaintance; he concealed it too from Alexey. That made it all the more embarrassing a few weeks later when, dropping in to see his brother, he beheld Mrs. Popov side by side on the couch with Olga, and Alexey steered him towards her, saying: 'And this, Vera, is my fine brother.'

She smiled and held out her hand. 'We have already met.'

'But how?' cried Alexey in astonishment. 'When? But Peter, why didn't you tell me?'

Peter sensed something menacing in his brother's astonishment, and for some reason or other his own beard quivered. He pulled at his ear and muttered: 'I . . . I forgot.'

But Alexey shamelessly waggled a finger at him, and cried: 'Just look—he's blushing, isn't he? That was a neat answer, upon my word, old boy! I should just think! Who would forget a lady like that once he'd met her? Look, his ears are burning—they're swelling!'

Mrs. Popov gave a kind smile, she was not offended.

They drank iced mead from tall cut-glass goblets. The mead was a present to Olga from Mrs. Popov. It had the golden gleam of amber, invigoratingly tickled the palate, and put on the tip of Peter's tongue extremely dashing turns of speech,—only he could not fit them in anywhere, while Alexey kept up a steady flow of restless talk: 'No, Vera Nikolaievna, my advice is, don't be in a hurry to sell. You ought to find somebody who is a lover of quietness— it's perfect as a refuge. What will an ordinary buyer give for it? There's no arable and only a little woodland, and that's not much catch. Besides, who wants woodland here-abouts, except the hares?'

Peter suddenly said: 'You shouldn't sell at all.'

'And why ever not?' Mrs. Popov inquired pensively sip-ping at her mead, then sighed—'I am obliged to.'

Peter did not like the penetrating way Olga was watch-ing him, nor the quiver of her lips as she suppressed a smile. With a scowl, he gulped his drink down, and answered Mrs. Popov with silence.

Two days after this, Alexey informed Peter of his inten-tion of making Mrs. Popov a loan against a mortgage on her property. 'The property's worth seven thousand ru-bles silver,' he said, 'and then there are the effects . . .'

'Don't do it,' Peter said very definitely.

'Why not? I know what it's all worth . . .'

'Don't do it, I say.'

'But—why ever not?' cried Alexey, 'I shall go over with a connoisseur, a valuer.'

Peter continued to shake his head. He would have given a great deal to dissuade his brother from the deal, but, being unable to invent a reason for this suddenly said: 'Let's go half-shares, you and me.'

Alexey gave a smile, looking his brother straight in the eyes.

'Going off the rails, eh?'

'Evidently the time's come,' Peter answered loudly.

'Take care—steer clear!' Alexey warned him. 'I've tried —she's cold as a fish.'

After two or three meetings with Vera Popov, Arta-monov had trained himself to dream of her. In imagination he would put her at his side, and in that very instant there would be created a life which was amazingly easy, comfort-able, beautiful to look at and sweetly calm inside, with no need to see dozens of people who did not enjoy their work, who were always dissatisfied with something, either complaining noisily or lying and trying to trick him, their insidious flattery exasperating him just as much as their ill-concealed, ever-greater hostility. It was easy now to create a picture of a life outside all that, far from the greasy red spider of the Artamonov works, which never ceased to enlarge its web. He saw himself then as something akin to a large tom-cat: snug and warm, with a mistress who was fond of him, always ready to cosset him—he needed no more than this, absolutely no more.

Just as once the Nikonov boy had been a dark point in his life, about which all that was difficult and unpleasant collected, Vera Popov was now a magnet that attracted only what was fine, cheerful thoughts and intentions. He refused to accompany his brother and a cunning little old man in spectacles when they went to her place to value it, but when Alexey had concluded the mortgage, and returned, he immediately said: 'Sell it to me.'

This was an unpleasant surprise for Alexey, who tried hard to get out of Peter what he wanted it for, then, at long last, said: 'Now listen here, I've no interest in doing it. She can't possibly pay the money back, and her things are worth a lot. Add a bit of a margin!'

In the end they agreed on the deal. Alexey, frowning, said: 'Good luck to you. You've a bargain.'

Peter also felt he had done a good thing; he had made himself a present of a refuge.

'Shall I say anything—to Natalia?' Alexey asked, with a wink.

'Suit yourself.'

With an inquiring glance at him, Alexey said: 'Olga has the impression you've fallen in love with Vera Popov.'

'Now, that's my business.'

'Don't bellow. At our age most men have a bit of a spree.'

Peter answered him bluntly, and angrily: 'Don't you meddle in my affairs!'

Before long he began to notice that Olga spoke to him in a more friendly way, though a bit wistfully too; he didn't like this, so one evening that autumn, when calling there, he said: 'Has Alexey been spinning a yarn about me and Vera Popov?'

With her gentle hand she stroked his hairy fist, and answered: 'Nobody shall know, but me.'

'Nobody shall know at all,' said Artamonov, banging his fist on his knee. 'It'll go no farther than me. You could never understand it. Not a word to her!'

In fact, he was devoid of bodily desire for Mrs. Popov. In his dreams she was not a female he wanted, but an indispensable completion of the gracious comfort of a home, of a decent, fitting life. When she had moved in to Dromov, he saw more of her in Alexey's house, and at last something staggering happened. Olga had fallen sick. He found Vera Popov at the bedside. The sleeves of her blouse rolled up, she was bent over a basin, soaking a towel; she stooped down, she straightened her back again; amazingly well proportioned, with small, girlish breasts, she was inexpressibly attractive. Peter stood speechless in the doorway, stealthily peering at her white arms, at the firm calves of her legs, at her thighs, and all at once he was stifled by such a fog of desire for her, that he could actually feel her arms round his body. When she greeted him, he returned her salutation only with difficulty, then went over to the window and sat there, to get back his breath, glowering and muttering: 'Whatever have you been up to, Olga? This won't do . . .'

It was the first time any woman had had such a powerful, devastating effect on him. He was really scared. In an obscure way he sensed something dangerous and menacing in it. He sent his coachman to bring Olga the doctor, and himself left the house at once, walking back to the factory.

This was at the end of February. The thaw was threatening a blizzard. A dirty grey haze hung low, blotting out the sky, and diminishing space to a cup upturned over his head, out of which a damp, chilly dust was slowly sifted, settling heavily on moustaches and beard, and making breathing difficult. Treading the half-melted snow, Artamonov felt crumpled and crushed, just as he had been that night when Nikita tried to commit suicide, and again when he killed little Nikonov. The similarity of the burden of those two moments was clear to him, and that made this third one seem all the more menacing. It was obvious that he would never succeed in making a lady like Mrs. Popov his mistress. What was more, he could already see that this physical attraction towards her which had suddenly flared up in him had destroyed and blackened something very precious within him, transforming her into a woman like any other. He knew far too well what women were, and had no reason to suppose that a mistress could be anything different, or better than his own wife, whose inevitable, brackish caresses had almost entirely ceased to excite him.

'What are you after?' he asked himself. 'Whoring? You've already got a wife.'

Invariably, when he had something hanging over him, Artamonov would be obsessed with a compelling urge to get the danger over as quickly as possible, to put it behind him, and never to look back. Facing a threat was like standing in the darkness of night on crumbling spring ice, with a deep river beneath you, a horror he had experienced once as a lad and to this day recalled in every bone.

After some days had passed in an oppressive, fumy stupor, he went out early one morning, having spent a sleepless night, and found the yard dog, Touloun, prostrate in the snow, bleeding. It was still dark enough for the blood to look black as pitch. He stirred the shaggy corpse with his foot. The dog too stirred and its grinning jaws and one staring eyeball leered at the human foot. Artamonov started back, opened the low-pitched door of the yardman's hut, and from the threshold demanded:

'Who killed the dog?'

'I did,' replied Vialov balancing a saucer of tea on the tips of his widespread fingers.

'And why, may I ask?'

'Bit somebody again.'

'Whom?'

'Zinaida . . . Seraphim's daughter.'

Artamonov reflected a moment, without a word, then said: 'I'm sorry about that dog.'

'What if you are? I brought it up. It had even begun barking at me. No doubt even a man would get mad if he was always chained up . . .'

'True,' Artamonov said, and closing the door very firmly walked away, thinking that there were times when even Vialov talked sense.

He stood for some while in the yard, listening to the mutter and drone of the factory. In the far corner showed a yellow patch—the light of Seraphim's quarters, built on to the stable wall. Artamonov went up to it, and looked in through the window. Zinaida, dressed in nothing but a slip, was seated by a lamp on the table, poking at something with a needle. When he went in, without looking up, she said: 'What have you come back for?'

Then raised her eyes. She flung her sewing on the table, stood up. 'Heavens,' she cried, with a smile, 'and I thought it was father . . .'

'Listen,' he said, 'did Touloun bite you?'

'I should think he did!' she said, almost boasting; she put

one foot on a chair, and raised her slip. 'Just you look!'

Artamonov cast one glance at the white leg, bound up just below the knee, went close to the girl and in a hollow voice asked her: 'And what were you doing running about the yard at daybreak? Out with it!'

She shot him one questioning look. Then immediately came a guessing smile. With one hard puff she put out the lamp: 'We must lock the door,' she said.

Half an hour later Peter Artamonov made his way without haste to the factory, pleasantly exhausted. Plucking at his ear and spitting, and recalling with astonishment the shamelessness of the mill-girl's caresses, he smiled; he felt as if he had very skilfully deceived someone, got the better of them . . .

He now broke into the wild life of the mill girls, like a bear attacking a colony of bees. At first he was astounded by the impudent nakedness of speech and feelings; that life exceeded anything he had ever heard of it; it was unbuttoned from top to bottom, every act was exposed with a challenging lack of shame. There were songs that lauded and songs that wept about the shameless attitude which Zinaida and her comrades called love; Peter Artamonov found in it an element of sharpness, with a mingled bitter tang; but it was more intoxicating than alcohol.

He learned that Seraphim's lean-to hut adjoining the stables was known as 'The Wolftrap' to the factory hands; Zinaida's nickname was 'The Suction Pump'. The carpenter's own name for his dwelling was 'The Nunnery'. Seated on the bench next the stove, with the inevitable guitar resting on an embroidered cloth draped over one shoulder and round his neck, he would give a dashing toss to his curly pate, his rosy cheeks all alive, and wink and shout: 'Make merry, my little nuns! They are nuns, aren't they, sir? They do penance to the jolly devil, and I'm their warden, a sort of priest, I'm the tinkling bones! Toss me a ruble, sir, for the laughter of life!'

When he got it he tucked the coins in his leggings and, strumming on the guitar, rakishly sang:

> "When the missus got to hell,
> She begged a bit of roasted ice
> But the devils poked the fool
> With a pitchfork for a tool!"

'You know a great many catches,' the master said, in surprise, and the old boy played the fool with bombast: 'A sieve, sir. I'm just a sieve; whatever muck you throw on me, I screen you a song. That's the sort of man I am, sir—a sieve!' And then he told the following yarn: 'It was some gents taught me, remarkable personalities they were, the Kutuzovs and a Mr. Yapushkin, also a tippler. Made out he was poor—a sly one!—tramped the roads with a hamper on his back, like a pedlar, and wrote down everything he saw or heard. He filled books and books, then went straight to the Emperor; look, says he, Your Majesty, what our peasants think about. The Emperor took a book, read a bit of those notes, saw the red light and had the peasants liberated, and said this fellow was not to be touched, but only transported to Souzdal and given as much vodka as he wanted at the State expense. Because, you see, Yapushkin wrote down a lot of other secrets about the people, only they weren't favourable to the Emperor and had to be hidden. When he got to Souzdal, Yapushkin drank himself to death, and of course his notes were stolen from him.'

'I think you're lying a bit,' Artamonov observed.

'Except women, I never lied to anybody, that's not my trade,' the old man said; it was difficult to tell when he was joking and when not.

Then he went on playing the fool. 'Who knows the

Bernard Duffield

truth, sir, or lies; but I can't lie, because I don't know the truth. That's to say, if you like, I'll tell you: I've seen a lot of truth in my time, and I riddle my rhyme like this: *truth's a woman, good so long as it's young.*'

Nevertheless, even without knowledge of the truth, he knew an infinity of stories of the gentry, their pleasures and misfortunes, their cruelties and richness, and, whenever he told any of these, would invariably add with open regret: 'Well, all the same, they're done . . . They've skidded off the point of life, they don't know themselves, they're broken!'

With his finger he drew a circle over his head, then swiftly dropped his hand and drew another circle just above the floor.

'They went just too far!' he said, and, with a wink, sang:

> "Once upon a time the gentry
> Guzzled from a groaning pantry
> Now the guzzling gentry lack
> Everything but the family scrag"

Seraphim had tales of bandits and witches, peasant risings and fateful love, of how fiery dragons visit inconsolable widows by night, and of all this he spoke so entertainingly that even his irrepressible daughter listened with the speechless, pensive eagerness of a child.

In Zinaida, Artamonov scornfully observed a combination of furious debauchery and calculating business. More than once little Nikonov's slander came to his mind—it had proved a prophecy. 'Now why did I choose just her?' he asked himself. 'There are prettier ones. I shall look fine if the son learns about her.'

He also observed that Zinaida and her companions took their pleasure just like soldiers faced with unavoidable duty; at times he felt that the shamelessness they showed was to deceive both themselves and their partners. Very soon he began to be repelled by Zinaida's persistent greed for money, her incessant wheedling. It came out in her more sharply than in Seraphim, who spent his money on a sweet wine called *Tenerife*—which for some reason he dubbed 'turnip wine'—and supplies of his favourite garlic sausage, jam and short-cakes.

The happy-go-lucky, entertaining old boy appealed to Peter; he was a skilled hand, and Artamonov was aware moreover that Seraphim was a general favourite, known all over the works as 'The Comforter'. He could see that there was more of truth than irony in the nickname, and even the irony had a kindly ring. But that only made Seraphim's friendship for Tikhon Vialov the more incomprehensible and displeasing, especially as Vialov apparently tried deliberately to increase his dislike.

When Vialov's name-day came round, after he had completed twenty years service with the Artamonovs, Natalia decided to turn it into a special celebration.

'When you come to think, how few there are like him!' she said to her husband, 'All these twenty years, and nothing to complain of in him. He glows steady as a wax candle.'

To show special respect for the fellow, Peter took him his presents in his own hands. In the yardman's hut he found Seraphim, in his best. Vialov stood behind Seraphim, head on one side, contemplating the master's feet.

'Here,' said Artamonov, 'a watch from me—and a length of cloth for a tunic from the mistress . . . And here is some cash too.'

'I don't want the cash,' Vialov muttered, then said: 'Thank you,' and offered Artamonov a glass of *Tenerife* which Seraphim had brought him. Of course, old Seraphim's tongue was ready: 'Mr. Peter, you know what we're worth, don't you—and we know your worth. We know a bear likes honey, but a smith forges the iron; the gentry were our bears, you are the smith. We can see—it's a big enterprise now, and a big worry.'

Thereupon Vialov, turning the silver watch over and over, examining it, said: 'An enterprise like that's a railing to a man. As you skirt the pit, you hold on to it.'

'That's it!' cried Seraphim, for some reason pleased by these words, 'how true! You mean, if not, you'd fall in.'

'Get away,' said Artamonov, 'you're both talking without your book, because you haven't got it on your hands, you can't understand.'

However much Tikhon's talk nettled him, the strong expressions which he needed eluded him. This was not the first time that Vialov had wrapped some stubborn, obscure idea of his in words like these, and it was beginning to get on Peter Artamonov's nerves. He looked down on the yard-man's rock of a head, with its thick coating of grease, and, tugging at his ear, and puffing, tried to find a crushing rejoinder.

'Of course, there's many kinds of doings,' Seraphim interposed pacifyingly, 'bad ones, and good ones . . .'

'So's a sharp knife good, but the throat doesn't like it,' Vialov growled.

Artamonov with difficulty suppressed an impulse to give the man a good dressing down.

'Still muttering your riddles about *doings*, then . . .' he said sternly. 'You never stop . . . who can understand it?'

With his eyes fixed somewhere under the table, Vialov agreed: 'It is difficult.'

Seraphim interposed his word again: 'Mr. Peter, it's only harmless doings he has on his mind . . .'

'Just a moment, Seraphim, let him speak for himself.'

Without moving from the spot, Vialov pointed to a

patch of his crop of hair, at the top of his skull, as big as a man's hand, which was bare and greyish. He sighed. 'The devil taught Cain doings . . .'

'There's a conundrum for you!' cried Seraphim, with a resounding slap of his knee.

Artamonov got up and with annoyance said to Vialov: 'You'd far better stop talking about what you can't understand; mark my words.'

He came away very indignant, telling himself he would have to sack the yardman. To-morrow, what was more. Well, perhaps not to-morrow, but in a week's time. He found Mrs. Popov waiting in his office. She greeted him curtly, like a complete stranger, sat down, tapped on the floor with her sunshade, and informed him she could not pay all the interest on the loan at once.

'It's a trifle,' Artamonov said calmly, without looking up, and then heard her say: 'If you can't agree to a postponement, you have the right to call in the mortgage.'

He could tell her by voice she was smarting under some offence. With another bang of the sunshade, she left him so quickly and unexpectedly, that she was already shutting the door before he could raise his head. 'Lost her temper,' it seemed, 'but why?'

An hour later he was seated with Olga, banging his cap on the couch and saying: 'You tell her I don't want her interest and I don't want . . . the money either. Why, it's a trifle! And she's not to have a care about it, see?'

Sorting out coloured skeins of silk and little baskets of pearls, Olga thought a while, then said slowly: 'I do understand, but I doubt if she will.'

'You see that she does. What are you for?'

'Thank you,' said Olga, with a flash of her spectacles, a glassy smile which exasperated him.

'It's no joke!' he snapped rudely, 'I've no intention of

pasturing my hog in her garden, I'm not after that, and don't think I am!'

'Oh, what a *mouzhik* you are,' Olga sighed, shaking her tight-combed head with wonder.

Peter shouted at her: 'Don't you take me lightly! I know what I'm saying . . .'

'Ah, but do you?'

It was a cry of real sympathy, and he knew it. He saw her eyes examining him sorrowfully almost tenderly, over the rims of her spectacles. But that only made him the angrier. He had to put it to her with convincing clarity, and could not find the words he needed; he stared at the window-sill; among the fleshy begonia leaves, like the ears of wild animals, hung exquisite clusters of blossom.

'I was sorry about her house. It's a wonderful place, I tell you. She was born there . . .'

'She was born in Riazan.'

'Doesn't matter. She's grown used to the place. In that house my heart found its first real repose.'

'First real awakening,' Olga corrected him.

'That's all the same to the heart,' he said. He also said a lot more which he himself could hardly understand. Olga, elbows on table, heard him to the end. When at last the flow of words dried up, she said: 'Now listen to me . . .'

She then told him that Natalia knew all about his liaison with the mill-girl, had been in tears to Olga about it. He was unmoved. 'She's crafty,' he said, with a grin, 'never a word to me to show she knew. And went wailing to you, eh? Hm! And behind your back, hasn't a good word for you!' He thought some moments, then went on: 'Zinaida's nickname's "The Suction Pump". She's certainly sucked all the rubbish out of me.'

'How disgusting,' Olga said with a frown, and sighed. 'I remember once telling you your own heart was like a step-child to you; well, it's true; Peter, you fear yourself like the devil . . .'

She had touched him on the raw. 'You're going a bit too far,' he said, 'am I a kid? You might remember one thing: I started this conversation and I've opened my heart to you, who else could I do the same to? Natalia? You can never talk seriously to her. At times I could hit her. But you. . . . Damn you, you women!'

He jammed his cap on his head and hastily left her. A speechless despair had suddenly descended on him when he had been reminded of his wife. For some time since he had given her no thought at all, scarcely even noticed her, although, every night, after a whispered exchange with the Almighty, she snuggled close in to his side, according to routine. 'She knows, and yet she offers herself to me,' he repeated to himself, with rage. 'The sow!'

His wife was a familiar pathway, on which he would not stumble even were he blind; he did not want to think of her. Then into his mind flashed the picture of Natalia's mother— Mrs. Baimakov was slowly dying. Propped in an arm-chair, her body swollen, her puffed-out face shapeless and purple —she had been eyeing him with increasing hostility; from her once lovely eyes, now dulled and watery, pitiable tears trickled; her twisted lips moved, but her paralysed tongue lolled between them, powerless to utter a word; the fingers of her half-dead, half-living left hand were pressed on him. She had sensed it all, and was sorry for her daughter.

Nevertheless, it required a tremendous effort of will to break off this disgusting affair with Zinaida. At the same time, once he had achieved it—in the very same instant, side by side with intoxicating memories of the mill-hand, new gnawing broodings appeared. It was as if a new Peter Artamonov was born, and lived beside the old one, concealed just behind him. He felt his double growing more and more tangible, a hindrance in everything that he himself, the real Peter Artamonov, was called upon and obliged to do. That other Artamonov took advantage of any moment-ary phase of thoughtfulness. In an instant he would blow up, like a gust of wind round a corner, bringing persistent, gnawing thoughts: 'You work like a horse—for what? You've enough for the rest of your days. It's time your son took over. You killed a boy for his sake. Then a gentle-woman pleased you—and you started loose living.'

Whenever that idea came to him, life became darker and more dreary.

He simply did not notice exactly when Ilia turned into a grown-up. This was not the only thing he failed to notice. Before he knew where he was, Natalia had married Elena to a cocky young fellow from Vorgorod with little black moustaches—son of a rich jeweller. Much in the same way, for that matter, his mother-in-law died at last, passing away one sultry June afternoon, while a storm was brewing. They were just in the act of laying her out when the first clap of thunder burst close by, scaring them all. 'Shut the windows and doors!' Natalia cried, and clapped her hands to her ears. One of her mother's huge legs, released, slith-ered from the bed, the heel banging on the floor.

As a matter of fact, Peter Artamonov simply did not re-cognize his son when Ilia first entered the room—a tall well-proportioned man in a soft grey suit, with a definite moustache on the swarthy, and now rather thin face. Yakov, broad and plump, in a *lycée* tunic, was more like himself. The two boys greeted him politely, and sat down.

'There,' Artamonov senior said, striding up and down the office, 'your grandmother's just died.'

Ilia said nothing, and lit a cigarette, while Yakov, in quite a new voice, said: 'Lucky it's the holidays, or I should not be here.'

Ignoring this silly pronouncement of his youngest, Artamonov examined Ilia; his features had changed considerably, they had grown firmer, and his forehead, with locks of darkening hair falling over it, was not so enormous; the blue eyes were more sunken. It was entertaining and also a little perturbing to reflect that he had shaken this pensive soberly dressed person by the hair; it was indeed not easy to believe it had ever happened. Yakov had simply grown taller and bigger altogether, remaining just as podgy as ever; nor had the radiant eyes changed in the least. His mouth too was just as infantile.

'You have grown, Ilia,' Artamonov said. 'Well, now you'd better be getting your hand in at the factory, so you can take the helm in two or three years' time.'

Ilia toyed with a leather cigarette case; the corner of the case was broken off; then, looking his father straight in the face, said: 'No, I am going on with my studies.'

'For long?' Peter inquired.

'Four or five more years.'

'Oho! And what are ye going to study?'

'History.'

It annoyed Artamonov to see his son smoking; moreover, that was a rotten cigarette case, he could have bought a better one. Still less did he like Ilia's resolution to go on with school, let alone the way he had announced it the moment he arrived. Peter Artamonov pointed through the window at the factory roof, where a small pipe could be seen puffing steam; a dull mutter of labour came from that direction.

'There's history for you, puffing away!' he said, trying to inspire Ilia, and speaking as gently as he could. 'Our job's to weave cloth, history isn't our job. I'm fifty, it's time you took over from me.'

'Miron will take over, or Yakov. Miron's going to be an engineer,' Ilia said; he stuck his arm out of the window, and shook the ash from his cigarette.

'Don't forget,' Artamonov said, 'Miron's my nephew, not my son. . . . But we'll talk it over some other time. . . .'

The boys went out; he followed them with his eyes,— he was astonished and hurt. What, had they really nothing to tell him? They stayed five minutes, one produced an idiotic observation, then yawned sleepily; the other had filled the office with tobacco smoke and wounded him right away. There they were, crossing the yard now. He heard Ilia say: 'Let's go and have a look at the river!' 'No,' the other replied, 'I'm tired. All that shaking on the journey.' The river, Peter thought angrily, would still be there to-morrow; besides, their mother, in grief on account of her mother's death, was full of cares about the funeral.

Mastering his habit of rushing to meet trouble half-way, so as either to ward it off as soon as possible, or circumvent it, Peter Artamonov gave his son a week's rest. During that week he noticed that Ilia spoke to the workmen as if they were his equals, and had long night talks with Vialov and Seraphim, sitting with them by the courtyard gate. One evening Artamonov caught Tikhon Vialov's miserable, life-less voice—he was pouring forth his usual idiotic chatter: 'That's it, I tell 'ee—a beggar's life means possessing no-thing. But, Mr. Ilia, if people weren't greedy, there'd be enough to go round.' And there was Seraphim ready with his cackle: 'I know that's true . . . I heard that long ago . . .'

Yakov's behaviour was more comprehensible, running about the workshops with a glad eye for the girls, or climb-ing up on to the stable roof, which overlooked the river, whenever the girls bathed in the dinner hour. 'The young cock,' Peter said to himself dourly. 'I must tip Seraphim a wink to keep an eye on him, in case he catches something.'

It was Tuesday, and a mournful, grey day, a pensive, hushed day. Early that morning there had been an hour of slow, drizzling rain, then at midday the sun had shown through, cast an unwilling glance at the factory and the fork of the two rivers, then vanished again behind dun clouds, plunging into their fluffy depths, like Natalia at night diving her rosy cheeks into her down pillows.

That evening, just before tea, Artamonov asked Yakov where his brother was.

'I don't know; he was sitting out there on one of the dunes, under a pine tree.'

'Call him. No, don't bother. How do you two get on together? Agree?'

'Not so badly.'

'No, come on—tell me the truth . . .'

Yakov looked down, thought a moment, then said: 'We see things differently.'

'What things?'

'Things in general, everything.'

'But how, exactly?'

'He always goes by books—I simply by what I think, what I see myself.'

'Hm!' said Artamonov, unable to ask any more.

Throwing an ulster over his shoulders, he took one of Alexey's presents—a walking-stick with a handle consisting of a silver bird's claw clutching a malachite sphere. When he left the gateway, he put hand to forehead to scan the rising ground towards the river—and there indeed, under a tree, in a white tunic, lay Ilia. 'With the sand damp to-day,' Peter Artamonov said to himself, 'the noodle may well catch a cold.'

Without haste, weighing over again and again everything he had to say to his son, he made for him, crushing under-foot the grey blades of grass, which rustled and cracked.

The boy was lying face downwards, reading a thick book, tapping the page every now and then. But at the sound of footsteps he turned his head lissomly and looked at his father, then, laying the pencil between the pages, slapped the book to noisily. He sat up, leaning against the trunk of the pine, examining his father, with kindly glance. The elder Artamonov, having got his breath, sat down beside him on a bare, arched root.

'I'm not going to talk about the factory to-day,' he said, 'just let's have a chat.'

But Ilia, clasping his knees, said softly: 'Well, Dad, I have really made up my mind to consecrate myself to learning.'

'Consecrate yourself,' Artamonov repeated the word— 'like taking holy orders.' He intended his words to sound joking, but himself caught the dour, almost angry note in them. This annoyed him, and he banged at the sand with his stick. In the same instant the incomprehensible had happened, which should never have happened: the blue of Ilia's eyes took on a darker shade, the clean-cut eyebrows puckered, the boy tossed the hair off his forehead and suddenly, with an unpleasant insistence, announced: 'I am not going to be a manufacturer, I'm not fitted for that sort of work . . .'

'Exactly the way friend Tikhon Vialov talks,' interposed Artamonov, with a smirk.

Paying no heed to this, the boy tried to explain why he did not want to be a manufacturer, or any sort of proprietor of any sort of enterprise. He spoke at great length, quite ten minutes, and there were moments when his father could spot some grain of truth, corresponding to his own obscure impulses. But on the whole he remained quite sure that his son was talking childish nonsense.

'Half a moment,' he said at last, poking in the sand about

the boy's feet. 'Not so fast, things aren't like that. That's all twaddle. There has to be somebody in command. The mass of people can't live without it. Without the incentive of gain nobody would work. Hence the common phrase— *what will I get out of it!* That's the shaft on which everything turns. Look at all the proverbs—"The matchmaker (*svat*) would be all holy (*sviat*), if he didn't want his rake-off." Or "Even a saint prays for something." Or, "An engine isn't a living thing, yet it wants oiling." '

He spoke quite calmly, and, as these fitting proverbs came to mind, liberally lubricated his words. He was glad he was not getting ruffled, but speaking easily, with ready flow of words, confident this talk would end well. The boy kept silence, sifting sand from one hand to the other, picking out from it rustly pine needles, and blowing them from his palm. But suddenly, just as quietly, he said: 'All this does not convince me. We can't go on living on that sort of wisdom.'

The elder Artamonov began to get to his feet, leaning on his stick. The boy did not assist him.

'So in other words, your father's wrong?'

'There's another right.'

'Nonsense. There is no other right.' And, waving his stick at the factory, the father said: 'There's your *right*! Your grand-dad began it, I've put my life into it, and now it's your turn. And that's an end to it. What do you want? Us do the work, and you idle? You'd like to be righteous on somebody-else's toil? Not a bad idea! History! Drop that tommy-rot! History isn't a wench, you can't marry it. What do you mean, anyway, by this idiotic notion of history? What's it for? Anyway, I'm not going to let you be an idler . . .'

Here he did feel that he had begun to show too much annoyance, so he made an attempt to smooth over his words: 'I quite see,' he said, 'you'd like to live in Moscow; it's more jolly, and your Uncle Alexey . . .'

Ilia took his book, blew some grains of sand from it, and said: 'Please let me go on studying.'

'I shall do nothing of the kind!' the father cried, and thrust his stick into the sand, 'and don't ask me to.'

Then Ilia too got up, and, looking past his father, with eyes that showed white, said in a stifled voice: 'Very well then, I shall have to do without your permission.'

'You dare not!'

'No man can be forbidden to live as he wants,' said Ilia, with a toss of his head.

'No man? You're my son, you aren't a man. What sort of a man are ye? Every stitch on you is mine!'

He saw Ilia flush red, saw his hands shaking, saw him, without success, try to hide them in his trouser pockets. Then, fearing that the boy might say too much, perhaps something irreparable, he himself hastily put in: 'On your account I once killed . . . perhaps . . .'

He had added that 'perhaps' because, the moment he uttered the preceding words, he realized that he could not say such a thing, at such a moment, to a mere stripling, who was plainly unwilling to see his point of view. 'The next thing he'll be asking is—who it was?' he said to himself, and strode rapidly down the shifting sand to the dune. Then he heard his son's voice, at his heels, deafening him: 'You haven't murdered only one man, look over there, there's a whole cemetery you and your factory have murdered!'

Artamonov stopped short, and turned about him—arm outstretched, Ilia was pointing with his book at the crosses against the grey sky. The sand crunched under Artamonov's tread; he recalled that only a few minutes ago he had heard something else offensive about the factory and the cemetery. He would have given anything to hide that word too many he had said—anything to have his son forget it; like a bear he made for the lad, brandishing his stick, thinking to scare him, shouting: 'What's that you say, you young scoundrel?'

Ilia leapt behind a tree: 'Come to your senses,' he cried. 'What are you thinking of?'

The stick came down on the tree-trunk and snapped in two. Artamonov threw his fragment at his son; it stuck sloping in the sand at Ilia's feet, the green sphere uppermost. He threatened Ilia: 'I'll have you clean the privies!' he cried, and stumbled hastily away, feeling his mind fumbling among words of grief and rage like a shuttle in a tangled warp.

'I'll disown him. Necessity'll compel him to come back. Then he will clean the privies. Yes, don't be a softy!'—He tore the fragmentary threads of thought off the whirling bobbin, at the same time aware that he had not behaved as he should; he had overdone it, he had made too much of his mortification.

Coming out on to the bank of the Oka, he sat wearily down on the steep sandy embankment, wiped the sweat from his forehead, and looked down at the river. In a shallow little backwater a shoal of dace were swimming along, like so many steel needles stitching the water. Then there appeared a bream, with dignified movement of its fins; after swimming a little way, it turned on its side, one little red eye peering upwards at the turgid sky, as it left a bright haze of floating ripples behind it on the water. Artamonov wagged his finger at it, saying out loud: 'I'll cook your hash for you!' and looked sharply round, feeling how falsely those words rang.

The tranquil flow of the river was washing his rage away; the warm, greyish silence insinuated into him a mood full of dumb astonishment. The most astonishing of all was that the son whom he loved, of whom he had thought uninterruptedly and anxiously for twenty years, had in a few brief moments slipped out of his heart, leaving only an angry hurt behind. Artamonov was convinced that he really had thought only of his son all these twenty years, day by day, living by his hope in him, his love for him, expecting from him something beyond the ordinary. Like a match he told himself, it had flared—and gone out. What had happened?

A touch of pink came into the grey sky; in one corner appeared a brighter patch, like the oily shine of threadbare cloth. Then a chunk of moon appeared, the air turned fresh and damp; mist crept like thin smoke over the river.

Artamonov entered the bedroom just as Natalia, already in nightdress, had put her left foot on her rounded right knee—with puckered brow she was cutting her toe-nails. With a sideways glance at him, she asked: 'Where have you sent Ilia?'

'To hell,' he replied, and proceeded to undress.

'You're so bad-tempered nowadays.' She sighed. He did not answer, but stamped and raged about, puffing and blowing. Rain began to spatter on the window-panes; a damp whisper swept through the garden.

'Ilia's all ambition about his studies,' she ventured.

'And his mother's a fool,' he snapped back.

She took a deep breath, crossed herself, and got into bed. As he finished, Peter continued to insult her with great satisfaction: 'What can you do? Nothing. The children don't respect you. What have you taught them? All you know about is eating and sleeping.'

Into the pillow she replied: 'And who sent them away to school? I told you . . .'

'Shut up!'

He too said no more; he listened to the rain lashing the leaves on the wild cherry that Nikita planted. Then he muttered: 'The hunchback made the wisest choice; neither children nor factory. Just bees. Better even not bother about the bees, let them find their own honey.'

Turning over on to her back as cautiously as if she were lying on thin ice, Natalia laid her warm cheek on her husband's shoulder. 'Have you quarrelled with Ilia?' she asked.

He was too ashamed to tell her exactly what had taken place; he growled out: 'Men don't quarrel with children—they tell them off.'

'He's gone to Dromov.'

'He'll come back. Nobody'll feed him for nothing. Let him see what want smells like, he'll be back. Go to sleep, don't worry me.'

A minute later he said: 'Yakov can leave school now.'

After yet another minute he added: 'The day after to-morrow I leave—I'm going to the Nizhny Fair—hear what I say?'

'Very well.'

'What on earth have things come to?' he asked himself, closing his eyes, but still seeing before him Ilia's features,—the lofty forehead, and that insufferably offended glint in the eyes. 'Telling off his father, like a workman, the young scoundrel! Spurning me as if I were a tramp . . .'

The incomprehensible swiftness of the break between them astounded Artamonov; it was as if Ilia had long made up his mind to it. But whatever could have driven him to do such a thing? He recalled the cutting, condemnatory language Ilia had used. 'That treacherous cur Miron put the idea into his head. And the notion that business harms a man, that he got from Vialov. Fool, fool! What advisers—after that schooling—what had he learned? Learned to pity the working class, but not his own father. Then sneaks off into a sly corner to be self-righteous!'

As he thought thus, the mortification Ilia had caused him flared up fiercer than ever. 'You're all wrong,' his heart cried, 'but you'll come to heel!'

Nikita flashed back into his mind—Nikita too had run away, found a quiet corner—they all of them got him, Peter Artamonov, well harnessed to the work, then they ran. But he immediately caught himself up on that thought. It was not true, because there was Alexey, who had not run away; Alexey loved the works, just as Peter's father had loved them. For instance, one day, when there had been a drunken brawl among the workers, he had remarked to Alexey that the men were deteriorating.

'Noticeably,' Alexey had agreed.

'Something's making them vicious. As if they all saw through one pair of eyes.'

Again Alexey had agreed. With a smile he had said: 'Also true. I sometimes remember Tikhon Vialov looking at father with the sort of eyes you mean, when he was wrestling with the soldiers at your wedding. Then he tried his hand against father himself. Do you remember?'

'Oh, nonsense,—Vialov? that poor loony?'

Alexey had gone on seriously: 'You seem to have that on your mind lately, it's always the men deteriorating. But that, old man, is not our job—that's for the parsons, the schoolmasters, and,—well, for all your doctors and government officials. It's their job to see to it the common people don't deteriorate—that's their stock-in-trade—we're only their customers. My dear fellow, everything is deteriorating a bit. For example, you're getting older, so am I. But would you, now, say to a young filly—don't you indulge in any love-making, my girl, you'll be an old woman some day!'

'He's full of sense, damn him,' Artamonov told himself, on that occasion, 'simply full of sense,' and whenever he listened to Alexey's dashing chatter, always seasoned with new popular wisecracks, Nikita would come to his mind—had their father thought Nikita would be able to help them through their troubles, yet Nikita himself got into trouble over a petticoat, and that was the end of him.

A great deal passed through the elder Artamonov's head that rainy night. Through the bitterness of his thought, like a wisp of smoke, threaded a string of other, alien ideas which might have been the insistent mutterings of the dark rain outside, hindering his every effort to justify what he had done.

'But how am I at fault?' he asked of the unknown, and, getting no answer, felt the question was a sound one. When day broke he came to a sudden decision—to drive over to the monastery to see his brother. Perhaps one living outside all temptation and trouble might have some comfort to give him, even precise guidance, what to do.

But when at last the two post-house horses brought him near the Priory, the shaking up he had received on the by-roads had exhausted him, and he thought how easy it would be to stand to one side—'You just try running about with the crowd! A cucumber keeps all right in the cellar, it soon rots in the sun!'

He had not seen his brother for four years. Their last meeting had been cold and strained; Peter had got the impression that his hunchback brother was depressed, and dissatisfied with his nest; Nikita had huddled and shrunk away from him like a snail into its shell; with a spiteful note in his voice he had spoken, not of God or even himself and the family, but of the monastery's wants, of pilgrims and of the poverty of the common people—even so he spoke with effort, unwillingly. When Peter had offered him some funds, he had said quietly and carelessly: 'I don't want any, give it to our Prior.'

It was obvious that all the monks had great respect for Father Nikodim—as Nikita was called. The Prior, a huge, bony, hirsute fellow, deaf on one side, was like a wild man of the forest dressed in a cassock. His dark eyes pierced Peter's glance uncomfortably, as unnecessarily loud he declared that: 'Father Nikodim is a great ornament to our poor dwelling.'

The Priory, tucked away on a small rise of ground in a clearing of bronze firs, dominated by their dense crowns, met Artamonov with the everyday jangling of its miserable bells, summoning to vespers. The gatekeeper, erect and lanky as a bean-pole, with a ridiculous childishly small head, topped with a faded and crumpled skull-cap, stammered and choked as he muttered: 'Ve-r-r-r-y w-w-w-well,' and then, with a whistle, and a sigh, 'p-p-p-please come-in.'

A bluish-grey cloud, which covered half the sky, hung stationary over the Priory and its surroundings, bearing heavily down on the whole country-side, instilling it with a dense, damp, all-stifling oppressiveness—even the brassy clang of the bells was powerless to shift it.

'I can't lift this by meself,' said the guest-house man apologetically, banging his forehead with his dirty little fist, after trying in vain to drag the box of presents for Nikita out of the chaise.

Dusty and fatigued, Peter slowly passed through into the close, making his way towards his brother's white cell, which was tucked snugly away amid an orchard of cherry and apple. As he went, he told himself that it had been foolish to come at all; he had done far better to go to the Fair. The rough road through the forest—driving over tree roots which sprawled across it—had churned up all his embittered feelings; now only a relentless depression remained, a yearning for repose and oblivion. 'I could do with a good night with some girls and drink,' he told himself.

He came on his brother seated on a garden bench in a semi-circle of young lindens, and facing him, for all the world like a familiar picture postcard, a dozen pilgrims seated on the ground. Among them was a swarthy-bearded merchant in an ulster, one leg in bandages and a surgical rubber boot; a fat old man, like a eunuch money-changer; a young fellow in soldier's overcoat, his hair long and with high cheek bones and fishy eyes; and there too, stiff as a gatepost, like a thief before the beak, that loose-living drunkard, the Dromov baker, Mourzin, who was just saying hoarsely: 'Quite right—the Lord God is very far away.'

Scratching the trodden ground with his thin white staff, and without looking up, Nikita continued his sermon: 'And the more degraded a man is, the farther removed is the Lord from him in the heights, for he is driven away by the stench of our corruption.'

'Comfort,' Artamonov senior said to himself, with an inward smile.

'God sees that we believe, yet do nothing about our belief —but what use is faith without deeds to him? Where is our charity one to another, where our love? And what are our prayers about? Nothing but trifles. Yet it is our duty to pray . . .'

Nikita raised his eyes, and gazed for some time at his brother without saying a word, staring up at him. Then, slowly, as if it were a great weight, he raised his staff, as though with the intention of striking somebody. He got to his feet, let his head drop on his chest, made the sign of the cross over the gathering, but instead of a blessing, he said: 'Look, here's my dear brother come to pay me a visit.'

A hairless old man opened his eyes wide, and looked at Peter with a certain malevolence, then with a deliberately demonstrative sweep of his arms, he crossed himself.

'The Lord God be with you,' Nikita responded.

The pilgrims made off in a loose group, like a flock driven from its pasture; the old man took one arm of the lame merchant, Mourzin the baker taking the other arm.

'Well, how are you?' Artamonov asked—'give me your blessing,' but Nikita swept aside the clenched fists which Peter had reached out to him, and, without any sign of pleasure, said quietly: 'I did not expect to see you.'

'You've aged a bit,' Peter observed, with some embarrassment.

'A thing we all have to expect. My legs have begun to trouble me too. The subsoil here is damp.'

Peter would have said that Nikita was more hunched than before; the angle of his back and his right shoulder had lifted, forcing the trunk nearer to the ground; thus shortening him, time had made him broader; he was like a spider with its head torn off, blindly creeping down the crunching gravel path. But in his cramped, though pleasantly clean cell, 'Father Nikodim' grew larger—and more alarming too; his cowl thrown back, he revealed his half-bald, bony skull—it gleamed white like that of a corpse, and the bald patch might have been skinless; over his temples and round behind his ears were straggling tufts of grey hair. The face too was all bone, the colour waxen; flesh was lacking, and the faded eyes failed to shed any light; they seemed only to see the tip of their massive, but flabby nose; below the nose the shrivelled lips kept up a soundless quiver; altogether, the mouth had grown larger, and now cleft the face with its profound hollow; there was something particularly unpleasant in the greyish mould of hairs on the upper lip.

To a puffy-faced serving lad, who might have been a public-baths boy, he said, in a very low voice, as if he were trying at the same time to catch some sound, laboriously too, as if it was an effort to remember the words: 'A samovar. Bread. Some honey.'

'You've lost your voice!' Artamonov said.

'My teeth have all gone.'

He sat down to the table in a white-painted arm-chair. 'All well with you?'

'All well.'

'Tikhon alive?'

'Yes. Why?'

'He hasn't been for a long time.'

Neither spoke for some time. Nikita, moving his arm, rustled his cassock, and that sound, like cockroaches running, depressed Peter still more.

'I've brought some presents for you. Tell somebody to bring the box here. There's some wine in it. Are you allowed wine?'

Nikita sighed and replied: 'The rule here is not strict. We have trouble. Some of the brethren have even become drunkards, since there's been so many pilgrims. They drink —what else are they to do? Peace reigns here—and poisons them. Monks are only human.'

'I hear a lot of people come to take advice of you?'

'By misunderstanding,' he replied. 'But they do come. They do the round. Looking for righteousness, or a righteous man. Some indication, how to live. "We've lived all these years, now—we don't know how to live. . . ." People can't bear reality.'

Feeling troubled by his brother's words, Artamonov senior muttered: 'Softness. They could bear serfdom, but freedom's too much for them.'

Nikita did not reply at once, then said: 'When they had masters, they did not go on the loose, they couldn't go off the road.' He shot a swift glance at Peter, and lowered his eyes again.

188

In this wise, finding it difficult to know what to say, and with many a long pause, they discoursed, till the serving lad brought a samovar, some sweet-scented lime honey and a warm loaf of bread, from which the yeasty steam was still rising. They attentively watched the fair-haired lad on the floor, clumsily opening the lid of the chest. Then Peter put a jar of fresh caviare and a couple of bottles on the table.

'Port,' Nikita read out. 'That's a wine the Prior likes. A clever fellow. Full of understanding.'

'Now that's just what I'm lacking in,' Peter confessed challengingly.

'You've got all you need,' Nikita said, 'what do you want more understanding for? It's harmful to know more than is necessary.'

Nikita suppressed a sigh. There was a bitter note in his voice. His cassock shone greasily, dirtily, in the gloom, which was barely broken by the flicker of the holy lamp in the corner and a rubbishy little oil lamp with chimney of yellowish glass on the table. Observing the calculating eagerness with which Nikita drained a glass of Madeira, Peter said to himself scornfully: 'Knows what he's drinking.'

After each glass Nikita broke off some crumb of the loaf with his dry, excessively pale fingers, dipped it in the honey, and slowly champed it. There was no sign of the wine going to his head, his muddy eyes merely brightened a little, but still remained fixed on the end of his nose. Peter drank cautiously. He did not want his brother to think he was a tippler. Drinking, he reflected that Nikita had not asked about Natalia—nor had he the last time. He was ashamed. He did not ask about anybody. People of the outer world. He was one of the righteous, men sought him out . . .

Peter sat scraping his beard over his waistcoat, and plucking at his ear, then suddenly said: 'You've fixed yourself up in a nice little refuge here. It's all right.'

'It used to be; now it's not so good; there are very many pilgrims. I'm always full up with appointments . . .'

Peter grinned. 'Appointments, eh? You're like a dentist.

'My desire is to transfer somewhere else, more out of the way,' said 'Brother Nikodim', carefully re-filling his glass.

'Where it's quieter,' Peter concluded, and grinned again, while his brother drained the glass, licked his lips with his dark-hued rag of a tongue, and, nodding his bony head, said: 'The number of people with the spirit of restlessness in them is growing noticeably larger. Hiding, to get away from their cares. . . .'

'I haven't noticed it,' Peter rejoined, fully aware he was not speaking the truth. What he would have liked to say was: 'You hid away.'

'But their cares, like their shadows, follow them . . .'

Automatically one reproach after another came to the tip of Peter's tongue. He would have liked to argue, even to shout at his brother. Then, thinking of Ilia, he said angrily: 'Man makes troubles for himself, he makes his own want. But if you do whatever your job is without trying to be too clever, you can get through peacefully enough.'

But Nikita could not have heard what he said, deafened as he was by his own inner thoughts. He suddenly shook his angular body, as if he had just waked up; the cassock draped in black ripples of cloth; Nikita twisted his lips and suddenly declared, very precisely, almost angrily: 'They come here and want to be instructed. How can I tell how to instruct them? I'm not wise by nature. I'm an invention of the Prior's. I am like an innocent man condemned—I really do know nothing about it all. I am condemned to instruct others—what have I done to deserve that?'

'That's a hint,' Artamonov senior grasped. 'He means that as a complaint.' He could indeed see that Nikita had reason to complain of his lot, and visiting him on previous

190

occasions he had been ready for such complaints. Now, tugging at his ear, he tried to ward his brother off it. 'Many people have to complain of their lot—but what good does it so?'

'Exactly. Contented people are very rare,' the hunchback observed, squinting into the corner at the ikon lamp.

'And of course, our poor departed father told you to be a man of comfort, didn't he? So you go on comforting.'

Nikita drew a wry mouth, clutched a handful of his grey beard and with it wiped the scornful look away, then continued to talk into the darkness, saying things that struck Peter and excited both his curiosity and a sense of danger, putting him involuntarily on his guard.

'They make out here, to me and the people who come, that I am a wise man; of course, it suits the establishment, it's a bait. But for me it's a wearisome task. It's no laughing matter. What can I offer to console anybody? Be patient, I tell them, though I can see quite well they're all sick to death of being patient. Live in hope, I say. What are they to hope for? The Almighty is not enough. There's a baker . . .'

'He's a Dromov man,' Artamonov senior put in, to change the conversation, fend off what he feared, 'Mourzin, a drunken sot.'

'He's got the idea into his head that he can judge God. In his mind God is not the master of this world. There are a number of daring characters like that about nowadays. And there's another one—clean-shaven—notice him? An evil character, bitter against the whole world. They come with their questions, and what am I to say? They come to catch me out.'

'Brother Nikodim' grew excited. When he recalled what his brother had been like on previous visits, Peter observed that Nikita's eyes had lost that guilty blink they once had had. He had always been relieved by that sense of guilt the

191

hunchback used to have—people who feel guilty don't complain. But here he was now, complaining, and declaring he had been unjustly condemned, and Peter Artamonov was afraid he might say: 'And it was you condemned me!' He frowned and toyed with his watch-chain, trying to find words of self-defence.

'Yes,' the hunchback continued, and seemed to be secretly pleased with the cause of his complaint. 'People are getting more arrogant, full of insolent ideas. A little while ago we had a scholar spend a week or two here—still a young man, but apparently not quite in his right mind, scared by something. The Prior gave me a hint: "You buck him up a bit with your simplicity," he said, "you say so-and-so, put it in such-and-such a way." But I've no head to remember someone else's ideas. Well, this scholar used to draw my nerves out alive, hour after hour, endlessly talking, without me being able even to understand the words he used, let alone his ideas. He said it was impossible to admit that Satan is master of our bodies, as that would be believing in two Gods, and that would be desecration of Jesus' body, with which we are in communion: *Accept of the body of Jesus Christ, consume the source of immortality.* He would blaspheme—he said God could have horns, so long as there was only one God, otherwise it would be impossible to live. He did give me a time, and I absolutely forgot all the Prior had told me, and cried: "Your flesh is a transformation and your soul destruction." The Prior was very angry with me about that. "What black magic nonsense was that you babbled to him?" Yes, that's how it stands . . .'

Peter found the story amusing and, since it put Nikita in rather a sorry light, it somewhat reassured him.

'It's not easy to talk about God,' he growled.

'It isn't,' Nikita agreed, then in an oily, but bitter way, he said: 'Remember how father would insist we were plain working people, and all this high-falutin wisdom was not for us?'

'I do.'

'Yes—and the Prior tries to get me to read books! I do read them, but to me a book is like a far-off forest, I fear it, but can't distinguish anything clearly. Books don't fit our time. There are ideas about to-day you'll never cap with books. Sects springing up all over the place. Men reason according to dreams—or in their cups. That man Mourzin, for example.'

Nikita swallowed a glass of port, took a mouthful of bread, but rolling it into a little ball, began poking it about the table, while he continued: 'The Prior says: all the trouble comes from the intellect; Satan has inflamed it; he has made it like a mad dog, and teases it, and it barks at whatever it sees. . . . He may be right, but it hurts to agree with that. . . . We've a doctor, too, a simple sort of man, cheerful too, who thinks otherwise. He says the intellect is a child, and everything it sees is a toy to it, a toy which amuses it. The intellect wants to find out how this or that's put together, what the works are like. Of course, that's going a bit far . . .'

'Don't you think that is dangerous talk?' Peter asked suddenly. His brother's words were once again worrying him, upsetting him, surprising him and alarming him, they were so out of the ordinary and penetrating. Again he felt a desire to crush Nikita, humble him. But he tried to calm himself. 'It's the liquor,' he told himself.

It had become stuffy in the cell, with an acrid odour of charcoal and colza oil, which quenched Peter's thought. The motionless leaves of a plant stood out like iron-work against the square of window. Meanwhile his spider-like brother quietly and insistently continued to spin his web.

'All ideas are dangerous. Especially simple ones. Take Tikhon Vialov.'

'A half-wit.'

'You're wrong there—the man has a very vigorous mind. At first I was really rather afraid to talk to him, I wanted to—but I was afraid! But when father died, Tikhon touched me very deeply. You know you were never as fond of father as I was. It didn't upset either you or Alexey to see him die like that, just at the wrong time, but it did upset Tikhon. You must know I did not lose my temper with that nun who read the prayers because of her stupidity, I was angry with God, and Tikhon saw it at once. See, he said, a gnat may live, but a man . . .'

'You're talking twaddle,' Peter interjected sternly. 'You've had too much to drink. What nun?'

Nikita continued tenaciously: 'Tikhon said that if God was master of the world, rain would come at the right time, to suit the corn and mankind. Nor is man responsible for all the fires—lightning sets fire to the forests. Why too did Cain have to commit sin, so that we should be mortal? What use are any misshapen things to God—hunchbacks, for example, what use to him?'

'Ah, now we're coming to it!' Peter told himself, smirking into his beard and conscious that all these complaints of his brother against God were most reassuring to him; it was a good thing his monk brother did not complain of his relatives.

'It's impossible to understand Cain. That's how Tikhon got me, and put me on a lead. It began from the day father died. I told myself that if I went to a monastery it would die out. Oh no. I still live by those same thoughts.'

'You used to hold your tongue about it . . .'

'Nobody can say everything at once. Besides, I might have held my peace all my life, had it not been for these pilgrims interfering. They stir up your conscience. That's dangerous—supposing Tikhonish ideas begin slipping off my tongue? Oh yes, he was really a clever man, though I'm not sure I like him. He's concerned about you too. There, he says, the man labours for his children, and they are strangers . . .'

'Here, what's this?' Peter cried angrily, 'what can he know about it?'

'He knows. The enterprise, he says—illusion . . .'

'I've heard all that. . . . The fool will have to be got rid of . . . Only he knows too much about our affairs . . .'

Artamonov said this in order to remind Nikita of that terrible night when Tikhon cut him down, but it was with the Nikonov boy in his mind. Nikita did not catch the hint; he brought his glass to his mouth, dipped his tongue in it, licked his lips, then went on in a metallic voice: 'Tikhon too had been outraged by someone, that was why he set himself apart, as if ruined . . .'

He simply had to get Nikita off this line of thought. 'So, in the upshot, you don't believe in God any longer, do you?' he asked suddenly. He was startled, because he had meant to put the question in a biting way, and had failed to do so.

'It's hard to know who does believe to-day,' said Nikita after a short pause. 'There's a lot of reasoning going on all round—but faith is not particularly noticeable. You don't need to reason, if you have faith. That fellow who spoke of God having horns . . .'

'Drop all that,' Peter advised him, looking about him. 'It all comes from boredom—doing nothing. They all need harnessing in iron yokes.'

'All the same, you can't have faith in two different things,' 'Brother Nikodim' insisted.

For the second time now the bell was tolling; the measured strokes beat on the black window-pane. 'Are you going to service?' Peter asked.

'I don't go. I can't stand long.'

'Do you offer prayers for us?'

The monk did not answer.

'Well, I'd like to go to bed, I had a tiring journey.'

Without a word, Nikita laid his long arms on the arms of his chair, carefully raised his nobbly body, and cried: 'Mitia, Mitia!'

He sank back again, saying apologetically: 'Sorry; I had forgotten—my serving-boy sleeps in the guest-house. I had told him he could go. I wanted to be able to have a chat without interruption—they're all spies and slanderers here . . .'

He gave his brother superfluous, long-winded instructions how to get to the guest-house, and when he found himself outside, under the thick, fine drizzle of rain, Peter Artamonov told himself that his babbling brother had not really wanted him to go. Suddenly, with a fear which was familiar, he once again felt he was walking along the edge of a deep abyss, into which he might fall at any moment. He hastened his pace, reaching out one arm in front of him, feeling the watery dust of this night obscurity on his fingers, and keeping his eyes on the oily blotch of a lantern in the distance.

'No,' he thought hastily, as he stumbled along, 'none of this is any use to me. I shall leave to-morrow. No use. What has happened? Ilia will come back. No, I must be harder. See how much rope Alexey has given himself. He could cheat me anyhow.'

He forced himself to think of Alexey, because he did not want to think of Nikita or Tikhon Vialov. But when he had stretched himself out on the hard pallet of the priory guest-house, oppressive thoughts about Nikita and the yard-man came back to him. Who and what exactly was Vialov? Vialov's shadow lay on everything; Vialov's expressions could be heard in his son's childish talk, and his brother was bewitched by Vialov's ideas.

'Fine consolation,' he said to himself. 'Now, Seraphim's a common carpenter, but he understands what comforting another really means.'

He did not feel sleepy; the mosquitoes kept biting, and three voices boomed through the wall. It must be the baker, Mourzin, the lame merchant, and the eunuch-faced man. 'Boozing, no doubt.'

From time to time the Priory night watchman banged on his gong, then all at once, at high speed, as if they were behind time and frightened, the monks were summoning to mattins, but to the sound of that bell Peter fell asleep.

Nikita came to him the next morning looking exactly as he himself had found him the previous evening, in the close —he gave the same alien and malevolent sidelong glance, from feet upwards. Peter washed and dressed at top speed, and told the servant he wanted a horse to take him as far as the nearest posting-house.

'Why so soon?' Nikita asked, though without a sign of surprise. 'I thought you'd be staying here a few days.'

'The work won't let me.'

They drank tea. Peter turned his thoughts over and over, wondering what he should ask Nikita. Then the idea came to him: 'So I suppose you'd like to leave this place?' he asked.

'I'm contemplating it. They wouldn't let me go.'

'Who wouldn't?'

'I'm profitable to them. Useful.'

'Hm! But what would you do?'

'I might become an itinerant.'

'On your invalid legs?'

'There are some get about without legs at all.'

'True enough—they get about,' Peter agreed.

They were silent for a time. Then Nikita said: 'Remember me to Tikhon.'

'Anybody else?'

'Everybody.'

'Right. I wonder why you haven't asked how Alexey is?'

'Why should I ask? I know he can make his way. I may leave this place very soon.'

'Not in the winter.'

'Why not? There are winter itinerants.'

'I suppose there are,' Peter agreed again. He offered his brother some cash.

'Thank you,' Nikita said, 'it will help towards the mill repairs. Aren't you going to call on the Prior?'

'I've no time, the horse is harnessed.'

Taking leave, the two brothers embraced. It was not easy to embrace Nikita. Nor did Nikita give Peter a blessing; his right hand got caught up in the cassock sleeve. It occurred to Peter that this was on purpose. His hump pressing against Peter's belly, Nikita said in muffled tones: 'Forgive me if I said too much last night.'

'What nonsense . . . aren't we brothers.'

'In the night hours, you think and think . . .'

'I know . . . well, fare thee well . . .'

When he had come out of the Priory gates, Peter turned his head, and against the white wall of the guest-house could see the silhouette of his brother, like a lump of rock. 'Fare thee well,' he muttered again, and doffed his cap, the fine rain peppering his bare head.

The road led through a pine wood; it was very quiet, the only life the glassy green of the pine needles under the pearly rain-drops. A monk was bouncing about on the driving seat of the chaise; the horse was a chestnut with curious bare ears.

'What things they talk of!' Peter thought, 'God not sending the rain at the right time . . . ! It's malice and envy and monstrosity at the bottom of it. And idleness. No worries. A man without worries is like a dog without a master.'

Peter looked about him, shivering. He agreed, the rains did indeed come at the wrong time. Once again gloomy ideas swarmed in on him, like a leaden cloud. In an effort to escape them, he drank vodka at each posting-house.

At evening, when the smoke of a town was showing in the far distance, a snorting train crossed the road in front of him; with a shriek, it billowed steam about itself and dived into the earth, disappearing into a semi-circular hole.

PART THREE

WHENEVER he thought of those tempestuous days spent at the Fair, Peter Artamonov shivered with incredulity amounting to terror; it was impossible to believe that he had really seen all that his memory brought before him, let alone that he himself had been stewed in that immense stone boiler, reverberant with the wail of music and song, with wild cries and drunken ecstasy and that dismal howling of men out of control, which shattered his spirit. The cook of it all had been a massive, curly-haired fellow in top-hat and tails, with owlish pop-eyes stuck into a bluish, clean-shaven face, who slobbered with thick lips, threw his arms round Peter, pushing, telling: 'Fool! Hold your tongue! The christening of Holy Russia, don't you understand? The annual christening on the Volga and the Oka!'

His physiognomy was indeed that of a cook—his attire suggesting one of those creatures that funeral undertakers hire to carry a torch beside the hearse. Peter had a vague recollection of having a fight with the fellow, then drinking cognac with him—cognac with a water ice beaten into it, and the fellow sobbing and babbling: 'Try to comprehend —the cry of a Russian soul! My old man was a parson, but I'm only a scallywag!'

It was a thick, trumpet-like voice, but soft at the same time, and out of it poured a dark stream of far-fetched talk which even against your will disturbed you.

'The corruption of the flesh,' the fellow had shouted. 'The struggle against Satan! Throw the swine his dirty tribute! Peter, old man, the revolt of your flesh—it wants assuaging! How can you repent if you don't sin? and how can you get salvation without repentance? Wash your spiri clean, old man! Don't we take baths to cleanse our bodies? Well, what about the soul then? Your soul wants its bath too. Let your good old Russian soul, the soul that sings, the great and holy Russian soul, let it have its bath!'

Peter slobbered too, he was very moved, he muttered: 'Poor little dear thing, poor little soul, it really is an orphan . . . all forgotten . . . we're too hard on it!' And the whole company shouted: 'True enough! That's well spoken!'

There had been a bald-headed, ginger-bearded man with cheeks aflame and ears purple, a tubby restless little balloon of flesh which flitted all round them like a spinning-top, shrieking wildly in a falsetto voice: 'Steve—it's the truth! I adore you. I'm mortally fond of you. There's three things I'm mortally fond of, that's you, dry wines, and the truth. The truth about the soul!'

He too then burst into tears and sang—'By death, death repair . . .' with Peter accompanying him with an undertone of loony Anton's song: '*Waggon's broke a wheel agen . . .*'

It had then seemed to him that he too was fond of dark-haired Steven; he listened to Steven's cries with enchantment, and though the far-fetched talk put him off sometimes, in the main what the man had to say disturbed him with a sweetness and seriousness, as if it was opening a door dividing a dark and noisy chaos from a serenely lit room.

He particularly delighted in the expression 'the soul of a singer'—there was something really genuine and moving in it—it ran into a definite picture in his mind: a sultry working day, a street in Dromov, with its usual filth, and a grey-bearded old man, a sheer skeleton, like Death, wearily turning the handle of his hurdy-gurdy, with a slip of a girl of about twelve in a crumpled little blue frock, standing, eyes closed, head thrown back, in front of him, grinding out mournfully in a broken voice the lines of Lermontov:

> "Nor do I hope for any more from life,
> My sole desire is to be free, and still . . ."

When that picture had come to his mind, Artamonov had stammered in the ear of the man with the purple ears: '*A soul of a singer* . . . he's—hit the nail on the head!'

'Steve?' the ginger-beard had squeaked back, 'Steve's always right! Steve knows the key to every soul.' And, swaying to and fro still more violently, the man had shrieked: 'Steve! Friend of all mankind! Let her rip! Mr. Lawyer Paradizov—take us all to the inaccessible den! I give you full powers!'

The friend of all mankind made himself guide and pastor to that company of industrialists on the ran-tan. Wherever he appeared, with his drunken flock, there was music to deafen you, and song—wailing and mournful songs to rend your heart to tatters and then dashing ditties to make it dance itself crazy.

The only detail of all that music that memory had managed to retain was the dull hollow beat of the huge drums and the hard thread of an infuriated reed-pipe. While the drawn-out, sorrowful songs were being sung it had seemed to Peter that the stone walls of the particular inn were pressing in on him, choking him; when the chorus set up a wild, dashing song and gaily dressed young men danced, the wind might have been fluttering the very walls and billowing them out like a tent. Tempestuously, it tore him this way and that, caught between sheer delight and ecstasies of despair, and there had been moments in which Peter Artamonov was so lapped and consumed in his enthusiasm that he became obsessed with the desire to do something completely outside the ordinary, something which would stun the world—such as killing a man and then falling at the feet of those who hemmed him round and grovelling on his knees, appealing to all and sundry to pass judgment on him and punish him with a terrible punishment.

They were at 'The Velocipede', a crazy café chantant where the floor with all its tables and company and waiters slowly revolved, the only stable points being the corners of the room, which was as full of guests as a pillow is of feathers—guests and noise. The edges of the floor whirled round, revealing in one corner a huddle of infuriated, brass-mouthed musicians, in another, the chorus, a crowd of multicoloured women with garlanded heads; in a third the glasses and bottles of the bar reflected the hanging lamps; the fourth corner was cut off by doors, through which there was an incessant flow of people who took their place in the revolving circle, swaying and falling, waving their arms, with deafening guffaws, as they were conveyed on else-where.

Swarthy Steve, friend of all mankind, had tried to en-lighten him. 'It's all very silly—but jolly good—the floor's supported on rafters like a plate on your finger-tips, the rafters are set in a pillar, and there are two capstans fixed in the pillar, with a horse harnessed to each, and they go round and round and turn the floor. Simple, eh? But—there's a meaning in it—Peter old man, don't forget, there's meaning hidden in everything, worse luck!'

He pointed to the ceiling. A greenish stone on the finger gleamed like the eye of a wolf. A strange, broad-shouldered business man with a canine head tugged at Peter's sleeve and stared with glassy corpse-like eyes into his face, only to inquire in a loud voice, as if Peter were deaf: 'But what will my Dounia say, eh? Who are you?'

Without waiting for an answer, the man had turned to his neighbour on the other side: 'Who are you?' he asked. 'Whatever shall I tell my Dounia, eh?'

Then he tipped back into his chair and snorted: 'To hell with it all!' and in the same breath yelled: 'Come along now, let's be going on somewhere else!'

Later, the man had turned out to be their driver; anyway, he was on the driving box of a chaise, with a pair of grey horses, addressing everybody they came to in the street in a loud voice, telling them: 'We're going to Paula's, coming along with us?'

It rained on the way. There were five of them in the chaise, one of them lying on the floorboards at Peter's feet, muttering: 'He cheated me, and I'll cheat him. He did me, I'll do him . . .'

They came to a square, rising in the centre like a cottage-loaf, and here the chaise was overturned, so that Peter had fallen out, hitting the ground with his skull and one elbow. He remembered sitting on the damp turf, watching the ginger-head with purple ears crawling over the hummock up to the fence round a mosque, howling: 'Out of the way, I'm going to become a converted Tartar, I'm going to be a Moslem, let me go!'

Steve had grabbed the man's feet, dragged him down back again, and taken him off somewhere, while a dense crowd of Persians, Tartars, and Bokharians flocked round them from stalls and inns, an old man in a yellow *khalat* and green turban threatening Peter with a stick. '*Ourussian deffil!*' he shouted.

A copper-cheeked policeman had established Peter on his feet again, declaring: 'Street scenes are prohibited.'

Then cabs had driven up, the drunken men had been got aboard and driven off.

In the front cab, standing erect, was the friend of all mankind, yelling and making a megaphone of his fist. The rain had ceased, but the sky was a dirty black such as it never is in real life; lightning flashed over the huge expanse of the

204

oriental market and its taverns, tearing flickering gaps in the darkness, and Peter remembered his sudden fear as the horses' hooves had drummed hollow on the wooden bridge over the Betancourt Canal—he had been convinced the bridge would give way and they would all lose their lives in the water below them, motionless, stagnant, black as pitch.

In all those tattered, nightmare memories Artamonov sought himself out, and found himself surrounded by men debauched to loss of reason; he hardly recognized the Peter he found. This Peter Artamonov drank lethal quantities, a-thirst all the time for that something-beyond-the-ordinary to happen, to burst over him, that something more import-ant and more glorious than anything else—to slump into a despair which knew no bounds, or to be raised to a de-light which knew no bounds, and would endure for all time.

The most horrible of all, a blinding spot in his memory, was the woman herself, Paula Menotti. He could see her —in a large, empty room with bare walls—one-third of the room was taken up by a table laden with bottles and many-hued wine glasses and goblets, with bowls of flowers and fruit, and silver buckets of caviare and champagne. There were about a dozen fair-haired, bald-headed, greyish-look-ing men sitting impatiently round the table, one chair—among a number of empty chairs—decorated with flowers. Steve stood in the middle of the room, holding up a gold-knobbed stick like a candle, shouting: 'You swine! Stop eating, you've time enough for that!'

Somebody else's voice had rung hollow: 'Hold your jaw!'

'Silence there!' yelled the friend of all mankind. 'I am in command!'

At that moment the room suddenly became darker, and

in the same instant a drum began to beat dully outside. Steve took one step towards the double doors and flung them wide; in staggered a fat man with a drum on his belly, waddling like a goose, beating out a tremendous *boum boum boum.*

Then five men entered, all equally serious and sedate in appearance. They were bent forward, pulling like horses as they dragged into the room—a grand piano, to which they were harnessed by towels tied to the legs—with a recumbent naked woman on the polished black top of the instrument, dazzling white and repellent in the shamelessness of her nakedness. She was lying on her back, arms behind her head; her dark, loose-flowing hair melted into the black shine of the polished wood; the nearer she came to the table, the more visible were the outlines of her body and the more impudently the tufts of hair under her arms and between her legs forced themselves on every eye.

The castors squeaked, the floor groaned, the drum throbbed dully on. Then the men harnessed to that heavy chariot came to a standstill and straightened their backs. Artamonov expected everybody now to laugh—that would have made all it more comprehensible—but instead the whole company rose to its feet and gazed in silence as the woman uncoiled and detached herself from the lid of the piano. One might have thought she had only just wakened from sleep, and beneath her was a fragment of the night, condensed to the consistency of stone; it was reminiscent of a fairy story. Once erect, she tossed her abundant hair behind her back and stamped her feet, turning the deep gleam of the polish dull with blotches of white dust; Peter could hear the piano strings humming as she stamped.

Two more persons came in: a grey-headed old woman in spectacles and a man in a tail coat. The old lady sat down, and at one stroke bared the black and white keys of the piano and her yellowed teeth. The man in tails raised his fiddle to his shoulder, squinted one eye, took aim, sliced the bow across the fiddle, and the thin, whining voice of the instrument cut in on the bass chant of the piano. The naked woman drew herself upright with a snaky motion, tossed her head, so that her hair was flung forward over her impudently outstanding breasts, concealing them. She began to sway to and fro and to sing—slowly, not very loud, nasally, with a distant, dreamy voice.

They were all silent, staring at her, heads erect, and all faces with the same expression—eyes like those of blind men. The woman sang indifferently, as if half-asleep, her excessively brilliant lips uttered incomprehensible words; her oily eyes were fixed beyond the heads of the company.

Artamonov had never guessed that a woman's body could be so harmonious, so terrifyingly beautiful. She cupped her own breasts and hips with her palms, and kept tossing her head; you could have thought her hair was growing denser —she seemed all of her to grow larger, both in size and luxuriance, blotting out everything else, so that she was the only object to be seen and nothing else had ever existed. He could remember precisely that not for one instant had she excited any desire to possess her; she merely gave rise to a sensation of awe in him, an oppressive feeling in his bosom, a shiver as of sorcery. At the time same he remembered equally clearly that, had the woman ordered it, he would have followed her and carried out her every whim. When he had glanced at his companions, he was convinced of it— every man jack of them would have done the same.

He had been getting sober, and wanted to slip away. At last he decided to do so when he heard somebody whisper loudly: 'A *charousa*. Bottomless pit of nature. See? A *charousa*.'

Artamonov knew what a *charousa* was. It was a patch of

greensward in swampy forest country, where the grass grew particularly silky and green, but if you set foot on it you were lost, sucked into bottomless slime.

All the same, he kept his eyes fixed on the woman, held by the inexpressible, dominating power of her nakedness. And when her heavy, oily glance turned on him, he stirred his shoulders uneasily, bent his head, looked to one side, and saw that the monstrosities of men round him, sodden with drink, all had the same stupid goggling amazement on their faces that the Dromov creatures had had when they stood gaping at the painter who had fallen from the church roof and smashed to death.

Black-haired, curly-headed Steve was sitting on the window-sill, his thick lips hanging loose, a shaky hand smoothing his forehead, looking as if he might fall headlong to the floor any minute. Just at that instant he had suddenly rent off a shirt-cuff which had come undone and flung it on the floor.

The woman's movements became faster, more furious; she writhed as if trying to leap down from the piano, but unable to; her suppressed cries became more and more loathsome and evil; what was particularly disgusting to see was the way her legs writhed, together with the jerkings of her head which sent her hair flying first over her breasts, then lashing over her back again like the tail of a snake.

All at once the music broke off, and she leapt to the floor; swarthy Steve wrapped her in a golden wrap and vanished with her, while the company set up a yelling and howling, clapping their hands, clutching one another, and the white figures of the waiters darted about like corpses in shrouds. There was a great clinking of glasses of vodka and wine, and they all gulped down their liquor as if it were a scorching hot day. They ate and drank disgustingly, heads bent over the table like so many hogs' muzzles in a trough.

Bernard Duffield

A crowd of gipsies appeared, sang salacious songs, and danced; the company began bombarding them with gherkins and napkins—they vanished—in their place Steve ushered in a whole crowd of women, and one of them, small but well-fleshed, in a red frock, plumped herself on Peter's knees, held a glass of champagne to his lips, clinked her own glass loudly on his, and with a glib couplet called on him to drink to somebody's health. She was as light as a moth, and her name was *Pashouta*. She handled the guitar nimbly, and sang most touchingly: '*I dreamed 'twas limpid, azure day . . .*' and when her ringing voice turned particularly pathetic as she came to the words: '*I dreamed of my youth that ne'er will come back . . .*' Artamonov gave her a friendly, almost paternal pat on the head and in an effort to comfort her, said: 'Now, now . . . no snivels! You're still a young-un, don't you worry . . .'

But in the night, while he held her in his arms, he closed his eyes tight to picture that other one—Paula Menotti,—as well as he could.

In the rare moments when he grew a bit sober, Peter had realized, with considerable astonishment, that this lewd little Pashouta was eating into his pocket to a ridiculous extent. 'The damned little moth!' he said to himself.

In point of fact, he marvelled at the ability of the Nizhny Fair women to suck out a man's money, and then to squander, in the most stupid way, the earnings of shamelessness, drunken night after night. He was told that the man with the canine face, a big shot in the fur trade, was spending tens of thousands of rubles on Paula Menotti, paying her three thousand every time she appeared naked; while the fellow with the purple ears made spills of hundred ruble notes to light his cigars, and tucked whole bundles under the arms of the women. 'Take it, old Dutch,' he would say, 'I've plenty.' He called them all 'Old Dutch'.

But Peter Artamonov began to see in each of them the came blatant lack of shame that Paula with the voluminous hair showed. All women were stupid and cunning he felt, crafty and insolent, hostile to him. Even when his wife came to his mind, he seemed to catch a note of craftiness and hostility in her. 'Moths,' he said to himself, as he examined the many-coloured chorus of beautiful and young females that his memory so vividly and brilliantly brought to his mind.

He could not understand the why and wherefore of it all. Men toiled, clanking the fetters that bind them to their work, even deafening themselves merely in order to accumulate as much money as possible and then—to burn that money, throw it away in handfuls at the feet of loose women. And what was more—these were all big figures, men of weight, married men, with families, proprietors of huge factories.

'I suppose father would never have behaved this way,' he told himself, with some conviction. He could not see himself as a real participator in that life of debauch—he was rather an accidental, involuntary spectator. Yet those reflexions went to his head worse than alcohol,—and only alcohol could quench them. He spent three whole weeks in a nightmare of debauch—only coming to himself when Alexey arrived.

The head of the Artamonov family was lying on the floor on a thin and hard straw mattress; beside him was a bucket of ice, bottles of kvass, and a plate of salted cabbage, well seasoned with grated horseradish. On the divan was sprawling Pashouta, her mouth half-open, just like Natalia's, and her brows arched; one leg dangling white with blue veins and toe-nails like fish-scales. Outside was the thousand-muzzled din of the great All-Russian Fair.

Through that drunken droning inside his skull and the dull ache of his poisoned system, Peter Artamonov was grimly clutching at what he could remember of the previous night's amusements, when there, all at once, was Alexey, as if he had sprung out of the ground. He limped up to Peter, stumping with his stick, and the words flowed freely from him: 'What, bowled over, on your back now, eh? And I spent all yesterday and all last night looking for you—I didn't feel too good myself this morning.'

Alexey had called a waiter at once, and ordered lemonade cognac, and ice. Then he hopped over to the divan and clapped his hand on Pashouta's shoulder: 'Up you get, missie.'

It was some time before the missie opened her eyes, then she growled: 'Go to hell. Leave me alone.'

'It's you're going to hell,' Alexey said, but without anger, and he raised her up by the shoulders, got her into a sitting position, gave her a shake, then pointed to the door: 'Scoot!' he said.

'Don't you touch her,' Peter ordered. But Alexey only smiled and reassured him: 'Don't you worry, she'll come again if we call her.'

'You buggurs,' the woman said; but she was already obediently putting on her blouse.

Alexey gave orders, like a doctor. 'Up you get, Peter, off with that shirt, take an ice rub!'

Pashouta picked her crumpled hat from the floor and set it on her tousled hair, but when she had taken a glance at the mirror over the divan, she cried: 'A very fine queen!' and flung the hat on the floor, by the divan. Then, with a long yawn, she said: 'Well, farewell, darling! Don't forget, you can find me at Simanski's, Room No. 13.'

Peter felt sorry for her. Still prostrate on the floor, he said to Alexey: 'Give her something.'

'How much?'

'Oh . . . fifty.'

'Oho, that's a lot.'

Alexey thrust a scrap of paper into the woman's hand, saw her out, and shut the door firmly.

'You're too mean,' Peter remarked challengingly. 'She gave more than that for her hat yesterday.'

Alexey settled himself down in the arm-chair, clasped his hands on his stick, leant his chin on them, and drily, like a police officer, demanded: 'What do you think you're doing?'

'Drinking,' the elder brother answered aggressively, as he got up and began to rub himself down with the ice, clearing his throat.

'*Kouzma, drink, so long as you can think* says the proverb—and you?'

'Well?'

Alexey went up to him and, looking at him as if he were a stranger, said very quietly, and acidly: 'Forgotten? Proceedings are being taken against you, for punching a lawyer's nose, for knocking a policeman into the canal . . .'

He went on so long with the list of offences that the elder Artamonov genuinely thought Alexey was inventing it, just to scare him. 'What lawyer?' he asked. 'Twaddle.'

'It's no twaddle, and that dark fellow, what's his name . . .'

'It's not the first time we've scrapped,' Peter said. He was sobering now.

'And what have you been slandering decent folk for? Your own folk too, eh?'

'Slandering?'

'Yes, slandering—saying things against your own wife, against Vialov, against me, and all about some boy or other, crying and shouting "*Abraham and Isaac and the lamb*"—what's it all mean?'

A flood of terror came over Peter; he sank down into a chair. 'I don't know . . . I was drunk.'

'That's no reason!' Alexey almost shouted at him, and bobbed up and down like a man on a lame horse. 'That's not what's on my mind. Out of the mouths of drunkards, you know, you get the truth, that's what I'm after. But babbling family affairs in brothels isn't the way—and what's the meaning of Abraham and the sacrifice and all that tommyrot? You're getting the business mixed up, you know, putting me in a funny light too. Stripping yourself bare like a man taking a bath . . . It was a good thing my old friend Loktiev was present at that escapade, and had the good sense to put you under with cognac, while he sent me a telegram. I've had all this from him. At the start, so he says, everybody laughed, but afterwards they began to prick up their ears, and take notice of what was being trumpeted about.'

'They all trumpet things about,' Peter muttered, half to himself. What his brother had to say had really bowled him over. It made him feel drunk again, especially as Alexey went on very quietly saying: 'They all trumpet one and the same thing, but you trumpeted *everything*! It was all right, with Loktiev having the wits to make you all as drunk as lords—they may forget it. But don't you forget all the things involved in it—whereas it was Loktiev this time, next time it might well be one of our enemies.'

Peter clung to his chair, with the back of his skull pressed against the wall. The masonry seemed to vibrate, it was so saturated in the infuriated noise of the street. He said nothing, hoping the vibration would drive off the fumy disorder that was confusing his mind, and expel his fear. He could not call to mind a single thing his brother mentioned, and it was mortifying to hear this magistral tone Alexey was taking, as if he were the senior; it was awesome too, not knowing what Alexey would say next.

'What's the matter with you?' Alexey went on probing, bouncing about all the time. 'You said, you were going to see Nikita. . . .'

'I did go.'

'So did I. When I telegraphed them, and they answered that you weren't there, of course, I popped over. Everybody's been very alarmed. After all, we don't live in the clouds; you might have been murdered.'

'Something started festering in me,' Peter confessed, in a hushed, guilty voice.

'So you had to show it to everybody, did you? Don't you forget you're putting the whole of Artamonov and Company in a funny light. What's all this business about a sacrifice? What do you think you are—a Persian? And this business of boys—who's the boy?'

Stroking his beard with both hands, and speaking through his fingers, Peter said: 'Ilia . . . all on his account . . .' slowly, indecisively, as if picking out a path in the darkness, he set about telling Alexey about his quarrel with Ilia. He did not have to say much. With sudden relief, Alexey cried: 'Peugh! But that's nothing at all! You see, Loktiev took the boy business in an oriental sense—you know what I mean . . . So it's Ilia worrying you . . . Well, now, Peter, you mustn't mind if I say it, there's no sense in it. The burgher middle class has to learn everything and master every aspect of life, and you . . .'

At great length, and with some vividness, he spoke of the need for the sons of merchants to become engineers, officials, officers.

The noise through the window was deafening: there were people driving up to the theatre, lemonade and ice sellers shouting their wares, though the most insufferable was the thunder of a band playing in a pavilion some Brazilians had made of iron and glass on piles over the waters of the canal. The beat of the drum brought Paula Menotti to Peter's mind.

'Something started festering in me,' he repeated, plucking at his ear, while with the other hand he poured a good shot of cognac into a glass of lemonade. Alexey snatched the bottle from him, warning him—'Take care, or you'll be tight again. There's my Miron learning to be an engineer, if you please. Wants to go abroad, if you please. All that's a gain to the family, not a loss. You must get into your head that our class is the main force . . .'

But Peter did not want to get anything into his head. While Alexey was running on he had been reflecting that here was a man who had somehow attained the respect and friendship of men who were richer and no doubt cleverer than he was, the mainspring of the commerce of the whole country; at the same time his other brother, who had retired to a monastery, was acquiring fame as a man of wisdom and righteousness, while he himself was at the mercy of a series of fortuitous things which rent him in pieces. Why? What for?

'So to suit your own looseness you blackguard decent folk, that's not quite right,' Alexey was saying, though more gently now, more timidly. 'But it's not looseness, it's excess of energy . . . That lawyer's a rascal, but he knows what's what, his head's screwed on straight. Of course, grown men, getting on in years, you might say, yet they're up to pranks like the young ones, and after all, the young ones do it because of the energy of their growing. And don't forget to take into account too that our womenfolk are a bit dull, they're not spiced or seasoned, they're dreary for us. I'm not talking about my Olga—she's one by herself. But there are some women who're so wise they're downright stupid, blind, you might say, to anything wrong. Olga's one of those. You can't hurt her feelings because she never sees anything nasty, she doesn't believe there's any evil in the world. You can't say that of Natalia, you hit the nail right on the head about her when you said she's a domestic machine . . .'

'Is that really what I said?' asked Peter grimly.

'Loktiev isn't one to invent things like that.'

Peter would have liked to ask Alexey some more, but he was afraid to remind him of things that Alexey no doubt had already forgotten. There was a feeling of dislike and envy of Alexey beginning to stir in him. 'Damn his eyes, he's getting too clever . . .' There was something of a horse whipped up at the races in Alexey—something of a fox too, twisting and turning. He was irritated by those hawk-like eyes and the golden tooth gleaming under the nervous upper lip, the grizzled moustaches, with their military upward twist, the dashing little beard, the claw-like fingers, and particularly the forefinger of Alexey's right hand, with which he was always sketching some fantastic outlines in the air. Also that short-docked, steel-coloured jacket which Alexey was wearing made him like a rascally little business tout. He was suddenly overcome by a desire to see the back of Alexey.

'I must have a sleep,' he muttered, closing his eyes.

'I don't doubt it,' Alexey agreed. 'You'd better not go out at all to-day.'

'Teaching me like a mere kid,' Peter said to himself with mortification, as he accompanied Alexey to the door. He went to the corner of the wash-hand stand, but stopped short when he suddenly caught sight of an inaudible man standing before him—a man who somewhat resembled him, but was miserably tousle-headed, his face all gone to pieces, his eyes starting, scared from their sockets; the stranger drew one red hand through his wet beard, and over his hairy chest.

For some seconds he could not admit that this was his own reflection in the mirror that hung over the divan. Then with a miserable smile he set to work once again rubbing the lump of ice over his face and neck and chest.

'I'll get a cab and go into Nizhny,' he decided, as he dressed, but before he had got his arm into one sleeve of his coat, he threw the coat back on a chair and pressed the bell button with all his strength. 'Tea,' he ordered the waiter, 'and let it be strong! And something salt. And some brandy!'

Looking out of the window, he saw that the wide doors of the booths were already padlocked—human shapes, weighted down to the cobbles by the sultry darkness, crept along the street; at the theatre entrance a milky lamp was burning; somewhere at hand he heard women's voices, singing. Yes, the moth had got into him.

'Can I do the room out, sir?' came a voice at his back. He swung round. It was a one-eyed old woman standing in the doorway with broom and rags in her hands. Without a word, he went out into the corridor. There he came on a man wearing dark spectacles and black hat; the man addressed a door which was ajar. 'Yes, yes, that's all,' he said.

Everything was wrong, everything forced him to think, looking for hidden meaning in the most trivial words. In a few minutes he was seated at a round table with a little samovar hissing in front of him, and the glass of a lamp over his head ringing lightly from time to time as if touched by an unseen finger. His head was full of the strange shapes of wildly drunken men, snatches of song, fragments of Alexey's dictatorial dressing-down, and the gleam of a pair of eyes he had noticed passing. Yet at the same time his brain remained vacant and full of gloom. It was as if the thinnest of quivering rays of light had made its way in, so that those human figures were dancing round like grains of

217

dust, preventing him thinking of something of great importance.

He took a drink of strong, hot tea, then a gulp of cognac, which burned his mouth. But instead of feeling it go to his head, he merely felt more uneasy, anxious to get away somewhere. He rang the bell. There appeared a foggily undulating creature, which had neither face nor hair but resembled a walking-stick with a bone handle.

'Bring me a little green liqueur, George,' he said, 'know what I mean?'

'Yes, sir; Chartreuse, sir.'

'Your name is George, isn't it?'

'No, sir; *Konstantin*!'

'All right, get along with you.'

When the waiter had brought the liqueur, Artamonov said: 'You're a soldier?'

'Oh no, sir.'

'You talk like one.'

'Similar duties, sir, and discipline, sir, orders to be obeyed.'

Artamonov considered a moment, then gave the man a ruble. 'Well, just stop obeying orders,' he said. 'Tell them to go to b——. You trade in ices! And quit!'

The liqueur was sticky as treacle and pungent as liquid ammonia. It made his head lift, cleared it; things solidified, and at the same time as things solidified inside him everything became quieter outside, rigid, breathing out a soft murmur, which rose and floated far, far away, leaving only silence in its wake.

'Discipline sir, orders to be obeyed, eh?' he reflected. 'Whose orders? I'm the boss, not a servant. Am I the boss or am I not?'

But all these reflections were suddenly cut short,—they vanished, dispelled by fear; he suddenly saw before him the very man who prevented him managing his life and being

218

carefree like Alexey and other irrepressible men—he was prevented by that broad-faced, bearded man seated opposite him, behind the samovar, sitting silent, with left hand clutching his beard and supporting his chin. The man was eyeing him sorrowfully, just as if he was bidding him farewell, and sorry for him at the same time, reproachful too; eyeing him—and crying—poison tears oozing through the fair-haired eyelashes; on the edge of the man's beard, right up against one eye, a large fly was busily waving its antennae; it had just crept on to the man's temples, like a fly on a corpse, but it paused on the eyebrow, looking down into the eye.

'Well, you scum?' he demanded of his enemy, but the other did not budge, or answer him, only moved his lips.

'Snivelling?' Peter Artamonov cried maliciously. 'Got me in a mess, and now whimpering about it? Sorry for yourself, are you? You . . .' And he snatched the bottle from the table and fetched the creature a smashing blow on his thinly-covered skull.

At the crash of the broken mirror and clatter of the samovar and crockery as they and the table tipped to the floor, a number of people came into the room; there were not many of them, but each divided into two, which floated apart from one another; the one-eyed old woman bent down and picked up the samovar, and at the same time stood bolt upright. Seated on the floor, Peter Artamonov heard complaining voices: 'It's night-time, everybody's asleep.' 'He smashed the lovely mirror.' 'Now, you know, this sort of thing won't do . . .' He waved his arms, floated off—he did not know where, himself—and bellowed: 'That fly . . .'

The next day, towards evening, that trotter, Alexey, came pit-a-pat in, and with great concern—like a doctor treating his patient or a coachman one of his horses,—he examined his brother. Then, brushing his own moustaches with a comical little brush, said: 'You're unnaturally swollen, you simply can't go home like that. Besides, you can be of use to me here. You'll have to have your beard trimmed, Peter, and buy yourself some new boots, too, those you've got on are coachman's boots!'

Grinding his teeth, but submissive, Artamonov senior accompanied his brother to the barber's, and Alexey gave stern and detailed instructions just how much of the beard to cut off, and how to do Peter's head, while at the boot-shop he chose Peter's boots himself. When that was over, Peter took a look at himself, in a glass, and found he looked like an estate bailiff; what was more, the boots pinched. But he did not say a word; he knew Alexey was right: he had to have his hair cut, his beard trimmed, and all the rest. Altogether, he had to pull himself together, and forget all the confused oppression that the debauch had left in him, bearing down on him like a real weight.

But with all the fog in his head and fatigue of his poisoned, lust-gutted body he still felt—as he followed all that Alexey did—an increasingly complex sensation, a mixture of envy and respect, covert mockery and enmity. This lean, thoroughbred man, with his natty walking-stick, keen of eye, emitted sparks and smoke as he glowed, with that insatiable thirst he had for business gambles. To his great astonishment, Peter saw that Alexey had pretensions to being a wit, striving to make rich men laugh, to amuse them; apparently they did not notice the clowning, but showed open fondness and respect for him, and paid careful attention to his grating magpie chatter.

Komolov, an immense, dense-bearded textile manufacturer, wagged a carrot-coloured finger at him menacingly, but then rolled his ox-like eyes, smacked his lips juicily, and said: 'You're a cunning one, Alexey old fellow, upon my word you're a cunning fox! You've done me . . .'

'Hah, Komolov,' Alexey cried in triumph, 'business rivalry, eh?'

'True. Look alive and trump the ace!'

'I'm trying to learn how,' Alexey replied.

Komolov agreed. 'That's the way,' he said.

'Now, you fellows,' Alexey went on, still triumphing, but with a note of cunning, 'my boy Miron's a clever lad, a future engineer, and he tells me there was once a very famous scholar in the town of Syracuse who told the King he'd move the whole world if he could only find the right fulcrum point.'

'Get away, you piebald . . .'

'Move the world, he said! Now, gentlemen—our class has a point of fulcrum—hard cash! We don't need wise men to turn things upside down for us, we've got whiskers too; all we need is a different set of officials! The nobility's at its last gasp, it's no hindrance. But we must have the State officials in our hands—all the people we need must be our own folk, merchant-class bred, if they're to understand what we're about, that's what I say!'

The grey-haired and bald, corpulent men all agreed gladly. 'That's right, old piebald!'

A scraggy little old man, with one eye and a sharp nose —Losev, who dealt in Lombard transactions—gave a polite snicker, and said: 'Artamonov's head's screwed on straight enough' (he punned on the Russian words for *intelligence* and *mice*) 'he knows where there's bacon to be found, and doesn't he just nibble, once he's found it! To his health!'

Glasses were raised, Alexey, happy, touching with them all, while Losev slapped Komolov's massive shoulder with his infantile hand and said: 'We·are beginning to get some brains among us, aren't we?'

'Always had,' was Komolov's haughty answer. 'My father began life as a stevedore . . .'

'I always understood that your father started by cutting the throat of a rich Armenian,' said Losev scornfully, to which the thick-bearded textile man roared like a bull and replied: 'Cock-and-bull yarn! We Russians are stupid—if a man gets on we conclude he must have been crooked! There's some funny stories about you too, my boy . . .'

'And me,' Losev confirmed, with a sigh. 'Lies are like flies, upon my word!'

Artamonov senior gave ear to it all, with only an occasional grunt. He ate heartily, trying to drink as little as possible, and among these men felt like a creature of a different species. He knew they were all peasants by origin; he could see in them a tough strain, something legendary, which they had in common with his father, and which commanded respect. There was no question but that his father would have been one with them in business and plying the bottle; no doubt but that he would have gone on the ran-tan too, just like them, burning money like wood shavings. Yes, that was what money was to these men, who never relaxed in putting every ounce into stripping it off the whole land, off one another, off the country-side.

But there was a certain difference between Alexey and these big men, and there were moments when, despite his antipathy to him, Peter felt that Alexey was indeed keener and more clever—even more dangerous—than any of them.

'Just think, all of you!' Alexey cried, beside himself with enthusiasm, 'what inexhaustible strength we command, with the countless millions of our peasantry—they provide the labour and they provide the market! Where else can you find such resources? Nowhere! And we don't need any of your Germans or other foreign technicians, we'll manage it all ourselves.'

'True,' these deep-throated, slightly inebriated men agreed.

Alexey spoke further of the need for an increase in import duties on foreign goods, about buying up the lands of the gentry, of the harmfulness of the banks run by the nobility—he knew about everything, and with all he said the others—to Peter's astonishment—agreed. 'How right Nikita was,' he said to himself enviously, 'Alexey does know how to live.'

Nor did the frailness of his health prevent Alexey doing his bit of debauch. It transpired that he had a permanent long-standing mistress, a Moscow girl, who had her own troupe of girl singers, a heavy, corpulent woman with a honeyed voice and flashing eyes. Peter was told she was forty, but her peach-like complexion made her look under thirty. She would call Alexey her 'pet falcon', show her sharp, foxy teeth, and spread her wings all over him, like a mother over her child. She cannot but have known that Alexey was not indifferent to having a nibble at the girls of her own troupe; of course she saw it; but that did not interrupt her comradely attitude to Alexey. More than once Peter was told that he consulted her about personalities and business, which surprised him, though he did recall his own father and Uliana Baimakov. 'He's a devil,' he thought, as he studied his brother.

Even Alexey's lighter side had its special twist. For example: the fat clown at the circus, a German named Meier, had a pig which did tricks. Rigged in a frock coat with long skirts, a top hat and broad jackboots, this pig waddled on its hind legs, representing a man of their own burgher class. This highly amused all the audience, even the burghers themselves, but Alexey's attitude was different. He found it insulting and he managed to persuade a band of bosom pals to steal the pig. They bribed the stable man, and stole the pig, and the company of merchants in triumph ate its meat, to the accompaniment of all the most recondite sauces the chef of Barbatenko's Inn could contrive. To Peter's ears came an obscure rumour that the clown had hanged himself from grief—a fact described by D. Boborykin in the *Russian Courier*. Indeed, everything which he observed in Alexey in those days at the Fair set very disturbing thoughts going in Peter Artamonov's mind. 'He's a common rogue,' he told himself. 'No conscience. He could drive me out loose on the world and never turn a hair. And it isn't greed makes him destructive, but pure devilry.'

Awareness of the danger which threatened him had a sobering effect and brought him back to normal living. He returned home alone—Alexey went on to Moscow. It was a wet, windy October when he drew near Dromov. With jingling bells and hooves smacking juicily into the sodden ground the post-house horses trotted eagerly between the ranks of the young fir trees which stood motionless, sentinel over the narrow strip of track through the marshlands. The whole sky was plastered with the grey dough of the clouds —it was just as grey and dreary in Peter Artamonov's still fuddled head. He felt as if he had just come from the funeral of somebody very dear to him, but of whom none the less he had been heartily weary. He felt sorry for the departed, but at the same time the thought that he would never come across him again was pleasant; the man who had gone would never more make him feel uneasy with those hazy demands, those unspoken reproaches or any of those things which had made life difficult for the real, the living Artamonov.

'I must get down to work, and that's the end of it!' he tried to persuade himself. 'It's work makes the life of a man, that's it.'

He did indeed set to work, to his full ability. The limpid days of an Indian summer set tranquilly in, with nostalgically bright moonlight by night. Wakening in the pearly half-light of autumn daybreak, the elder Artamonov would listen to the insistent factory siren; half an hour later the irresistible rustle of the works would begin, a muttering, the noise of labour which, though hushed, was full of power, and familiar to his ear.

From daybreak to late evening there would be the yelling of the peasantry, men and women, delivering their flax at the storehouses. Down at the inn, which one of the innumerable Morozovs had opened on the shore of the Vataraksha, there would be tipsy singing and the drone of an accordion. About the yard went Tikhon Vialov, ponderous, reliable as a machine, stern towards the workers, always with broom or shovel, or axe in hand. Taking his time he would sweep and dig and hew, or shout at the peasants or the workers. Seraphim, always all blue and spick and span, flitted about.

Indoors, another machine, Natalia would be busy. Natalia had been very pleased with the expensive presents her man had brought her from the Fair—still more pleased at his taciturn but unruffled calm. Everything was now running smoothly, everything seemed firmly established—factory, men, even the horses—it might have been clockwork wound up to run for ages.

With his head down the senior Artamonov charged through the shops and about the yard like a bull, strode through the workers' hamlet, scaring the kiddies, but wherever he went now he was aware of a novel and peculiar sensation—that he was almost a superfluity, an onlooker, in this vast enterprise. It was pleasant to observe that Yakov was getting hold of the workings, even seemed enthusiastic about them. The way Yakov behaved not merely served to distract him from thought of his eldest—it even reconciled him to Ilia. 'I can rub along without you, clever-head—you stick to your books!' he told himself.

Yakov was a small-boned rosy-cheeked lad, with kindly eyes which seemed to reflect all colours of the rainbow just like soap bubbles, when he smiled. He bore his plumpish flesh with dignity, and though at close hand he was peculiarly like a pigeon, from a distance he gave the impression of a skilful and business-like master. The workgirls had indulgent smiles for him; he would twitter to them and peer at them in a sugary way, and sidle round any one of them, his outward show of solidity powerless to conceal the saucy young cockerel in him. His father would pluck at his ear and grin and think: 'You little booby, if only you could see Paula.'

It afforded Peter Artamonov some satisfaction, too, that when Yakov was down at Alexey's he never got drawn into the endless discussions that Alexey's boy Miron carried on with that down-at-heel, restless Goritzvetov boy. Miron now bore no resemblance whatsoever to the son of a member of the merchant class. Lean and big nosed, wearing spectacles and dressed in a tunic with gilt buttons and a monogram on the shoulders, he rather suggested a magistrate. He walked and sat upright as a soldier, had a supercilious and haughty way of talking. But for all that Peter was aware his nephew always had something clever to say, he could not take to the lad. 'My dear fellow,' he would say, with his hands in the side pockets of his tunic and his elbows bowed out, 'all this philosophizing and wisdom-mongering comes from feebleness and lack of ability.'

As far as Peter Artamonov could see, the Goritzvetov lad too talked quite well, not at all stupidly. He was small, wore a black shirt under a student frock coat which he would wear carelessly unbuttoned, always had his hair unkempt, and swollen eyes, just as if he had not slept for some days, set in a swarthy sharp-featured and pimply face; he was given to shouting, without listening to what others said, gesticulating wildly, and quarrelling with Miron.

'You'll succeed in the end in making the sun rise to your factory sirens, and your smoky day dawn in the swamps and forests to the command of your machines,' he cried on one occasion, 'but what are you going to do with *man*?'

Miron arched his brows, frowned, straightened his spectacles, and hammered out in a dry, unruffled voice: 'More *feeble-sophy*—more poetry! My dear fellow, it's all verbal masturbation and philo-superstition. Life in itself is a struggle; lyricism and hysterics are out of place, even ridiculous . . .'

The language of these lads quarrelling stood out like white pigeons in a flock of blue pigeons. 'No getting away from it, new birds and new songs,' was Peter Artamonov's thought.

He grasped only hazily the essence of this dispute. When he looked at Yakov, with great satisfaction he saw his son stroking the fair flue of down on his upper lip to conceal his scornful smile.

'That's right,' he thought, 'but what would Ilia say?'

Goritzvetov cried: 'When you've put iron fetters on the land and on men, and made men slaves of the machine. . . .'

Waggling his nose, Miron interrupted: 'The kind of men you're worrying about are idle men. They will perish, if they don't grasp to-morrow that their salvation is in the development of industry . . .'

'Who is right? Which way is the better?' Peter Artamonov tried to figure out.

He disliked Goritzvetov even more than he disliked his nephew—there was something watery and hopeless in him, he was so clearly afraid of something, with his wild shouting. He had no manners either. As if intoxicated, he would take his seat at dinner before the elders, start shifting his knife and fork spasmodically to and fro, then gobble his food, burn himself, choke. He was just like Alexey, always leaping forward, always in the way, and at times malevol-

ent. There was a blindness about the dark pupils of his inflamed eyes; when he met Peter he would merely stick out
his scaly, hot hand without any polite *how-do-you-do*, and
quickly jerk it back again. In short, he was altogether a
nuisance, and it was hard to understand what Miron could
see in him.

'Steve, eat your dinner and don't talk so much,' Olga
once said to him, only to get the crashing reply: 'I can't,
while destructive heresy is propagated under my nose.'

Peter was astounded by the silent attention Alexey would
give the two students' arguments, with only occasional support for his own son: 'That's right enough, power does
mean authority, and power to an industrialist . . .'

Olga, her temples now marked with crowsfeet, the tip
of her nose red, weighed down by thick rimlesss spectacles,
would sit down at her embroidery frame by the window and
and silently, persistently, embroider endless dazzling flowers
in beads. Peter felt more comfortable in Alexey's home
than his own; there was more to interest him, and his
brother kept a good cellar.

On the way home with Yakov on one occasion, Peter
asked: 'Do you understand these discussions?'

'Of course,' was his son's curt answer.

In order to hide his own incomprehension, Artamonov
adopted a stern tone. 'Let's see if you do,' he said.

Yakov's answers were always brief and unwilling, but
clear. According to his account on this occasion, Miron
thought Russia should adopt the same way of life as all
Europe, while Goritzvetov believed that Russia had her
own way.

Here the elder Artamonov had felt a need to demonstrate
to his son that he, his father, had his own ideas on the matter,
and said weightily: 'Now if foreigners lived better than we
do, they wouldn't to so anxious to come here . . .'

But this was one of Alexey's ideas—did that mean that he had none of his own? Peter frowned with mortification. Then, as if to make it worse, Yakov said: 'We could manage without all this showing off of intelligence, all this talk . . .'

Peter Artamonov grunted: 'Oh, of course, we could . . .'

Shocks from petty hurts and surprises came his way with greater frequency nowadays. They seemed to thrust him to one side, making a permanent onlooker of him, bound to see everything and think about everything. Meantime, everything about him was rapidly though unnoticeably changing —on all sides, in speech and action, there was an insistent new note, an insistent uneasiness.

One day, over tea, Olga suddenly said: 'Truth is when your heart is full and you want nothing more.'

'True,' said Peter.

But Miron, his spectacles flashing, tried to teach his mother: 'It's not true,' he said, 'that is death! Truth is in doing things, in action.'

When Miron had left the room, taking with him a thick sheet of paper, rolled in a tube, Peter turned to Olga— 'Your boy's very rude to you.'

'Not in the least.'

'But I see that he is.'

'He's cleverer than I am,' Olga replied. 'After all, I've no education, and often say silly things. Children as a whole are cleverer than we are.'

Artamonov refused to admit this, and said with a smile: 'True, you are saying silly things. But I'll tell you one thing —our old folk were cleverer than we are—their proverb was "*sons bring trouble—daughters, double*", get me?'

This thing she had said about the intelligence of their children got him right under the skin—clearly she was thinking of Ilia. He was aware that Alexey was helping

Ilia with funds, and that Miron wrote to him regularly, but from pride he would never inquire either where his son was, or how he was. For that matter, Olga cleverly managed to inform him, as she understood his pride. From her he had learned that for some reason Ilia first went to Archangel, but was now abroad. 'Well, let him,' he thought—'it will sharpen his wits, and he'll see how foolish he was.'

Sometimes, thinking about Ilia, he marvelled at this son's stubbornness—all around people were getting cleverer— what did Ilia think he was going to find?

Frequently at Alexey's he met Mrs. Popov and her daughter; the widow was still as beautiful and melan- cholically calm and alien to him. She had little to say to him, and what she did say was spoken in much the same manner as he used to adopt himself to Ilia when he had said something which offended him. She froze him. In calmer moments, he would recall her image, but it only excited surprise—that there was a person whom he liked, of whom he often thought, but without ever being quite clear what she meant to him, and with no more possibility of con- versing with her than with a deaf mute.

Yes, everything was changing. Even the workers were getting more and more moody, fouler in temper, more tubercular, and their womenfolk more quarrelsome. The noise in the Artamonov hamlet was now more restless. At night you could even imagine sometimes that a pack of wolves was howling there, even the litter-befouled sand snarled. There was a marked reluctance of the workers to stay settled, a passion for wandering. Young fellows whom nobody had done anything against in any way would sud- denly come to the office and ask to be paid off.

'Where do you mean to go?' Peter would ask.

'See what other places are like. . . .'

'What devil has got into them?' Peter asked Alexey.

230

With a foxy grimace and a smirk Alexey assured him that the working class was restless everywhere. 'We are pretty well off here so far—but up there in Petersburg, ugh! . . . We've not got the right men in the government, or the administration.' Alexey went on to make assertions so daring and so stupid that Peter told him off fairly bluntly.

'Utter twaddle!' he said. 'It's the gentry who see their advantage in grabbing power from the Emperor, because they're losing their money. Whereas we're making money, without any power. On holidays your father went about in tarred jack-boots, and here you are wearing imported button boots and silk scarves. We ought to be the Emperor's workers, not his pigs. The Emperor's our oak tree—it's from him we get our golden acorns.'

Alexey, hearing this, smiled. That only outraged Peter still more. Altogether, the elder Artamonov was of the opinion that people were nowadays given to too much smiling anyway; there was something rather ominous and quite stupid in this new fashion. In any case, there was not one of them could make a fellow laugh as heartily or as lightly as that immortal old fellow Seraphim the carpenter.

Peter Artamonov had become a very fast companion of the comforter. From time to time now Peter's fits of gloom returned and excited in him an invincible urge to drink. He was ashamed to get drunk at Alexey's house; there were always visitors there, and he was particularly anxious for Mrs. Popov not to see him drunk.

At home, on days like that, Natalia would hang her head sullenly and maintain an oppressed silence—it would have been easier if she had attacked him, as he could then have sworn back at her. But as she resembled somebody who had just been robbed, and excited no malice, she simply stirred up feelings akin to pity, and he would go straight off

231

to Seraphim. 'Methuselah, I want to get tight!' he would say, and the cheerful carpenter would smile and support him. 'It's the most natural thing, like sun in summer,' Seraphim told him on one occasion: 'You're clearly tired, you've worn yourself down. Well, well, take a dose of medicine. It's a big works, yours is, it's not like a pimple on your cheek.'

For the master Seraphim kept a number of unusually flavoured vodkas and sweet wines, and would produce bottles of all colours from one corner and another, boasting: 'This is my own idea, the wife of a deacon makes it for me, a peppercorn of a wench. Now you test it for me—it's a steeping of birch catkins with the spring sap in them, now how is it?'

Seraphim then setttled down at the table, plugging away at his own beet-wine, and mumbling: 'Aha, that's it, a deacon's missus. A most misfortunate female. If it isn't a lover, it's a thief—she can't ever do without lovers, there's such an intolerance in her veins . . .'

'That's nothing,' Peter assured him, 'there was one I saw at the Fair . . .'

'I don't doubt,' Seraphim hastened to comply. 'Now, there you'd get choice goods from the whole country. I know!'

Seraphim knew everybody and everything—he could tell many an entrancing tale of the domestic life of the factory hands—all in the most kindly way, about his own daughter too, as if she was nothing to him. 'The little devil's settling down. She's living with locksmith Sedov now, and upon my word they get on well together! Oh yes, there's never a beastie but finds its hole in the end.'

It was fine in Seraphim's clean little room, full of the re-sinous scent of wood shavings, with a warm twilight which the tin lamp on the wall did little to dispel. When the drink

had mellowed him, Artamonov would expose his griev-
ances against humanity; the carpenter would try to comfort him.

'That's nothing, that's all right! Men are taking a run,
that's the core of it. They've been lying quiet long enough,
turning things over, now they want a change. Let them
have their run. Dont' you get down-hearted; have faith in
men. You've faith in yourself, haven't you?'

Peter said nothing, wondering whether he really had any
confidence in himself, while Seraphim's buoyant little voice
drubbed away its song of consolation: 'Don't you keep
looking out who's no good, who's all right, this doesn't
stand firm, it used to be all right, it's all wrong to-day.
I've seen it all, Peter Artamonov, the bad and the good;
God, what a lot I've seen! Look! for example—I used to
reckon so-and-so was fine, but now he's no more! I was
there all right, but suddenly he was no more, like a bit
of dust the wind blows away! And here I am still! Now,
after all, what am I? I'm only a tiny fly in the whole
scheme, you can't even see me. As for you . . .' Seraphim
broke off and raised his finger very significantly.

Artamonov got a double pleasure out of Seraphim's talk
—first of all, it really did afford him consolation, because
it entertained him, but at the same time he could clearly
see that the little old creature was playing a part, lying—he
did not say what was in his heart but what his calling of
'comforter' demanded. And, grasping this game, 'What a
cunning rascal the old boy is,' Peter said to himself, 'Nikita's not a patch on him.'

To his mind came various comforters he had known—
women at the fair, devoid of shame; circus clowns and
tumblers; conjurors and animal tamers; singers and musicians—and black-haired Steve, 'friend of all mankind'.
Alexey too had something in common with them all—

something of which Tikhon Vialov had not a trace, nor Paula Menotti.

The drink was going more and more to his head. 'You don't mean a word of it, you old devil!' he cried. But the carpenter slapped at his bony knees and, very solemnly, said: 'Oh yes I do . . . how am I to invent if I don't know the real truth? I tell you from my heart of hearts, I don't know the truth, so how can I be false?'

'Then hold your tongue!'

'Am I a dumb man?' Seraphim countered gently, his rosy cheeks aglow with a smile. 'I'm well on in years,' he said, 'I'll manage the little left me without any truth. That's for the young folk, bothering about the truth, that's why they have to have spectacles. Master Miron always wears them, so he's sure to see right through where things belong and what a man's place is.'

Artamonov was pleased to find out that the carpenter did not like Miron, and he roared with laughter when the old fellow suddenly strummed his guitar and with great dash sang:

> "There's a woodpecker in the works to-day
> Wearing great big spectacles,
> I'm the clever one here, he would say,
> And all the rest are ninnies . . ."

'That's right,' Peter said. Then the carpenter, also a bit tipsy, tapping out his beat evenly, improvised again:

> "Is't a hawk, is't an owl
> Pinching all the birdies?
> Alexey's the name o' the fowl,
> For a sainthood worthy . . ."

This too was to Peter's taste. Then Seraphim sang a dirty ditty about Yakov:

> "Masha under Yasha lay
> But he didn't know the way . . ."

234

And so they would go on, sometimes all night, till at day-break there would be Tikhon Vialov at the door, to waken the master, if he'd fallen asleep, and—as if nothing was un-usual—say: 'Time to be getting home, the siren's just going to blow—the men'll see you, and that wouldn't do.' 'Why wouldn't it do?' Peter would answer him, 'am I not the boss here?' All the same, he would do as the yardman said, stagger home and go to bed, sometimes sleeping through to the following evening, and then spend another night with Seraphim.

The good-humoured carpenter died at work. He was making a coffin for the son of the one-eyed surgeon, Moro-zov, who had been drowned, when he suddenly collapsed and was dead. Artamonov determined to see the old fellow laid to rest, and went to the funeral service. The church was cram full of workers. He listened to ginger-haired parson Alexander who had taken the place of the quiet Reverend Gleb (who had suddenly for no known reason abandoned the Church and gone nobody knew whither) sternly read-ing the prayers for the dead. The church choir, trained by the teacher of the factory school—one Grekov, a fellow like a tom-cat—sang magnificently, and there were very many young people present.

'It's Sunday,' Artamonov said, to explain the great gather-ing.

The light coffin was carried by four young weavers; the serious elder men held aloof. Her brow knit, but dry-eyed, Zinaida followed. She was wearing a blouse of unseemly bright colours, and was accompanied by broad-shouldered locksmith Sedov, dressed in his best, with Tikhon Vialov lumbering along nearby. There was bright sunlight, the choir sang lustily and harmoniously, and altogether the funeral was marked by a peculiar lack of grief.

'He's having a good burial,' Peter observed, wiping the sweat from his face. Vialov stopped short, and gazed at his feet. Then, after a moment's thought, he said: 'He was a good fellow; as full of fun as . . .' He waved his hand. 'The old boy used to carry her about, and the kiddie would sing . . . It did us good.' Then, quizzing Peter with a severity devoid of all respect and most disturbing, he added: 'He gave us all many a teaser—never a man he hurt—though his way of living was not decent.'

'Decent, decent'—Peter mocked the man's tone. 'You're chained to your stupid ideas. You take care, or you'll go mad like Touloun . . .' And, swinging round, Artamonov left the yardman and went home.

It was still early, about midday, but very hot already; the sand of the roadway and the blue depths of the atmosphere were getting hotter and hotter. By evening the sun boiled up mountains of white cumulus, which were sluggishly floating over the horizon towards the west, increasing the sultriness. He went for a stroll in the garden, then out through the gates. Vialov was just tarring the hinges; the spring rains had rusted them, and they squeaked badly.

'What's the idea, greasing to-day, it's a holiday,' Artamonov inquired lazily, sitting down for a minute on the bench. Vialov rolled the whites of his eyes towards Peter and in low tones said: 'Seraphim was harmful.'

'How do you mean?'

In answer to Peter the following strange pronouncement crept like a swarm of beetles: 'He had such a memory, he never forgot a thing. He remembered everything he saw. But what could he see? Bad things, dreary things, trifling things. And it's them he told everybody about. He's been the root of much trouble. I can see it.'

Vialov poked some of his grease into the eyes of a hinge, and continued still more querulous: 'Men ought to have

236

their memories destroyed. Memory breeds bad things. Things ought to be so that when one lot have had their lives and died, all their ill doings and follies die with them. Then a new lot be born, with no memory of evil, only good. I too suffer from my memory. I am old and long for peace. But where is it? Only in loss of all sense . . .'

Never before had Tikhon Vialov spoken at such length, or so perturbingly. Even though what he had just uttered was as stupid as anything else he said, somehow, at this moment, it particularly aggravated Artamonov. He looked closely at the man's tangled beard, his watery, shifty eyes, and the stony, wrinkled forehead, and marvelled at the ever greater monstrosity of the man. The wrinkles were unnaturally deep, like the folds on the leg of a jack-boot; the face with its prominent cheek-bones, laid bare by the years, had acquired a grey pumice colour; the nostrils were flabby, like a fungus.

'He's got very feeble,' Peter said to himself, and the thought pleased him. 'His mind's begun wandering. He's no worker. I ought to pay him off. I'll give him a gratuity.'

Greasing-stick in one hand and bucket of tar in the other, Vialov turned round to him; with his greaser he pointed to the works—dark red, colour of raw flesh—and muttered: 'You should pay attention to the things that are being said there; dandy Sedov, the lopsided Morozov and his brother Zahar, and Zinaida too,—they say outright that any enterprise built on the labour of others is bad, and should be destroyed . . .'

'It might almost be Mr. Vialov himself speaking,' Artamonov said ironically.

'Me?' Vialov shook his head. 'Oh no. I don't accept schemes like that. Let each man work for himself, then there would be no wrong. But they say "we're the ones that made it, we're the real masters". Now, when you come to think of it, it is so, isn't it, they did make it all . . . They harnessed you to the factory, and you pulled it out on to the right road. And now . . .'

Artamonov gave a serious grunt, got to his feet, stuck his hands in his pockets and, with great determination, even though a little scared of what he was going to say, stared into the clouds beyond Vialov and said: 'Listen here, of course, I quite see, you've spent your whole life with me, that's right enough; but you're getting on now, you can't help finding it hard. . . .'

'And Seraphim saw it like that too,' Vialov said clearly paying no attention to what Artamonov had been saying.

'Just a moment! It's time you had a rest . . .'

'There's a time for everything! But what is the right time?'

'Wait a moment. . . . You're a . . . difficult fellow . . .'

In the end Tikhon Vialov showed no surprise at hearing himself dismissed, merely muttered calmly: 'Well, there it is . . .'

'Of course, I shall make you a gratuity,' Artamonov assured him. He was a bit troubled by Vialov's calm. The man did not say a word, merely smeared his dusty boots with the tar mixture. Then Artamonov said, as firmly as he could: 'So it's farewell.'

'All right,' the man replied.

He went down to the river, hoping to find it cooler there, —under the pine where he had quarrelled with his son, Seraphim had built him something like a throne of birch brushwood. From that point of vantage there was a good view of the whole factory, together with the house, the outbuildings, the factory village, the church, and the grave-yard. The large windows of the factory infirmary and the school gleamed in the sunlight. All over the field of vision, miniature human beings flitted to and fro like little boats, weaving the endless woof of the Artamonov business.

Similarly, although not so many of them, they were moving about the sandy alleys of the factory village. Beside the churchyard wall, a toy flock of goats was browsing among the grey trunks of the alders, watched over by one-eyed surgeon's assistant Morozov, who was a nephew of the old weaver, Boris Morozov—the factory women bought great quantities of goat's milk for their children. On the far side of the infirmary there was a bare square of ground with railings round it, where miniature men in yellow gowns and white chimney-pot hats, like lunatics, were grazing. All round the factory there were numerous birds—sparrows, crows, gulls, noisy starlings, whirling from place to place, the white of their side-feathers flashing like silk—they were especially numerous round the inn on the bank of the Vataraksha where the peasants bringing in flax put up.

But for some time all this extensive estate had ceased to excite the least pleasure or pride in Peter Artamonov. It had become merely the source of all manner of mortifying circumstances. It was mortifying to observe how his brother, his nephew, and a number of other men of that circle would argue, waving their arms and shouting like gipsies at the fair, without even noticing him, the head of the whole business. Even when the conversation turned to the factory, he was forgotten. If he did bring himself to their notice, they would hear him without a murmur, as if in complete accord with him, although doing everything, important or trifling, in their own way.

This had begun long enough ago—from the point, in fact, at which he had given way to their desire and the Artamonov Mills Electric Power Station was erected. It had taken him very little time to see that the power station was both more profitable and less dangerous, but the thing still rankled. There were, indeed, endless petty mortifications, and they were constantly being added to, and hurting more sorely.

The conduct of Alexey's son Miron was disgustingly insolent. He had finished his studies, and was now dressed in an outlandish, un-Russian fashion, wearing short leather tunics. From his gold spectacles down to his yellow boots he glittered, and he would squint and frown at Artamonov and say: 'That's out-of-date, Uncle. Times have changed, Uncle.'

You would have thought he was afraid of time, like a lackey fearing a stern master, but this certainly was all he feared—in everything else he was unbearably insolent. On one occasion he even said: 'You've got to face up to it, Uncle, with men like you Russia can't go on.'

This gave Artamonov such a hard jolt that he even forgot to ask why. He was so offended that for some weeks he did not go near his brother, or even speak to Miron, if he came on him about the factory.

Miron was supposed to be going to marry the Popov daughter, now as tall and well-proportioned as her grey-headed icy mother. This girl had the same displeasing grin as the rest of them. She had a way of jerking her neck as she stared quizzingly at anything with her large, shamelessly wide-open eyes,—which no doubt believed in nothing. From morning to night she would be humming through her teeth, like a buzzing fly, and spoiling good canvas by smearing miserable, bright-coloured pictures on it. Her straw hat, worn with a ribbon under her chin, was always dangling on her back, against her straw-coloured hair. She dressed carelessly, showing her legs under her skirt—it was almost knee-high!

That idler Goritzvetov was loathsome; he flitted about like a sand-martin, always popping up or disappearing unexpectedly, attacking them all like a snapping little pet dog, repeating at the top of his voice: 'You would like to turn Russia, with her rich spiritual heritage, into a soulless America, you are making a trap for mankind . . .'

Sometimes Artamonov caught a note of truth in what Goritzvetov had to say, but usually he detected a quality of kinship with Vialov's nonsense,—though he knew no two persons more dissimilar than this unpredictable, scalded little jumping jack and the cumbrous, indifferent figure of the yardman.

There was Goritzvetov, rushing up to Elizaveta Popov (the daughter) and shouting at her: 'Why don't you say something, you, a person of the spirit?'

The Popov girl smiled; her features were haughty and immobile, only her grey autumnal eyes smiling. Artamonov caught words he had never heard before, and did not understand.

'The death-throes of romanticism,' Miron declared, painstakingly cleaning his spectacles with a piece of chamois leather.

Alexey was rushing about Moscow; Yakov was growing fatter, remaining soberly aloof, with little to say, but therefore, no doubt, sensible, since what he said irritated Miron and Goritzvetov equally. Yakov had grown a thick-set ginger goatee, a ginger tuft with which his scornful humour noticeably increased: it was a delight to Peter to hear him drawl to the cocky ones: 'You'll sit in the mire yet, riding to be gentlemen—you'd better live a bit more simply.'

He was highly amused too—and could see Yakov was likewise—when Elizaveta Popov suddenly slipped off to Moscow, and married Goritzvetov. Miron was savage, and could not hide it. He twisted at his sharp-pointed beard—so unlike a son of the *bourgeoisie*—and, as if dragging the dry words out of it, said, with obvious insincerity: 'Men like

Stephen Goritzvetov belong to a race that is dying out. You could not find such useless creatures as he and his like anywhere else 'in the world.'

Yakov, to prod him on, said: 'All the same, one of them knew how to snatch a morsel you'd set your heart on, right under your nose too.'

Miron shrugged his shoulders. 'I'm not romantic,' he replied.

'What's that? Who do you say?' Peter Artamonov demanded, but Miron hammered out, like a judge pronouncing sentence: 'Nobody really knows what a romanticist is, so you can't expect to understand, Uncle. It's in part to do with aesthetic pleasure, like a wig on a bald head, also in part a matter of caution, like a trickster with a false beard.'

'That's one in the eye for you!' the head of the Artamonovs said to himself with inward satisfaction.

These trifling moments of satisfaction in some measure reconciled him to the innumerable hurts he received from these hearties who were more and more getting their own grip on to things and elbowing him aside, into isolation. Even in his isolation he invented—perforce—a meed of bitter satisfaction; and through this he made the intimate acquaintance of a new Peter Artamonov, with whom he had already been on nodding terms—a very different sort of man, of different cast from himself.

This other Peter Artamonov was quite a decent fellow, who was terribly hurt. Life had treated him unjustly—like a stepmother her stepchild. He had begun life the submissive, speechless lackey of his own father, from whom he had obtained no delight of any kind, if he was not to count his stupid and dreary wife. That father had then suddenly shifted to his shoulders this huge and worrying enterprise.

Oh yes, his wife loved him, and the first year of life with

her had not been bad at all. But now he knew that even the
lecherous mill-girl Zinaida could be more entertaining and
more temperamental in love,—not to speak of the clever
insensate women of the Fair. All her life his wife had been
afraid—first of Alexey, then of oil lamps, then of electricity
—when an electric light was switched on she would leap
back and cross herself. She had made a fool of him at the
Fair, when they were in the gramophone shop. 'Oi, no,
you mustn't buy that!' she had implored him. 'For all you
know it's Satan inside, his spirit hidden there.'

To-day it was Miron she was afraid of, Doctor Yakovlev,
and her own daughter Tania. She had grown terribly fat,
and did nothing for days on end but eat. His brother Nikita
had nearly committed suicide on account of her. The
children had no respect for her, and when she was trying one
day to persuade Yakov to get married, he merely answered
scornfully: 'Mamma, you'd better have a bite of something.'

She did not quite see what he meant, and answered him
submissively: 'I would, dear, but I don't think I really want
to'—and of course did eat something.

Peter took Yakov to task. 'What does this mean, making
a laugh of your mother? It is time you married.'

'It's too early to tie myself with a family,' was Yakov's
business-like opinion.

Peter lost his temper. 'Why are you all so scared of
time?' he cried. Yakov did not answer, merely shrugged his
shoulders. He also added: 'You just can't understand, Father.'

He said it softly enough, but after all, how could a father
understand less than his son? People don't live by to-
morrow, but yesterday . . . everybody.

His eldest, Ilia, his favourite, had altogether disappeared.
Out of love for Ilia he had done something he could not
bear to recall.

His eldest daughter, Elena, broad-faced and broad-buttocked too, thoroughly spoiled by the money of her drunkard of a husband, was a complete stranger. She would come to see her parents occasionally, lavishly dressed, with a multitude of rings on her fingers. A-jingle with little gold chains and trinkets, her satiate eyes peering through a gold lorgnette, in a weary voice one day she said: 'What an unpleasant smell there is about this house! It's mouldy throughout, you ought to rebuild. Anyway, who lives on top of their factory nowadays?' Another time Peter overheard her saying to her mother: 'Is Daddy still the same? How dull you must find it with him. My man's a drunkard, but he's full of fun, he's jolly.'

She had a particularly irritating passion for cleanliness. Whenever she sat down she would first dust the chair with her handkerchief, and she scented herself so strongly that it made you want to sneeze. She behaved with such mortifying rudeness whenever she came that he would have given anything to know how to revenge himself on her for exasperating him so—when she was there he would go about the house, even outside, in his underclothes and an unbelted dressing-gown, his bare feet slipped into goloshes, and at dinner he chewed deliberately loudly and belched like an oriental.

'What *is* the matter with you, Father?' Elena would ask indignantly, which was just what he was after.

'I beg your pardon, Madame,' he would reply, 'but didn't you know I was a simple peasant? After all, I'm only a common *mouzhik*.' And belched and champed all the more savagely.

Elena had been abroad, and in the evening would tell her mother all sorts of nonsensical stuff, in a petting, oily, lazy voice, all about the women scrubbing the outer walls of the houses in one of the towns she had been in with soap and water, and somewhere else where the fogs were so thick, winter and summer alike, that street lamps were on all the time, but still you couldn't see a thing. In Paris the whole population sold ready-made frocks, and there was a tower so high you could see towns overseas from it.

With her younger sister, Tatiana, Elena used to quarrel, sometimes very badly. Tatiana had turned out rather a miserable thin little thing, sallow and embittered because she was so unprepossessing. She made Artamonov think of a church sexton, perhaps because of her truncated pigtail, flat bosom, and purple nose. She lived with Elena, for some reason never got her school-leaving certificate, was afraid of mice, agreed with Miron that the Emperor's authority should be limited, and recently had begun to smoke cigarettes.

When Tatiana came to stay in the summer she would shout at her mother as if she were one of the servants, talked through her teeth to her father, spent the whole day reading books, and the evenings in Dromov at her uncle's, whence Dr. Yakovliev, with his gold teeth, would see her back home. At night virginal yearnings kept her awake, and she could be heard smacking on the walls with her slipper, like pistol shots, killing mosquitoes.

The whole world about him, in other words, was becoming alien to him, noisily and exasperatingly senseless, from Miron's challenging pronouncements to the nonsense ditties of one of the stokers, a man named Vaska, a lame peasant with a dislocated hip and a head like a mop. On holidays this Vaska, who was courting the cook, would hang about under the kitchen window, close his eyes, twiddle up and down on his accordion, and yell:

> "You are so unhappy now . . .
> I am used to you
> I want to see you every hour
> That sweet little phiz your face . . ."

It was now a long time since Olga gave him any news of Ilia, and the new Peter Artamonov, Artamonov the mortified, thought more and more about his eldest. It seemed clear that Ilia has already suffered a full penalty for his hot-headedness—the changed attitude towards him in the Alexey household showed that clearly enough. It was one evening when he had come down to his brother, and was taking off his coat in the hall, that Peter overheard Miron—just back from Moscow—saying: 'Ilia's one of those people who see life through the printed page and can't tell a live horse from a cow.'

'Nonsense,' Peter said to himself, but found a sort of consolation in his nephew's hostile opinion of Ilia.

Alexey asked: 'Is he in the same party as Goritzvetov?'

'He's still more harmful,' was all Miron replied.

Entering the room, Peter in his thoughts warned him. 'You just wait, he'll come back and he'll show you a thing or two . . .'

Miron had begun talking about Moscow, angrily complaining too of the government's lack of gumption. Then Natalia and Yakov came in, and Miron turned to speaking about the indispensability of building their own papermill—he had been tiresomely insisting on this for some time.

'Uncle,' he said, 'we've money lying idle.'

Natalia flushed so red that even her ears seemed to swell, and cried loudly: 'Where's it lying? Who's looking after it?' And Peter was at once overcome by gloom.

It was as if the door of a room in which he knew every single object had suddenly been thrown open before him, but at the same time he was so sick with everything that the room might have been bare. This sudden, physical gloom would descend on him, from outside, like a fog, stopping his ears, clouding his eyes, filling him with a sensa-

tion of weariness and frightening him with the idea of illness and of death.

'You make me sick,' he said. 'When will you let me have
a bit of peace?'

Yakov growled: 'We've enough trouble with what we've
got. . . .'

Natalia added her cry: 'And you've spoiled the men so,
it's impossible to go out of the house, what with their
drunkenness, and the foul language . . .'

He went to the window. There was Vialov in the garden!
He was pointing up into an apple tree, showing a little girl
something. 'You damned Adam!' Peter said to himself, and
that stirred him out of his gloom.

Far-fetched ideas like that often came to him, and their
unexpectedness tittilated him; he liked them also because
they did not disturb him at all—they flashed in, vanished
again—and that was the end of them.

Vialov too: Peter had been very indignant to see that
Alexey had taken the man on—after he had vanished completely for more than a year, only to turn up again with the
bad news that Nikita had left the Priory and nobody knew
where he had gone. Peter was convinced that Vialov knew
where Nikita was, and would not tell only in order to cause
unpleasantness. He had had a stand-up row with his brother
over Vialov, even though Alexey did find a convincing
enough argument, saying: 'Think for a moment, the man
worked all his life for us, and then we turn him out—was it
decent?'

Peter knew very well it had not been decent, but having
Tikhon Vialov about the place made matters even worse
for him. And, as far as he could remember, for the first time
in their life Natalia took Alexey's part, and with a firmness
unusual in her, said: 'It's not decent, Peter, even if you were
to strike me, I'd still say, it isn't decent!'

Together with Olga they succeeded in talking him round and calming him, though the man of mortifications had his final crow, saying: 'Well—have your own way—but it's nobody's law . . . see?'

This man of mortifications was becoming ever more visible, ever more palpable to Peter Artamonov. Cautiously he bore his body, which weighed heavy on him, up the hill to the seat under the pine tree, where he sat down to dwell on the man of mortifications and genuinely grieve for him. There was sweetness as well as bitterness in building up this picture of a man who was unhappy, inscrutable, wanted by nobody—yet a good fellow. It was as easy to conjure him up as those little wisps of cloud would suddenly form, out of nothing in the blue depths of the sky over the marshes, on hot days.

The man of mortifications looked down on the factory and all it had created, and whispered: 'You could have lived a different life, without all these complications.'

Then Artamonov the manufacturer objected: 'Tikhon Vialov's talk!'

'The Reverend Gleb used to say the same, Goritzvetov too, and many another. Yes, men are like flies struggling in a spider's web.'

'You can't get through life as easily as that,' was the involuntary retort of the manufacturer.

Sometimes this silent debate between two men in one turned into a savage battle, and the mortified one would become merciless and almost shout: 'Don't forget, when you were drunk, at the Fair, you told them of your remorse because when you sacrificed your son, as Abraham did Isaac, somebody substituted the little Nikonov boy for a lamb, remember it? It's true, true! And for this truth you flung a bottle at my head. Ah, you did for me then, you killed me. You sacrificed me too. To whom—to whom did you

Bernard Duffield

sacrifice me? That Divinity with horns that Nikita spoke of?
That God? You, you . . .'

At the height of disputes as savage as this, the manufacturer Artamonov closed his eyes tight, to hold back the
angry, shaming, bitter tears. But the tears, not to be restrained, would stream out, and he would wipe them with
his hands from cheeks and beard, then rub palm against
palm till his hands were dry again, and stare blankly at his
swollen, purple paws. He would swallow huge draughts of
Madeira, straight from the bottle.

But in spite of those tears of sorrow which he squeezed
out, that man of mortification was beloved by Peter Artamonov, and indispensable to him. He seemed like the
Turkish bath attendant, when the latter takes a soft loofah,
dips it in water of the right temperature, soaps it with sweet-
smelling soap and scrubs you in just that patch of your back
which your hand cannot reach.

Suddenly, far, far away, farther than Siberia, a powerful
fist was raised—and began to beat Russia.

Alexey danced about, waving his newspaper, shouting:
'Brigandage! Pillage!' He raised his bird's-claw of a hand
ceilingwards; the fingers writhed. 'We'll show 'em . . .
we'll show 'em . . .' But the doctor with the gold teeth
stuck his hands into his pockets. Standing with his back
firmly up against the warm tiles of the stove, he murmured:
'Perhaps they're going to show us . . .'

This large, copper-haired fellow of course was only being
facetious—he was always facetious, whatever the subject.
He even mentioned illnesses and deaths with the same
facetiousness that he spoke of a wrong card in a game of
preference. Peter Artamonov looked on him as a foreigner,
given to smiling from embarrassment, simply because he
fails to understand another people. Peter did not like the

249

man, had no confidence in him, and himself consulted the Dromov doctor Kron—a taciturn German.

Twisting anxiously at his beard, and frowning as if his head ached, Miron paced from one corner to another like a stork and tried to teach everybody. 'We should have made an alliance with the English before beginning the job . . .'

'Yes—but what job do you mean?' Peter inquired. But neither his bouncing brother nor his clever nephew could give him any clear reason exactly why this Japanese war had suddenly flared up. He found the confusion of these self-assured know-alls a pleasing sight—his brother seemed the silliest of all. Alexey was behaving so incomprehensibly that one might really have supposed this unexpected war primarily touched him, hindering him personally in some very important task.

There was a special church procession through the town. Pompously and piously the merchant community with their heavy feet trod the thick fall of snow and, close-packed one to another, followed the chain of gilt-clad priests; ikons and banners were carried; the united choirs of all the churches of the town chanted loudly and impressively: '*Almighty God, spare thy people* . . .'

The words of the prayer, akin to a demand, emerged from the 'O' of their mouths in the form of white vapour, which formed hoar frost on the beards and moustaches of the bass voices and also settled on the beards of the burghers, who were discordantly supporting the choirs. The town mayor, Voroponov—son of the carter—sang with particular penetrating power, insistently too, but out of tune with the choirs; obese and rubicund, with eyes like mother-of-pearl buttons, he had inherited in addition to his father's estate an untamable hatred for all the Artamonov brood.

There were seven of them, all together; at the head Alexey, with his limp, arm-in-arm with his wife, then

Yakov with his mother and his sister Tatiana; then Miron, with the doctor; behind them all, in soft leather high boots, strode the head of the family, Peter.

'The nation . . .' Miron said in a low voice.

'A review of our strength,' was the doctor's answer.

Miron took off his spectacles, and wiped them with his handkerchief, while the doctor added: 'You'll see—they'll kindle the blaze!'

'Hm! this green timber'll be a long time burning . . '

'Silence!' Peter Artamonov commanded his nephew. Miron cast a sidelong glance at him and, first feeling for the right place, put back his spectacles on his long nose.

'*Almighty God, spare thy people . . .*' came Voroponov's demand emphatically loud, bringing out the word *people* with a peculiar explosiveness; then he craftily turned round, sweeping his glance over the whole concourse of citizens, and for some reason waving his beaver cap at them.

The full-bosomed forty-year-old daughter of Pomialov, still fresh and plump, sang with a fine rich voice; she was now a third time a widow, and first in the town for scandalous, shameless living. Peter caught her giving Natalia a whispered word of advice: 'You'd do well to send your hubby to the war, he's enough to frighten anybody, and the Japs would run away if they saw him.' She turned to Yakov: 'Well, godson, my little cock, not marrying yet?'

Peter shook his head. These things he heard were like flies, they hindered him thinking of something important. He went to the side, and, once on the pavement, slackened his pace, letting the stream of the procession overtake him, unusually black to-day, against the masses of white snow. On they trod, like so many steaming samovars.

There was Vera Popov, stony-faced, at the head of her pupils. Snowflakes glittered on her grey hair. Her eyelashes, white with hoar, quivered an instant when she bowed her rich, bared head. Artamonov was sorry for her —how stupid she was to harness herself to bringing up young geese.

A long wave of short-cropped heads swept past him— the united pupils of the Dromov schools; then, like a heavy grey machine, a half-company of soldiery moved forward, led by brave Lieutenant Mavrin, famous throughout the town for his daily bathes in the Oka, which began at high spring flood and ending with the first frosts. It was also notorious that he lived on the Pomialov woman's money— she was his mistress.

Pompously, like a well-fed gander, came Nesterenko, an officer of the gendarmery, with Chinese moustaches; his ailing wife was arm-in-arm with her brother, Zhiteikin, son of the former mayor and owner of a leather tannery. It was said of Zhiteikin that though he lived with nuns in sin, he had read seven hundred books and also was a master of the kettle drum, even in secret teaching army recruits the art.

Next followed Stephen Barski, with his drunkard son-in-law and squint-eyed daughter; lost in fat, he was borne by in a sleigh. There were then the common people, a long, confused dark chain—craftsmen, tanners, weavers, carters, beggars, and a number of superfluous old women, like rats. Slowly the snow powdered the bared heads; from the distance came the irrepressible, insistent voice of Voroponov: '*Almighty God, spare thy people!*'

'What on earth can God want with these people?' Artamonov asked himself—he could not understand. He did not love the townspeople, and had very little to do with them, apart from business connections. He knew that he was not liked in return—they thought him haughty, and surly—but Alexey enjoyed great respect, on account of his passion for town improvement—for having the main street paved, the square embellished with lindens, and a park laid out on the riverside, with a boulevard. They were afraid of Miron, and even of Yakov, considering them excessively greedy, out to get everything about them into their grasp.

As he watched the slow procession of these people, with their worried faces, Peter Artamonov frowned—many a face he did not know and far too many eyes, of all sorts, looked at him with equal hostility.

At the gates of Alexey's house, Tikhon Vialov saluted him. 'So we're at war, eh? old boy?' said Artamonov.

Without a word, with a familiar movement of his clumsy paw, Vialov scratched his head. This was the very first time in all his life that Artamonov had asked him something as if he had confidence in his answer. 'What's your opinion?' Artamonov asked.

"Tis nought but trifles,' Vialov answered in a flash, as if he had been expecting the question.

'Everything's a trifle to you,' Peter said·indecisively.

'Then what? Dogs, are we?. We're not animals.'

Artamonov continued his way, through the fine sifting snow. It was falling thicker now, and the distant crowd of people, among the white mounds of trees and houses, were almost concealed.

Now that Seraphim the Comforter was no more, Peter had taken to finding relaxation with the widow of the deacon, a woman of uncertain age named Thais Paraklitov— a thin creature, resembling a young lad, or a black nanny-goat. She was quiet, and invariably agreed with him about everything. 'That's so, darling,' she would say, 'oh yes, darling, oh yes.'

He was drinking heavily, but taking a long time to get drunk, and he was exasperated to find that it took so long for his dismal, obsessive ideas to melt away, dissolved in

Thais's powerful and tasty vodka concoctions. The first few moments of intoxication were usually unpleasant. The alcohol merely made Peter's thoughts about himself and others still more pungent and bitter, and the whole of life was stained an angry marsh-green hue by it, and set into seething motion. He got the impression that this ebullition turned him, spun him about, only, a moment later, to send him flying over a sort of boundary line.

To-day, gritting his teeth, he tried to hear and see every detail of that sombre revolt within himself. Suddenly he shouted at the woman: 'Well, why don't you say something? Tell me something!'

Like a little goat she leapt on to his knees. She was marvellously light and warm. Opening wide before him an invisible book, she read out: 'Mrs. Pomialov's dismissed Lieutenant Mavrin. He lost again at cards—three hundred and twenty-two rubles. She's going to protest a bill—she has got a promissory note he signed. The reason the gendarmery officer Nesterenko keeps his wife here is that he has taken on a mistress in the town and not that his wife's ill . . .'

'This is all dirty and petty,' Peter said.

'Dirty and petty, darling, and how dirty and petty!'

Her tales about the dirty and petty doings of Dromov frightened Peter's ideas away, by giving him reason and right in his hostility to the dismal sinners of Dromov. In place of his thoughts there would rise a circle of pictures of the wild debauch of the Nizhny Fair—a dance of insensate men, their thirsty but insatiate eyes rolling, men who burned money and, devoid of any sense of restraint, were beside themselves in every possible way in a crazy infuriation of the flesh, as they strove towards that large, dazzlingly white and shamelessly naked woman against the black background . . .

In dead silence Peter Artamonov gulped down vodkas of all possible shades and hues and chewed the tart, slippery mushrooms, feeling with his whole drunken body that the dearest thing of all, ominously powerful and real, was concealed in that shameless troll of the Fair who showed her naked body for money and on whose account famous men were prepared to squander fortune, shame, and health. Yet all that remained in life for him was this swart little nanny-goat.

'Take off your clothes!' he roared suddenly. 'Dance!'

'How can I dance without music?' she asked, as she unfastened her clothes. 'You ought to get Noskov in, he'd be willing, he's a good accordion player.'

Time paced unnoticed in these pleasures, and there were occasions when out of the flow of turgid days something otherwise quite unattainable would arise. One day that winter news came that the workers in Petersburg had tried to rush the palace and kill the Tsar.

Tikhon Vialov muttered: 'It'll come to pillaging the churches yet. Is it surprising? People aren't made of iron.'

When the summer came round there was talk that a Russian warship was steaming about in Russian waters, firing broadsides at the towns.

Vialov said: 'Is it surprising? They've got accustomed to making war.'

There was a new church procession in Dromov. Voroponov wore a reddish frock-coat and carried a portrait of the Tsar, while he chanted: '*Almighty God, spare Thy people!*'

This time he chanted louder than ever before, and more savagely too—yet nevertheless the final note of the appeal for help sounded tremulous.

Zhiteikin was quite drunk. Hatless, a double-barrelled

shot-gun in his arms, his purple bald pate a-shine, he led his
tanners and yelled wildly, shockingly, such things as: 'Boys!
Don't let the Yids get our Russia! Whose Russia? Our
Russia!'

'Our Russia,' the tanners responded in tune with him,—
they too were not sober, and whenever they came up
against the weavers, who were traditional foes of theirs,
they fell to blows. Doctor Yakovliev was struck with a stick,
and the old chemist was thrown into the Oka. Zhiteikin
ended by a long hunting of his own son about the town.
Twice he let off both barrels at him, without getting in a
hit, only Bruskov (the tailor) receiving a slight back wound
from the buckshot.

The factory closed down. In spite of the attempts Miron
and some other sensible fellows made to talk them out of it,
and the cries and wailing of their womenfolk, the young
men rolled up their sleeves and made off for the town.

The Artamonov works were deserted. The spirit had
gone out of them. They might have been shrivelled by the
wind, which was rioting too; it howled and whistled, lashing everything with iced rain; it plastered the chimney with
sleet, then blew it off again, dried it away.

Peter sat at the window staring dully at the dark little
figures of men and women hustling like ants into the town
and out again. Through the glass came their cries; they
seemed to be enjoying themselves. There was an accordion
being played by the gates—a crowd of workers; among them
the lame stoker Vaska Krotov, singing:

> "Now the world is getting tight
> With the Japanese we're fighting—
> They are giving us a hiding
> But we're hitting back with ikons!"

From Dromov the wind brought a dull mutter, as if a
mammoth samovar, holding a whole lakeful of water, was

bubbling there. Alexey's trap came cantering into the yard, with one-eyed Morozov driving—Olga leapt out, a shawl about her. Peter forgot the pains in his legs and in great concern leapt to his feet and hurried towards her. 'What has happened?'

Shaking herself just like a hen, she answered: 'All our windows smashed—the tanners . . .'

Artamonov stood aside, to let her pass. He gave a smile as he growled: 'There you are . . . that's what your idle chatter's brought you! You shouted at me. Now you see . . . Whatever you may say, the Emperor . . .' But before he finished there came the loud rejoinder, furious, unlike Olga: 'That's enough! He's dishonest, your Emperor.'

'A lot you know about Emperors,' he said awkwardly, and his hand went to his ear. This burst of rage of the *petite* old lady in spectacles, who was always so calm and never breathed a word against anybody, amazed him—there was a devastating note of seriousness in it, however superfluous and pitiable it might be—it was like a mouse squeaking against a bull which, without either seeing what it was doing or wanting to do it, had trod on its tail. He sank into his chair and was lost in thought.

It was a considerable time—some weeks—since he last saw Olga. He had been avoiding meeting her son, as he had quarrelled with him. It had been back at the end of the summer, when he had taken to his bed with swollen legs, that Voroponov, perspiring and triumphant, had come to see him, and with much clobbering with his thick, blue lips, asked Peter to sign a telegram to the Tsar—a plea not to delegate his prerogative to anybody else. Peter had been much surprised by this daring move of the mayor's, but he signed the telegram. He did this because he was sure it would displease both Alexey and Miron—also because no doubt Voroponov would get a good ticking-off from Petersburg for it: you thick-lipped fathead, don't poke your nose in other people's business, don't get a swelled head!

Tucking the form into the pocket of his frock-coat, and fastening every button, Voroponov had then begun to lay complaints against Alexey, Miron, the doctor, and all those who, prompted by the Jews—some blindly, others out of personal ambition—were turning against the Emperor. Peter had heard these complaints out with something like satisfaction, egging Voroponov on; it was only when Voroponov's purple lips began maliciously attacking Vera Popov that he said—severely:

'Mrs. Popov's nothing to do with all that.'

'How do you make that out? We are informed . . .'

'You're informed of nothing.'

'Then go on falling till you come a cropper,' said the mayor threateningly, and was gone.

The same evening Peter was assailed by his nephew and his daughter—they burst in on him like wild dogs, barking at him, making no allowance for his years.

'Here, Dad, what are you about?' Tatiana yelled, her crazy eyes starting from her ugly face. Yakov was standing at the window, tattooing on the pane. Peter had the impression that Yakov too was against him. Miron demanded bitingly:' Did you read what was written on that document?'

'No, I didn't,' Peter had replied, 'I didn't, but I know—it said young pups should not be let loose!'

It was good to see Miron and Tatiana losing their tempers, but Yakov's silence disturbed him; he had confidence in his son's business qualities, and sensed that he had acted against his own interests. But pride would not let him drag Yakov into the dispute and ask his opinion. He lay still, snapping and snarling, while Miron, nose wagging, hammered away: 'Get this into your head—the Tsar's surrounded by a band of rogues, we've got to get some honest men in their place . . .' ·

Artamonov knew that Miron pictured himself as one of the honest ones, and that Alexey had been going to Moscow to try to get somebody to put Miron forward as candidate for the *Duma*. It was both laughable and alarming to think of that stork-like creature his nephew close to the Emperor. Then in had come Alexey, his hair tousled, his coat unbuttoned, and set a-dancing and yelling: 'You lunatic, what do you think you're doing?'—shouting as if dealing with one of his men.

'Go to hell!' Peter had suddenly shouted back. 'You teach me? To hell with you all! Get out!'

He had even frightened himself by this sudden burst of rage.

And now, seated in his corner, hearing Olga's naïve account of the riots in the town, he recalled the quarrel and tried to get clear who was right—he or they? He had found Olga's childishly angry words specially disturbing. Now she was talking quite clamly, almost sweetly: 'Our weavers are good lads! You should have seen how soon they cleared away the Voroponov crowd and the tanners. They've stayed down there to protect the house . . .'

Natalia, terrified, complained angrily: 'It's your house started all this trouble. It serves you right. You're to blame for it all!'

Miron came in and, without so much as how-d'you-do, began prancing up and down the room, full of threats: 'All these Voroponovs and Zhiteikins shall pay dearly for teaching the people to riot like this! This won't go for nothing, this will have its recoil. There have been quite enough lessons in rioting from the friends of Mr. Ilia Artamonov, and if these people now start . . .'

But Peter did not say a word.

After the quarrel over the Voroponov petition, Miron had become absolutely and irrevocably repugnant to him, but he could see that the whole works were entirely in the young man's hands. Miron was managing the business with skill and assurance—the workers obeyed him, or were afraid of him; they were less riotous than the town men.

The wind had dropped, lost in the thick snow. It was coming down heavily and straight, in large flakes, and had laid a white curtain over the window, so that nothing could be seen outside. Nobody spoke to Peter, and he sensed that all of them, except his wife, considered him the culprit for everything—for the riots, the foul weather, and the Tsar's mismanagement.

'But where is Yakov?' Natalia asked, with alarm. 'Where is Yakov, I say?'

Miron rudely blew his nose, then, without looking at his aunt, said: 'I suppose he's taken refuge in town, in his hen-house.'

'What? Where?' mumbled Natalia timidly.

'I suppose the fool doesn't know Yakov has a mistress,' was Peter's thought, then suddenly aloud: 'Well, this is what I say: do as you think fit! Carry on! Yes. I really don't understand it all. I'm an old man. And in all this . . . in all this . . . there's Satan's fingers. For all my long years, I can't make head or tail of it . . .'

PART FOUR

TILL he was twenty-six, Yakov Artamonov had lived decently, quietly, with no particular troubles. But then time, that enemy of those who live a quiet life, began playing a dirty, tangled game with him. It had begun in April, during the night, three years after the riots which had stirred up the long-suffering people.

He was lying on the sofa, smoking, enjoying the sensation of satiety, which excluded all other desires, a sensation he valued more than anything else, seeing in it, indeed, the purpose of life. He found it equally pleasing after a good dinner or after possessing a woman.

The woman in the case, a well-proportioned, rounded little person, was standing in the middle of the room, against a table, dreamily watching the angry, lilac-coloured flame of the spirit-lamp under the coffee-machine. Her bare arms and childlike face, lit by the light of a lamp with a red shade, took on the colour of a well-baked piecrust. Her dark hair, falling loosely, made a pretty picture flowing over her neck and shoulders. A gold-yellow Bokhara house gown was drawn over Pauline's naked body; on her feet were green morocco-leather slippers. There was something very aerial, un-Russian, in her; she had the sweet little face of a young boy, with pouting lips and impudent eyes, round as cherries; even at this moment, when Yakov was satiated with her, he liked her. She was of course incomparably better than all the other girls or women he had known, and had she not been so stupid she would have been perfect.

261

'I don't want coffee, my Little Orange,' Yakov said, speaking through a thick film of cigarette smoke. Without a look at him, Pauline replied: 'What about me?'

'I don't know what you want,' he replied, with a lazy yawn.

'Oh, yes you do,' she caught at his words, with a shake of the head and a sudden break in her voice.

For a minute Yakov turned over those four sharp-hooked, prickly words, then sat up, threw his cigarette on the floor, put on his boots, and said, with a sigh: 'I can never make out why you have to spoil a good mood. You know well enough I can't marry till my father dies . . .'

Then, as usual, Pauline poured a stream of insults over him. 'Of course, you spider, all that matters to you is your good mood. I know, for your comfort you'd be ready to sell me to any old Tartar buying up old clothes, you're absolutely devoid of principles . . .'

Yakov particularly disliked having her call him a spider —at petting time she had a quite different name for him— 'Salty-pie'. Moreover, he thought that to-day at least she might have kept from quarrelling—just two hours before this he had given her a hundred rubles.

'You'll get nowhere by carrying on,' he warned her calmly, as he put on his hat and held out his hand. 'So long!'

'Filthy pig! Throwing your cigarette ends on the floor again, too . . .'

Outside there was a stiff, damp wind; the shadows of the clouds swept over the ground as if trying to wipe the puddles dry. The moon for a moment, and the water in the puddles, with a thin film of ice, gleamed like brass. This year winter was stubbornly refusing to give way to spring; only yesterday there had been a heavy fall of snow.

Yakov Artamonov walked slowly, hands in pockets, his heavy stick under his arm, thinking how inexplicably and strangely stupid people were. What did that dear little ninny, Pauline, really want? She could live quietly, without a care in the world, getting quite a lot of presents, dressing well, spending about a hundred rubles a month. Yakov was aware that she liked him—he could sense it. So what more did she want? Why did she want marriage?

'She's as stupid as a mouse in a jam-pot,' he concluded, with his favourite saying of his own invention. Life seemed simple to him, making no demands on a fellow beyond that which he possessed.

After all, in essence it was simple; everybody strove to obtain one and the same thing—complete tranquillity. The turmoil of the day was merely a rather unpleasant overture to the tranquillity of the night—to those hours when you could be alone with a woman and at last, pleasantly fatigued by her caresses, sleep a dreamless sleep. This was really the only significant reality. People were stupid because nearly all of them, either secretly or openly, thought they were more clever than this. They invented all manner of unnecessary things. Possibly this was due to a sort of blindness, each of them wanting to be quite different from the others, and afraid of being lost among them, and losing himself.

Ilia was stupid, because he had got caught up in books even when he was still only a schoolboy, and now he was knocking about somewhere among the socialists. He had been obliged to put up with a lot from Ilia, yet not so long ago he had had to send him some money somewhere in Siberia.

His mother was unbearably stupid—though she was comically so; still more unbearably stupid—quite insupportably so—was his grim father, an old bear, a dirty old drunkard who did not know how to get on with other people. That fussy jumping-jack Uncle Alexey was ridiculous in his stupidity; he would have liked to be a Member of the *Duma*, and with that in view fed greedily on the newspapers, and had turned insincerely pleasant to everybody in Dromov, playing up to the factory workers, too, like a bawdy old woman.

In his own peculiar way, and that somehow terribly oppressive, even that beaky woodpecker Miron was stupid. Counting himself the first mind in all Russia, it seemed he now pictured himself a future minister, nor did he make any effort to conceal that he alone knew what ought to be done and what people should think. He too was trying to make up to the workers, organizing all manner of entertainments for them, football teams, and a library—feeding wolves on carrots!

The workers wove first-class cloth—and dressed in rags, living in filth and drunkenness. They also were *en masse* bewitched by a special kind of stupidity, insolently so—a brazen stupidity—devoid even of that rather nice simple, patriarchal cunning that every *mouzhik* had in himself.

Yakov Artamonov had to think more about the workers than anything else, as he came into direct contact with them every day, and long since—from his early days— they had inspired him with feelings of hostility. At that time he had had many a clash with the younger weavers over girls, and to this day, it seemed, some of his old rivals had not forgotten the old sores. While he was still beardless, twice at night stones had been flung at him. More than once his mother had been obliged to silence a woman's tongue and avoid a scandal with money; then she would try to get him to be good in the most ridiculous fashion: 'What are you thinking of, like a young cockerel—you ought to wait a bit till you marry, then find a girl for yourself and begin life! You'll have them complaining to your father, and he'll turn you out, like Ilia.'

During two or three years of social trouble, Yakov had

not noticed anything particularly threatening at the factory, yet Miron's talk, the agitated sighs of Uncle Alexey, the newspapers which this younger Artamonov hated reading, but which with persistent obligingness and open, malicious menace told the story of the working-class movement and printed the speeches of the workers' representatives in the *Duma*—all this together inspired Yakov with a feeling of hostility to the factory people, together with a mortifying sense of dependence on them. He thought he had found the way to keep these feelings well hidden under petty concessions to their demands, and smiles and a humorous approach.

So, taking all in all, things were not going too badly, although he would sometimes all at once be overtaken by a sort of embarrassment which he found oppressive—a feeling as if he, Yakov Artamonov, the master, were only a sort of guest of the men who worked for him, a guest who had long outlived his welcome, so that there was a dismal reticent attitude on their side, and glances which seemed to say: 'Why don't you take your departure? It's high time.'

Whenever he experienced that feeling, he would have a dull, ominous foreboding that at the works there was something fermenting invisibly in secret, something smouldering which was extremely dangerous for him—for him personally.

Yakov was convinced that man is a simple structure—that the thing man prefers is simplicity and that man himself never invents or fosters a troublesome notion. Such ideas, likely to lead to loss of balance, existed somehow outside man, so that anybody infected with them thereby became disturbingly incomprehensible. It was better not to know anything about such combustible ideas, nor to exacerbate them. But, though hostile to such thought, Yakov did sense its existence outside himself, and saw that these ideas not only did not loosen the tight knots of universal stupidity, but made a still worse tangle of that simple, clear life he liked to live.

The man who seemed the cleverest of all the people he knew was old Tikhon Vialov. Observing Vialov's tranquil attitude towards his fellow-men, and his gracious service, Yakov envied the man. Vialov even slept wisely, one ear pressed into the pillow, as if to catch something unknown.

One day Yakov asked Vialov if he dreamt. 'Why should I?' Vialov replied, 'I'm not a woman,' and Yakov felt there was something solid, firm, so strong it could not be shaken, in that reply.

'Old women's dreams,' Yakov said to himself, whenever he listened to the discussions and pronouncements made in his Uncle Alexey's house, and pondered them, with an inward smile.

Altogether, thought came with difficulty to him, and if he did begin thinking it made his movements torpid, as if he was carrying a great weight; his head would droop to one side, his eyes be fixed on the ground.

In this wise, that night, he left Pauline. This was why he simply did not notice a sombre, squat form appearing before him, swinging one arm high in the air. Then he quickly dropped to one knee, drew a revolver from his coat pocket, pressed into the leg of his assailant, and fired. A dull, faint report followed, but the man leapt back, striking against the fence with his shoulders, uttered a howl, and slithered down to the ground.

It was only after all this had happened that Yakov realized he was mortally afraid, so afraid that though he wanted to shout, he could not. His hands were shaking and his legs would not obey him when he tried to get up. A couple of paces away, writhing on the ground, also trying to get up, was the man, capless, curly headed,

'I'll shoot, you scum,' Yakov said, in a hoarse voice, and stretched out his arm, with the revolver. The man turned his broad face to him and muttered: 'You've already shot me . . .'

Then Yakov recognized him, and in amazement he exclaimed, also in a mutter: 'Noskov; you scoundrel—you?'

Yakov's fear swiftly gave place to a sensation akin to delight, a feeling caused not merely by the knowledge that he had succeeded in foiling the attack, but also by the circumstance that the assailant was not one of the factory workers, as he had thought, but an outsider. It was Noskov, one by himself, who lived by trapping, playing the accordion at weddings, and lodged with the deacon's widow, Mrs. Paraklitov; so far he had never heard a bad word about the man.

'So that's the sort of thing you get up to,' Yakov said, standing up and looking about him. It was quiet, only the wind shaking the dry branches of the trees above the fence.

'And what do I get up to?' Noskov suddenly demanded loudly. 'A practical joke, giving you a scare, that's all! And you straightway draw and shoot. You won't get a testimonial for that, you'll see. I was frightened myself . . .'

'Oh, really?' Yakov Artamonov said ironically, with the air of a victor. 'Well, up you get, and we'll go to the police station.'

'I can't move, you've crippled me.'

'We'll see about that when we get there—up you get!'

'I've nought to fear,' Noskov repeated. 'How will you prove I attacked you, that it was not you got scared and attacked me? That's point number one.'

'Yes—and number two?' Yakov demanded, with a grin, yet somewhat surprised at Noskov's calm.

'There is a second point. I can be of use to you.'

'A fine yarn—story-book stuff.'

And, pointing the revolver point-blank at the accordionist's face, with sudden fury Yakov threatened him: 'I'll blow out your brains in a minute!'

Noskov looked up, then lowering his glance again at his cap, said suggestively: 'Don't you start a public row. You can't prove anything, even though you are rich. I tell you, I was out to play a joke. I know your dad, I've played the accordion many a time for him.'

With a sharp movement he clapped his cap on his head, bent forward, and pulled up his trouser leg, groaning through his teeth as he did so; he then drew a handkerchief from his pocket and set about bandaging the leg, which was wounded above the knee. All the time he kept up an indistinct mutter. But Yakov paid no attention to what he was saying; he was once again scared by the strange conduct of this would-be brigand.

He reflected. At unusual speed he concluded that, of course, the thing to do was to leave Noskov where he was, up against the fence, and go into town to summon the night watchman, to mount guard over the wounded man, while he went to the police, to report the assault. But then the inquiry would begin, and Noskov would tell all he knew about his father's debauches with the deacon's widow. The man might have friends, cut-throats like himself, and they might try to take their revenge.

Yet it was impossible to leave the man without some sort of retribution. . . .

The night was getting colder; the hand in which he was holding the revolver was aching from cold—it was a long way to the police headquarters—a long way and, of course, they would all be asleep. Yakov snorted angrily, unable to decide, regretting he had not at once killed this wiry fellow, with such bandy legs you'd think he's spent his whole life straddling a barrel.

Then all at once he heard something which staggered him, it was so unexepcted.

"I'll tell you straight, though it's a secret,' Noskov said, still tending his leg, 'it's for your sake I'm here, to keep an eye on the workers. It may have been a lie, saying I wanted to frighten you, but as a matter of fact I was out to catch somebody else, I mistook you . . ."

'Well—I'm damned,' Yakov gasped. 'What do you mean?'

'This—I suppose you don't know that the Socialists foregather in Mrs. Paraklitov's bath-house, reading pamphlets and talking of an uprising again . . .'

'You're inventing,' Yakov said weakly—yet believed him. 'But who are they? Who foregathers there?'

'I can't tell you that. You'll learn when they're arrested.'

Holding on to the palings, Noskov got up. 'Give me your stick,' he said; 'I can't walk without . . .'

Yakov bent down and picked up his stick, handed it to him, looking about him, and asked feebly: 'But, then, how was it . . . what did you attack me for?'

'I did not attack you at all. I mistook you for somebody else. I wanted somebody else, not you. Don't you worry about that. It was a mistake. You'll soon see that I'm speaking the truth. You must give me something to pay for treating my leg. That's how it stands . . .'

Holding on to the fence, and supporting himself with the stick, Noskov began to move slowly, on his bandy legs, away from the gardens, towards the obscure houses of the outskirts, and as he went he seemed to drive away the cold shadows of the clouds. But when he had gone about ten paces he called back quietly: 'Mr. Yakov!'

Yakov went quickly up to him. Noskov said: 'Not a word to anybody about what's just happened, not one word—or—you can see. . . .'

He gave a flourish with his stick and went on his way, leaving Yakov flabbergasted.

There was so much to think about at the same time—he had to make up his mind at once whether he had done what he ought. Of course, if Noskov was spying on the Socialists he was useful, even indispensable. But what if that was all a lie, and Noskov had tricked him, to gain time —then to take revenge for his failure—and for the wound!

It was a lie that Noskov had mistaken him for somebody else, or wanted to scare him; so much was clear. But— what if he had been bribed by the men to kill him? There was a large group of hot-heads among the weavers, ready for anything, but it was difficult to imagine they were Socialists. The more sober workers, such as Sedov, Kikunov and Maslov, had quite recently insisted on the management dismissing one of the more untamable scoundrels.

Yes, most likely Noskov had tricked him. Should he tell Miron all about it?

He could not imagine what would happen if he did tell Miron, except that his cousin would submit him to a detailed cross-examination, like a judge, then level some sort of accusation against him; and, most likely, one way or another, make a mock of him. If Noskov was a spy— probably Miron already knew all about it. Finally, it was still not quite clear who had made the mistake—Noskov or he himself. Noskov had said: 'You'll soon see that I'm speaking the truth.'

He watched Noskov till the man had vanished in the night shadows. One would say it was all simple and understandable enough—Noskov had attacked with the clear purpose of robbing him. Yakov had then shot at him —whereupon had begun that disturbing complex business, just like a nightmare, with Noskov's strange movements as he followed the fence and the strange shadows crowding in on his heels; never before had Yakov seen shadows drag so heavy behind a man.

Shaken up by his own thoughts, and fatigued by them, the youngest of the Artamonovs decided to hold his tongue and wait. He could not get Noskov out of his head, and went about frowning, feeling really ill. At dinner-time, when the men were leaving the shops, he stood at the office window and peered out at them, striving to guess which of them were Socialists. Could it be stoker Vaska, a slovenly, lame fellow, who had learned from Seraphim the art of cunning composition of quatrains?

It was a few days later that Yakov, taking out for exercise a horse which was stable-bound, observed the gendarmery officer Nesterenko, on the edge of the forest, in a Swedish jacket, and tall high-boots, a shot-gun in his hand and a bag full of birds over his shoulder. Nesterenko was standing, back to the road, facing the forest. Head down, one hand up to his face, he was just lighting a cigarette. The sun was shining on his red leather shoulders, and they looked like iron. Yakov determined in that instant what he had to do—he rode up to Nesterenko and bid him a brusque good day.

"I had no idea you were here,' he said.

'Since the day before yesterday', Nesterenko replied, 'my wife, my dear sir, is getting steadily worse; yes, sir!'

He made this sad communication very cheerfully, and the next instant clapped his hand to his bag. 'As for me— not bad, eh?' he added.

'I wonder if you know Noskov—the trapper?' Yakov asked quietly.

The officer's fair eyebrows rose in astonishment, and his oriental moustaches quivered. He took hold of one moustache and squinted up into the sky, which led Yakov to conclude that he was going to lie—but in what sense?

271

'Noskov? Who's that?' Nesterenko asked.

'A trapper. Curly headed, bandy-legged fellow . . .'

'Hm! I believe I have seen somebody of that description about the woods. Carries a rotten old shot gun . . . Well, what about him?"

Now Nesterenko looked into Yakov's face with a persistent, inquiring expression in his grey eyes, and a sort of bright spark in the centre of the pupil. Briefly Yakov told him about Noskov. Nesterenko heard him out, his eyes on the ground, tapping a fir-cone into it with the butt of his gun—heard him out, and thereupon, without looking up, said: 'And why did you not report all this to the police? My dear fellow, that's their job—and your duty to report it.'

'But I'm telling you why; he made out he was keeping his eye on the men, and that's—your business . . .'

'True,' Nesterenko agreed, putting his cigarette out against the barrel of his gun, and then, once more squinting straight into Yakov's eyes he began an instructive but rather confused story, the upshot of which was that Yakov had acted illegally, hiding an attempted robbery from the police, but that now it was far too late to report it.

'Now, if you had dragged him off there and then to the police station, everything would have been simple. But even so not quite simple. But how could you prove now that he attacked you? His wound? Pah! You can shoot a man from fright. Or by accident, out of carelessness. . . .'

Yakov felt that Nesterenko was being crafty, making it seem confused, even trying to do so to get either himself or Yakov out of the whole business, and when Nesterenko spoke of it being possible to shoot from fear, Yakov's suspicions were confirmed, he knew the officer was lying.

'Yes, sir. Of course, my dear chap, the man will pay for giving himself out as an informer. We shall ask him what

272

he knows.' And, placing his hand on Yakov's shoulder, he said: 'Look here, will you give me your word of honour that this will go no further? Is that all right, your word of honour?'

'Of course, if you wish it.'

'You won't tell either your Uncle or Miron anything about it—you really have not spoken to them? All right then. Let's leave the business to take its own course. And— not a whisper to anyone! All right? The man wounded himself, you've nothing to do with it.'

Yakov smiled; it was now another man talking to him, a cheerful, good-hearted man.

'Good-bye then,' said Nesterenko. 'Don't forget, you've promised.'

The youngest Artamonov returned home somewhat re-assured. The same evening his uncle suggested a trip to Vorgorod, and he was only too pleased to get away—but, a week later, back home and dining at his uncle's, a new wave of alarm came over him as he listened to Miron's story.

'It seems Nesterenko hasn't been so inactive as I thought —he's caught three in the town: a teacher named Modestov and some others.'

'And our men?'

'Our men? Sedov, Krikunov, Abramov and five of the younger men. Though the arrests were carried out by gendarmes from Vorgorod, of course it's Nesterenko's work, his wife's chronic illness has been to our advantage. Yes, he's no fool. He's afraid they might bump him off...'

'Nowadays men have stopped killing,' Alexey observed.

'Hm, perhaps you're right!' Miron replied. 'Yes—and in Dromov, they've also arrested that trapper fellow...'

'Noskov?' Yakov asked feebly, in terror.

'I don't know his name. He lodged at Mrs. Paraklitov's

273

and right there, in her bath-house, these revolutionaries used to organize their congresses. While in her house—with her too—as you know, your own father was having his pleasure. A pretty shabby coincidence . . .'

'Don't I agree,' said Alexey, shaking his bald head. 'What's to be done with him?'

Everything went black before Yakov, and he could no longer hear what his uncle and cousin were saying. He could only think of Noskov being arrested—clearly the man was a Socialist too, not a brigand—the workers had ordered him to beat up, even to kill, the master—workers whom Yakov himself had considered the most sober and reliable: Sedov, always so cleanly dressed, not a young man either; locksmith Krikunov, polite and cheerful; Abramov, a pleasant fellow, a singer, and skilful, handy at anything, and a good worker. Was it possible that these men were also his enemies?

He also got the impression that in the week which had passed his uncle's house had become still more noisy and uneasy. The gold-toothed doctor, Yakovliev, who never had a good word about anybody or anything, but took a lofty view of everything, supercilious and aloof, had become more prominent and seemed to rustle his newspapers menacingly.

'Yes,' the man said, his teeth flashing, 'we're stirring, we're waking up! People are now like servants who have been lazy, but the moment they get news that the master of the house is unexpectedly returning, begin bustling round sweeping and cleaning in an attempt to put the neglected house in order; it's fear of the reckoning drives them.'

'Very ambiguous, doctor,' Miron observed, with a frown. 'This anarchism, this scepticism of yours . . .'

But the doctor merely raised his voice, and lectured at

greater length, and what he had to say disturbed Yakov very much. Apparently everybody was afraid of something; people were threatening one another with misfortunes, fanning their own fears, so you might even imagine that they were afraid precisely of what they themselves were doing—afraid of their own thoughts and of the things they said.

To Yakov this seemed like an increase in the universal stupidity. He himself was living in a fear which was no invention, a very concrete fear, every nerve alive with the sensation of a noose already being on his neck, an invisible noose, but one which grew tighter and tighter, as it dragged him on towards a great misfortune which he could not avoid.

His fears increased still more about two months later, when Noskov reappeared in the town, and Abramov came back to the factory, his head shaven clean, yellow-skinned and thin.

'Won't you take an old man like me on?' he asked, with a grin, and Yakov dared not refuse him.

'What, was it hard in prison?' he asked.

With the same smile Abramov replied: 'Very cramped. If typhoid had not helped the authorities I don't know where they would have stowed us all.'

'Yes,' Yakov said to himself, as he saw the weaver out of the office, 'you may smile, but I know what you're thinking . . .'

The same evening, on Abramov's account, Miron made a really painful scene, shouting at him, even stamping his foot, as if Yakov were his valet: 'Have you gone out of your senses?' he shouted, red from rage to the tip of his nose. 'First thing to-morrow, pay the man off . . .'

One morning, a few days later, while he was taking a bathe in the Oka, he was overtaken by Lieutenant Mavrin and Nesterenko. They were in a boat bristling with fishing-rods. The brave lieutenant gave Yakov a curt nod, then without a word rowed out into mid-stream, while Nesterenko, stripping, said softly: 'It was wrong of you not to take on Abramov, I'm very sorry I was unable to give you a tip in advance.'

'It was Miron.' Yakov muttered, sensing the vodka in Nesterenko's breath.

'Was it? You were not responsible?'

'I was not.'

' That's a pity. That lad would have been useful. As a decoy—live bait.'

Eyeing Yakov conspiratorially, as he stood naked in the sun, all aglow, his skin flashing like the scales of a carp, Nesterenko asked again: 'And your friend—seen him—the trapper, I mean?' He gave a quiet, self-satisfied little laugh. 'Do you know why he tried to make you his prey? He wanted to buy a gun—a double-barrelled shot-gun. In everything, old boy, it's passions control men, I assure you. Now if I keep a tight hold on his throat he'll be very useful, thanks to that little mistake with you . . .'

'What mistake, if as you say . . .'

'I said mistake, my dear sir, and I mean mistake,' Nesterenko repeated. Splashing some water over his chest and making the sign of the cross he entered the river, striding like a horse.

'God damn you all,' was Yakov's gloomy thought.

All at once, just like closing the door of a room full of noise, death appeared. Yakov was wakened in the night by his mother, sobbing—'Get up, quick, Tikhon's just run up to tell us—your Uncle Alexey's passed away.'

He was on his feet in a jiffy. 'How can that be?' he stammered. 'He wasn't ailing, why . . .'

His father appeared in the doorway, unsteady on his feet, breathing stertorously. 'Vialov, you say?' he growled. 'Where that man is there's bound to be trouble. See, Yakov. All of a sudden . . .'

Barefoot, a dressing-gown thrown over his night clothes, Peter Artamonov stood plucking at his ear, looking all round him, as if he did not know where he was, and groaning.

'But what could it have been?' Yakov questioned.

'Without a priest, to repent to,' his mother said; she was like a huge sack of flour.

They drove down in the *brichka*, Yakov on the driving-seat, whence he could see Vialov bouncing on the horse's back, while to one side their shadow was stretched out, dancing, as if trying to bury itself in the earth.

Olga met them outside. She was pacing to and fro in a white petticoat and bed jacket, between stable and gateway. In the moonlight she looked bluish and transparent; it was strange to see her silhouette casting a dense shadow on the paving stones of the yard.

'Now my life is done,' she said, with pitiful weakness. Close at her heels hung their black dog, Kouchoum.

On the bench under the kitchen window sat Miron, bent double—in one hand a cigarette was smoking, from the other he swung his spectacles, the glasses flashing, thin gold threads radiating from them. Devoid of spectacles, Miron's nose looked larger than ever.

Without a word Yakov sat down beside him, while his father, taking his stand in the middle of the yard, looked up at the open window like a beggar expectant of alms. Olga, staring heavenwards, told Natalia all about it, in a high-pitched voice: 'I didn't notice when it happened . . . All at once his dear shoulder was deadly cold—his dear mouth was wide open. My darling was not able to say his last

277

word to me. Yesterday he had begun to complain of stabs about his heart.'

Olga's voice remained low; each word seemed to cast its shadow.

Miron threw down his dead cigarette, butted his head into Yakov's shoulder and howled plaintively: 'You just don't know how wonderful he was.'

'What can you do?' Yakov replied—he could think of nothing else to say. He ought to say something about his aunt, but—what could you say? So he held his tongue, staring into the ground, fidgetting with one foot. His father gave a gasp, and cautiously went indoors, Yakov following on tiptoe.

His uncle was laid out under a sheet; from a cloth tied round his jaw two horns stuck up; the sheet clung round his big toes so that it looked as if they would break through. The moon, one edge of it melted away, shone brightly in at the window, and the muslin curtain stirred; Kouchoum howled outside. Then, as if in answer to the dog, the eldest of the Artamonovs, crossing himself suddenly with a great sweep of his hand, said, in an unnecessarily loud voice: 'Life came easy to him, so did death.'

Through the window Yakov noticed that Vera Popov was now walking to and fro with his aunt; she was all in black, like a nun, and Olga was once again telling the story in a high-pitched voice: 'He passed away in his sleep . . .'

'Don't be silly!' came a low cry from Vialov. Vialov was wagging his head to and fro, to prevent the horse biting at his ear, while he rubbed it down with handfuls of straw; Peter also looked out, and growled: 'That fool again, he can't understand a thing . . .'

'Better not say anything,' Yakov said to himself, and he went out on to the porch, and watched the shadows of the two women, one white, the other black, brushing the dust from the stones; the stones took on new light. His mother was talking to Vialov in a whisper, and he was obediently nodding his head; the horse too agreed; there was a copper spot in its eye. His father came out, and his mother said to him: 'A telegram ought to be sent Nikita,—Tikhon knows where he is.'

'Tikhon—knows, does he!' his father grunted angrily. 'Send a telegram, Miron . . .'

Miron got to his feet, started off, bumped into the door-post with his shoulder and then tenderly felt the post.

'Send one to Ilia, too,' the senior Artamonov called after him.

From the dark hole cut in the wall Miron replied: 'Ilia won't be able to come.'

'You see, I've lived thirty years of my life with him,' Olga was saying—and was herself surprised at what she said. 'And four years we were together before we were married. What will happen to me now?'

Peter Artamonov went up to Yakov. 'Where is Ilia?'

'I don't know.'

'You don't?'

'This is not the moment to discuss Ilia, Father.'

Doctor Yakovliev came hurrying into the yard. 'Is he up-stairs in the bedroom?'

'The fool,' thought Yakov, 'as if you could bring him back to life.'

He was oppressed, because it was impossible to avoid these dismal moments. Everything about him bore down on him, pointlessly—people, what people said, the chestnut horse, gleaming like bronze in the moonlight, and this black dog, with its speechless grief. It was as if Aunt Olga was boasting of her lovely life with Uncle Alexey. His mother was sobbing in the corner, lettering herself go completely, but it was all false. His father's eyes were fixed, his face

279

wooden. Everything was worse and more unbearable than it need be.

On the day of the funeral, when the coffin had just been lowered into the grave, and they were throwing in hand-fuls of the yellow sand of the cemetery, Uncle Nikita arrived.

'The last straw,' Yakov said to himself, as he peered at the monk's angular outline; Nikita was leaning against one of the birches he himself had planted.

'You're late,' Peter said to him, wiping away tears as he approached his brother. Like a tortoise, the monk with-drew his head under his hump. His appearance was beg-garly; his cassock had faded in the sun, his hat taken on the colour of an old tin pail; his boots were down to the uppers. His dusty face was swollen; with dull eyes he was looking at the backs of the group about the grave, and speaking to Peter in an inaudible voice, his little grey beard quivering. Yakov looked slyly about him—dozens of eyes were con-ning the monk in curiosity—no doubt they were all seeing the misshapen brother and uncle of rich men, and expect-ing some sort of scandal to begin. Yakov knew the town was convinced that the Artamonovs had hidden their hunchback away in a monastery after the father's death to be able to make use of his share of the property.

The fat, good-natured priest, Father Nikolai, in a kind of tenor voice, was trying to convince Olga: 'Let us not offend our Lord God with lamentations and tears,' he said, 'for His will . . .'

Olga replied, in a high-pitched voice: 'But can't you see, I'm not crying, I am not lamenting.'

Her hands were trembling, and making spasmodic move-ments as if to straighten her skirt, or hide in a pocket the fragment of handkerchief wet with tears.

Skilfully Tikhon Vialov filled in the grave, assisting the

cemetery verger; beside it, straight and still as a post, stood Miron; in a low, plaintive voice the hunchback monk said to Natalia: 'Oh, how you have changed—I wouldn't have known you!' Then, pointing his finger at the chest bulge of his deformity, he added clumsily, superfluously: 'Nobody could help recognizing me. Is this your boy—Yakov? And that tall one—Alexey's? Miron? Well, I never . . . Well, let us go, come on . . .'

Yakov stayed at the cemetery. A few moments before this he had caught sight of Noskov in the crowd of workers. Noskov had passed near him, together with the lame stoker Vaska, and, as he passed, had looked him in the face with a malevolent, inquiring glance. What were that man's thoughts? Of course, he could not but will ill to the man who had shot at him and might have killed him.

Tikhon Vialov came up to Yakov, brushing the sand from his tunic, and said: 'Well, you see, despite all Mr. Alexey's efforts, after all . . . Mr. Nikita too looks poorly . . .'

'There's one . . .' Yakov suddenly said, then broke off.

'What?'

'The workers are full of grief . . .'

'But—what were you going to say?'

'There's one man here—Noskov—the trapper,' Yakov tried again, 'I'd like to tell you about him . . .'

'If a horse dies, you're sorry for that too,' Vialov said pensively. 'Mr. Alexey lived at high speed, and died the same. As if he ran slap into something. Only the day before he died, he was saying to me . . .'

Yakov was silent. He felt that nothing he said would penetrate Vialov's mind. He had made up his mind to tell him about Noskov because he simply had to tell somebody about the man; having Noskov on his mind was more oppressive than anything else which was happening. The day before, in Dromov, that brutish-faced bandy-legged creature had suddenly appeared from nowhere and, taking off his cap and peering into it, at the lining, said: 'There's a little debt you owe me—you promised to pay for treatment of my leg. And now your dear uncle had just died, so —you might give a bit for the repose of his soul. I've a chance too of buying a wonderful accordion, to amuse your dear Papa . . .'

Yakov had gaped at him, dumbfounded, but said nothing. Then Noskov, insistently and didactically, had added: 'And seeing how I serve your cause, against the enemies of Russia . . .'

'How much do you want?' Yakov had asked him.

After a moment's thought, Noskov had said: 'Thirty-five rubles.'

Yakov had then given him the money and hurried away, extremely upset and afraid. 'He thinks I'm a fool, he thinks I am afraid, the scoundrel! Let him just wait!'

Now, as he made his way slowly homewards, all Yakov could think of was—how to free himself from the creature, who quite clearly intended to bring him like an ox to slaughter.

The wake dragged on for ever. Those present made a real party of it, forcing the deacon Kartzev and the choir to chant an 'eternal memory' to the departed man. Zhiteikin got so drunk that, waving a fork in the air, he came to singing, most unseemly and ominously:

> "Warriors recall the days that are past,
> And battles they fought through shoulder to shoulder.

Stephen Barski, when his flabby body, just like a huge cushion, was being squeezed into his carriage, was loud with praise. 'Peter Ilitch Artamonov,' he said, 'truly you were fond of your brother. A funeral spread like this takes a lot of forgetting.' Yakov caught his father—very full of

liquor—answering with grim humour: 'You'll soon forget
everything, you'll soon burst!'

Zhiteikin, Barski, Voroponov, and a few other of the
élite of Dromov had been invited by Peter on his own account, against Miron's wishes, and Miron made no secret
of his indignation; after half an hour only at the funeral
feast, he rose and strode away on his long stork legs. After
him, Olga too disappeared, unnoticed, then Nikita, who
was obviously sickened by the shower of questions of half-
tipsy men about monastery life. But Yakov's father, Peter,
behaved as if out deliberately to offend everybody, and the
whole time, right to the very end, Yakov was apprehensive
of a quarrel breaking out between him and the town party.

His mother was offended because Mrs. Popov looked
after his aunt Olga, so she drove off in a huff. Inexplicably,
his father then insisted on sleeping the night in Alexey's
study. To Yakov all this seemed like one unseemly superfluous caprice after another, and still more upset him. After
lying about two hours on the sofa, he went outside, and
there, on the bench under the kitchen window, found Vialov and the dark outline of the monk, curiously reminiscent
of a broken piece of machinery. Without the tall orthodox
hat on his bald head, Nikita was shorter and broader, and
his pale, puffy face was childlike; in one hand he held a
glass; on the bench beside him was a bottle of kvass.

'Who is this?' he asked in a gentle little voice, then himself gave the answer: 'Why, it's Yasha—come and sit with
two old men, Yasha my boy.'

And, holding up a glass to the moon, he examined the
turgid liquid in it. The moon slipped behind the church
tower, lapping it with a misty silver light, strangely em-
phasizing it against the warm darkness of the night. Clouds
hung over the tower, like dirty patches cobbled on to stuff
of deep blue velvet. Alexey's pet, the heavy-jowled hound

Kouchoum, was wandering moodily about the courtyard, snuffing at the ground—all at once it would break off its search, raise its head to the skies, and utter a broken, questioning wail.

'Shh! Kouchoum!' Vialov commanded, in a hushed voice.

The dog went up to him, thrust its broad muzzle into his knee, and whined.

'He knows,' Yakov observed. Nobody made any response. He longed to talk, to drown his thoughts. 'I say—he knows,' he insisted.

Vialov rejoined quietly: 'Well, and why not?'

'At Souzdal the monastery dog could tell a thief by his smell,' Nikita recalled.

'What are you talking about?' Yakov asked him.

The monk took a draught of kvass, wiped his mouth with the sleeve of his cassock, and in his toothless way, like somebody coming down a ladder, said: 'Tikhon was just observing that the people are once again inclined to rebellion. I don't doubt—he's right. There's a broody quiet about everywhere . . .'

'It's things getting them down,' Vialov interposed, toying with the dog's ears.

'Send that dog away,' Yakov ordered him, 'it'll give us fleas.'

Vialov took Kouchoum's paws off his knees and with one foot pushed the dog away. It tucked its tail between its legs, sat down and gave a couple of barks. The three men looked at it, and the thought flashed into Yakov's mind that Vialov and the monk were perhaps far more sorry for the dog than they were for its master, now buried in the ground.

'There'll be trouble,' Yakov observed, and looked cautiously into the corners of the yard. 'Don't forget, Vialov, Sedov and his band have been arrested.'

'Well, what of it?'

The monk drew a metal box from a pocket in his cassock, took a pinch of snuff from it, and said to his nephew: 'See, I've taken to snuff. It's good for the eyes, my sight was getting poor.' He sneezed, then continued: 'They're even arresting peasants all over the place . . .'

'Spies everywhere now,' Yakov said, endeavouring to sound natural.

'Everybody's watched.'

Tikhon Vialov grunted: 'If you don't watch, you can't find out anything.'

Then Yakov, after his tongue had itched to say it for some moments,—and shivering, whether from the freshness of the night or from fear,—said: 'We've got spies here, too. I've heard unpleasant things about Noskov—that trapper fellow . . . to the effect that it was he who informed against Sedov and the Dromov people . . .'

'You—numskull,' Vialov suddenly said, after a short pause, reached out his hand towards the dog, then at once let it fall back on his knee, and Yakov felt how foolish he had been to speak, wasting his words on nothing. Without quite knowing why, he warned Vialov: 'All the same,' he said, 'don't you say anything to anybody about Noskov.'

'And why should I? He's nowt concerning me. Besides, I haven't anybody to tell, nobody believes anybody.'

'True,' Nikita agreed, 'there's little belief about; after the war I had some talk with wounded soldiers, and I could see they didn't even believe in the war! Yakov my boy, it's iron everywhere, machinery! Machinery does the work, machinery sings, machinery talks. Now the very stuff of life is manufactured with iron, we need a new sort of men —iron men. There are many who know it, I've come across more than one. We'll show you pappy creatures, they say —though there are others all against it. They say people are used to the idea of another man bossing them, but being bossed by iron metal, that's against nature. They're used to anything you can manage with your hand, like an axe or a mattock, but there you've got something weighing a ton, which might be alive.'

Vialov grunted; to Yakov's surprise, never having seen it before, he even laughed, then said: 'Cart before the horse, damn it!'

'Besides that,' Nikita continued, speaking very softly, 'there's many a man turned real angry. I've been all over the place these last three years, and I've seen; phew, how angry they are—at the wrong address, too—angry one with another. After all, they're all at fault, whether it's wisdom or stupidity. The Reverend Gleb said that to me once—'twas well said!'

'Is the parson alive?' Vialov asked.

'He's no longer a parson,' Nikita replied. 'Gleb has left the church; he's peddling books now round village fairs.'

'He was a decent parson,' Tikhon Vialov said. 'I used to confess to him. Decent. Only he was just pretending to be a parson, out of poverty, he didn't really believe in God at all, that's what I think.'

'You're wrong, he believed in Jesus Christ. Every man has his own way of believing.'

'That causes all the confusion,' Vialov said firmly, and laughed again maliciously. 'That's your thinking . . .'

Peter Artamonov came noiselessly out on to the porch, barefoot, in his nightshirt. He looked up into the pale sky and said to those under the window: 'Can't sleep . . . That dog keeps me awake . . . And you muttering there . . .'

The dog was sitting in the middle of the yard, its ears alert, whimpering, staring at the dark hole of the open window, no doubt waiting for its master to call to it.

'And you, Vialov, same old story!' Peter Artamonov be-

gan. 'See, Yakov, what happens—a *mouzhik* gets hold of
an idea—and he's like a wolf in a trap . . . your brother was
just the same. Have you heard about Ilia, Nikita?'

'Yes.'

'Well, it's true—I turned him out. He leaps plump into
the wrong saddle, and Heaven alone knows where he's
galloped it. Of course, everybody can't renounce his wealth
like that, and live no one knows how . . .'

'Alexey the saint did,' Nikita gently reminded him.

Peter raised one hand to his temples, and was silent a
moment. Then, turning to Yakov, he said: 'Bring me an
eiderdown and some cushions to the summerhouse, perhaps I shall be able to get a bit of sleep there,' and he made
for the garden.

All in white, a lumbering figure, his hair awry, his puffy
face a muddy brown, he was almost terrifying. He paused
half-way across the yard. 'You're all wrong about machinery, Nikita. What do you know about machinery? God's
your business. Machinery doesn't stand in our way . . .'

Disrespectfully, Tikhon Vialov bluntly interrupted him:
'Machines have made life dearer and more noisy,' he said.

The only reply was a scornful wave of the hand, as Peter
slowly continued his way to the garden, while Yakov, going
ahead with the pillows, angrily and dismally thought:
'They're my relations—father and uncle—but what are
they to me? They can't help me.'

Peter Artamonov did not offer to put Nikita up, so he
made his quarters in Aunt Olga's house, in the attic. He
assured her: 'I shan't stay long, I'll soon be gone . . .'

He might almost not have been there, and never entered
the house, unless invited. He pottered about the garden,
trimming out dead wood from the trees, crept over the
lawn like a tortoise, rooting out weeds; he seemed to be

shrivelling up, a mass of wrinkles, and spoke very softly to everybody, as if confiding important secrets. He was an unwilling churchgoer, always making the excuse of ill-health, prayed little at home, and did not like religious discussions, plainly wriggling out of them.

Yakov saw he had struck up an intimate friendship with Olga, and that taciturn Mrs. Popov respected him. Even Miron showed no sign of irritation while he heard out his uncle's stories of his wanderings, and about people, although in general, since his father's death, Miron had become still more supercilious and curt, issuing instructions at the works as if he were the senior, and snapping at Yakov as if he were only an employee.

When Nikita's eyes fell on Natalia's shapeless, ruddy face, his expression was just as kind as when he looked at anybody else, but he had less to say to her than to the others—she herself, for that matter, was gradually getting out of the way of talking at all. Her eyes had grown dull and motionless; it was only rarely that a flicker of concern for her husband's health, of fear of Miron, or affectionate pleasure when she caught sight of sober, plump Yakov, appeared in them.

For some reason, Nikita had fallen out with Vialov; they had taken to snarling at one another; though they did not exactly quarrel, they passed each other by like two blind men.

This sombre, angular person, his monkly uncle, had brought yet another shadow into Yakov's life; the very sight of him gave rise to forebodings which weighed Yakov down; the gloomy, imprecise features made him think of death.

Yakov Artamonov viewed everything in his personal life from the superior angle of concern for himself alone, and now cares were growing every day greater, and there were

Bernard Duffield

ever more things to worry him in his intimate affairs. The sensitivity of a man experienced in love matters had begun to tell him that Pauline was cooling towards him, and brave Lieutenant Mavrin confirmed his suspicions. Now whenever he met the lieutenant, the latter merely gave a careless touch of one finger to his cap and screwed up his eyes as if examining some very distant and very small object—whereas formerly he had been much more polite and obliging.

When on occasion in the club he had borrowed from Yakov during card playing, or asked for a little more time to pay back a debt, more than once he had remarked approvingly: 'Artamonov, you've the figure of an artilleryman,' or said something else of a pleasing nature.

Yakov had been flattered by the rather rough good humour of the brave Mavrin, who might have been cast in rubber, and was the wonder of the whole of Dromov on account of his scorn for cold, his agility, his physical strength, and the desperate courage which he certainly possessed. Mavrin would look people straight in the face, his eyes round and hard, and say, in a husky, commanding voice: 'I am a cool person and cannot stand exaggeration.' When he quarrelled with the Postmaster, Dronov, for example, an ailing but spiteful old man, feared by the whole town, Mavrin said to him: 'I will not exaggerate, but you are a senile fool!'

With this suspicion that the lieutenant had become a rival, Yakov Artamonov began to be afraid of meeting him, but he had not the least notion of giving Pauline up to Mavrin—she was becoming more and more attractive to him. At the same time, he more than once gave her a word of warning—'Look out, if I notice anything between you and Mavrin—it's the end!'

Parallel with this developed the nagging worry caused by Noskov. Noskov would lie in wait for Yakov on the outskirts of the town, near the little bridge over the Vatarak-ska; he would suddenly appear as if springing out of the ground, and with the insistence of a creditor—looking into his cap the while—demand money.

There was something strange and unpleasant in the man's always appearing at exactly the same spot, out of a thick growth of nettles, burdock, and other weeds under two crooked willows. Two years ago this had been the site of the house of a gardener named Panfil. Panfil was murdered by an unknown assailant and the house burned down. The willows had been scorched, and the clayey soil, mingled with cinders and ash, was now well trodden down by hop-scotch players. Among the ruins of the brick foundations was a stove, complete with stove-pipe. On clear nights, low in the sky, a greenish star shimmered above the pipe. Without haste, rustling through the nettles, Noskov would come from behind the pipe, slowly drawing his cap from his head.

'I'll be at your service,' he said one night. 'There's a new group of conspirators forming in your works . . .'

'The new group is no business of mine,' Yakov replied with annoyance, and in answer heard Noskov's nagging: 'Of course, you are not the organizer, but nevertheless, it does concern you.'

Time and again in the past, and on this occasion too, Yakov regretted not having killed the man the first time he came up against him. Handing him some money, Yakov said: 'Now, you be more careful!'

'All right.'

'Don't involve me.'

'Why should I? You need not worry.'

'Of course,' Yakov told himself, 'he thinks I am a fool.'

Grasping that Noskov was a useful man, Yakov was nevertheless convinced that that bandy-legged flat-faced youth would not fail to take revenge for the bullet in his leg. That was what he was really after. He would involve him—or with the money he got from him, would bribe one of the workers to murder him. Yakov even imagined that latterly the men had begun to eye him more keenly and with more malice than previously.

Miron more and more frequently said that the men were not in rebellion to improve their conditions, but because the most unseemly, crazy idea was being instilled into them from outside—the idea that they should take command of the banks, the factories, and the whole industry of the country. When he spoke of this, Miron would stretch himself erect, to his full height, and pace the room with his lanky legs, then wriggle his neck and put a finger down his collar—although his neck was thin enough and the collar of his shirt big enough.

'It's no longer a question merely of socialism, but I'm damned if I know what,' he declared once; 'and, what's more, one of the supporters of this fine notion is none other than your own brother Ilia. And our government of old women . . .'

Yakov understood that everything Miron said was intended to convince his listeners—and himself—of his right to a seat in the *Duma*, yet all the same it left a residue of fear in Yakov, which intensified his consciousness of being personally defenceless among hundreds of workers.

One morning he even experienced something very akin to an attack of sheer terror: he was wakened by a hullabaloo in the factory yard. Raising his head from the pillow, against the smooth white wall of the warehouse he saw a seething crowd of shadows, leaping, waving their arms, and seeming to lift the whole building into the air. He came out in a dense sweat, his heart crying out: 'They're rebelling!'

The stream of shadows, which for some reason was more terrible than real people, swiftly vanished, and he realized that it had merely been one of the ordinary Monday fights at the factory gates—there were always fights after a holiday, yet that ominous rush of dark, howling blotches would not leave his memory. Altogether, he became so uneasy that he could not bear to see a newspaper, let alone read it. All that was simple and clear had vanished, and in its place, from all directions, trouble had poured in and new faces.

His sister Tatiana had suddenly appeared from Vorgorod, bringing a fiancé—a skinny, ginger-haired little fellow dressed in engineer's uniform. Light and nimble-footed, and extremely cheerful, he was two years younger than Tatiana, and immediately the whole house, following her example, called him Mitia. He played the guitar and sang, and one song, which he was always singing, seemed to Yakov to be insulting to his sister and also very much upset his mother. The song was to the effect that his wife was *in her grave*, and would the Lord God please *fix his slave* up with a nice place *by way of prize in Paradise*!

But Tatiana was not in the least offended; she found this fellow as entertaining as everybody else did, and even Yakov's mother would quite frequently simper: 'Oh, you song bird, you're a real Pagliacci!'

Mitia could eat like a pigeon—endlessly. Old Peter Artamonov examined him, as if he were a dream, in astonishment, blinked, and said: 'With your make-up, you ought to be a drinker. Do you drink?'

'I do,' this son-in-law replied, and at supper proved that he was a master-drinker.

He had been everywhere: down the Volga, in the Urals, in the Crimea and the Caucasus; he knew innumerable amusing saws, anecdotes, turns of phrase; he seemed to have come from a country of eternal merriment and carefree life.

'How beautiful life is!' he would declare. He immediately found his place in the incessantly revolving wheel of the enterprise. The workers took a liking to him, the young men laughing, the old weavers nodding kindly; even Miron, as he listened to that flow of words sparkling with laughter, would coil his tongue round the smiles which came to his thin lips.

Yakov watched Mitia and Miron when they went over the new shop which was building. They crossed the yard to that fifth finger of the red-brick Artamonov claw which had only just got its grip of the ground: there stood Mitia, amid the scaffolding; the carpenters were busy on planking, their adzes glittering silver; Miron's eye-glasses flashed gold; Miron extended an arm, like a general on an old twopenny print; Mitia nodded and waved his arms too, as if laying out something on the ground.

Yakov too liked his brother-in-law; it was jolly in his company, you forgot things which weighed you down. He even envied Mitia his temperament. Yet at the same time he felt a strange mistrust of the fellow; he had the impression that this man would not last long—to-morrow he would declare himself an actor or a hairdresser or completely vanish as suddenly as he had appeared. Still, he had another good quality—he was clearly not greedy, never inquired what dowry Tatiana would get—though it might be that this concealed a piece of Tatiana's cunning. But their father, sober-minded, grumbled: 'So I've worked for that little ginger fellow . . .'

Miron too got married. 'Allow me to introduce you to my wife,' he said, returning from Moscow, and he pushed forward a blue-eyed, podgy doll with her curly head held askew. She was of toy dimensions, but put together with particular precision, which made her seem to Yakov not a real woman, but something like the china figure mounted

on Uncle Alexey's favourite clock. The head of that figure
had been broken off, and stuck on again a trifle to one side.
The clock stood on the shelf under a mirror, so that the
figurine was turned away from the room, to face the
glass.

Miron announced his wife's name as Anna, and said she
was eighteen, but he omitted to mention that he had acquired a quarter-of-a-million dowry and that she was the
only daughter of a paper manufacturer.

'That's the way to get married,' the father growled, his
red eyes on Yakov. 'And God alone knows what you're
mixed up with. And Ilia we've wiped off the balance-sheet,
he's been a dead loss.'

Peter Artamonov now walked with great difficulty, the
movements of his flabby, obese body painful. Yakov had
the impression that his body made his father angry, and
that he took special care to expose to people, as demonstratively as possible, the oppressive indecency of his senile flesh,
showing himself off in his night clothes, his dressing-gown
loose, his slippers on his bare feet, his flabby breast bare, just
as he had once done to his daughter Elena, to make her
angry. He would on occasion put in an appearance in the
office, and sit there a long time, hindering Yakov with his
complaints—how he had given his whole life to the works
and his children, living his whole existence out choked by
the smoke of cares and harnessed to those granite shafts of
the Artamonov business, with no pleasure at all.

Yakov would hear him out, without saying a word,
observing how all these complaints, which soothed his
father, swelled and exaggerated him in his own eyes to the
dimensions of the church tower—first seen by the morning
sun, before the homes of ordinary men, and the last thing
seen at night. At the same time Yakov drew an instructive

conclusion for himself—there was no sense in living as his father had done.

Further, he always observed that when satiated with complaints, a burning itch, a restless desire to offend other people and make mock of them, would take possession of his father. Peter would go and find his ageing wife, sitting at a window looking into the garden, her useless hands on her knees, her vacant eyes fixed on one point. He would sit down beside her and the itch would begin: 'What are you thinking about? You're big enough, but nobody ever sees you. Your own children never see you. Tatiana has kinder words for the cook than for you. Elena's quite forgotten you, she never comes now, does she? It's obvious she's got a new lover. And where's your Ilia?'

But bullyragging his wife was dull. Her purple face was easily sweated into tears, which seemed to be exuded, not only from her eyes, but from every pore of the tight-drawn skin of her cheeks and the flabby double chin, oozing out too from about her ears.

'Oh, dry up,' the old man would growl scornfully, and, waving his arms at her as if driving smoke away, would leave her. There was no amusement to be found there.

He never bullyragged Yakov, but Yakov had the impression that his father looked at him with a painful sort of pity. He would sigh and say: 'Oh, you vacant-eyed block!'

Miron was untouchable in this way, and Peter Artamonov quite obviously kept timorously out of his way—Yakov saw that quite clearly. Miron was generally feared, both at the works and at home, from his mother and his china wife down to Grishka the page-boy. When Miron crossed the yard his long shadow seemed to create silence about itself.

Nor was there any pleasure to be had from mocking his ginger-haired son-in-law. Mitia was quite good at mocking himself, and clearly liked to get in the first blow. Tatiana was now pregnant, and swelled enormously, pouting her lips with importance, lying down after dinner, reading three books at once, then going out for walks, with her husband trotting at her heels like a poodle.

The senior Artamonov would then have the carriage brought round and go to town to bullyrag Nikita and Tikhon Vialov. Yakov heard it all many times.

'Well, Mr. Monkly Student, ferreted out God yet?'—he would force himself on Nikita, and Nikita's hump would writhe, while he stroked his knees with his hands and pitiably muttered: 'Oh, why must you . . .'

'What do you mean—why must I? You're dressed wrong, you're falsely got up. From top to bottom. You're no monk.'

'That concerns my own conscience.'

'Taking snuff? No, you've lost, you made a mistake. You should have married a poor girl in good time, an orphan, and she would gratefully have borne you children, and you'd be a grandfather like me to-day. But you let yourself . . . remember . . . ?'

Slowly, like a huge tortoise, Nikita would creep away, and then Peter would go in to Olga, and tell her stories of Alexey's debauches at the Nizhny Fair. Even this afforded him no amusement. After her husband's death the little old lady became infected with restlessness, always on her feet, moving furniture about, shifting things from one place to another, peering out of the window. As she went about she held her head stiffly, and though the thick-pebbled spectacles were always on her nose, she lived by feel, prodding the floor with her stick, groping in front of herself with her right hand. And whatever nasty story the old man told, her answer was the same: 'Say what you like, no mud would stick on the Alexey I knew, and there's nothing good to be added.'

'He was right about you,' Peter told her, 'you see with only one eye.'

'I scarcely see with either,' she said. 'I see so badly, I broke his favourite porcelain mug yesterday.'

Peter tried to bullyrag Tikhon Vialov, but that was not easy either. Tikhon never lost his temper; he would look away, grunting from time to time, or giving unruffled, terse replies.

'You're living a long time,' Peter Artamonov said to him one day.

Vialov answered sensibly: 'Men do live longer.'

'But let's hear what you've lived your life for? Come on, speak up!'

'Everybody lives his own way.'

'Of course—but everybody doesn't spend his whole life sweeping yards and clearing away rubbish . . .'

Vialov had his own ideas. 'You come into the world, so you go on, till you die,' he said.

But Peter paid no attention to what he said, he went on: 'Now, you've spent your whole life broom in hand. You've neither wife nor children, and no worries either. What's the purpose of it? My father used to offer you other work, but you wouldn't take it, you refused it. What's the meaning of your stubbornness?'

'You're late with your question, Mr. Peter,' replied Vialov, looking away.

Peter began to lose his temper; he insisted: 'Just think how many people made their pile in your lifetime. Everybody trying to do better for themselves, get a bit of money together . . .'

'*Kopil, kopil, da chorta i koupil,*' Vialov punned, playing with the words with biting sarcasm—'Get a bit of money, yes, and then buy the devil . . .'

Yakov quite expected his father to fly into a rage and

blaspheme at Vialov, but the old man was silent for some moments, then muttered something under his breath and turned his back on the yardman.

Though gradually breaking up—bald and all of one earthy sort of hue—Vialov, since he refused to give way to any of the artifices of old age, was still as sound physically as he had been; he had even acquired a certain nobility of bearing, and spoke with more importance, in an instructive manner. Yakov thought he seemed to carry himself more like the *master* of it all than did the real master.

Concerning himself, it was becoming clear to Yakov that he was superfluous in the family, where the only pleasant person was a complete stranger,—Mitia Longinov. He did not find Mitia either stupid or clever—he would not fit into either of these categories, but stood out as one by himself. His importance was confirmed by the attitude Miron adopted towards him; Miron the hard-headed and authoritative, who had bossed them all, lived on comradely terms with Mitia, and though they frequently failed to agree, they never quarrelled—they even argued cautiously. In the home, from morn to night, there was one call to be heard, in many voices—Tatiana crying 'Mitia!' his mother asking, 'Where's Mitia?'—even his father leaning out of the window, shouting, 'Mitia, time for dinner!'

Mitia scurried about the works like a fox, and with his nimble brush, with comical words and merry quips, managed to wipe away the traces of Miron's biting severity with workers and office staff alike. He called the workers '*brothers*'.

'Here, brother, that's not the way!' he would say to a stolid bearded carpenter-foreman, and drag from his pocket a little red-leather notebook and a pencil—or he would sketch something on a plank and say: 'See? All right? And then—so—get me? Ready?'

'That's right enough,' the foreman would agree, 'of course, we've been doing everything the old way . . .'

'Won't do, my dear chap, we've got to get used to the new way, it's more profitable.'

The foreman agreed. 'That's right enough.'

In the dashing way he attacked the work, Mitia resembled Yakov's Uncle Alexey, except that there was no proprietorial greed noticeable in him. In his tendency to play the fool about things, he was very much like the old carpenter, Seraphim—as Peter Artamonov himself observed. There was an occasion one day at supper—Mitia has just smoothed out and dispersed a disputatious atmosphere at table. Peter smiled and growled: 'Ugh, we used to have another Comforter—Seraphim . . . Upon my word!'

On another occasion Yakov heard that after one of the usual clashes between his father and Miron, Mitia had said to Miron: 'The combination of something petty and both disgusting and terrible, with something pitiable—is a purely Russian sort of chemistry!' following this without a pause by these soothing words: 'No matter, though, it'll soon be forgotten and altered. We're improving . . .'

One Sunday evening, at tea in the garden, the old man had complained that *he* had had no sort of holiday,—when there was his son-in-law, flying up like a rocket, with a golden tail of sparkling words: 'That's all your own fault, and nobody else's. Man makes his own holidays. Life's like a beautiful woman—it needs presents, entertainment and, all sorts of relaxations—you have to enjoy living. A man can always find something, every day, to delight him.'

He went on at some length, and skilfully—as if playing a pipe—the whole table spellbound. It was always the same —when Mitia spoke up, everybody was motionless. Even Yakov felt the spell of his pronouncements, saw there was real truth in them, though he would all the same have liked to ask Mitia why he married a stupid, ugly girl like Tatiana.

In Mitia's attitude towards his wife Yakov detected a false note—he was too tender, his concern for her was excessive. It seemed to Yakov that Tatiana too felt the falsity of it; she was always gloomy and taciturn, too easily irritated, and much more often conversed with Miron about politics, and with more animation, than her cheerful husband. Politics were her only subject.

There were times when Yakov would think it was a mistake to imagine that Mitia Longinov had originated in some cheerful, carefree land; rather had he appeared from some dark, miserable pit, and by sheer force managed to reach people he did not know, and then, out of delight at having succeeded in struggling through to them, was dancing before them and entertaining them, full of admiration and amazement at their plenty. It was in Mitia's air of astonishment that Yakov found a rather idiotic strain—he was like a child standing astonished in a toy shop, except that the child would be more intelligent, and distinguish at once which were the better toys.

Among them all—that is, the family circle and the factory community as well—there were two who definitely did not like Tatiana's husband: Uncle Nikita and Tikhon Vialov. When Yakov one day asked him what he thought of Mitia, the yardman calmly replied: 'Not trustworthy.'

'How?'

'Like a fly. He'll alight on any muck.'

Yakov most persistently, and for a long time, cross-examined the old man, but could get nothing more precise out of him: 'You'll see, Mr. Yakov,' he declared. 'Why, look, the man invents shapes.'

His uncle—the monk—said almost the same: 'He makes a lot of dust,' Nikita said with a sigh. 'I've seen many a chatter-box like that in my time. They muddle people. They muddle themselves with their own tongues in the end. You say *peace* to him and he'll start jabbering about *peas* and *beans* . . .'

It was strange to hear the gentle little cripple talking so angrily, almost bitterly, not at all like himself. Still more surprising was this unanimity between Vialov and his uncle concerning Tatiana's husband—otherwise the old men never agreed, there was a sort of open, if silent conflict between them, they hardly ever spoke, but avoided each other. In this, once again, Yakov saw that human stupidity of which he was so sick. How could two men whom death would mow down any day fail to agree?

Uncle Nikita was dying. Yakov would have said that his father was most heartily trying to assist him in it—nearly every time the two met, Peter would maul and crush the old monk with reproaches. 'I have spent all my life in the world, slaving like an ox—you, snug as a tom-cat. Everybody's concerned to see you're nicely warm and softly bedded, and even don't seem to see your hump. I'm reckoned to hate everybody—*Me*, when all my life . . .'

Drawing his head into his hump, and clearing his throat, Nikita said: 'Don't be so angry.'

A feeling of scorn for his father, for that bare chest—it might have been moulded from lathered soap, with its mould of grizzled hair—also darkened Yakov's life; it was a feeling difficult to hide. There were times when he had to remind himself by force that the old man was his father, to whom he owed life. But this of course did not improve the old man, nor quench Yakov's sense of scorn for him, in which there was a mortifying element of degradation.

His father drove down to Dromov practically every day, as if he wanted to be able to see Nikita actually meet his death. Moving with difficulty, out of breath, the eldest of the Artamonovs would mount the stairs to the attic and sit down at Nikita's bedside, staring at him with inflamed red eyes. Nikita would not say a word, merely cough faintly from time to time, his leaden gaze fixed on the ceiling. His hands were restless now, jerking at his cassock, stripping something invisible from the cloth. Sometimes his cough would choke him, and he would get up.

'The death rattle?' Peter would ask.

Nikita crept to the window, clutching at his brother's shoulders, the head of the bed, the chairs. His cassock hung loose on him, like a sail on a broken mast. He sat down by the window, mouth opened wide, and gazed beneath him at the garden and beyond, in the distance—at the sombre, angrily bristling forest.

'You take a bit of rest,' Peter said, and plucked at the lobe of his ear. Then he went down and informed Olga that now it wouldn't be long, the death rattle had begun.

A stout monk, Father Mardary, came and tried to get them to send Nikita to the Priory—according to some ecclesiastical regulation, he should die there, and nowhere else, and must also be buried there. But the hunchback had his way with Olga. 'You'll take me there after, when I'm gone,' he said. Pitifully, too, he begged, on three occasions: 'Please have my coffin made with a high lid, so it doesn't press on me. Don't forget, please!'

He died four days before the 1914 war began. The evening before, he had asked them to inform the Priory. 'Let them come to take me—I shall have time to die just before they get here.'

On the morning of his death, Yakov helped his father climb up to the attic. Peter, crossing himself, fixed his gaze on the dark, ashen features, the half-closed eyes, the drooping mouth. Unnaturally loud, Nikita said: 'Forgive me.'

'Whatever do you mean? For what?' Peter Artamonov growled.

'My brazen ways . . .'

'You forgive me,' the elder said. 'More than once, lately, I've made fun of you . . .'

'God will never condemn that,' Nikita assured him, in a whisper.

After a moment's silence Peter said: 'So that's that. How do you feel now? How's it going?'

'I had forgotten,' Nikita suddenly began, speaking quickly. 'Yakov, my boy—tell Tikhon to take down that maple by the summer-house, it'll never do, I'm sure . . .'

Yakov found this unnecessarily clear voice, and the sight of the bones of that chest stuck up so inhumanly, like the corner of a wooden box, quite unbearable. There was in fact nothing at all that was human left in that little heap of immobile bones draped in black, or in those hands clasping a cross of beaten brass. He was sorry for his uncle, but nevertheless could not help wondering what was the purpose of this custom of old men—or any relations—dying in front of the rest of the household.

Lingering a while, in case Nikita still had something to say, at last Peter left, holding Yakov's arm, his head silently sunk on his breast. Once downstairs he said: 'He *is* dying.'

'Oh yes?' said Miron, who was seated at the table, concealing half of himself behind a huge page of newspaper. He did not even look up as he put his question—then tossed the newspaper down on the table and turned to his wife and said: 'I was right—just read it!'

His round little wife rolled quickly up to the table, and their mother, sitting by the window, said, with great alarm: 'Not really, Miron, not really war?'

'That will be the second for us,' Peter said loudly.

'All lies, of course,' declared Miron to his wife—or

303

Yakov, who also had now bent over the newspaper, reading the alarming telegrams, and puzzling how all that could affect him.

Peter Artamanov, waving his hand as if to say don't bother me with all that, went outside. The sun had made the cobble stones so warm that he could feel the heat through the soft soles of his cloth boots. Through the window he could hear Miron's dry voice laying down the law. Yakov from the window, where he was examining the paper, saw his father raise a purple fist, threatening someone.

Two days later, early one morning, the monks arrived; there were seven of them, of all possible sizes and girths, though to Yakov they looked all the same, like so many newborn children, except that one of them seemed to have no face at all. He was the tallest of them, and very thin, with an extremely dense beard and a voice which was not at all fitting to the occasion, either in its loudness or its cheerfulness; he went in front of the others, carrying a black cross; he was bald and his nose seemed to have run all over his cheeks—the only other marks on his face were a pair of dark little pittings placed midway between the bald pate and the beard. He walked raising his feet so slowly, he might have been blind; he produced three different voices as he chanted:

'*O Holy God*,' came from deep down, nearly bass; '*O Holy and Mighty*,' came higher, more like a tenor; then '*Holy and Immortal One, have mercy on us*,' came in such a penetrating high-pitched voice that the little boys, who were keeping just in front of the procession, stared in amazement at the beard which could contain such an invisible triple-voiced mouth.

When the procession had turned out of the street on to the square, they found it packed with the citizens of Dromov, the militia reserve, Lieutenant Mavrin's command, a sprinkling of the town administration, with the priesthood in the centre of the crowd. Monumental, in parade style, the brave lieutenant stood in front of his men, in full sunlight; the priests and the deacons were like conical gilded statues, in their gold mantles, which melted and flowed in the sunlight, the reflection of their robes casting additional light on Lieutenant Mavrin. In front of a lectern was a fat officer with a tiny head, dancing about and brandishing his forage cap.

The triple-voiced monk flourished his black cross, came to a stop at the wall of humanity, and in his bass voice commanded: 'Make way!'

The crowd did not make way for him, but for the tall, red horse of Ekke, the assistant chief of police. Waving a white glove in the air, Ekke bore down on the monk, manoeuvred his horse athwart the street and cried out in injured, reproachful tones: 'Where are you going? Can't you see? Turn back!'

The monk raised his cross. '*Holy Go-o* . . .' he began.

'Hour-ah!' yelled the officer, and the whole crowd, with a thousand throats, yelled madly: 'Hour-rahhh!'

Ekke rose in his stirrups, and shouted: 'Mr. Artamanov, if you please, go by the side street! Make a detour! Mr. Miron, I beg you! To-day's the National Manifestation—what are you thinking of?'

Peter, from his position by the head of the coffin, where he stood, supported by Natalia and Yakov, took one look up into the wooden features of Ekke, then grimly turned to the monks acting as bearers: 'Please turn back, Fathers . . .' he said, then adding with a sob: 'Clearly the last time I give any orders . . .'

To Yakov all this seemed most unseemly, if not a trifle ridiculous. But when they had turned into the side street, which happened to be the one in which Pauline lived, there was Pauline herself striding rapidly towards the funeral procession. She was all in white, with a pink sunshade—hastily making the sign of the cross over her prominent, tightly gloved bosom.

'Off to admire Mavrin,' he thought at once, and was so infuriated that he sucked in a good mouthful of dust.

The monks increased their pace, the black-bearded one chanting more softly, pensively—the choir had ceased altogether. Outside the town, exactly opposite the slaughter house gates, stood a peculiar kind of farm waggon, covered with a black cloth, a pair of piebald horses in the shafts. They laid the coffin in this waggon and began the service of the dead, while from the street behind them, as out of a funnel, came the triumphant roar of brass as the band played: 'God Save the Tsar,' the bells of the three churches pealed and a dusty, smoky roar of 'Hourah!' welled over it all.

Yakov thought he could catch Lieutenant Mavrin commanding: 'St . . . and . . . ea . . . syyyy!'

After the service they had to go back to his aunt's, and sit endlessly at the wake table, listening to his father grousing: 'I wonder what fool had the waggon wait opposite the slaughterhouse?'

'The police, the police,'—Mitia tried to calm him, explaining—'it was a bit awkward, you see, with the national manifestation on, to have a hearse come by—it would have been out of keeping . . .'

Licking the smile from his lips, Miron turned to Doctor Yakovliev, who was always in the front place on trying-difficult occasions. 'But if we all put our guts into it, like Mitka in *Prince Serebriany* . . . After all, everything in this world is decided by the relationship of forces . . .'

'By technical knowledge,' the doctor objected.

'Technical knowledge? Well, yes . . . only . . .'

It was not till after nine that evening that Yakov was able to get out of that tiresome atmosphere and run round to see Pauline—full of an alarm such as he had never hitherto experienced, with the foreboding that something unusual was going to happen. Of course, it did.

'Ohhh!' Pauline's cook cried out when Yakov strode across the yard and entered the kitchen—and with that cry sank in a heap on the seat by the stove.

'You miserable pimp!' Yakov replied, and halted at the door into the sitting-room, his ear taking in precise military steps and a familiar military voice. 'So there you are, you must decide—one way, or the other. Come on!'

'He's talking formally in the plural,' Yakov considered, 'perhaps nothing has happened yet.'

But when he had opened the door, and stood on the threshold, he could see immediately that everything had already happened—the brave lieutenant stood with beetling brow in the middle of the room, his tunic unbuttoned, his hands in his pockets, his braces showing, one button undone; Pauline was seated on her bed, one leg thrown over the other, the stocking on one leg concertinaed, her bold eyes unusually round, and her face slowly turning purple.

'What does this mean, sir?' demanded the brave lieutenant, thus finally confirming all Yakov's suspicions. Yakov took one step forward, threw his cap down on a chair and in a breaking voice he could not recognize said: 'I've come from the funeral . . . the funeral supper . . .'

'Indeed,' was the lieuteant's respon, questioningly, and in the tone of one who is master of the house. Pauline took such a deep breath that her cigarette sputtered. Then, as she puffed out the smoke, she said—but not guiltily, rather offhandedly: 'Mr. Mavrin is trying to persuade me to join the sisters of mercy—to nurse the wounded.'

'Sisters of mercy? Not half!' Yakov brought out ironically. Then the brave lieutenant stepped up to him, and asked very clearly: 'What does that sneer mean? May I ask you not to forget that I do not like exaggeration. I cannot bear it.'

In these two or three minutes Yakov had felt as if burning currents of mortification and rage had passed right through him, leaving him with the crushing, almost distressing certainty that this little woman was as indispensable to him as any part of his own body, and that he could not allow her to be torn from him. That realization brought back his wrath in a flash—he went cold all over and rose to his feet—thrusting his hands in his pockets he warned the lieutenant: 'Keep your distance!' feeling his own eyes bulging out till they pained him.

'And why, may I ask?' the lieutenant demanded, and took another step. He had a disgusting trick of doubling his consonants and separating one syllable from another, which Yakov had always disliked, but now it made him mad—he made to pull one hand from his pocket as he shouted: 'I'll kill you!'

Lieutenant Mavrin seized the wrist of that hand and crushed it painfully—the revolver went off in Yakov's pocket, then with a blinding stab of pain Yakov's arm seemed to snap at the elbow, his hand came out of his pocket, the lieutenant took the revolver from his fingers, flung it into an armchair, and said: 'Didn't come off!'

'Yasha, Yasha!' Yakov heard a loud whisper, 'Mr. Mavrin—gentlemen, are you both mad? What is this about? This is really impossible. What on earth for?'

'Well?' the brave lieutenant said, in a deafening voice, grabbing Yakov by the beard and tugging it down, so as to make Yakov bow to him: 'Ask my pardon, you fool!'

With every syllable he gave the beard a tug, then with a light blow on the chin made Yakov raise his head again.

'*Oi*, shame, shame, *oi*!' whispered Pauline, grabbing the lieutenant by the elbow.

Yakov could not move his right arm, but he gritted his teeth and pushed the lieutenant off with his left; he bellowed, and tears of humiliation streamed down his cheeks.

'Don't you dare lay your hands on me!' barked the lieutenant. He gave Yakov a hard shove, so that Yakov plumped into the armchair, on to his own revolver.

He covered his face with his arms, to hide his tears, and sank into a half-faint, through the din inside his head, scarcely hearing Pauline's cries.

'Dear God, how common! You, of all people. Such behaviour. And why?'

'Go to hell, Missie,' the lieutenant said, in a cast-iron sort of voice. 'Here's a ruble for your services—I'm through! I cannot stand exaggeration, and you are simply a common little trollop. . . .'

With this, Lieutenant Mavrin stamped heavily out of the room, banged the door, and was gone, leaving in his trail the faint tinkle of the glass of the hanging lamp and a broken squeal from Pauline. Yakov stood up, his legs giving way, his whole body quivering, as if from cold. In the centre of the room, under the lamp, stood Pauline, her mouth open, sobbing and staring at the dirty little piece of paper in her hand.

'You dirty little bitch!' cried Yakov. 'What did you do it for? And all your talk . . . You deserve killing . . .'

The woman shot him a glance, threw down the note and in astonishment brought out: 'What a rotter!'

She sank into the chair, doubled herself up, clutching her head in her hands, while Yakov thumped on her

shoulder, shouting: 'Out of the way! Let me get my
revolver!'

Without stirring, still in amazement, she asked him: 'You
love me so much?'

'I detest you!'

'No . . . you love me now!'

She leapt at him so swiftly that Yakov had no time to
ward her off. She flung her arms round his neck and with
savage purposefulness seared him all over 'with biting
kisses, breathing heavily into his eyes and mouth and
whispering: 'No, no, you love me. And I love you . . . my
dear, soft, Salty-pie.'

Salty-pie was her pet petting word, which she only used
when she was very much worked up, and it always went to
Yakov's head, calling out a specially sensual, yet tender
savagery in him. So it was this time—he crushed her,
pinched her, kissed her, muttering, breathless: 'You bag-
gage. You little trollop. When you knew . . .'

An hour later he was sitting on the bed and she was
lying on his knees; he was rocking her, and in thought
marvelling how rapidly it was all past. She was saying
drowsily: 'I went all bitter, I wanted to throw you over.
You were always bothered about your family and your
funerals—it was so dull. And I never knew whether you
really loved me. Now you will love me more and you'll
be jealous, because, when there's jealousy . . .'

'If we could only get away from this place . . .' said
Yakov wearily.

'Yes . . . to Paris . . . I know French.'

They had not lit the lamp and the room was dark and
stifling; outside soldiers of the reserve and women were
shouting, though it was late, past midnight.

'Now we couldn't go abroad, because of the war,' Yakov
recalled. 'Damn the war!'

The woman began her thoughts again. 'Only dogs love without jealousy. If you think, all plays and novels are made of jealousy . . .'

Yakov gave a smile and a start. 'Lucky the way that gun went off,' he said; 'it might have hit me in the leg, but there's only a hole in my trousers.'

Pauline stuck her finger through the hole then, with a sudden sob, and subdued, but intense malice said: 'Oh, how sorry I am you did not manage to shoot him. Right in his hard rubber belly.'

'Don't say that!' said Yakov, and gave her a good shake, but she went on hissing, just as bitterly: 'The scoundrel! The things he said to me! Oh, you men, you don't know a thing about women!' Turning back her swollen lips and revealing her tight-clenched foxy teeth she completed her thought: 'Because even if a woman is unfaithful, it doesn't in the least mean that she has stopped loving you.'

'Stop, I tell you,' cried Yakov, and squeezed her to him so hard that she groaned. 'Oi, now I feel you do love me . . . Yasha, my Salty-pie. . .'

He left her at daybreak, stepping lightly, with the feeling of a man who has played a dangerous game and won something of great value. This tranquil holiday which had come in his heart was further strengthened when, asking Pauline, as he left, for the revolver she had hidden, she refused to give it up.

He was forced to tell her that he was afraid to go without it. He told her all about Noskov. Her alarm afforded him great pleasure, and the concern she showed convinced him that he really was precious to her, beloved to her. With many cries and much gesticulation she reproached him for never having confided in her before. Then, still troubled, thinking aloud, she said: 'Of course, it's very interesting, too, his being a detective. There's Sherlock Holmes, for example, have you read about him? But I suppose even detectives in Russia are also scoundrels?'

'Of course,' Yakov confirmed.

When she did let him have the revolver, she insisted on making sure he could shoot well, and persuaded him to fire a shot into the opened door of the stove. To do this, Yakov had to lie down on the floor; she lay down with him. He fired, and there was an angry puff of ash from the stove. Pauline gasped out and rolled away, then, raising her hand, said in a hushed voice: 'Look!' In the painted part there was a deep little oblique hole. 'And when you just think that was death!' she said, with a sigh, frowning her sharply pencilled brows.

Never before had Yakov seen her so charming, or felt her so near to him. There had been a look of childlike wonder in her while he told her about Noskov, not a trace of evil on her keen, youthful features. 'She doesn't feel any guilt,' Yakov had said to himself. He was amazed, but also pleased.

As she saw him off she had stroked his beard and murmured: 'Oh, Yasha, Yasha . . . So that's how it stands, is it? We're serious. Oh, heavens! . . . But that scoundrel!' She clenched both her fists in one and shook them with indignation. 'Oh God, how many scoundrels there are!' she cried. Then all at once she seized Yakov's hand, frowned as if in thought and said softly: 'No, just a moment—there's a young lady in the picture—oh, of course!' Her whole face lit up, she made the sign of the cross over him, and—'Off you go, Salty-Pie!' she said.

It was a rather cold morning with heavy dew; the day-break breeze blew up, the greenish-pearly sky was redolent with apples.

'Of course, she deceived me like that out of spite, and I

ought to marry her as soon as father dies,' Yakov mag-
nanimously told himself—when a curious thing Seraphim
had once said to him came to his mind: 'Every lass', the old
man had said, 'if she's drowning, will clutch at a straw.
That's when to catch her!'

The brave lieutenant came into his mind, and disturbed
him—but Mavrin was no straw. He had been very angry,
and would no doubt do something nasty. But he was sure
to be sent to the front. Yakov was even calmer now concerning Noskov, though he did keep looking suspiciously
about him, ears alert, hand gripping the revolver butt in his
pocket—it was just at this time of day that Noskov most
often waylaid him.

About two weeks later his fear of Noskov enveloped
him again in a dense cloud. On Sunday he was inspecting
the trees they had bought for felling from Voroponov,
when he caught sight of the trapper making his way through
the thick undergrowth; he was strung with his gear, a sack
at his back.

'A fortunate meeting for us both,' Noskov said, as he
came up, and doffed his cap. He wore this now soldier-
fashion, cocked down over his right eye; to take it off he
did not grasp the peak but the top.

Without answering this strange greeting, in which he
sensed a threat, Yakov gritted his teeth and nervously
clutched the gun in his pocket. Noskov too remained silent
for some moments, picking at the lining of his cap, without
looking up at Yakov.

'Well?' asked Yakov Artamonov. Noskov's dog-like
eyes looked up. Drawing his hand over his stiff, bristly hair,
he brought out, very precisely: 'Your love, I mean Miss
Pauline, has struck up acquaintance with the daughter of
the Reverend Sladkopevtzev, now you tell her to drop it.'

'Why?'

'Because . . .' And, listening a moment to the sound of the town bells, the trapper added: 'I'm giving you a piece of advice from the heart, wishing you well. And you can give me some little rubles . . .' He shot a glance at the sky, reckoning—'Thirty-five,' he said.

'I ought to shoot the dog down,' Yakov Artamonov said to himself, as he counted out the money.

The trapper took the notes, swung about on his bandy legs, with a jangle of his traps, and, without putting on his cap, plunged back into the undergrowth. Yakov felt the fellow had become still more irksomely repellent.

'Noskov!' he called softly, and when the man halted, half hidden by the arms of the firs, he said: 'You ought to drop all this!'

'For what reason?' Noskov demanded, thrusting his head forward, and Yakov caught a glint in the man's eyes either of some kind of fear or of evil.

'It's a dangerous business,' Yakov explained.

'You have to know how,' Noskov said, and his eyes went dull. 'If you don't know how, anything's dangerous.'

'As you will.'

'You're talking against your own advantage.'

'Where's the advantage, with this feud,' muttered Yakov, sorry now he had tried to talk to the spy, only an idiot would do it.

Noskov said sagely: 'Men can't live without it. Everybody has his own feud, his own necessity. So long!'

He turned his back on Yakov and plunged into the dense greenery of the firs. Yakov listened for some moments to the man forcing his rustling way between the prickly branches, and the dry brushwood crackling, then returned hastily to the ride where his chaise was awaiting him and drove straight into town, to Pauline.

'There's a scoundrel!' Pauline cried, almost with pleasure

as well as surprise. 'He's already found out that she comes to see me. Just think!'

'Why do you make friends with people like that?' Yakov reproached her, with annoyance, but she got annoyed too, and plucking at the scarf of yellow muslin she was wearing at her neck, began to lecture him: 'First of all, I have to, for your sake. Secondly, would you rather I kept cats, or dogs, or a Mavrin? Here I live, all alone, as if I were in prison, nobody to go out with, and she's very interesting, she fetches me novels and magazines, and she follows politics and tells me everything. We went to school at Mrs. Popov's together, only we had quarrelled . . .'

She drummed on his shoulder with one finger, then went on, still more indignantly: 'Do you think it's easy being a secret mistress? She says a mistress is like a pair of goloshes, you only want her when it's muddy, so there! She's having an affair with your doctor, and they don't hide it, but you treat me as if I was a sort of ailment; you're ashamed, as if I were hump-backed or lopsided, whereas I'm not at all misshapen . . .'

'Do be patient,' Yakov said, 'and I'll marry you! I really mean it, though you are a dirty . . .'

'And that's a question, which of us is the dirtier,' she cried, then burst into childish laughter at the unwitting pun she had made, as the words might also have meant 'which of us is the more at fault'. 'My tongue's tied in knots,' she ran on. 'My Salty-pie . . . darling, you're not greedy . . . Some people wouldn't have said a word . . . After all, the detective's useful to you . . .'

As usual, Yakov left her in a mollified frame of mind. A week later, early in the morning, the sign-painter Elagin, a pock-marked little man with a crooked nose, brought the news that at daybreak, when some weavers were drag-netting for fish, one of them, Mordvinov, had nearly drowned himself trying to save Noskov the trapper, and was now in the infirmary.

When he heard this miserable story. Yakov stretched out his legs, so as to be able to hide his hands deeper in his pockets, they were shaking so.

'They've done him in,' he said to himself, but, picturing good-natured Mordvinov, with his soft, womanish face, could not believe the man would kill anybody. 'It's a lucky accident,' he told himself, heaving a sigh of relief.

Pauline was of the same opinion—it was a lucky accident. 'Of course, that was the best thing,' she said solemnly, with a frown, 'because, if they had done it any other way, there would have been a fuss.' But she was also sorry because: 'It would have been more interesting to catch him and make him repent, than hang or shoot him. Have you read . . .'

'You're talking nonsense, Polly,' he cut her short.

A number of tranquil days followed. Yakov made some trips to Vorgorod, and then Miron returned, his brow overcast, full of worry. 'We've had another fishy business,' he said. 'Ekke's received instructions from up top to make an inquiry into the circumstances in which that trapper fellow was drowned. He's arrested Mordvinov, Kiriakov, and that clown, Krotov the stoker—the whole band who went fishing with the trapper. Mordvinov's face was all scratched and one ear torn. They suspect a political motive. . . . Not the torn ear, of course . . .'

He paused by the piano, balancing his pince-nez on one finger, and peering into the corner. In creased Swedish tunic, brown trousers and dusty knee-boots, he was like an engine-tender; his clean-shaven bony cheeks and close-clipped moustaches suggested a military man; his rather immobile features scarcely changed, whatever he was saying, or whatever his mood.

'A crazy time, this is,' he said pensively. 'Here we are plunging into a new war. We're going to war, as usual, to take our attention off our own stupidity; we can't fight that, we're too feeble. Yet our only problems are really internal ones. The workers' party in a peasant country dreams of seizing power! In the ranks of that party is a son of the burgher class—Ilia Artamanov—born in the class destined to accomplish the great task of bringing about the industrial and technical Europeanization of our country. Folly upon folly! Treachery to the interests of one's own class should be punishable as a capital offence—in fact, as high treason . . . I can understand your intellectual like Goritzvetov, who has no obligations at all, and nothing to do with himself, because he's no brains and is incapable of working, so all he can do is read and jabber—altogether, as I see it, revolutionary activity in Russia is the only thing for men with no brains to occupy themselves with . . .'

Miron was talking as if he had a room full of people in front of him; he screwed up his eyes more and more, till he had entirely closed them. Yakov stopped listening to what he was saying, and thought of his own affairs: what would be the end of the inquiry into Noskov's death—how might it affect him?

Miron's pregnant wife, bulky as a chest of drawers, came into the room. She gave him one glance, and said wearily: 'Off you go, and change your clothes!' Miron humbly stuck his pince-nez back on his nose and went.

About a month later all the arrested men were released. Severely, in tones which brooked no discussion, Miron ordered Yakov to pay them off, all of them. Long since, without noticing it, Yakov had got into the way of submitting to all his cousin's dry commands. It was really rather to his advantage, since it diminished his responsibility for the factory affairs. But now he said: 'We ought to keep on the stoker.'

'Why?'

'He's a cheerful fellow, and he's been with us a long time; he keeps the men amused.'

'Does he? Very well, then, let's keep him.' Miron moistened his lips. 'You're right, clowns are useful.'

For some time it seemed to Yakov that on the whole things were running smoothly. The war had subdued the men. Everybody was more thoughtful, quieter. But Yakov had grown accustomed to trouble, and had a foreboding that his worries were not at an end—indeed, he hazily expected new ones.

He did not have to wait very long. Nesterenko reappeared in Dromov, with a tall woman resembling Mrs. Popov. Meeting Yakov in the street, Nesterenko looked right through him till he got nearer, then went up to him, exchanged greetings, and said: 'Could you drop in and see me in an hour's time? I'm staying with my father-in-law My wife's dying, you know. So please don't come to the front door, it would disturb her—come in the back way.'

It was a troubling hour, an unnaturally long hour, and when at last Yakov Artamanov wearily took a seat on a chair in a room lined with bookcases, Nesterenko, in a low voice, his ear on the alert for something, said: 'Well, my dear sir, so they bumped our friend off. No doubt about it, though it couldn't be proved. A neat job, worthy of praise. Now listen here: the lady of your heart, Miss Pauline Nazarov, is acquainted with Miss Sladkopevtzev, and Miss Sladkopevtzev was arrested in Vorgorod the other day! Am I right about the acquaintance?'

'I don't know,' Yakov replied, and immediately came out in a sweat. The gendarmerie officer put his finger to his nose, then examined his nails and said:, very calmly 'You do know.'

'I believe she does know her.'

'Exactly.'

'What can he want?' Yakov wondered, slyly examining the flat, grey face with its little red veins, its squat nose, and dull eyes, from which intense boredom seemed to drip, and run in sharp little trickles of liquory breath.

'I'm talking to you off the record, as a friend who wishes you well, and who isn't foreign to your business interests,' Yakov heard the hoarse voice say. 'You see, this is what I have in mind, my dear—er—marksman . . .' He grinned, then, after a moment's pause, went on to explain: 'I say *marksman* because I happen to know of another case of your being unsuccessful in handling firearms. So now, you see— there's Miss Sladkopevtzev acquainted with Miss Pauline Nazarov, the lady of your heart. Now, just put two and two together—the particular line of activity of the trapper, Noskov, could have been known to nobody but yourself and myself. I am excluded from this chain of acquaintanceship. Noskov was no fool, even if he was slack and . . .'

Nesterenko sighed and looked under his chair. 'Nothing is eternal. But we still have . . . you . . .'

Yakov Artamonov felt that Nesterenko's mouth was emitting not words, but fine, invisible little threads, which lapped round his neck and choked him so sharply that there was a cold at his heart, which was ceasing to beat, while all about him was swaying and howling like a winter blizzard.

Meanwhile, Nesterenko continued with deliberate slowness: 'I think—I am almost sure—you have allowed yourself a certain lack of caution in your speech, don't you think so? Now just try to recall it!'

'No,' Yakov said, very quietly, fearing his voice would give him away.

'Really?' Nesterenko demanded, and spread his moustaches with gestures of his beefy fingers.

'No,' Yakov repeated, shaking his head.

'Strange. Very strange. But it can still be put right. Listen to me: Noskov's place must be taken by a man just like him—useful to you. A man called Minaiev will report to you—you'll take him on—all right?'

'Very well,' said Yakov.

'That's all. Matter terminated. Be careful, please. Not a word to any fair ladies—not one syllable. Understand?'

'He talks to me as if I were a child, or a fool,' Yakov said to himself. Meanwhile the gendarmerie officer had begun talking about the nearness of the autumn migration of some birds, of the war, and of his wife's illness, saying that his sister was now looking after her.

'Only, we must be prepared for the worst,' Nesterenko declared, taking hold of the ends of his moustaches and lifting them right up to his ear lobes, so that he also pulled up his upper lip, laying bare the yellow teeth.

'I must clear out,' thought Yakov. 'He'll get me mixed up in it all. I must get away.' And later, as he took the river road, 'God damn you all,' he said to himself, 'What do I want with any of you? What do I get out of it?'

A fine drizzle, harbinger of autumn, was slowly damping the earth, and the yellow waters were wrinkled with fine ripples; there was something in the very atmosphere, warm to the point of stuffiness, which still further deepened Yakov's misery. Was it really not possible to live a quiet, simple life, without all these superfluous, senseless anxieties?

But the months, like a convoy moving through a winter

blizzard, dragged on, one after the other, over-burdened with surprising new anxieties.

One of the Morozovs came back from the war—Zahar. On his breast was the St. George Cross; his head was bald and covered with angry sores, where he had been burned; one ear had been torn off, and in place of his right eyebrow was a red scar, with a strangely smashed-in, dead eye beneath it; but the other eye still looked keenly out, severe and watchful.

Morozov instantly struck up friendship with the stoker Krotov and that lame pupil of Seraphim the Comforter danced and sang the following quatrain:

> "Rain beats, winds howl,
> In a trench lie I—
> I am helping, like a fool
> Fighting Europe till I die . . ."

Yakov asked Morozov—'Tell me, Zahar, are we fighting badly?'

'We've nothing good to fight with,' the weaver answered him. There was an insolent bark in his voice, and an echo of the desperate shamelessness of the stoker's ditties in what he said. 'We've no boss, Mr. Yakov,' he said straight to his own boss, 'only rogues at the head.'

This man and Vaska the stoker began to stand out like lanterns lit in the depths of the autumn night. When one day Tatiana's gay husband rigged himself out in trousers of a sort of Turkish style, with a ridiculously big, baggy seat, exactly the same colour as Zahar's faded old army topcoat, the stoker, with one glance at him, sang:

> "Here are breeches guaranteed
> Tell two men apart—
> Some grow bigger in the head
> Others in the arse."

To Yakov's amazement, his brother-in-law was not in

the least offended by this quip, but roared with laughter, and made no bones about egging the stoker on to more such literary efforts. The workers all laughed too, and the factory was particularly amused when Morozov turned up with a shaggy pup with a fluffy tail turned stiffly over its back—and on the end of its tail, tied on with bast, dangled his little white metal George Cross. Miron could not pass by a thing like that; Morozov was arrested, and Vialov took charge of the dog.

Men with all manner of disablement—legless, armless, eyeless—appeared about the town in soldiers' great-coats; the whole world took on the suppurating hue of their uniforms. Under the command of Vera Popov, thin as a rake, the élite ladies of Dromov took the broken, ruined men out for walks. Mrs. Popov tried to persuade Pauline to take part in the work, but Pauline tossed her head and was loud with her complaints. 'Oh no, I can't do that! The idea! Look, Yasha, they are all young and healthy, but disfigured, and they smell so, I can't. Yasha, let's go away somewhere!'

'Where?' he asked dismally, seeing that his mistress was becoming more and more a bundle of nerves, smoking terribly hard, so that her breath was strong with it.

Altogether, all the women, both in Dromov and at the works in particular, were becoming more spiteful, constantly whining and grumbling about the high cost of living, while their husbands, with derisive whistles, came demanding a rise of wages, though the quality of their work was going down. The Artamonov village was a-buzz now every evening, with an angry mutter which was quite new.

Omnipresent among the workers was Minaiev, a sober locksmith of about thirty, with black hair and a Jewish sort of nose. Yakov kept cautiously out of the man's way, and tried never to meet his eyes: Minaiev's dark eyes stared at everybody in turn as if he had forgotten something which he was trying to remember.

Yakov's father drifted about the courtyard, a dirty mass of flesh; he could scarcely move his diseased legs. He now wore, dangling from his broad shoulders, a travelling fox-skin coat, in patches worn quite bare. He would stop a man and ask him sternly: 'Where are you going?' And when he got his answer, he would wave his hand and mutter: 'Off you go, then. Idlers! Bugs and bloodsuckers!'

His purplish, swollen cheeks would be drawn back squeamishly, his lower lip drooping. Yakov was ashamed to have the men see the old man.

Tatiana now spent the whole day rustling the news-papers. She was so full of apprehension that her ears were always red. Miron kept flying off to Vorgorod, Moscow or Petersburg. On his return he stamped the broad heels of his American boots and told malicious stories of the drunken, debauched *mouzhik* Rasputin who had battened like a leech on the Emperor.

'I simply don't believe he exists,' insisted Olga—now half blind—sitting beside Tatiana on the couch, where the latter's two-year old son, Platon, was sprawling and shrieking. 'He's been specially invented, to warn us . . .'

'Marvellous! Stupendous!' cried Tatiana's gay husband. 'Then the countryside will have its revenge, won't it!'

He rubbed together his plump little hands, with their flue of ruddy hair. He was the only one confident that everything would be right one day.

'Heavens alive!' cried Tatiana, with some annoyance, 'what you see to be pleased about, I can't understand.'

Mitia opened his mouth in astonishment and croaked: 'What's that? You can't understand? Well, get this into your head, then—the countryside will have its revenge for all it has suffered. In the personality of Rasputin it has produced its own self-destructive poison . . .'

'Just a moment,' said Miron, with a frown. 'It was only the other day that you were saying . . .'

But, scarcely able to control himself, swallowing half his words, Mitia babbled on in a subdued whisper: 'He's not a mere *mouzhik*, he's a symbol! Three years ago they celebrated the three-hundredth anniversary of their accession to power, and so . . .'

'Twaddle,' said Miron sharply. Doctor Yakovliev gave his usual laugh, while Yakov wondered what would happen if Nesterenko heard of the things that were being said. . .

'Why do you say these things?' he asked. 'What's the point?' and tried to persuade them to stop.

He observed that even Miron was unusually distracted and anxious, and this particularly upset Yakov. In the end the only one who remained unchanged was Mitia, all over the place, as before, with his little jokes, or strumming his guitar when evening came, singing:

"My wife is dead . . ."

But Tatiana no longer liked these ditties. 'Oh, how you make me sick with your songs,' she would say, and busy herself in the nursery.

Mitia was a great hand at quieting the workers—he suggested to Miron buying up flour, millet, beans and potatoes round the countryside, and selling them to the workers at a special price to cover solely cost and transport. The workers appreciated this, and it was obvious to Yakov that they had more confidence in that merry soul than in Miron; he also observed a greater tendency for Miron and Mitia to fall out. . . .

For example, one day Miron, making no attempt to

conceal his malice, said plainly to Mitia: 'I suppose you're trying to keep your ear to the ground?'

Mitia smiled and replied: 'The will of the people is the people's right . . .'

'I wonder exactly who you think you are?' shouted Miron.

'That's enough shouting there,' grumbled the senior Artamanov, though in his father's dimmed eyes Yakov could detect flickers of satisfaction; the old man liked seeing his nephew and son-in-law at loggerheads, and whenever he heard Tatiana's exasperated high-pitched voice he would smile, just as she would smile when Natalia timidly asked 'Tania' to 'pour me a cup of tea, dear, please'.

It was now one new anxiety after another, one after another without rhyme or reason. All at once Aunt Olga, grown wholly blind, caught a chill—and two days later was dead; only a few days after her death a clap of thunder broke over town and works—the Tsar had abdicated!

'What shall we have now?' Yakov asked his brother, whose nose was buried in delight in the paper—'a Republic?'

'Of course, a Republic,' was Miron's reply, as he bent over the table, his hands resting on the spread-out paper with all his weight, till with a crack the sheet suddenly split in two, in which of course Yakov saw a bad omen. But Miron straightened himself, with a most unusual expression on his face, and in a strange voice, strained, but gentle, cried: 'Russia has entered on the road to recovery and reconstruction, that's what this is, my boy!'

He flung his arms wide, as if wishing to embrace Yakov, then lowered one arm and with the other still outstretched, picked up and straightened his pince-nez, then, with his arm once more outstretched, so that he looked like a semaphore, announced that the following evening without fail he was going to Moscow.

Mitia also waved his arms, just like a cabby trying to get warm, and shouted: 'Now everything will go swimmingly; now at last the people will have their say—long has it been ripening in their hearts!'

Miron gave up bickering with him; he grew thoughtful, smiling and moistening his lips all the time. To Yakov it seemed that they were quite right—everything did go swimmingly, everybody was glad. Mitia stood on the porch, addressing the workers gathered in the yard, telling them what was taking place in Petersburg; the workers shouted *hourah*, then seized Mitia by the arms and legs and tossed him. Mitia huddled into a huge ball, and flew high in the air, but when they tried to do the same to Miron, he somehow came to pieces in the air, as if his limbs would fall off. A crowd of workers gathered round Mitia, and massive, wiry weaver, Gerasim Voinov, shouted to his face: 'Mr. Mitia, you're a decent fellow, a decent fellow, understand? Lads, give him a cheer!'

They cheered him, and then, dancing a step, Vaska the stoker, his bald head gleaming in the sun, yelled, as if he were drunk:

> "Hi! the people stood far
> From the throne of the Tsar
> When they went near the show
> They found an old crow."

'Go ahead, Vaska!' they shouted.

They would have tossed Yakov too, but he ran off and hid indoors, being sure that they would toss him all right, but just wouldn't catch him properly, so he would smash to the ground. That evening he was in the office, when outside, under the window, he caught Vialov's voice.

'What have you taken the pup away for? Sell me him. I'll make a good dog of him.'

'Eh! old fellow, is this the time to be thinking of training dogs?' came Zahar Morozov's answer.

'Then what are you doing? Sell it—I'll give you a silver ruble, come on!'

'Get away.'

Yakov poked his head through the window. 'What about the Tsar, Tikhon, huh?'

'You're right,' the old fellow replied, then, with a glance at the angle of the house, gave a hushed little whistle. 'He's turned out, and no mistake.' He bent down to give a pull at his boots, then, speaking to the ground, said: 'Now they've got going. That's what Anton used to mean— *Waggon's lost a wheel . . .*' He straightened his back and went round the corner, calling softly: 'Touloun, Touloun!'

A chain of merry weeks went dancing by; Miron, Tatiana, the doctor, and all the men as well became more gentle to one another. Some strangers came from Dromov and took the locksmith Minaiev away with them. Then spring arrived, sunny and warm.

'Tell me, Salty-pie,' said Pauline, 'I still don't quite understand what has happened. The Tsar abdicated his throne, all the army is beaten and disabled, the police disbanded, and unknown civilians in command—how shall we get on? Every devil can do whatever he wants, and that means Zhiteikin won't let me alone. Neither he nor any of the others who were after me, and I refused. I don't want to live here, I can't live here now everybody's equal, I must go somewhere where nobody knows me. And, after all, now it's done—revolution and liberty, I mean—it must have been so that people could live where they wanted.'

She was getting more insistent, more persuasive. Ykov felt there was something indisputable in what she said, so he tried to soothe her, saying:' Wait just a little, till things settle down a bit, and then . . .'

However, he had no confidence that the disturbance all round would settle down. He could see the factory getting noisier and more threatening every day. A man whose habit it is to be afraid will always find something to be afraid of. Yakov began to be afraid of Zahar Morozov's burned skull. Zahar was going about like a little king, and all the workers following him like sheep. Mitia was like a toy magpie fluttering round him.

Actually, Morozov acquired a likeness to a large dog which has learned to walk on its hind legs. No doubt the burn scars on his head had broken out again, as he appeared with his head wound in a turban made of a Turkish towel of Tatiana's which Mitia had given him. His enlarged head seemed to crush him down and make him shorter of stature. He had an important stride, like Police Inspector's Ekke's fat assistant, and a way of tucking his thumbs behind the belt of his tattered army trousers, wagging the other fingers like little fins, and shouting out: 'Order, comrades, order!'

He tried three lads for stealing cloth. He cross-examined them in a loud voice which could be heard all over the yard: 'Do you understand from whom you've stolen it?' And himself gave the answer: 'From yourselves, from us all! How can you thieve now, you bastards?'

He issued orders for the thieves to be flogged, and two workers with great satisfaction gave them a birching, while Vaska the stoker danced and madly sang a ditty about the way vermin were dealt with to-day, now that there was a just magistrate . . . but then suddenly broke off his song, flung his arms wide, and cried:

"Almighty God, save your people!"

'Bravo!' cried Mitia.

Mitia was wearing dull grey breeches and a leather cap tipped back on his head. His gingery face was sweaty, and there was a tipsy, sickly delight in his eyes. The night before this happened he had had a sharp quarrel with Tatiana—

Yakov had heard first a loud whisper, coming from the window of their room which opened on to the garden, then a loud cry which broke from Tatiana: 'You clown! You don't know what honour is! Your convictions? Beggars have not got convictions. . . . All sham! A month ago your convictions . . . It's the limit! I shall go to town to-morrow and live with my sister . . . Yes, and take the children with me . . .'

Yakov was not a bit surprised. He had long noticed that Mitia with his gingery hair was getting more and more unbearable. He was only surprised—even a little proud—of having been the first to observe what a hopeless creature the ginger-haired little type really was. Now even his mother—who only the other day had been as fond of Mitia as of a pet cockbird, was grumbling. 'I can't make it out, he's always against us now, he might be a Yid. There you are, people bite the hand that feeds them . . .'

Mitia, on the other hand, trumpeted about: 'Everything's marvellous! Life is like a beautiful, clever woman! Only, my dear Tatiana, you'll have to get out of your head all these fables about the wolf lying down with the lamb—they're badly out of date.'

Upon which, Miron—bitter and curt—asked him: 'And what wisdom shall we hear from you to-morrow?'

'Life will prompt me,' Mitia replied. 'Oh yes; and the next question?'

Tatiana and Miron avoided close contact with him as carefully as if he were covered with soot. Only a few days after this Mitia moved to town, taking his property with him: three big bundles of books and a basket-trunk of linen.

Now, on all sides, Yakov observed an agitation devoid of purpose, like that at a fire; everybody seemed wrapped in the smoke of his own crass stupidity, nor was there anything to promise any near end to these lunatic days.

'Well,' he announced one day to Pauline, 'my mind's made up; we're going! First to Moscow; when we get there, we'll see . . .'

'Oh, at last,' the woman cried with delight, flinging her arms round him and kissing him.

The July evening, filling the garden with a ruddy twilight, breathed against the windows the pungent breath of rain-soaked soil that the sun has warmed. It was good, if melancholic. Yakov, lost in thought, removed from his neck Pauline's hot, moist arms, and said: 'Cover your bosom . . . Put something on properly—we've got to be serious.'

She leapt down from his knees, with two bounds reached the bed, wrapped a dressing-gown about herself, and sat down businesslike beside him.

'It's like this,' he began, rubbing his beard against his cheek so hard that the hair rustled loudly. 'We've got to put our heads together, and find somewhere—some country —where things are quiet. Where you don't have to understand or worry your head about matters that don't concern you. That's the question!'

'Of course,' said Pauline.

'We've got to move very cautiously. Miron tells me the trains are full of deserting soldiers. We must pretend to be very poor . . .'

'Only don't forget to take a good bit of money with us.'

'That goes without saying. I shall travel so that the family have no idea where I'm going. I shall pretend to be going to Vorgorod, see?'

'But why this concealment?' Pauline demanded with astonishment and suspicion.

He could not say why—the idea had only that minute come into his head, yet he was sure it was sound. 'Well, you see . . .' he said, 'father and Miron would want to know everything . . . We don't want anything of that. Once we get to Moscow I can get money, a lot . . .'

'Only let's go soon,' she begged him. 'You can see now we can't go on here. Everything's so dear, and the shops and market are empty. There's sure to be robbery soon, or how could people live?' With a glance behind her at the door, she whispered: 'Why, you know how good cook was, now she's turned insolent, you'd think she was always drunk. She might kill me in my sleep—why not, everything at sixes and sevens as it is? Yesterday I heard her whispering to somebody. Dear God, I said to myself, it's begun! But when I opened the door just enough to peep through—there she was on her knees, muttering away—horrible!'

'Not so fast,'—Yakov halted the swift flow of her troubled whisper—'First I shall get away . . .'

'Oh no,' she said loudly, bringing down her fist on his knee—I shall go first—you'll let me have some money and then . . .'

'Do you mean you don't trust me?' he demanded with anger and mortification, and received the very firm answer: 'No, I don't. I'm honest, and I tell you straight, I don't trust you. Do you think you can trust anybody, now they've betrayed the Tsar and everything else? Whom do you yourself trust?'

Her voice was convincing—still more so the bosom showing between the folds of the half-open house-coat—and Yakov Artamonov gave way. It was decided that she would begin to get ready the next morning, then go to Vorgorod, and wait for him there.

But the following day Yakov complained of stomach trouble and pains in the head, which was quite possible, since latterly he had become very thin and limp and distracted, with no light left in his radiant eyes. A week later he slowly drove out from Dromov to the station, keeping on the edge of the ruined cobble surface, with its enormous potholes full of dried-out, cracked hillocks of mud. Behind him lay a life similarly broken and misshapen; ahead, a whitish blotch, a miserable lifeless sun peered out of a spongy abyss in the heart of the smoky clouds.

A month later, Miron Artamonov, returning from Moscow, brought the news. Head on one side, he examined the palm of his hand, and said: 'I'm afraid I've got some rather sad news for you: while I was in Moscow that silly hussy Yakov lived with came to see me . . . she told me that "some men"—what does that mean to-day?—beat Yakov up and tipped him off the train . . .'

'Oh no!' cried Tatiana, trying to get out of her chair.

'While the train was moving . . . Yakov died two days later . . . He was buried in the village graveyard near Petoushka station.'

In silence, Tatiana pressed her handkerchief to her eyes, her sharp shoulders quivered suddenly, and all at once her black frock slipped off them, just as if the thin, long-necked body had begun to melt.

Miron straightened his pince-nez and stood, wiping his hands and cracking his finger joints, listening to a lonely bell tolling for vespers. Then, striding to and fro, he said: 'What's the use of crying? He was absolutely useless to the family. And, if you don't mind my saying so, he was disgustingly stupid. Of course, one is sorry—that goes without saying.'

'Dear God!' cried Tatiana, her red-lidded eyes snapping; she moistened a finger and smoothed her eyebrows.

'Meanwhile that brazen hussy,' Miron continued, hands in pockets, 'is playing the grieving widow, though her smart clothes make it clear enough she fleeced him. She assures me she wrote to us.'

Bernard Duffield

THE ARTAMONOV BUSINESS

Tatiana shook her head.

'She didn't? I thought as much. My idea is—we shouldn't tell his father or mother about it—let them think he's alive. Agreed?'

'Yes, that's best,' Tatiana agreed.

'For that matter, I think Uncle's quite lost his understanding, but his mother would weep herself to death . . .'

Nodding her head, Tatiana said: 'We shall all of us perish soon enough.'

'That's possible, if we stay here. But I'm sending the wife and children away at once, and my advice to you is to clear out too, without waiting for Zahar Morozov to start . . . So it's settled, not a word to the old folk. If you don't mind, I'll run along now, Anna's poorly. . . .'

He held out his lanky arm and shook his sister by the hand. 'Travelling's incredibly difficult now, the roads are in a frightful state!'

The senior Artamonov was living in a state of semi-coma, which was steadily deepening. He spent the night and most of the day in bed, the remainder of the time in an arm-chair pulled up to a window. Outside was the azure profundity; at times this was plastered over with cloud. The mirror returned a picture of an obese old man with swollen face, swimming eyes, and knotted grey beard—he would examine that face and think: 'What a nightmare!'

His wife, Natalia, came into the room, bent over him, stirred him, whined: 'You ought to go away and take a cure.'

'Go away,' Peter Artamonov dragged out. 'Go away, you cow! . . . Sick of you . . . Let me be.'

Alone again, he strained to catch the festive sounds of the crowd—in the courtyard, in the garden—everywhere—but there was no sound from the Artamonov Works.

His customary companion—the man whom life had cheated—who used to stimulate him with injections of his petty thoughts—had vanished, died. It was a good thing he had done so—the old man found it difficult to reason—did not even want to, in fact, had long ago grasped that reasoning was useless, because you could never understand anything.

Sometimes he would ask Natalia: 'Has Ilia come home?'

'No.'

'Not yet?'

'No.'

'Nor Yakov?'

'Nor Yakov.'

'Hm! On the ran-tan, and Miron draining the business dry.'

'Don't you bother your head about that!' Natalia counselled.

'Go away!'

She withdrew into a corner and sat there, her filmy eyes examining the thing that was once a man, with whom she had spent her whole life. Her head shook, her arms might have been disjointed, she could not control her hands, she had gone thin, guttering like a tallow dip.

From time to time, and with increasing frequency, Peter Artamonov was wakened by a strange disturbance in the house. Then some complete strangers came into the room. He peered at them, striving to comprehend their noisy, disconnected babble, and heard Natalia pitifully crying: 'But what do you think you are doing? And why? Don't you know that's the proprietor there—we are the proprietors! At least, let me take him away, he ought to go to town, to see doctors. But please let me take him away . . .'

'Wants to conceal me. What's the sense of that?' thought Artamonov. 'Fool. Always was a fool. Yakov takes after

334

her. And the rest. Only Ilia takes after me. As soon as he gets back, he'll straighten things up . . .'

It rained, it snowed, it froze hard everywhere, blizzards howled and shrieked.

Then a sharp sense of hunger suddenly stirred Peter Artamonov out of his semi-coma. He found himself in the garden summer-house. Through the windows, between the wet branches, showed a ruddy sky, strangely close to him. He had the impression it was suspended just beyond the trees, and if he reached out his hand he could have touched it.

'I'm hungry,' he said, but nobody answered.

The garden was full of a damp, bluish fog. Outside the summer-house were two horses, one grey, the other black, each with its head on the other's neck. On the bench behind them sat a man in a white shirt, untangling a large bundle of cords.

'Natalia—listen—bring me something to eat!'

Before, whenever he woke from his oblivion and called his wife, she was there in an instant, she was always somewhere at hand; to-day—no Natalia!

'Can it really be . . . ?' he asked himself—then his mind cleared a bit—'Or perhaps she's fallen sick.'

He raised his head. Something flashed through the shrubbery by the bath-house door. Then he saw it was a rifle with bayonet attached, on the shoulder of a greenish soldier, indistinguishable among the foliage. Somebody outside shouted: 'Comrades, what's this, what are you playing at? Is that the way to keep horses? You can't even keep pigs like that? Want a spell under lock and key in the bath-house, do you? And why wasn't the hay brought in— you've let it get wet.'

The man in the white shirt threw down the cords and stood up. 'So there you are, out of the blue—I'll be damned!' he muttered.

'We've more commanders now than ever before,' the soldier answered.

'And who appoints the devils?'

'They appoint themselves. Nowadays, brother, everything happens of itself, like an old wives' tale.'

The man went up to the horses and took hold of their manes. Peter Artamonov shouted as loud as he could: 'Hi! there! call my wife!'

'Hold your row, old man,' was the answer he got. 'The idea—wants his missus . . .'

The horses went. Peter Artamonov brought hand to face and drew it over the cheek and beard, till his chilly fingers touched his ear. He looked round him. He was lying against the blind wall of the summer-house, the wall with no glass in it, under the apple tree, on which red apples hung in dense clusters, like rowan berries; the couch was hard; as covering he had the mangy old fox coat and a short winter jacket. Still he was not warm. He could not make out why he was there. Perhaps they were cleaning up indoors, for some festival . . . what Saint's day was it? But the horses in the garden and the soldier at the bath-house? And who was that shouting in the courtyard. He could hear: 'Comrade, you're a regular milksop—where's your gumption? What's that? The men tired? Let 'em get up betimes—clear out the fools . . .'

There was shouting afar-off, but it set up a din inside his head, and deafened him. He felt as if he had no legs; he could not move them below the knee. That apple tree on the wall was painted by a painter called Vanka Lukin—he was a thief, robbed a church, and died in prison.

Into the summer-house stumped a very broad man wearing a shaggy fur cap; with him came a cold shadow and a pungent odour of tar.

'Not you, Vialov?'

'Who else?'

That reply, growled at him, also deafened him. The aged yardman stretched out his arms as if he were floating over the creaky floor.

'Who's shouting?'

'Zahar Morozov.'

'What's that soldier for?'

'It's war.'

After a short silence, he asked: 'Has the enemy got as far as us, then?'

'It's war against you, Mr. Peter.'

The master of the Artamonov Works said sternly: 'Don't try to be funny, you old fool, keep your place!'

He then heard the calm response: 'This is the last war, they won't want any more. As for my place,—now we're all comrades together. And I really am too old for a fool.'

It was clear that Tikhon Vialov was jeering at him. Now, without more ado, the man actually sat down on the foot of the couch, not even taking off his cap. Outside could be heard the hoarse, broken commands: 'After eight at night —not a man to be seen outside!'

'Where's my wife?' Peter Artamonov asked.

'Gone to forage for bread.'

'What do you mean—"forage for bread"?'

'Well, why not?—bread isn't a stone—you don't find loaves lying about just anywhere.'

The dusk in the garden grew steadily more dense and blue; the soldier at the bath-house gave a noisy yawn; the man himself was now completely invisible; only his bayonet flashed—like a fish in the water.

There were many things Peter Artamonov would have liked to ask Tikhon Vialov about, but he held his tongue; even if he did ask, he would get nothing out of Vialov. All the same, there were the questions, dancing about, a confused tangle, in which it was impossible to tell which was the most important. He was also frightfully hungry.

Tikhon Vialov suddenly growled: 'You call me fool, but I saw the truth before anybody else. Now you see how it's all turned about. I said it would be universal penal servitude —and now they've got it. Swept it all away like dust with a rag; like sweeping away shavings. That's how it stands, Mr. Peter. I tell you. Satan used the tool—and you helped him. And all to what purpose? One long chain of wrong, no counting it. I watched it all; marvelled—and when would be the stop to it? Now you've got your stop! All you did, cast in lead. *The waggon's lost its wheel* . . .'

'Delirium,' Peter Artamonov assured himself, but none the less he asked: 'Why am I here?'

'You're turned out of your house.'

'Miron?'

'You're all turned out.'

'But . . . Yakov?'

'No sign of him, a long time.'

'Where is Ilia?'

'I hear he's with the new folk. Must be, since you're still in the living—that's him being with them, otherwise . . .'

'Delirium.' Peter Artamonov was still not convinced, and so said no more. 'You've come to losing your senses, you miserable old creature. You ought to have known you would come to it in the end,' he said to himself.

Tiny, glimmering stars were scattered over the sky; it seemed they were different from the stars that used to be. There were not so many either.

Vialov took his cap, and, crushing it in his hands, started again. 'All that crafty folly of yours you've had to throw up. It's easier for beggars.' Then all at once, in changed tones, asked: 'Remember that little kid—son of the clerk Nikonov?'

'Well, and what if I do?' Peter could not tell if this unexpected question frightened him, or merely suprised him. But he did know, as soon as Vialov said: 'You killed him just as Zahar killed the pup. But for what?'

Now he understood. At last Vialov had denounced him and so, ill as he was, he was under arrest. But this did not frighten him very much; rather, it made him indignant, it was so inhumanly stupid. Supporting himself on his elbows, he raised his head a little, then, conscious of a bitterness on the tongue and a dryness of the mouth, he said, with quiet reproach and scorn: 'You know it's a lie! Besides, any crime has its period, and after that it lapses. You're too late by far, I tell you. You're mad, too. Anyway, you've forgotten—you saw for yourself, you said so at the time . . .'

'Now—what did I say?' the old man interrupted him. 'Of course, I saw nothing, but I guessed. Just to see, I said,— what'll you do? I told a lie, but you were glad and you snatched at my lie. I kept a watch on you, waiting all the time . . . You were all the same. Alexey prompted that drunkard his father-in-law to set fire to Barski's Inn, and when your father guessed, he had the drunkard beaten to death. Nikita knew that, he too guessed everything, by reason. He should have held his tongue, but he hated you so, he told me. I said: you're a monk, you should forget all this, I'll remember for it you. You harried him with fear, with your doings. Put his head in a noose, then into a monastery, to "pray for us"! And he too terrified to put in a prayer for you, so he lost his faith in God . . .'

It was as if Tikhon Vialov could have gone on talking as long as he lived. He spoke softly, dreamily—and, so it seemed, without malice. He became almost invisible in the dense, hot darkness of late evening. His lisping language, which suggested the nocturnal rustle of cockroaches, did

THE ARTAMONOV BUSINESS

not alarm Peter, but rather bore him down under its weight, leaving him speechless with astonishment.

He gradually became more firmly convinced that this strange creature had gone mad. Now Vialov heaved a long drawn-out sigh, as if he had tipped a great burden from his shoulders, and continued in the same monotonous voice, pointlessly decanting the past, drop by drop:

'You Artanonovs destroyed the faith in me too. Through you, Nikita put me off it, made me too into a godless man ... You believe in neither god nor devil. You keep an ikon in your house just for deceit. What have you got in you? Nobody can tell. Yet there seems to be something. You're receivers. You have lived by deceit. Now it's all visible, they've stripped you naked ...'

Shifting his flesh only with difficulty, Peter got his terribly heavy feet to the floor. But the sole of the feet could not feel the floor, and it seemed to the old man that his legs had come off, left him, and he was suspended in mid-air. This did frighten him. He grabbed at Vialov's shoulders.

'What do you want?' the yardman cried, and roughly shook the hands off him. 'Hands off me. You've no strength left, you'll not strangle me! Your father was a strong man—and that strength he blew, boasting. I tell you, you robbed me of faith, and I don't know how to meet my death. I have grown like you, you demons ...'

Peter was getting hungrier and hungrier, and his legs frightened him badly. 'Am I really—dying? I'm not three-score years and ten yet. Oh Lord ...'

He tried to lie down again, but he was too weak to raise his legs. So he ordered Tikhon Vialov to help him.

Laying the dead legs of his former master on the bench, Vialov spat out a gob, then sat down again, poking about inside his cap. In his hand he held something which flashed. Peter concentrated his gaze on it. It was a needle.

340

The man was sewing his cap in the darkness, thereby making it quite clear he was mad. Over him fluttered a grey moth. Out in the garden there were three bars of light in the air, and a voice some distance off said, quite clearly: 'Comrades, there's no turning back for us . . .'

Vialov drowned the voice: 'Your father too; he killed my brother,' he said.

'You lie,' Peter cried involuntarily, but immediately went on to ask: 'When?'

'Huh! Now you want to know when!'

'What do you tell all these lies for, you madman?' Peter suddenly demanded, indignantly, feeling that his hunger was sucking at him and drying him up. 'What do you want? Are you my conscience, my judge? Why did you say nothing all these thirty-five years and more?'

'You see, I said nothing. So I was thinking.'

'Gathering malice? Be damned . . . Off you go, then, fetch the police!'

'There isn't any police.'

'Tell them—all my life he fed me, see—now put him on trial! I suppose you've already denounced me! Then what else do you want of me? Grind me down! Try to frighten me—extort money, eh?'

'You haven't got any money. You haven't got anything. You never had. To hell with magistrates, I say. I am my own judge.'

'Then what are you holding over me, you delirious fool?'

But evidently Vialov held nothing menacingly over him, so Peter obscurely sensed. The man only muttered: 'It's an end to all Cains. What did you kill my brother for?'

'That's a lie, about your brother.'

The old men began to speak more quickly, constantly interrupting one another.

'A lie? I was with him when . . .'

'With whom?'

'My brother. I ran away when your father landed him that blow. It was for him your father bled to death. Why else should he bleed . . . ?'

'Too late . . .'

'And so, now you see, they've overturned you, you're down and defenceless, whereas me, who was always of no account . . .'

'You're out of your mind!'

Peter felt the one time navvy was driving him back into a corner, towards a precipice, over an abyss in which nothing was to be distinguished, there was no knowledge, only horror. Persistently he repeated: 'Too late! You never had a brother, you're lying, people like you don't have anything . . .'

'Only a conscience.'

'You were the cause of my boy Ilia going wrong.'

'You Artamonovs were the cause of me going wrong— Nikita Artamonov infected me with his folly.'

'He used to say you put him wrong.'

'You'll never know how often I was prompted to kill your father. I once nearly smashed in his skull with a shovel. . . . You're crafty . . .'

'You yourself . . .'

'You ruined Seraphim. There's another one confused my mind, never harming a man, yet always living wrong. How can that be? Craft all round . . .'

'Who's there? Where are you going?' came a loud, angry cry in the darkness. 'You buggurs, haven't you been told, no movement after eight o'clock?'

Vialov stood up, went to the door, and dropped away through it into the darkness. Peter Artamonov, crushed to nothing by excitement, hunger, and fatigue, saw something broad and green flit through the three bands of oily light in the garden. He closed his eyes, expecting something completely horrible to happen now.

'Get any?' Vialov asked of somebody.

'This is all.'

It was Natalia's voice. Where had she been, why had she left him alone with this old man?

He opened his eyes, raised himself on his elbows, staring at the door, which was blocked by two human shapes. All at once it came to his mind that throughout his life he had wondered who was to blame, whose fault it was that his days had been so terribly tangled, and full of a kind of deceit. In this instant it had suddenly all become clear to him.

Natalia came up to him, bent over him, whispered: 'Oh, God Almighty be praised . . .'

'There, Vialov,' he cried, 'this is who is to blame for it all,' and heaved a decided sigh of relief. 'She with her greed, egging me on, I tell you!' Triumphantly he yelled out: 'It was through her my brother Nikita was ruined. You know that yourself, don't you . . .'

His breath gave out. It was strange to see that his wife was not offended, nor frightened, and did not shed a tear. With a shaky hand she stroked the hair of his head and whispered anxiously, but so kindly: 'Shhh! don't shout, there's enemies all round . . .'

'I am hungry . . .'

Into his hand Natalia put a cucumber and a heavy hunk of bread; the cucumber was warm—the bread stuck to his fingers like dough. He was astounded. 'What is this?' he cried. 'This all you give me?'

'Not so loud, for the love of God,' Natalia whispered, 'there is no food anywhere, you know! Even the poor soldier boys . . .'

'You give me this—for all I . . . for all the anxiety . . . for a man's whole life . . . ?'

He balanced the bread on his hand, muttering, but beginning to guess that something insupportably and finally mortifying, for which even she, Natalia, was not to blame, had come to pass. And he sent the bread flying towards the door. In hollow, but firm tones he declared: 'I don't want it.'

Vialov picked the bread up, muttering and blowing on it. Natalia once again tried to press a piece into her husband's hand, whispering in his ear: 'Do eat a little bit, just a little bit, don't be angry . . .'

Pushing aside her hand, Peter Artamonov closed his eyes firmly, and, with blinding rage, repeated through set teeth: 'I don't want it. Go away!'

This book, designed by
William B. Taylor
is a production of
Edito-Service S.A., Geneva

Printed in Switzerland